for Boris, my son,
and also for Malou

KU-771-549

Part One

What I must do is: make a space – that's right, that's what I must do, make a space in the overcrowded brain so that my thoughts, those that need to, can toss and turn like insomniacs, without disturbing the others. The others must not be disturbed. (Why have I returned to Vienna?)

My other thoughts are fine, concerned with practical matters, affairs of business, real things, tangible and of the present. It is the unsleeping thoughts, the troublesome ones, for which a space must be made. Consider this, Kazakh: some of your thoughts are so secret you don't know yourself you are thinking them, you only discover afterwards, like this business of suddenly deciding to return to Vienna. When did you come to that decision? You swore you'd never go back, and now you are here, disturbing yourself. Memories, useless, what use are they? Can you mend what's past? Or remember, even? Yes, that's a point. Time is an exasperating thing. (Divide a second by 10^2 and it takes an eternity to boil an egg.) When I see myself in time I think, always, was that me? Rarely was I altogether myself, I was – oh all sorts of – all sorts of – But then, if this is so, where are you to find yourself, Kazakh? since you were so infrequently yourself, since you have deposited yourself all over the place.

This business of coming back to Vienna; it started with my buying the hat (didn't it?), the grey Persian lamb hat you bought one day for no apparent reason (I never wear hats, never); oh you looked fine in it, it'll be fine for Vienna, you decided. That was the first you knew of your decision to go back to Vienna, you weren't surprised, no, I wasn't surprised, Kazakh was not surprised, next day he told the maid that he had to go to Vienna on business. Had to: those were my words. Where was the compulsion? One uses the imperative loosely, I know, but still I did feel that I had to go to Vienna, that it was not a purely arbitrary decision on my part.

If I could think this through, Stefan Kazakh thought.

On my first day back in Vienna I visited my father's grave. Now that's a peculiar thing for me to have done, highly peculiar, you are not someone who attaches much value to ceremonial acts. You gave up your religion a long time ago; yes, it is true, I did, when was it I stopped praying to God? As a very small child I used to get a lot from prayer, a sort of bargaining went on between God and myself, if I did such and such (or else refrained from something) then it was only fair that He should reciprocate by granting – whatever it was I wished to have granted at that particular time. I put a great deal into my praying, and I asked only for what I was entitled to. I was quite sure my requests would be granted, they were very reasonable. What characterized my relationship with God was its exclusiveness; although I had to accept that I was not His sole preoccupation, I did believe that my relationship to Him was unique, that there was a very special intimacy between us (which, for instance, permitted me to be quite cheeky sometimes in my requests) and that if it were not for the fact that God was incapable of favouritism (divine justice was absolute) I would have been his favourite. Standing by my father's grave, I felt nothing – what was I expecting to feel? – except a sense of amazement that I should be here, performing this little ritual of mourning in which I did not believe. Was that why I was here? To visit my father's grave? – is that in character? Ah, what is?

So many of my remembered actions seem totally – Was that me? Did I do – feel, think that, say that, or was I only wearing my robes?

Impossible, it is not like me at all –

What a peculiar fellow you are, Kazakh; always amazing yourself.

Predictable as well, I would say.

Especially to others – predictable, that is.

Not to yourself (it would be more useful if you were predictable to yourself).

There is definitely something most peculiar about you, I would say.

Telling yourself stories – and such stories. Tell me, is that an occupation for a grown man? with affairs to attend to, people to see, memoranda to –

Ah well! (I always used to say ah well! all the time, as an expletive, whether it was appropriate or not –) Ah well! In due course no doubt you will tell yourself why you have come back to Vienna, patience Kazakh, be patient, you are overexcited.

Until yesterday I was calm; indeed, becalmed is probably the word for the state I was in: nothing in me moved, my thoughts were clear and consecutive, orderly, instead of jumbled up as they now are, pulling in all directions at once.

Yesterday, I suddenly felt cold, began to shiver, as if I had fever; there was no heating in the room – I looked around: no radiators, no heating vents, it was disgraceful, in winter, in a first-class hotel! The shivering in my body was like some living organism twisting and wriggling under my skin. On the phone, the concierge said I must be mistaken, the heating was on. Where was it coming from, this mythical heating? I demanded: where were the radiators, the vents? It was coming from the ceiling, he said. From the ceiling! I climbed up on the bed, and with my hands extended above my head trudged through the soft high eiderdowns, into which my feet sank as into a snow drift, testing the air above me for warmth. No heat was coming from the perforated ceiling, of that I was sure. Returning to the phone, I snapped into it, 'You must be mistaken. There is no heat coming from the ceiling. Please have an electric fire sent up to me,' and I put down the phone, and wrapped one of the puffy eiderdowns around my shoulders and began to pace. Was that yesterday, or the day before? Yesterday was when I got so tired. And it was yesterday I had the dream, yesterday afternoon when I lay down after lunch because I was so tired. I was back in the flat in the Obere Donaustrasse: from one of the windows I could look out across the canal, dark turbid water slapping against the rafts of the fish market, fishmongers in rubber aprons covered in scales and blood, the big fish convulsed in an ecstasy of dying, the futile flapping of their tails; in the dream the window was boarded up, I could see the Stephansdom projecting amid the green domes of the city, reassuring vista: how many hours I spent as a child looking out of windows; but now, in the dream, the emotion was of trepidation, the flat was a shambles, as if a bomb had hit it, there were rents in the walls, pipes protruded like entrails torn out, lumps of moulding like pieces of wedding cake littered the floor, thick black dust filled every cavity and lay on every ledge, a ceiling lamp of smoky white glass, in the form of a flower with drooping petals, had fallen to the floor, and shattered. The flat was in a terrible state, terribly damaged, but not recently, a long time ago this damage had been done, and then the dust had settled on the old trunks, the raffia fruit basket, the oil stove, the roller blinds: there was no furniture in this flat in my dream. I could see out into the back area, and on the other side of the cobbled courtyard the windows were as dark as a blind man's eyes. I hadn't locked and chained the door, and as I was planning to spend the night in this place I thought I had better lock up. The door was ajar, and when I tried to close it I felt the pressure on the other side, not very great, might have been caused by some minor obstruction, but when I put more weight against the door it still gave only a centimetre or so, and then it gave no more. I threw all my weight against it, frightened as a child in the dark – though I was a grown man in my dream – but still the door didn't move, I had only a child's strength in me, and I could not dislodge whoever was on the other side. I wanted to scream for help, but who was there to help me in this ruined place? That was yesterday, yesterday after lunch. The impulse to go to the Obere Donaustrasse and see where our flat had been was irresistible, though I knew perfectly well (but for some reason didn't remember this then) that the entire building, much of the street in fact, had been destroyed by shell fire in 1945 – how could I have forgotten? Later yesterday I walked through the streets of Vienna and felt calmer. The sharp air, pure and clear and with the taste of clean cold ice on it, made me calmer. Almost I understood myself. For a moment I thought – I actually understand myself, marvellously. Stefan Kazakh smiled and paused in the street, and one or two people glanced at this tall Jew, aged fifty-two, wearing a Persian lamb fur hat that did not suit him, that made him look not as he thought Russian, but like an Englishman over-equipped for the cold, it was an English fur hat. (It was possibly not even fur, but Acrilan.) Stefan Kazakh's smile went on, illuminating him, it was a smile of remembrance that distinguished him from a tourist and atoned for the Acrilan fur hat. I was happy walking by the canal yesterday. Surfaced in frost Vienna shone dull as old silver, it had aspects that were lovely to me. The canal, and the bridges over them – have always loved bridges. Such beautiful things to look at; the silent struggle of opposing forces going on inside them, in their essence, but the structure bearing this tumult. (By and large. Bridges collapse only infrequently.) I was crossing the Aspernbrücke; looking in the direction of the Prater, I saw that the Riesenrad was not turning, presumably it didn't operate in the winter. Used to love the Prater: that ride through the sky on the Giant Wheel – the feeling of being astride the city, everything below, nothing above: the love of heights I have retained, together with a fear of them, the queasy apprehension that informs all my loves. (One cannot be comfortable in love, what I have I can lose.) That great wheel in the sky – a sign, what did it mean to me? Of course I used to see it all the time as a child, every time I crossed the Aspernbrücke to go home, and from other parts of the city too, segments of it were visible from many places. I saw it again in '45, the iron skeleton of something unimaginable, without its carriages, black, charred – what could it have been? A children's ride – on this battlefield? The slow drift of the smoke from the burnt-out tanks derided such a possibility. No, it was a medieval contraption of war, a catapult for hurling death at the enemy, a monster wheel. Did I ride on that? All the bridges across the canal had been destroyed by the retreating Germans. Along the entire length of this gently curving waterway the stumps of the wrecked bridges projected their tangled ends for varying distances towards the opposite bank, the curiously contorted tram rails seemed to be reaching out with epileptic arms. I had loved those bridges, hadn't I? Their destruction pained me more than any other damage caused to the city, about the rest I did not care, was almost glad in a vengeful way, but I was sorry about my bridges. Now they have all been rebuilt, they have plaques to commemorate their restoration, but for me, yesterday, there was no alleviation in that, the converse in fact, and I walked on across the Aspernbrücke, so solid under my feet, as if it had never been a tangle of iron and stone, ends without a middle, and I felt resentful that it should be so easy for a city to be restored; to see everything intact, whole, offended me, it would have eased something in me to see signs of irreparable damage, like in my dream, now there was damage beyond reparation. Kazakh felt despair flourish in him. He walked heavily, not conscious of the snowfall. That's right, it was snowing all day yesterday and I didn't realize it walking around the city until I became conscious of the white-swollen statuary, and then – that must have been before I crossed the Aspernbrücke – I paused, you paused Kazakh, and watched the city change with the snow, losing its italianate aspect, showing its easterly face. My father's father came from Belorussia, my father was born in Budapest, my mother in Krakow. Which makes me – what? I was born in Vienna, but it is not my city, it has not nurtured me, only given me an accent, a demeanour,

perhaps some gestures. On picnics up in the Kahlenberg I saw –
often – the perpetual mist on the Hungarian plains, my forbears
have strange names, I like to think they were horsemen (on
account of my name) and free, but really I know nothing of
them. My memory can skim only the surface of my inheritance,
the rest is conjecture. This much is reasonable to suppose: the
craft of survival is in my constitution, there are instincts in me,
and devices, that bear out such a supposition. Kazakh, you are a
romantic – the only horse you ever rode was a wooden one, on
the carousel in the Prater, and the rocking-horse your father
bought you, and then much later you did ride a mule, the one
that generously deferred dying under you for five whole days,
that was a noble thing for that animal to do. Was that me? Lake
Bojh tiny as a coin in a well, a glitter through the tall spruce
trees, was it me who sat on that skinny mule and survived?
Yesterday I walked again in the Prater, how shabby and desolate
it was, the Giant Wheel looked smaller than I remembered it,
not ominous as in '45, nor enticing with promise as once it was.
The Prater yesterday was gloomy, the stalls and booths shuttered;
nobody about; the Planetarium was now a cinema, closed too, a
poster advertised a Hollywood film called *The Great Waltz*,
though there was no way of telling if this was the most recent
film to have been shown there or if the poster was just an old
poster that had not been plastered over for some reason. It was
definitely colder here, close to the river; the way I'd always remembered it the Prater was not like any other fun fair with a
Ferris wheel, which is all it was yesterday; for me it had been –
once – a unique place, my playground, where I had adventures
and made discoveries and fell in love with a wooden horse.
Kazakh, you are a fool, what is the point of these memories?
Such things as these are beyond recall. Be thankful there are
memories you will never have, there is consolation in that – and
despair, why despair? If you could think it through, give absolute freedom to your thoughts, and think them through: do
you dare do that? Do I dare? Traces I must have left of myself
somewhere. Do I dare?

I was thinking about that all yesterday, walking around Vienna,
through the snowfall and the sudden cold sunlight, the domes
turning from green to black.

12

'Morality is the invention of men without honour,' Wirthof used to say, ad nauseam. And, 'A man with honour does not require a moral code, he has only to consult his honour to know how to act in any situation.' How pompous you were about your honour, Wirthof. Must I think about you? It's funny: I have always been drawn to people who could do me harm, as evidence of which: my wives. And those others I sought out, pursued even, my mad-eyed ones, I never loved any of you. If you were anti-Semites, so much the better. Your betrayals consoled me, something in me chortled with satisfaction – so I was right all along, right to distrust, right to give nothing of myself, except the one thing whose giving on my part and taking on theirs meant no more than a politician's slippery handshake. Must you think about all that, Kazakh? Still, you have survived, that's some consolation, survived the holocaust and the whores, it is a knack you discovered in yourself. The knack of your race? 'Where are their empires now?' the rabbi used to say: the Babylonians, the Persians, the Egyptians, the Romans, the Spaniards he was referring to. The whores – where are their empires now? And you, Kazakh, horseman of the carousel, have survived. Still, it was quite a close thing, wasn't it?

I must have walked for hours around Vienna yesterday, my mind adrift, exhausting myself.

'You're tall for your religion.'

'Yes, I am, that's true.'

I'm over six foot, thin and quick, and already then I was tall, I must have been ten then, a tall ten, taller than Wirthof though he was two or three years older than me.

'My father's tall, you see.' Oh my father was a lovely man. He had a thick black moustache that spread out richly from his upper lip as if to encircle his mouth but stopped just short of his lower jaw to lie snug inside his smile. It had a natural untended look, his moustache. He had a very soft gentle voice for such a big man. I loved to hear him talk, though I regret to say he was a fool, a Don Quixote, with some highly peculiar ideas: a bit cracked, I'm afraid. He lived deep inside himself. Thoughtful, but without any common sense at all. An idealistic socialist, than which there can be no worse kind of fool. He could see beauty in sewers, in their construction, and he said the large intestine was a wondrous organ, not exclusively concerned with the elimination of waste, more remarkable in some respects than the heart. There was nothing fanciful about him however, he was strong, but he had peculiar ideas.

Wirthof saying how tall I was for my religion: of course he was an anti-Semite, which somehow made him more interesting to me rather than less – I always have been drawn to people who could do me harm (as evidence of which: my three wives).

On the old unlevel cobbles a horse and cart went by, piled with little bundles of firewood. Smell of horse dung. The afternoon growled from time to time: hot and heavy it was. The driver cracking his whip for the entertainment of the tall child (who was me, amazing as that seems) as he went by.

What does religion have to do with being tall or short? The fact is that people have often been surprised to learn that I am of Jewish blood (my mother wasn't, of course) and there are those of a slanderous bent who – because I am tall, and because it suited them and because my mother was a beautiful woman, Jadwiga was her name –

Stefan Kazakh was ten years old in the spring of 1925 when he raced Konrad Wirthof from the magician's booth in the Prater to the Aspernbrücke, and beat him hollow. My first encounter with Wirthof, who had such an intimidating air – even then – of being able to excel you at everything (it was his boastful manner) but somehow, when it came to it –

After the horse and cart with the firewood had gone by, the tall child – Stefan Kazakh – felt in his pockets for something to eat. All he could find was a dirty-looking peppermint, which he put in his mouth and crunched up with his teeth instead of sucking it. It tasted stale and of the contents of his pocket, and he spat it out immediately, making a face. He sat on the steps leading down from the embankment to the canal: to have a pretending game. Who shall I pretend I am? Dr Boess? Boring. Felix? He didn't much like Felix, that superior smirk of his when Dr Boess asked a difficult question to which, naturally, Felix, being Felix, knew the answer. Conceited. Still, it would be interesting to be Felix, there was a servant girl who sometimes came to fetch him from school, and Felix had once confided that she gave him baths, that she bathed him all over. Must be very nice to be bathed all over by Felix's servant girl, and Stefan imagined that. He screwed up his eyes against the steely glare of the sunless sky, he was feeling a bit sick, must be the old peppermint. Felix was such a liar, always boasting and lying. Stefan was not enjoying his pretending game today. He wished he knew somebody really fantastic. The trouble was there weren't any fantastic people any more, they were all dead, like Napoleon and Bismarck and Genghis Khan and Bar Kochba and Moses and Solomon – pretty interesting to have been Moses, leading your people out of captivity, receiving the commandments straight from God, how did he know it was God? Supposing it was the Devil. Must be interesting being the Devil, rather like being Herr Hülle, who everybody said was so wicked. He sat for a long time on the steps of the canal dreaming of God and the Devil and Herr Hülle, and wondering if he would ever get through these boring years, wishing he could find a way of getting through them more quickly. Most things you could get through more quickly if you hurried, if you were fast enough, and Stefan was fast; it was un-fair that the one thing he wished desperately to be able to get through, time, wouldn't be hurried. There ought to be a way of getting through it faster. His behind was aching from having sat too long on the stone step. Getting up, his eyes rose to the Prater Wheel beyond the Aspernbrücke and above the rooftops, turning slowly through the sky. He wouldn't mind seeing the magician, he thought, the one who swallowed razor blades. He began to run, very fast, he was good at running, his long legs with their strong calf muscles gave him a useful turn of speed, he ran all the way to the Prater and arrived, chest heaving, lengths of spittle hanging out of his mouth. His hair was all over the place, and the inside of his thighs felt sore from where the coarse material of his trousers rubbed against them when he ran. Inside, it was not very full; some of the small children, held in the arms of their mothers or nurses, cried: stupid little brats, always bawling, sob, sob, sob, what was the matter with them? Those fat-bosomed nurses, they looked severe; when he was very small he'd had a woman like that looking after him, because he had no mother, Tante Ilse she was called though she wasn't anyone's aunt, he hated her, she had such a rigid expression on her thin face, as if smiling would break her jawbone, which he wished it would. 'Come along, young fellow, a young man doesn't cry, does he? A young man is brave, a young man doesn't shed tears because he's going away from his papa for a short while, not a young man who deserves the name of young man.' 'Papa, Papa, Papa, Papa, Papa . . .' Tante Ilse ran a kindergarten outside Vienna, in the hills, it was a nice house with thickly wooded grounds and the air was wonderful; after four days he couldn't stand it any more, the cooking at Tante Ilse's made him sick for one thing, so he'd knotted his bed-sheets together, climbed out of the window, and walked back to Vienna, the first child ever to escape from Tante Ilse's kindergarten. After that, his father didn't send him away again. The magician was doing a trick with cards – boring. Stefan wanted to see him swallowing razor blades, that was what he had come to see, he had seen it often but it never ceased to enthrall and astound him. The magician was a fat man, old under his make-up, with bulging cheeks. He suffered from shortness of breath, his eyes rolled like marbles around his face. The card trick was going on and on: Stefan was beginning to feel cheated: supposing he didn't swallow razor blades any more, supposing it was too dangerous and he'd given it up. Stefan moved his weight from one foot to the other. The inside of the booth smelled of wet tarpaulin. Now the magician was doing a trick with eggs, producing them from different places in his clothing, Stefan knew how that was done, nothing to it. If he doesn't do the razor blades trick next I'll go and have a ride on the carousel, that's what I'll do. But when the next trick wasn't the one he was waiting for, he decided to wait until the one after, and then for the one after that, his galloping impatience making him hate the fat magician. And then, finally, of course it was always his final trick, the razor blades were brought on and the magician selected one from a heaped dish and sharpened a pencil with it until he had produced a superb point, and then popped the glittering blade into his mouth, and munched and chewed. Stefan smiled with pleasure, and relief. Now a frown had appeared on the face of the fat magician, he smacked his lips together rapidly like a chef tasting – something lacking: of course, pepper and salt. From behind his left ear he conjured up a salt cellar, from thin air he created a pepper-mill, and with a gluttonous expression on his fat face salted and peppered the glittering mound, selected a single blade, tasted it on his tongue, mimed satisfaction, and began to chew and swallow. As an afterthought, he offered the dish to the audience – arousing laughter – and was comically offended by their refusal. Very well, he would eat it all himself. One after the other, in rapid succession, the blades went in his mouth, Stefan was so delighted he couldn't keep still, the magician's eyes glinted greedily, once or twice he belched and covered his mouth coyly. When he had devoured the entire plateful, he stood beaming happily at the audience; as the applause began, a look of distress came over his face, one hand went to his stomach, the other to his mouth, and in a moment he was vomiting out a daisy-chain of shining steel razor blades. Applause and laughter; Stefan was aware of someone else applauding as loudly as himself, but the way this person was calling out 'Bravo, bravo' was so – so scoffing. Turning towards this sound, he saw a boy of perhaps eleven or twelve, his hands fully extended before him, applauding with the large motions of someone banging cymbals together, and looking around the audience in search of support; his eyes meeting Stefan's were aglitter with occult knowledge, ah – he had such things to tell, such things. The applause was beginning to diminish, people were leaving, but this boy was continuing to slap his hands together as loudly as before, and presently he was the only person still applauding, and the fat magician, sweat trickling down the side of his face, was bowing to him alone, to this vociferously applauding child, again and again he bowed, detained by the continuous hand-clapping: slap, slap, slap, slap: he winced once or twice, becoming suspicious, his professional jollity hardening into a painted smile: slap, slap, slap, slap, slap. He was breathing hard, and bowing, and as the last of the audience filed out he fumbled for a handkerchief and dabbed at his neck, and discovering those mocking child's eyes still on him, he gave an angry flick of his hand, a man brushing away hornets.

Outside, the scoffing boy turned to Stefan. 'You know how it's done?'

'Well, no, not exactly.'

'I know.' It wasn't only the secret of this magician's act that he knew, his manner hinted at the possession of all sorts of knowledge that nobody else had access to.

'Yes?'

'Y-e-e-s, I know how it's done. Magnets.'

'Magnets?'

'Of course, magnets. Didn't you know that? *Magnets*. Yes. In the cheek. Didn't you see how his cheeks were bulging?'

'You can't know for sure.' Stefan felt disappointed, cheated, he'd never come to see the magician again.

'I know about magic,' this scoffing boy said. 'I know all about it. You didn't know it was done with magnets? You thought he swallowed the razor blades?'

'No, of course not.'

'You did, didn't you? You believed that!'

He was a very pale child, with dark rings under his eyes, smaller than Stefan and of slighter build, not at all strong looking, but with natural authoritativeness. He was very neatly dressed, wearing long trousers with a perfect crease in them, his hair was a light colour, parted on the right and brushed down very flat.

'Wirthof,' he said, bringing his heels together and giving a mechanical bow from the neck.

'Kazakh.'

'You don't want to believe everything you see, Kazakh.'

'I don't.'

'I've seen real magic.'

'You have?'

'Oh yes. This – here – is for children.' He began to stroll, assuming – correctly – that Stefan would follow; he was looking around all the time with the eyes of an overseer, as if all the people milling around came under his jurisdiction, had to be watched, would later be the subject of his report. His movements were precise and elegant, next to him Stefan was conscious of his own cumbersomeness, of his long legs which got in each other's way and sometimes made him stumble, of his dishevelled appearance; his scalp was itching and tingling with pins and needles, but he was ashamed to scratch himself in front of this meticulous boy. He felt as selfconscious as if he were in the presence of one of his schoolmasters. There was nothing child-like about this Wirthof, he had the self-possession of an adult, and the look on his face said there were things he knew that even adults didn't know: a little prince schooled in command. Stefan had seen royal princes on the newsreels possessed of this kind of inbred assurance. Perhaps this boy, Wirthof, *was* a young prince, or an aristocrat at least, he had the haughtiness and the grace that Stefan would have expected of someone like that.

The booths and stalls they passed seemed to interest him little, the Lilliputbahn simply brought forth his scoffing laugh, the marionette theatre was given a passing glance only, but at the rifle range he stopped, took out his leather purse, shook some coins into the rimmed flap, carefully selected one and tossed it on to the counter; the attendant showed him a stool to stand on, for he was too small to be level with the target, but he waved away this offer, loaded the rifle from a box of pellets, fired, reloaded, fired, reloaded, and fired again, each of his shots hitting the inner circle of the target, and the last neatly denting the bull's eye. By the time the attendant was examining the target, Wirthof was already walking away, showing no interest in the fact that he had won a prize.

'You're a good shot,' Stefan said admiringly.

'Oh,' he replied dismissingly, 'I've fired real guns.'

'I wish I could shoot like that.'

'It's easy. I'll show you.'

'Yes?'

'When I get time. You want to have a ride on one of the round-abouts?' He asked this as if such childish pastimes had no attraction for him, personally, but for Stefan's benefit he was prepared to go along.

'I don't mind,' Stefan said.

'You ought to be a good horseman, with your name.'

Stefan couldn't be sure if he was being mocked. He laughed.

'I'm not,' he said, 'I don't know how to ride. Can you ride?'

'Yes, I can ride.' It was not said boastfully, it was a matter of course; when the sun shone it picked out the fair flecks in his hair and made them shimmer.

The light was changing all the time, one moment everything was dull, an indeterminate greyish-blue-green without lustre, and Stefan felt invaded by this dullness, felt it lying on his stomach like strange food, and then the sky opened fractionally in some place, the colours ignited as if a match had been put to them, the rows of chestnut trees, the painted designs on the roundabouts, the signs on the booths, the people strolling and looking and laughing all blazed, all except this new friend of his whose pallor was of some deeper, older origin, and, evidently, not curable by sunlight. They had ambled up to the steps of the carousel, the revolving platform was just coming to a halt and children were being lifted off their horses, some of them screamed, not wanting to get off – that awful moment of loss, Stefan remembered his own pangs, of course he was a lot, lot younger then: fighting back the tears, clinging to the lovely, glazed neck, the soft hair of the mane against his cheeks: mine, mine, mine: the horse so beautifully made, a lovely thing: my feet snug in the stirrup irons, backside supported by the pommel, all the leather parts new-smelling, the brow band, the cheek straps, the nose band, the headstall, the curb rein and the snaffle rein, the throat lash, the stirrup leather: bushy tail, glass eyes, gaiters, truly in every respect a horse: mine. His father had promised him a rocking horse, or he'd never have got off, he'd rather have died. How very childish, he reflected, aged ten, casually getting up on a horse alongside the one Wirthof had chosen.

Wirthof shot him a sidelong glance, smilingly critical of Stefan's inexpert posture. 'You wouldn't stay on long if it was a real horse. You've got to grip it with your knees, not your heels. Not your heels, Kazakh. Watch me.' The platform was starting to turn, music was blaring, Stefan felt himself bobbing up and down with the simulated motions of the canter, Wirthof was laughing, alternately they rose and dipped, the platform turned faster, the spectators' faces were boneless flesh, elastic, stretchable and shrinkable, the sky was in its dark phase and Stefan was riding into thunder under a black overhang towards a distant point of illumination that was now in front of him now behind him: a Kazakh riding free, a marauder, the terror of the vast plains, sparing no one. None shall be spared. The scoffing eyes upon me all the time, violet eyes; his neck quivered, giving a proud tremble to his head. Wasn't it all going to be magnificent? His birthright. He was going to be a general before he was thirty. *The flags are high, the lines of men are serried* (high gruff male voices rising to a sweet pitch); *the SS are marching, tread full of purpose and strength*, and so on and so forth, as they sang later, all the time. He never sang it himself, as it happens, because – one of his peculiarities – he couldn't sing, couldn't sustain the simplest tune, not even the simple tune of the SS song: so he'd just mouth the words and pretend he was singing.

All too soon the ride on the roundabout was coming to an end, the platform slowing, the whizzing balloons decelerating, Stefan's hands felt sticky, his behind was itching; and all those elastic faces, of which none would be spared, were becoming solid again, bony, firm, impervious to me and to him. Indifferent, you might say if you wanted to rub it in. The common masses, as Wirthof invariably referred to them, or the *Lumpenproletariat*. What doesn't kill me, strengthens me: that was one of the dicta he'd throw at me, inviting me to agree with him. He was always inviting me to agree with him, but without really wanting me to: I think if I had agreed with him ever, and I don't think I ever did, our relationship would have foundered, run out of fuel; we never called each other by our first names, it was always Wirthof and Kazakh.

Wirthof was dismounting. It was a shame having to get down off the horse. The sun was shining, but the dullness was back in my stomach, and with it a feeling of sickness which might have been caused by the roundabout. He felt awkward with Wirthof, could think of nothing to say to this princely boy whose silence, unlike Stefan's, had a quality of superiority. They left the Prater together.

'Where d'you live, Kazakh?'

'Obere Donaustrasse.'

'I live on the other side of the canal. Stubenring.'

So he lived in the 1st Bezirk. Naturally, being a prince. 'You good at sports, Kazakh?'

'I play football.'

'Football.'

'Full back?'

'No, left wing.'

'So you can run?'

'Yes.'

'I'll race you to the canal. All right?'

He didn't feel like racing, the sickness in his stomach made his legs feel wobbly, and he was tired. 'What are we racing for?'

'For? What d'you mean for? For sport, Kazakh.' The faint sneer in his voice riled Stefan.

'I'll race you,' he said.

'Right.' Wirthof was off before Kazakh was ready to go, but he didn't mind, and a slow smile came over his face as he watched the other boy shoot across the tramlines, just clear of a long (three-coach) tram that was beginning to move, thereby gaining a goodish start. Stefan didn't mind giving him this start, maybe he couldn't ride and shoot, but he felt sure he could outrun Wirthof any day. When the tram had gone by he saw Wirthof already a good distance ahead, going all out, his legs moving with stiff precision. Idiot, Stefan decided, going after him with easy, loping strides, he'll be beat after five minutes. He didn't try to catch him up immediately, but ran steadily, saving himself, carefully weaving through the heavy traffic at Praterstern, getting into the long Praterstrasse, which went all the way down to the canal, even farther behind Wirthof than at the start. He wasn't worried. He could tell exactly how much speed he needed to overtake Wirthof, and he judged it to be well within his capacity, even allowing for the fact that he was feeling sick and that there was a trembling in his leg muscles. He was playing a game; how much of a lead should he give this scoffing boy before catching him up? Then he decided to stop playing; it was not just a matter of beating Wirthof, he had to inflict a crushing defeat on him, really show this cocksure princeling, or whatever he was. All right. Head back, arms going like paddles, he started to really move his long legs, he felt exhilarated by his own speed; there was pain in his chest and in his head and in his legs, but the speed took care of that, and he forced still more out of himself, and was thrilled by the rapidity with which he was catching up; his feet smacked against the pavement with stinging impact. The sound of panting made Wirthof turn, amazed, and in a minute Stefan was ahead, going like a steam engine, he didn't bother to look back, his speed was carrying him through pain; he knew he was way ahead. In front of him was the slight rise going up to the bridge, and on the other side, looking far nearer than it was, the huddled Inner City was blocking out the sun; a diffused light, reddish mauve, tinted the clouds and domes and spires and the water of the canal. At the bridge he stopped, and slid immediately into a sitting position on the ground, with his back against the embankment, and settled back to enjoy his victory. It was spoilt somewhat by the fact that as soon as Wirthof saw he had been beaten, he stopped running, and covered the remainder of the distance at an easy walking pace; he arrived not at all out of breath, looking cool and neat, whereas Stefan was sweaty and hot and full of pains. Took his defeat graciously, managing to be superior even in that. 'You run well, Kazakh,' he pronounced with the air of an adjudicator bestowing a prize. 'A very good effort. I congratulate you.' And he extended his hand, which obliged Stefan to scramble to his feet to take it. His own hand was so dirty and sticky he was hesitant about giving it, but not wanting to seem churlish he did give it, after first wiping it on his trouser leg. 'I'll have to beat you at something else,' Wirthof announced. 'How good are you at chess?'

'Not very good.'

'Just good at running.' It made Stefan smart, the way it was said.

My cousin Zavius. I have some knowledge of this particular cousin of mine (I must have had twenty or thirty of them all told, at least, considering that my father had six brothers and three sisters, all of whom married); of the others I have no information, but cousin Zavius writes to me from time to time, asking for money. During the war he escaped from Sofia and somehow – I forget all the incidents – made his way to Istanbul, where he married his first wife, who died in tragic circumstances, when they were trying to get to Palestine on one of those illegal immigrants' ships: his wife drowned, I believe. Later, in Palestine, he became a member of the Irgun terrorist organization, and married a second time, a fellow terrorist. They have four children, two boys and two girls. It appears he does not earn very much, and they are always hard up.

When I think of my twenty or thirty cousins, all of whom must have had stories, not to say tragedies, to relate, when I think of their suffering, or their happiness, I am ashamed to say I feel quite detached. I can guess at their fate; since they do not write to me for money it is unlikely that they are still alive. Whenever I do think of them, I think of them in a very general way – those unfortunate ones, the victims, the ones who went under, and I feel sorry for myself for having lost them. What a tragedy to have befallen me that I should have lost all twenty or thirty of my cousins, not to mention uncles and aunts, leaving only Zavius and myself to propagate the seed Kazakh, towards which he has done a certain amount whereas I, as far as I know –

I feel very sorry for myself when I think of my unfortunate cousins.

When someone has done me an injury for which no immediate redress is available for one reason or another, I have a strong impulse to resort to violence (I am quite capable of exacting revenge); that I desist, most of the time, does not seem to me particularly creditable, for it seems to me that I desist for the wrong reasons. I assert that I do not believe in an eye for an eye, though I suspect that I do, and I have to conclude that it is my indifference rather than my forgiveness which makes me stay my hand. No, it is not exactly indifference; it is, rather, that there is a failure of my rage, which is strong only for a moment and then subsides, and usually I discover an element of justification in the person who has done the injury to me, and this produces a sort of relief of the pain, for after all if I have deserved the injury, if it is just, if I have taken an eye myself either now or on some previous occasion –

The Obere Donaustrasse was to me a dingy street – working-class Jewish – but it had a fine view across the canal to the Inner City. That low sad dreary period before dusk when everything on my side of the canal was becoming dim, and women sat working by their windows in the dark, not switching on their lights because it was bad for the eyes – so it was said – to work in twilight. On the other side of the canal Vienna began to glow flickeringly like candles in the wind, faintly at first, then more strongly with the hard sparkle of a night city. This time, however, Stefan's low mood was overcome by a feeling of excitement. He said good evening to Herr Fielker, who with a long pole was pulling down his roller shutters, only three-quarters of the way down so he could get back under and inside, he and his wife lived in the back of the shop. Stefan knew all the shops, and all the local tradesmen – he knew exactly, better than the shopkeepers sometimes, where different commodities were kept on the crowded shelves and counters, the tins and the packets were stacked right up to the ceiling, and in front of the counter at Fielker's there was scarcely space to turn with all those open sacks of coffee beans and lentils and rice and dried fruit and soap flakes, all with their little metal serving shovels. Overhead, suspended from the ceiling, hung long slender strips of fly-paper, which most warm nights had a considerable catch, some of the insects still twitching and struggling against their gluey doom. He wondered what it must feel like, being a fly trapped in this way. Must be a horrible death. Still, perhaps it was a normal enough death for a fly and not so awful from the fly's point of view. I wouldn't like to be a fly, he thought. I wouldn't mind being Wirthof – no, I wouldn't like being him, snooty pig, can't run for toffee, but those clothes of his, that suit, his shiny hair, rich little swine, he wondered how he could get to be friendly with him, it'd be a feather in his cap to have a friend like that, an anti-Semite.

He was approaching the place where he lived, a plain building, unornamented, the lower part defaced by the scrawls and knife marks of the kids who played around there, and the ka-ka of the dogs. He went in through the high entrance arch, and up the dark stone steps. He lived on the top floor, sometimes he ran all the way up but tonight he was tired, and he felt he had a winner's right to take it easy. He hoped Papa was home already, he hated coming into the empty flat, especially when it was dark, it smelled so of . . . darkness, and emptiness. He wished he had a mother like other people, it seemed shameful not to have one, he didn't like to talk about it, because people always asked him what had happened to her and he didn't know, and he didn't like to say that he couldn't even remember his mother. There would be an excuse if his mother were dead, if she had died soon after he was born, he knew of other boys whose mothers or fathers were dead, but he didn't know of any whose mother had gone away. Even so, he should have remembered something of her, but all he knew was that she had a beautiful name, Jadwiga, and that she lived in Frankfurt, and that she'd gone to live in Frankfurt when he, Stefan, was four, that was when she'd gone permanently, once or twice before that she'd gone, but then it wasn't permanent, it wasn't permanent until he was four. There was something he remembered about her – she had very white skin and black hair, not just dark brown, but really black black. And there was something else, a smell, a sort of warm delicate comforting smell, quite different from the harsher, beardy smell he now became aware of as he let himself into the dark and silent flat with his own key. Papa wasn't home yet, he was often late, probably he'd stopped somewhere for a beer. Stefan went immediately to the window, the one that looked out across the canal, to see if there was any sign of his father at the bottom of the street. Not a sign. He sighed, and went into the small kitchen and peeled himself a banana, put it between two thick chunks of black bread and took a big bite. Clutching his banana sandwich he returned to his place by the window and settled down to wait and watch. 'Please God,' he prayed, 'make Papa come home quickly. I'm hungry. Thank you. Oh yes – I forgot – thank you for letting me win the race, thank you for giving me strong legs for running. And make Papa come home soon, please make him come home soon, make him be the next person to come round the corner.' He concentrated hard on getting this request through, putting all his energy into it, screwing his eyes up tight with the effort. 'Well, the next then,' he said with a sigh, seeing that the man who had just turned the corner was not his papa. 'One of the next three men,' he added, to make it easier for God. It was half an hour later, and after quite a number of people had come round the corner, that he spotted his father approaching, but he reckoned that among those who had turned the corner there had been several women and children, and maybe there hadn't been more than three *men*, so he was prepared to give God the benefit of the doubt. 'Thank you, God,' he said a little curtly, to show he wasn't altogether convinced his request had received the attention it deserved.

Stefan followed his father with his eyes, all the way from the corner right until he disappeared inside the entrance of the building, and then the boy ran to the door, opened it and stood on the landing listening for the footsteps which he could distinguish from anybody else's footsteps, his father never took long coming up the stairs, sometimes taking them two at a time, with those long strong strides of his, as deliberate as a mountaineer's. Coming up the stairs didn't make him out of breath, as it did other people who hadn't so high up to go, who had to pause and rest on one of the landings, his father never had to do that. And when he got near to the top and saw Stefan waiting for him, a big smile came over his face; Stefan loved to see that smile – and he ran to meet his father, who increased his stride to take three steps at a time, and at the top swept the child in his arms and lifted him high. 'Papa, Papa, you're so late,' Stefan said scoldingly.

'I know, I know. I'm sorry. I was detained.' He kissed the boy, and stooped so that Stefan could get on his back and be given a piggyback into the flat. Happy, happy – hanging on to his father's neck, feeling the bristly texture of his cheek, touching the thick black moustache that lay snug inside his smile.

'You did the shopping, Stefan?'

'Yes, Papa.'

'Good. I'm starving.' He put the boy down on the kitchen table, went to the larder and took out the large loaf of black bread that Stefan had bought earlier in the day at Fielker's, and holding the loaf against his middle began to slice it, thickly, with a long knife, its edge curved from much honing.

'Come on, Stefan, get the sausage and the butter and some beer.'

He loved seeing his father cut bread, all his movements were so exact and strong, there was nothing wasteful in his movements, he was like a good carpenter in the way he used his hands, they were very large with thick ridges of hair coming out from under his shirt sleeves and continuing as far as the knuckle of the little finger. His whole body was densely covered in this thick curly black hair. The various sausages and the pickled cucumbers were unwrapped from their greaseproof paper, laid out on the table; they didn't bother with plates, and they both sat down, knife in hand, and cut themselves slices of whatever they fancied, and ate seriously and in silence until the immediate hunger was allayed.

Staszek Kazakh ate with appetite; his jawbone worked vigorously, his Adam's apple, which was prominent and to which the mat of hair on his chest sent up a few exploratory tendrils, bobbed as he swallowed, especially as he drank down his beer. The line of foam it left on his moustache he wiped away with the back of his hand. While eating, he smiled often.

'Did you work on bridges today, Papa?'

'No, Stefan. You know the department is not making bridges for the present.'

'You said they might make another one over the Donau.'

'That's a big project, Stefan. Nothing's been settled. I've told you that.'

'What did you work on, Papa?'

He smiled. He knew that Stefan was disappointed, the child always asked about the bridges, he would have liked to be able to tell his friends that his father was working on the construction of a wonderful new bridge with a great span, a suspension bridge perhaps, with massive towers at each end. As it was, he could only tell his friends, vaguely, that his father was a construction engineer who worked for the municipality, to say that he made sewers was embarrassing, once he'd mentioned something about that to Felix and the little swine had said – oh, so he's a plumber.

'You know, Stefan, there's nothing shameful about making sewers. Bridges are more beautiful perhaps, to the eye. It's more romantic to make bridges, and when I worked on bridges, before you were born, I enjoyed it very much, but I also enjoy the work I do now. You know, Stefan, you mustn't think of a sewer as being something nasty. If you lived in a country like Palestine you wouldn't think of it like that. There they use the water from the sewers to cultivate the soil, they make the desert fertile with water from the sewers, and it's a wonderful experience to see things growing where nothing grew before. People are squeamish about the function of the large intestine, as if it's shameful, as if all it contains is waste, but that's not so, you know, it's a very remarkable organ, you'd be amazed what intricate and marvellous processes it handles, it doesn't only contain waste matter. It's as remarkable as the heart in many ways, a really remarkable piece of engineering. I love bridges, as you know, Stefan, but a sewer also can be a beautiful thing, any structure that fulfils its purpose in the simplest possible way has a certain beauty, if you can see it.' Stefan wished he could explain it like that to his friends, but he knew they would laugh at him for saying such things.

'Are you never going to make another bridge, Papa?'

'I wouldn't say never. But to be a bridge builder you've got to go wherever you're needed, and live there while the bridge is being made, which can be a matter of years, and that's not a good life for a boy, I want you to have an education. I want you to go to university.'

'I'd rather go to Africa with you, and see you build bridges.'

'I know you would, I know, but I have to think of your future, Stefan.'

Supposing we had gone to Africa, or Canada, where they needed bridge-builders –

In mid-summer, the air was so still; the water wagons sprinkled the streets regularly, leaving a glistening trail that rapidly became obscured again by the dust.

He was nineteen at the time, Stefan. And almost as tall as his father. How I shot up!

He saw the large cheap but no longer new-looking suitcase in the space between the wardrobe and the window. The ashtrays in the room were full, not only of cigarette ends but of the black ash of recently burned paper. His father was fully dressed, his overcoat lay on the bed. He looked at his wristwatch. 'I have to go out,' he said.

'Where? Where d'you have to go in the middle of the night?'

'Try not to ask, Stefan.'

'I have tried.'

'It won't be long, not too long now.'

'Papa, how do I know what you're doing is best?'

Staszek Kazakh laughed. Stefan's eyes went to the suitcase, the overcoat on the bed, the overflowing ashtrays. His father looked at his watch again. 'What can I say to you, Stefan? Any explanation would require me to discuss with you things that at the moment you shouldn't know about, that it's best you don't know about. Besides, there isn't time now. Trust me. Just trust me.' He smiled.

My father had a lovely smile, it would flash suddenly below that thick untended moustache of his like silvery fish rising up to the surface of a still pond – there's one, and another and another, I used to watch out for his smiles, they illumined my world. The time I saw him with one of his women: he threw himself into the love act like a man throwing himself into a cool lake on a hot day, and afterwards my spying eyes saw the fragile smile floating on his face, undulating with the waves, his chest going like a deep storm. How furious I was – hypocrite! betrayer! – that he could give away my love, my due, to fat-bellied whores.

They were all girls of a certain class, shop girls or servant girls, who giggled a lot.

I loved the sound of my father's voice, it was so soft.

He could see from his father's expression that there was no time at all, that he had to leave now. They embraced silently, Staszek Kazakh smiling and calm, and Stefan felt restored partially by the confidence that came from his father. The tall man with the Russian moustache and the brilliant eyes, on whose back I had ridden joyfully, pulled on his heavy overcoat, and picked up his suitcase, its weight pulling his left shoulder out of alignment with the right. Stefan went to the window, as he used to do as a child, and waited for his father to come out of the building. It was February, cold and dry. The street was a hard white, the furrows of horse carts set solid by frost. He watched his father walk rapidly in the direction of the Aspernbrücke, that lopsided walk. Oh God, he thought, oh God!

He turned back into the flat, switched on the light in his bedroom and lay down on the bed, outside the bedclothes, keeping his overcoat on. He'll be all right, yes, he'll be all right; Stefan put all his power, all his magic, into the vow. He slept deeply for a couple of hours.

He dreamt he was at a railway station, trying to find a seat on a crowded train. He was rushing along the platform, slowed down by the weight of his luggage. It was a choice between leaving his luggage behind or missing the train, either was unthinkable. There was only one porter, a feeble old man bent almost double from the luggage already on his back, who kept turning to look at Stefan inquiringly, offering his services. Absurd to think that this wretched old man could take any more luggage on his back, but he seemed to be moving faster than Stefan, and he had a cheerful expression on his face.

It was almost seven when he woke, and still dark outside. He dressed without washing, did not eat breakfast, and went straight to the window. First light, and the city had no shape: a texture of dull metal, hoar frost giving a wintry patina to roofs and spires, obscuring window panes. In the slow seeping light the city was rebuilt, domes, steeples, office blocks, apartment buildings, bridges formed amoebically in a cold creation; the usual activity of morning – the surge towards the tram stops, motor-car engines spluttering and wheezing, schoolchildren with satchels on their backs running, blowing on their hands, skating on icy patches, yelling, disappearing from view, dray horses smoking at the mouth, their driver muffled up to the eyes in a ragged balaclava. The Stephansdom had appeared like an iceberg, suddenly. Stefan blew on his hands to restore some mobility to numb fingers; his toes too were stiff; drink something hot, he thought, but made no move.

The normality of the morning was disturbing, a prolongation of the anticipatory dread that had begun last night; he wished something would happen to end the waiting. Perhaps it had happened already, but if so there would surely be some sign of unusual activity, it was an ordinary morning, like any other. Perhaps it has been called off, he thought, whatever was due to happen, any moment now I shall see Papa coming round the corner. He kept watching out for him, hopefully; the next man to come round the corner will be him.

By ten o'clock, though there was still no sign of any unusual activity, he had to abandon the idea that nothing had happened, if that were so his father would be back by now. Perhaps he's been arrested; the possibility of that was almost a relief. He became mesmerized by the everyday routine of the street. Trivialities compelled his attention: the death of a fly.

How could such a tall man as my father have had such a soft voice?

'The feeling of helplessness is a state of mind, it's a surrender, it's saying there's nothing I can do about it – so let it happen, whatever. But it's hardly ever a true picture of how things really are, except perhaps in some great natural calamity, an earthquake, an avalanche. Situations that are of human origin are capable of human solution. A human being, Stefan, has means at his disposal. Perhaps he doesn't use them, or he doesn't use them well, that has to do with the sort of person he is and the kind of allies he has made for himself. Not only outside himself – inside too, they're also inside you. What I am warning you against is indulging that feeling of helplessness which for us especially, as Jews, is a very dangerous feeling, and easy to succumb to, a very insidious feeling, Stefan. There were Jews in Russia at the time of those pogroms who said – What can we do? We are weak, *helpless*. God is our only help. Trust in God. It's true there wasn't anything spectacular any of them could do – nothing to equal the hope of divine intervention, a flaming sword in the sky to strike down our enemies, there was nothing on that scale that any of them could do. But there were things they could do. For one thing they could read, they could read the writing on the wall, and act accordingly – get out, go somewhere else. My own father did that, your grandfather. There were many others like him who saved themselves and their families. But those who waited for the flaming sword in the sky, for the Angel of Death who would strike down their enemies but exempt them, many of those unfortunate, foolish people perished.'

He became aware, first of all, that his watch was wrong; it said eleven fifty whereas the electric street clock showed eleven forty-six, he was about to make the adjustment when he saw that the trams had all stopped.

How could such a tall man have had such a soft voice?

'When you're certain of something, that's the time to be wary. Conviction isn't the same as certainty, conviction is saying – of that I am convinced, and I will act accordingly, though it is possible I am wrong. Acting out of conviction always has in the background the worry that you may be wrong, and the man who acts out of real conviction doesn't deny that worry, he accepts it, lives with it. The man who acts out of certainty is not worried, because he knows he can't be wrong, and that's somebody to be wary of, and it's also something to be wary of in yourself. I'd say to you, Stefan, that when you are certain of something, that's the moment to hesitate. On the other hand, when you're convinced but worried, that's the moment to have the courage to go on, in the absence of certainty.'

The trams had not stopped at their normal stopping places, and drivers and conductors, and presently passengers too, were getting out and regarding the stricken vehicles, heads shaking, puzzled, slowly realizing it wasn't only their tram that had ground to a halt. The lights in the office buildings on the other side of the canal had gone out, and there were faces at windows, and in his own street shopkeepers had come out of their shops and were looking around and calling to each other.

He went into his father's room, and looked around like someone searching for a mislaid object, what it was he did not know; the room was uninformative, some of his father's working drawings in their thin cardboard canisters lay under the long table.

He opened a deep cupboard, its shelves crammed with loose papers and objects, and he pulled at a dusty stack, extracted an old exercise book; opened it at random. 'A bridge', he read in his father's schoolboy handwriting, 'is as beautiful as it is strong. Beauty arises out of structure, it can never be added on, nor can it be striven for. To strive for beauty is a contradiction in terms; beauty is the feeling created by the successful resolution of conflicting forces. When this is achieved, the result is experienced as beauty. This is as true of the human anatomy as of mechanical structure. When the human body is drawn without knowledge of its inner structure, it is lifeless and ugly, however prettily the external features are rendered. The outer form of objects is determined by their inner structure; when artificial form is imposed to disguise structure the result is deceitful decoration, and ugliness. There is no ugliness in nature, only deformity; there are no ugly people, only ...'

Stefan put back the exercise book exactly where he had found it; he wished his father had left something more useful in this room, a gun for instance. A treatise on beauty, in the firm, confident handwriting of the bright schoolboy, what use was that? ... If only my father had taken me into his confidence.

Where was the evidence for the existence of allies? Stefan began to empty the ashtrays; it was an oversight on his father's part not to have done so, if the police came they would see immediately that some kind of meeting had been held there. Stefan watched the second hand of his watch make its slow revolution, his heart racing it.

Unable to do anything else, he returned to his place by the window, to continue his watch. The trams had emptied; some of the passengers were standing about, stamping their feet, irritated at being delayed, but clearly expecting the trams to start up again at any minute; whoever was responsible for the trams running would presumably see to that, it was nothing to do with them, they were passengers. Others, perhaps those with shorter distances to go, had begun to walk.

At ten minutes past noon a police van, its lights flashing, pulled up at the tram stop on the Schwedenbrücke, and a dozen policemen armed with rifles jumped out and began to clear the bridge, gesturing to the still waiting passengers to get off the street. Some of them argued with the policemen, who seemed fairly good natured and argued back, leaning their rifles against the parapet. Farther away, on the Marienbrücke and the Aspernbrücke, much the same sort of thing was happening. As the passengers of the stranded trams began to walk towards one or other bank, open army lorries full of soldiers in combat uniform rumbled on to the bridges from the Franz Josefs-Kai. They aroused only limited interest; such troop movements were not uncommon, it might be an exercise, or possibly trouble *was* expected in this vicinity from hotheads, such things happened, nothing so unusual in that. The steel-helmeted soldiers getting out of their lorries appeared to be of the same opinion, they were in not too much of a hurry as they set up their barbed wire roadblocks at the approaches to the bridges and placed their machine guns and their sandbags. Anyone approaching the bridges, whether on foot or in a motor-car or on a bicycle, was turned back by the sentries who, however, kept their rifles slung on their backs and became quite conversational if the person seeking to cross over happened to be an attractive girl. There was some confusion about who was and who was not allowed to cross; a senior police officer lost his temper with a sentry who sought to bar his way, and the commanding officer of the unit, a thin, serious-faced youth, was called, and he insisted – Stefan gathered this from the gestures – that nobody was

allowed to cross, his orders were explicit, not even a senior police officer was exempt. But when the police officer lost patience with him, brushed him aside, and proceeded to walk across, the young lieutenant didn't seem to know what to do, frowned angrily, muttered something in a sharp voice to the sentry (evidently not an order to shoot for the sentry made no attempt to unsling his rifle) and walked fiercely to the parapet from where he frowningly studied the canal's dark-brown flow.

For the next two hours the only activity consisted of policemen telling people to get off the streets, and firmly steering those who protested they had nowhere to go, that they lived on the other side of the canal, or else had business there, back in the direction from which they had come. Most of the shopkeepers in the Obere Donaustrasse and in the Untere Donaustrasse had pulled down their shutters, partly as a precautionary measure but also because there was after all no point in remaining open.

Stefan did not eat. It was a little like a Jewish fast day, Yom Kippur, the Day of Atonement.

In the late afternoon there was a light snowfall, then the sky darkened rapidly, the day folded into itself and was over, and nothing had happened, except that his father had not come home.

He was standing in the dark holding his breath, if he breathed everything would come tumbling down on top of him, and crush him: one is never helpless my father said. Stefan sat quite still, watching the movement of darkness inside the room, coming from the far wall, an outgoing tide lapping his feet, joining with the darkness outside. He saw the flicker of candles in windows, but he did not light a candle himself, even such a small action was perilous, a possible disturbance of the precarious balance of forces that held him up.

From time to time he rose and walked painfully up and down to restore the circulation to his legs, after which he returned to his watch, his eyes never long away from the corner around which his father would have to come. There was no question of going to bed, the watch had to be maintained, and when against his will his eyelids began to fall he dug his fingernails into his thighs to keep awake. This insufficient pain filled his head to the exclusion of all else; he was empty; a single cell organism incapable of the simplest thought.

When he saw that twenty-four hours had gone by since his

father's departure, he got up, buttoned the collar of his overcoat across his neck, and went down into the street. The shock of the cold night air reactivated the processes of his halted body. The city, devoid of landmarks, still, its surface unruffled, its darkness faintly patterned with cats' eyes of light, had nothing to communicate; the light snowfall had set to a concrete hardness; abandoned trams loomed up like shipwrecks everywhere; Stefan picked his way through the dark, he did not need to see, nor did he need to make much effort to avoid the soldiers, their guard posts were in the most obvious places, easily avoidable. He had no plan, only a strong impulse. He handed himself over to instinct. He made his way along the side of the canal, by-passing the roadblocks at the bridges by doing a small circuit of back streets, and after the Salztorbrücke he climbed over the parapet at a point where he knew the embankment wall to be pitted, providing hand-holds for the descent. He lowered himself by his fingers to within ten feet of the bank, and dropped down the rest of the way. He kept close to the wall until he came to the place opposite the fish market where a punt was always tied up. He untied it, stepped in. The old wood had a skin of hoar frost, and reeked of fish. Paddling a diagonal course, he reached the other bank below the Morzinplatz: there were no guards on this side and he was able to take the public steps up to the Franz Josefs-Kai. Candles and oil lamps flickered in a few windows of the tall apartment buildings lining the boulevard, The immobilized trams formed odd clusters and chains, a de-energized molecular structure. A solitary tank stood in the middle of the Schwedenplatz, turret open, motor off, its occupants warming their hands on mugs of steaming coffee. Stefan walked quickly across the street, and up narrow steps to the little piazza with the old church in the Ruprechtsplatz. From there he had a wide view of the canal, the Kai, the guarded bridges, there was no sign for him here, and he carried on through the second-hand clothing district of the Judengasse and into Marc-Aurel Strasse and Tuchlauben.

Usually the various routes he took through the town were governed by his loves; he had to see this one when she caught her tram at eight in the morning and that one when she left her office in the early evening and another when she locked up shop – to see was everything. It was not necessary that the objects of his love should be aware of him; on the whole he preferred it if they were not, for once they became conscious of his enraptured gaze he felt embarrassed and had to give them up.

The girl who lived in the Untere Donaustrasse and often was sitting by the window, sewing, when he came home from school had in the end become aware of him standing against the embankment wall gazing up, though he tried to give the impression of just looking around at nothing in particular. At first she had been puzzled, then amused, then for several days she hadn't come to the window at all, and he'd waited around in vain for a glimpse of her; but a few days later she was at the window again and he was overwhelmed, and in the succeeding days he became convinced she was actually looking out for him, waiting for him to appear, and actually leaning out, when she did lean out as she sometimes did, for his benefit. One evening she sat by the window brushing her hair, there was such excitement for him in her brushing movements. She had not looked at him directly, but he was convinced she was brushing her hair for him, and every brush stroke increased his passion; attaining the peak of daring he gazed straight at her without pretence, waiting for her to return his look, which was all he needed, all he asked of her. Look at me, he begged her silently, look at me; but she didn't.

As he penetrated deeper into the Inner City and approached the area in which government buildings were situated, he saw more soldiers, armoured vehicles, hastily constructed machine-gun posts at street corners, armed police; but he was not challenged. At the top of the Graben there was a hot sausage stand. As he ate hungrily, he said to the corporal next to him, 'It's quiet. Nothing going on?' The corporal shrugged, and said without looking at Stefan, 'I'm getting frozen, that's what's going on.' 'What's happened?' 'How would I know.' He laughed at the simpleness of civilians. 'They don't tell *me*. There's no electricity, I know that.' One of the civilians said to Stefan, 'It's a general strike, it'll be over by tomorrow. The Austrian worker has no stomach for Bolshevik revolutions. General strike . . . well . . . so called.'

The Hotel Imperial was full of excitedly gesticulating men. Candlelight flickered against red figured damask walls. Snacks were being served. There was a great deal of coming and going. The little groups were constantly re-forming as someone came in with the latest news. 'It'll be over by tomorrow.' 'I'm not altogether so confident.' 'I wager it will have blown over by tomorrow.' 'These revolutionaries – hah!' 'So much for the solidarity of the workers – eh? Isn't that what I said?' 'They say there is heavy fighting in Linz.' 'Yes, yes, I had heard.' 'It is of course typical of the workers that –' 'My information is that Deutsch has bolted.' 'The workers' settlements, that's where the trouble is going to be.' 'Those places are arsenals.' 'It was the Socialists who built them, naturally they have made fortresses of them.' 'The city workers are different. Waiter! Herr Obers!' 'The Viennese worker has no stomach for revolution.' 'Only one thing Dollfuss can do.' 'What is that?' 'Blast them out. Howitzers will blast them out.' 'These Socialists, when there is a little dying to be done – ah-ah! Where are these men of steel, hmm?' 'And of course they all have their little bank accounts in Switzerland. What do you think?' 'Do you know what Brimmer said –'

The tall youth aroused some stares. He looked as though he was about to be sick. Who had let him in here?

Running, through streets no longer familiar: I was possessed of the instinct of a mole and the terror of a child.

How many hours?

Like a mad dog, down this street, up that one, asking everyone where was the fighting. Nobody seemed to know where the fighting was. Some said Linz, others Dobling, others Floridsdorf – back across the canal, and then across the Floridsdorfer Brücke over the Donau. 'That's where they say the fighting is.' But nobody knew for sure. There was no sound of guns.

The soldiers were kind to the tall wild-eyed boy who came up to them and demanded where the fighting was. He looked distraught and ill. They told him to sit down for a minute and have a drop of something, but he wouldn't hear of that, he had to find out where the fighting was. Something about his father.

Only in Vienna could there have been such a civil war – well, they called it that later, it was only a small civil war of four days, only two or three hundred killed, a handful hanged, there were people who lived in Vienna and didn't know it had happened. The *Schutzbund* was supposed to have taken the Inner City in the first few hours, mounted on a fleet of mobile incinerators supplied by the municipality, picturesquely smoking, no doubt, as they encircled the Ballhausplatz, but Bauer, the great procrastinator, had cabled Bernaschek, 'Anna is ill, don't undertake anything,' and then argued until ten a.m. before conceding that his hand was forced and handing out the weapons. And then, a few hours later – while I was staggering through the dark streets sicking up lumps of sausage, a maniac demanding where the fighting was – he had already taken to his heels, abandoning what was scarcely begun, 'left in the lurch by the masses' as he said, and scurrying across the border to safety in Czechoslovakia. And in the morning, the black scum of night drifting from the rooftops, the war was already lost, and I was still looking for the fighting.

The cafés were open, people were going to work, and presently the electricity came back on, the trams began to move again, government newspapers were on sale in the streets, Dollfuss was broadcasting every half hour promising amnesty for all who laid down their arms, all except the ringleaders would be pardoned. There was hope again; the night was over. It was possible for me to eat.

Always the waiters made a fuss of the small child, brought him a cushion to sit on, poured his soup out of a heavy silver cup – he looked with such adoration at his father; his shoulders went up and down as he tackled his soup, soup spoon clutched tightly, the vermicelli reaching his mouth in a conglomerate mass, having to be unpicked like stitching, disentangled, reduced to scalding plaited strands before he could get them in his mouth.

There were foreign newspapermen at a near-by table, American and French, and they were discussing the fighting, and then another came in and said that there was a story going around that Dollfuss was bringing in howitzers against the workers' settlements. 'Come on, let's go see,' one of the Americans said. Suddenly the word Floridsdorf crystallized in my mind out of the whisperings of a wall. Floridsdorf, the wall had said again and again, Floridsdorf.

Stefan followed the newspapermen out of the café; one was going to Dobling, another to Ottakring, and the American said he'd see what was doing at Floridsdorf; they signalled to taxis. Stefan said, 'Could I come with you to Floridsdorf? I think my father is there.' The correspondent looked at the boy sharply but not unkindly – I must have had the appearance of a tramp. 'Sure,' he said, 'come on. Hey – are you all right, son?' Stepping towards the taxi, Stefan had stumbled and almost fallen. 'Yes, I'm all right,' Stefan said.

I was all right as shattered glass. I was having an awful job keeping my eyes open, but when I closed them everything was in the wrong place, earth, sky, the taxi; the inside of the moving car sometimes seemed absolutely vast, a rolling plain, and a small bump felt like a great turn on the Prater's Wheel and I had no hold on anything.

The correspondent, seeing how pale the boy was, gave him something to drink from a chrome hip flask; it made his fever, if that it was, burn more fiercely, but also dealt a blow to that part of himself which was running in a maze. Once or twice their taxi was stopped by policemen or soldiers and the correspondent showed his papers. Stefan was not conscious of crossing the canal, but presently he saw the wide gash of the river, the frost-skinned superstructure of the massive bridge, heard the gunfire at the same time as he felt the wind catch them exposed above the brownish water. At the correspondent's insistence, their driver overtook the tanks and armoured cars and troop vehicles; ahead of them a ministerial car with motor-cycle outriders had cleared the way, and they followed in its wake. The small-arms fire was a constant pitter patter, it sounded like hail. The other sound they heard when three-quarters across the bridge, a very formal sound preceded by a bugle call, the sound of ceremonial salutes, making the air shudder and the bridge move as if shaken by a giant casta-net player. Following the ministerial car, all roads clear for them, they drove on, the American correspondent with his head stuck out of the window. Arriving, they pulled up a few metres behind the ministerial car, having passed through the cordon with it, on a patch of iced-over ground. The low, white complex of the Floridsdorf workers' tenement, the pride of municipal socialism, lay slightly below them, with a steel-corseted gas storage tower behind. One white wall had a lump torn out of it, as if someone had stuck a dirty hand into an iced cake. An artillery major opened the rear door of the ministerial car, stepped back and saluted as an elderly man in a long overcoat with a broad fur collar got out, followed by a thin elegant man in frockcoat and striped trousers, holding a silk hat; he had the air of having been dragged from a conference room unprepared. The statesmen nodded gravely, and surveyed the scene with the air of men who do not shirk their duty, even if it is an inconvenience.

The howitzers, four of them, were positioned twenty feet apart, covering the east to west spread of the tenement; they pointed across an area of uneven ground without trees or shrubs (but with a children's swing and some poles serving as goal posts), pitted, and with many ice patches, occasional reflectors of sporadic sun. To the left and the right and some little distance to the fore of the field guns the buildings directly overlooking the tenement had been occupied by infantry, and there was the continuous pitter patter of rifle and machine-gun fire. A mild sound. The howitzers were out of range of the small-arms fire of the workers.

The statesmen surveyed the situation, and consulted with the artillery major who pointed in various directions, and loaned his field glasses to the man in the striped trousers, and held this man's silk hat so that hatless he could better survey the battle-ground. A junior officer had asked the American correspondent for his credentials and now took them to the major, who examined them and said something questioning to the two statesmen.

After a discussion the elder of the two men was escorted to a signals vehicle and given a hand microphone. He took out his glasses, placed them on his nose, unfolded a piece of paper, and read into the microphone, his voice carried by loudspeakers across the treeless playground. 'Fellow citizens, workers of Vienna, this is the Minister of Internal Security speaking to you. I appeal to you to lay down your arms and bring to an end this senseless bloodshed. The ringleaders of this treacherous attack on the legal government will be called to account for their treason. But everyone else who surrenders now will be pardoned. No action will be taken against any of you who lay down your arms and surrender now, I make you this offer in the presence of a representative of the American press. Lay down your arms, workers! You have ten minutes before the artillery fires the next round. A bugle call will signal the commencement of this period and another the expiry. After this you will be given a further minute of grace, followed by a third bugle call which will be immediately followed by the next round of artillery fire. This procedure will go on throughout the day, until you surrender. I ask you, for the sake of your women and children, whose blood will be on your head, to surrender now and avoid this senseless slaughter.'

Solemnly he handed the microphone back to the artillery commander, folded his statement and returned it to his pocket; the statesman in the striped trousers gave him a congratulatory handclasp. The junior officer jumped to attention and saluted. The bugler issued his first call, and the statesmen, the officers, and the American correspondent, all looked at their watches. The Minister of Internal Security said, 'I can only remain ten minutes.'

From the tenement a machine gun spat a forlorn reply, the bullets lacerating a patch of frozen ground some fifty metres or more in front of the gun emplacement. The American correspondent took a swig at his chrome flask, offered it to Stefan, who took a long gulp. 'You think your father's in there?'

The minister had taken out his watch again and clicked open the lid. The gunners were standing ready to the side of their guns, clear of the recoil. The major was studying the tenement through his field glasses. The bugler was rubbing his lips, which were numb from the cold. The frozen declivities on the playground glittered dull as dead eyes.

If he could hide inside people's eyelids he would be able to see everything, and he would know everything, they wouldn't be able to keep anything from him. But then – if the person in whose eyelid he was currently hiding should happen to blink; it was a perilous adventure hiding inside people's eyelids. The nose might be roomier, but even more dangerous; just imagine what a sneeze could do to you, blow you to pieces. The ear then. Yes, maybe the ear. Safe enough there – hear everything, and also look out and see, yes, that would be a good place to be, inside Papa's ear, a good comfortable place, warm with all that hair, quite protected there, and a good vantage point – all the things he could whisper from there, having Papa's ear, a powerful position.

One is never helpless. Situations of human origin are capable of human solution. I made alliance with the unfeeling sky. My new ally darkened with the passage of clouds, and I closed my eyes in emulation. I demanded another swig of the correspondent's flask, that was another ally I could rely on, it burned the sharp edges of my dread. One must make allies; yes, I opened my eyes, the bugler was passing the back of his hand across his lips, he was nervous. My allies gave me a measure of calm, I had the one inside, burning my stomach and chest, and the other was dimming its light, throwing a shadow over the white façade of the tenement, obscuring the faces at the windows. The bugler was issuing his call. When it had died away, the major stood with wrist raised, counting the seconds on his watch. The statesman with the striped trousers stood erect, chin raised, silk hat under his arm, a ceremonial stance. The old minister shook his head and kept his eyes on his pocket watch. Then the major issued the command, and the gunners in rapid succession pulled the firing cord of their howitzers, standing well clear of the recoil. The deep roars seemed to have no causal relation with the effect; the first shell of the enfilade tore a neat hole in the main façade of the building, the second widened it, ripping out one storey for a distance of about four metres on either side of the point of impact. But they were thick, solid walls, and they did not totter; the third shell, aimed higher, took off a section of the upper storey and roof, the fourth shot fell somewhat short and merely smashed a lot of windows, the falling glass could still be heard after the other sounds had stopped. The minister said, 'Repeat the amnesty offer before every round,' and turned towards his car.

In the comparative silence after the shelling, when the slow shattering glass sounded to deafened ears like the soft tinkling of chandeliers, a human yell was heard, not of pain or surrender or fear but of attack, of men urging themselves on; so somehow inappropriate was this human yell after the booming of the big guns that it startled the minister on the way to his car, and made the major turn, without field glasses for once, in the direction of the sound. A group of perhaps a dozen men had come out from the tenement and were running – making this yelling sound – straight towards the gun emplacement. It took the major and the infantry officers on his flanks some moments to grasp that this was a kind of counter-attack, and by then the attackers were already past the children's swing and almost level with the goal posts and sweeping forward – perhaps this was suggested by the goal posts – like the forwards of a football team. Up in the gun emplacement they had recovered from their momentary surprise and the heavy machine guns had opened up, and to the left a lieutenant of infantry, pistol in hand, was leading his men in a dash across the playground to cut off the workers before they could get within range of the howitzers. The minister was appreciating the situation and frowning, as if to say that such an eventuality had not been presented to him in advance. The major, recovering, drawing his pistol, was urging the statesmen to take cover behind their car, gesticulating to them urgently. The artillery crews had sprawled flat on the ground and were unslinging rifles. The workers, spread out, weaving, were not pausing to fire their weapons, but running with straining necks – running like athletes. The minister refused to get down, unaccustomed to such indignity, but the other statesman had dashed behind the protection of the car, dropping his silk hat as he went, and it had rolled to the edge of the decline, and was over it, rolling down towards the runners on the playground, rolling over and over, black and shiny, spun and whipped along by gusts of wind. From the flanks the government troops were converging in a claw movement on the little group of runners, clouds opened momentarily, and all over the treeless playground the ice patches glittered before dimming again. A woman's scream from the tenement; a burst of machine-gun fire from the roof, wild and useless, an overflow of rage. On the treeless playground the runners' feet made the ice crackle like stiff brown wrapping paper, I saw my father among the runners, he was the tallest of them. The government troops, greatcoats flapping, heavily belted and cross-belted, bent low with soldiers' caution, were pausing every so often to fire into the little bunch of workers. When the government troops were hit they went down like sacks, but the workers, their speed offering more opposition, careered like berserk skaters.

A hundred metres from the gun emplacement, all except three of the workers still alive threw themselves on the ground, firing their sub-machine guns into the enclosing claws of the crab, while the three kept straight on for the head, the gun emplacement, hands high in frantic semaphore. The three, zigzagging crazily, were within thirty metres of where the ground began to rise slightly. Stefan saw his father in the lead, taller than the others, saw his long arm sweep forward from the horizontal to the vertical in a powerful throw forward, the believer in human solutions for human predicaments – saw the small dark round object rise in a high arc, saw the major, shooting arm rigidly extended, fire twice with the accurate deliberation of someone in a shooting range; and I saw my father arrested in the posture of an athlete breaking the tapes, an agony of accomplishment on his dying face, and I saw the other bullets from all sides hit the slow falling body, twist it this way and that, make a whirligig of it, and allow it, finally, as the grenade landed some three metres short of the first howitzer, to complete its interrupted fall. The slight rise below the gun emplacement threw back most of the blast, toppling the other two before they could throw, and as they fell the government crab closed its claws, firing unnecessarily into the little group, all of whom were already dead.

In the gun emplacement one of the gunners had had his steel helmet blown off by blast. Below, a sprinkling of government troops lay dead or wounded.

Stefan Kazakh ran forward, breaking free of the American correspondent who had sought to detain him, ran to the edge of the decline, and there was held back by soldiers, all energy going out of him he hung on their arms like wet washing. Blood had left my father's body from so many places that he had shrunk – the great frame seemed to have shrunk up into itself, the white shirt was a rag of holes, and his sweet fool's face – ridiculously – was illumined with accomplishment.

He did not say *Kaddish* for his father, nor did he sit *Shivah*, nor did he go about in stockinged feet; he did not believe in all that rigmarole, not shaving, making a tear in his clothes, all that. He did not even wear a black arm-band. He did not see the point of mourning. His father was dead and that was all there was to it.

Wirthof called to express his condolences: he was meticulous in such matters. He talked all that pompous rubbish about honour and a soldier s death, as if there were some kinds of death to be preferred to others. You were just as dead however you died. God, how I was sick of all this Austrian posturing, attitudinizing!

I never understood what my father meant when he talked about allies, that's something you never comprehended, Kazakh. About enemies I understood, yes, yes, from the beginning; with enemies I knew where I stood, could look after myself, I was quick. But allies? Where were these mythical allies? My father was a crazy man, a man who could see beauty in sewers, in the large intestine, a crazy man, a fool, a Don Quixote. Lovable, yes. But what a fool! Did you go to Vienna to visit the grave of a fool, Kazakh? More fool you. But you are not such a fool, Kazakh. (Trust no one, that's the secret, whom did I ever trust? Myself, my quickness. Nothing else, nobody else, even when I was most trusting.)

Yesterday . . . what was the matter with me yesterday? How many hours did I walk around Vienna, getting myself exhausted. A man with business to attend to, with serious matters to occupy him, looking at fun fairs, standing on bridges. Next you'll be looking at girls in windows. The Stadtpark though was beautiful in the snow.

'My father used to talk about having allies – good allies, that was what one had to have. You see what good allies he had. What a fiasco that so-called revolution was. The sheer incompetence of it takes one's breath away. I have my own theory about allies, Wirthof – pick strong ones, not fools and Don Quixotes. If you're going to fight, pick allies with howitzers, those are allies worth having.'

'Oh absolutely,' said Wirthof.

What colour was Wirthof's hair? It was the yellow of dead leaves, as a child his hair was darker and it just had these lighter flecks in it, but later it became the colour of dead leaves, it had that texture too – perhaps he used dye, perhaps that's what it was – and you felt that if you touched it, his hair, it would disintegrate in the hand, that can happen if you use poor quality dye, in those days they probably didn't have such good dyes, that could be the explanation. Kazakh, have you come all this way to Vienna in order to concern yourself with the question of whether or not Konrad Wirthof used to dye his hair? (Why would he dye his hair?)

What makes me feel that I knew Wirthof so well? (We never even called each other by our first names, there was always a curiously formal aspect to our relationship.) I have the feeling that I have always known him, but this is simply untrue. I met him only occasionally when we were children, half a dozen times perhaps, the period when we were closer came later, but why, then, do I think of him almost as my constant companion? Because I can remember nobody else? What was there about the other companions of my childhood that my memory should so effectively have consigned them to oblivion?

Yesterday when I was walking around Vienna looking at all the rebuilt bridges, I suddenly remembered I had wanted to build bridges too, that had been my earliest ambition, one that occupied me for months, years, it was a real passion in my life, nights I dreamed of bridges, my thoughts turned to them whenever my spirits were in need of lifting, and in my imagination what fantastic structures they were, I was going to build bridges such as nobody had ever built before, spanning unheard of distances. It passed, this passion of mine. Something must have changed in me. Quite suddenly, or so it seems now, I no longer wanted to build bridges, nor were my father's words unquestionable any longer. I left the Technische Hochschule – very abruptly. I remember, in response to the overwhelming feeling that I was going wrong.

In the fish market on the canal: the fish being hauled out of the tanks: wriggling and flapping; being put in wooden tubs for weighing; and then they were loaded on to the waiting lorries. (In 1927 I was twelve.)

'Oh it's you, Kazakh? Buying fish?' (He managed to make it sound something shameful.)

'Yes. You?' Ridiculous to ask such a question of a prince, princes didn't shop, of course not, people like him had servants to do that sort of thing.

'I like to look around,' he said.

'Oh I see.'

'Ever been to a slaughter-house?'

'No.'

'That's interesting. They tie up the cow's legs, then they hit it on the head till they've got it on the ground, and then they slit its throat. You should see the blood. Rivers of it. I'm vegetarian myself,' he added. 'I've taken it up recently. I think it's the only honourable thing one can be. Don't you agree?'

'Well, I don't know, I'm not.'

'You any good at discussions, Kazakh?'

'What sort of . . . ?'

'I like to have discussions. It's interesting. Keeps your mind alert. Now for instance, we would have a very good discussion about vegetarianism.'

'I don't know anything about it.'

'You don't have to know anything about it. All you have to do is discuss it. You can attack it, and I'll defend it, or vice versa, as you like, and we'll see who wins. If vegetarianism doesn't interest you, we could discuss the Jewish question. Now that would be a first-class subject. The problem of the Jews. We might discuss anti-Semitism, Kazakh. One day, when you come to my house, you agree?'

A medium-sized carp was what Stefan wanted (his father loved carp) and the fishmonger delved in the water and fetched one out that looked about the right weight; it was flapping violently as he removed it from the net and carried it to his slab, where he killed it, cleaned the scales off, filleted it and wrapped it up in newspaper. Stefan was conscious of the smell of the fish as he walked with Wirthof along the side of the canal; carrying his school satchel and several loose books in one hand, and trying to transfer the fish from the hand closest to Wirthof to the other, so as to minimize the smell, he got himself in a tangle, and the books, the satchel and the fish fell to the ground. He went red, he was sure Wirthof was smirking – pig! Stooping down, he retrieved his things, trying to be casual about it. Of course Wirthof made no attempt to help; naturally; the pig; only the memory of having beaten him at running eased the humiliation. They parted at the bottom of the next lot of steps, Wirthof calling to him, 'Mind you don't go falling in the canal, Kazakh.'

Next time he saw him it was winter, snowing: very cold. Wirthof wore a long grey overcoat reaching almost to his ankles, it had a high fur collar that could be turned up, as it was now, to cover his ears. He was standing at a street corner, hunched inside his voluminous coat, stamping his feet, his face paler than ever, his eyes glutinous from the cold, spasms of shivers shaking him periodically. Stefan called out to him.

'Oh, it's you, Kazakh.' (He always looked astonished to see me.) 'God, it's cold, isn't it? I've been waiting for a cab for half an hour, I'm frozen.'

'Why don't you walk? You'd get warmer.'

'Hate walking. You don't mind the cold?'

'Not too much.'

'I hate it. I shall live in a warm climate, and fry in the sun. Tahiti. Have you ever been to Tahiti?'

'No.'

'Neither have I. But I've been to Venice. The Italians are highly sympathetic, don't you think?' He was dancing around, stamping his feet, looking quite comical.

'I don't think I know any Italians.'

'You don't know very much, do you, Kazakh?'

At last a cab came in sight, and Wirthof rushed into the middle of the street, stamping, waving his arms about. Stefan didn't know any other boys of their age who travelled by cab.

'You want to come with me?' Wirthof asked when the cab had drawn up.

'Where to?'

'Where I live, my flat. We can have a discussion. Or a game of chess, if you prefer.'

'Oh all right.'

'Get in then. Come on, come on, I'm frozen.'

It was only a short distance to where he lived, he could have walked it easily in ten minutes. Still, Stefan enjoyed the cab ride and was sorry it didn't last longer. Wirthof paid the driver from inside the cab, head sunk in his fur collar, and when he'd received his change made a quick dash across the pavement and through a narrow high door set in a much larger one. Stefan, following him, had an impression of a richly ornamented building, very different from the one in which he lived, with stone lions and female figures grouped around the entrance; inside, there was marble on the floor, a statue in an arched niche, a wrought-iron staircase.

Wirthof lived on the ground floor. He opened the door; it was of a shiny dark wood, panelled, and had a dark brass plate and a spy hole at eye level. The entrance hall was dim and silent, and their boots made a harsh noise on the floor. Wirthof put a cautionary finger to his lips. 'My mother's an invalid, you see, we mustn't make any noise. Better take your boots off, Kazakh.' He had begun to unlace his own. There was a strange – alien – smell in this flat, it smelled of the lives of people quite unlike any that Stefan knew. The smell of the *Yocks*, Stefan deduced – lavender-scented furniture polish, formaldehyde, old clothes chests. 'My mother's highly sensitive to noise,' Wirthof explained, creeping in his stockinged feet across the hall and gesturing to Stefan to follow. He opened a pair of mahogany doors that gave on to a large room in semi-darkness, its curtains three-quarters drawn, its dark furniture disappearing into darker walls. Stefan followed Wirthof in silence, polished parquet under his feet and the smell of disuse in his nostrils. At the end of this room there was another pair of identical doors, and they went through these and through another unused room; he didn't know how many such rooms and such doors they passed through to the accompaniment of the grave serial ticking of unseen clocks before they reached a room into which some daylight penetrated. This was Wirthof's own room, formerly the nursery; it contained a bed, a wardrobe, a marble-topped washstand, which he was using as a desk, and two straight-backed hard chairs. Wirthof squatted down on the floor, and began to arrange chessmen on a board.

'Come on, Kazakh, you have to give me a chance to revenge myself, for that beating you gave me at running. It's only fair. You must give me satisfaction, if we're to be friends.'

Stefan didn't feel like playing chess. 'You've got lots of rooms here,' he said.

'Oh, yes. Plenty of rooms. And they're a good size. I like rooms to be a good size. I like high ceilings. Of course, it's useful to have some small rooms as well. You don't want to have all large rooms, do you?'

'No, that's true.'

'You have large rooms, Kazakh?'

'Not very large. Not as large as yours. What d'you do with all these rooms?'

'Those rooms are reception rooms,' he said, indicating with his head the direction from which they had come. 'Only we receive very rarely now, which is why they're hardly ever used. We don't see many people now, except family. You have family, Kazakh? God, I hate relatives, they're impossible. Always telling you how much you've grown, what do they expect you to do – shrink? I've got one uncle who's interesting, you can have an interesting discussion with *him*, he's a State's Prosecutor. That's something that interests me. Criminals are highly interesting, wouldn't you agree? People who've committed murders or colossal swindles, or rape. You'd be amazed, Kazakh, how many people commit rape. It has to do with the blood sugar level in the brain, did you know that? Yes, it's well known, if your blood sugar level falls below a certain level, you can go mad, that's a fact, it's a good idea to carry a lump of sugar in your pocket, as a safeguard. Of course, there are some people who are just of the criminal classes. They're different. Jews are supposed to be a very sensual race, would you agree?'

'That's just iniquitous propaganda.'

'Is that so? I've wondered sometimes. The Jews do seem to be a very peculiar race from what one hears. I don't think I've ever met a Jew – except you, that is. I don't suppose you're typical of them. My father is always talking about the Jewish problem, he says there's an international brotherhood of Jews who control everything. Is that true? He says the Pope is a Jew.'

'That's not true, he couldn't be.'

'Well, Jesus Christ was, wasn't he?'

'I suppose he was.'

Stefan didn't like the turn their talk was taking; he didn't know very much about such things, but he knew from experience that people who started talking about the Jews in this way were usually anti-Semites.

'Is your father an advocate too?'

'Oh God no. My father is a general, Kazakh. He got his legs blown off. In the war. Stick-grenade. They're monsters. If it hadn't been for the horse – the horse took most of the blast – he'd have been dead. I'd rather be dead myself, wouldn't you? What's the point of being alive with no legs? All he does all day long, my father, is play cards. With his cronies – they're in there now. You should see them, the cripples brigade. Some of them have only got one arm, or one eye, they're a sight when they come trooping in. My father, when he hasn't got his stumps on' – Wirthof suppressed a giggle – 'he's smaller than I am, without his stumps. He used to be quite tall, but without his stumps he's smaller than I am. Tell you what,' he added, 'I'll go and find Katty, that's my little sister.' He got up, took a short run, and slithered to the door.

Now Stefan had a chance to have a good look round, which he had been dying to do all along. On the washstand, next to a blotting pad: pencils laid out in order of size, all sharpened to a fine point. A compass box. A ruler. India rubber. Pencil sharpener. An open exercise book – he took a peep: each line began exactly at the ruled margin; each fresh paragraph indented the same amount as the preceding one, very neat, no blots, no erasures, no slovenly formed words, all very neat. Textbooks formed piles on the washstand; other books stacked on the floor. Many contained red-tasselled markers – and these were mostly between a third and a half way through the books. One book actually had a marker a few pages before the end, but it was the exception. Pinned up around the walls were his drawings – botanical drawings, showing plants in section, with Wirthof's precise handwriting naming the different parts, practical chemistry drawings showing experiments to prove a particular equation, and a few still-life sketches. The sketches looked as if they had been made with a ruler and compass, everything in them formed geometric shapes – cones or circles or triangles; and each drawing was symmetrical, the principal object at dead centre, the others grouped around it, the shapes on the left side corresponding in mass to those on the right. It was like looking at part of the repeating pattern in silks and wallpapers and on friezes.

Stefan heard voices, then they came in, Wirthof first, his sister behind him, concealed by him except for her arms which were around his waist. 'She's shy, my little sister,' he declared, 'come on, show your face, little.' With bashful obedience she stuck out her head, looked at Stefan, giggled, and quickly hid herself again. 'All right,' he said firmly, 'all right, little, enough of that now. Go and say hello, little.' She murmured something into his back, and he said, 'Don't do that, that tickles. I told you not to do that, little.' Applying force he separated her hands, freed himself of her arms, and reaching behind pulled her out. 'Go on, little, say hello to my friend, Kazakh.' She stood quite still, head hanging, face solemn, and then shot a quick glance not at Stefan but at her brother, and giggled again, continuously this time. 'Take no notice of her,' he advised, 'she's in one of her giggly moods. Now shut up, little. Behave, or you'll get slapped.' He made a face slapping motion with his hands, screwing up his features into a fierce expression, and abruptly she became quiet. She said something to him appealingly, in a low voice, and he replied sternly, 'No. No, you can't. You can go and fetch Father's medals, I want to show Kazakh. Go on.' He clapped his hands together close to her face. 'Go on.'

When she had left the room, Wirthof said in a confidential voice, 'You can't have anything like discussions with her, she's not brilliant. Women are not very brilliant, are they? But one thing I will say for Katty, she's obedient, you can tell her what to do and she'll do it. You have any sisters, Kazakh?'

She returned to the room after a short while, and Wirthof's face darkened when he saw that she had had the audacity to pin the medals on herself; she looked very pleased; the medals jiggled and jingled, Wirthof was furious. 'Who said you could wear them! I never said you could *wear* them! I said to fetch them, not to *wear* them. Those are Father's medals. You're not *entitled* to wear them. Take them off at once.' He began to pull at the medals on her chest.

'Don't, Konrad, don't, you're tearing my dress.'

'Serves you right.'

'No, don't, Konrad. I'll take them off. Honestly I will, Don't tear my dress.'

'Go on then, take them off.'

She began to unpin the medals, fumblingly, pricking herself once and crying out, and she handed them over one by one to her brother who took them solemnly. When he had them all, he laid them out carefully on the floor, in two rows. He sprawled on his stomach, his head supported on cupped hands, and studied the medals intently. He touched them reverentially with his fingers.

'That's the German Cross in Gold,' he explained, 'it's intermediate between the Iron Cross First Class and the Knight's Cross. Quite a lot of those were awarded. But now this, Knight's Cross to the Iron Cross, that was rarer. And this – Oakleaves with Swords; weren't many of those awarded. After that there's only the Oakleaves with Swords and Diamonds.'

A shadow passed across his face; he suddenly had become bored with the medals.

'You better take these medals back, little,' he said. 'If Father finds out you've taken his medals he'll be furious.' He scooped them up from the floor, quite unreverentially now, and pressed them into his sister's hand. 'Go on, put them back. Neatly. See you do it neatly. You don't want him to find out you took them . . .'

'You told me to, Konrad.'

'You took them, little. You did it.'

'I only did it because you said to.'

'Go on then, put them back. Fast. Fast.' Again as earlier, he clapped his hands at her, and she responded, to his evident satisfaction, with dispatch, slithering over the polished parquet to the door. 'One day,' he said to Stefan, 'I'll show you my father's uniforms and guns. He's got a whole closet full. Locked, but I know where the key is. I'll show them to you one day, Kazakh.'

He went to the door, opened it and listened intently; finger to lip, he cautioned Stefan to keep still. 'I'm going to see what's going on,' he said, and Stefan watched him creep along a narrow corridor, open a door, continue silently across another large unused-looking room and then place his ear against the double doors at the end. He stayed in this position for a while, gesturing to Stefan to keep absolutely still. Having peered through the keyhole he motioned to Stefan to approach, at the same time gently pressing down the door handle. His sister was standing on top of library steps, replacing a presentation case on the upper shelf of a bureau; the curtains in this room were fully drawn and it was dark; as Stefan came in he knocked against something, making a slight, sharp noise which startled her, she half turned and in doing so the presentation case slipped out of her grasp, fell to the floor and burst open, scattering the medals. In the stillness of the flat the noise was shattering. From the room beyond came the rasp of a chair being pushed back; a silence, various creakings, movements that were not footsteps; and then the doors were thrown open, letting in light and the thick aroma of cigar smoke. The man supporting himself on crutches in the open doorway had a magnificent head, placed on distorted shoulders, his face was reddish, there was a cigar end wedged in his lips. He wore the trousers of an army officer, with a broad red stripe down the side, a collarless shirt, braces; as he swung forward rapidly on his crutches his trouser legs flapped about.

'Katty, Konrad – what are you doing in here?' He saw his medals scattered all over the floor. 'What have you been doing? I've ordered you not to come in here. Aren't there enough rooms in this flat? Hmm? Hmm, young sir? Do I have to lock this door? Well, young sir?'

'I wanted to show your medals, Father. To my friend, Kazakh.'

Stefan saw the group of men around the card table, a low-hanging ceiling lamp with a fringed green silk shade, which cast a circle of light on the table; the rest of the room was in semi-darkness.

'Katty, pick up those medals and put them away. There's no call to show my medals to your friends, Konrad. But if you do wish to do such a thing, you must first obtain my permission. D'you understand? There's no reason for you to go to my cupboard like thieves. Don't permit it to happen again.'

'Yes, Father.'

'Have you been to see your mother?'

'Not yet.'

'You know she likes to see you when you come home. Go and see if she needs anything.'

'The maid is here,' Wirthof retorted.

'That's not the same, Konrad. Instead of creeping into my room like a thief you'd do better to concern yourself with your mother's needs. Have you offered your friend some refreshments?'

Wirthof said nothing. 'I see that you haven't. Is that the way we treat a guest? Well, young sir? I offer my apologies for my son's lack of manners,' he said to Stefan. 'I trust next time you visit this household we shall not be so lacking in hospitality. There's ice-cream in the ice box in the kitchen, if you're interested. Konrad, take your friend to the kitchen and offer him some ice-cream. And take some in to your mother. Off with you now, go on, go on.'

He turned adeptly on his crutches and swung back into the card room, which received him with a short burst of male laughter that was abruptly cut off by the doors closing. Wirthof was grinning. 'It's lucky you were here,' he said. 'We'd have been in trouble if you hadn't been here. We'll have to be careful when I show you the uniforms and the guns. After lunch, that's a good time. He always sleeps after lunch, doesn't hear a thing then.' He made a swigging gesture with his hand, and gave Stefan a wink. 'You'd like to see the guns, wouldn't you, Kazakh?'

It was 1931 or 1932 that the Bodenkreditanstalt failed; and it was around this time I first heard Wirthof's militaristic ideas. He must have been about eighteen. Already then, I seem to remember, he was suffering from headaches, his pale face with its deeply ringed violet eyes would be screwed up as if he were peering through a sandstorm. 'What you have to understand, Kazakh, and few people do, that is the whole trouble, you see it is not grasped, not grasped at all, even by the so-called experts – for whom I don't have much time –' He was inordinately fond of explaining to me the follies and inadequacies of almost everyone. 'Military thinking, so-called, is perfectly archaeozoic. They have no conception of the meaning of strike power. In the next war, Kazakh, all tactical thinking will centre on the deployment of armour. The generals still think in terms of infantry as the prime factor in a battle. Old fools! Puerility of thought, Kazakh! In their senescence they can't see what stares them in the face. They can't see the *possibilities*. I tell you, Kazakh, I would know what has to be done, I've studied it, I've given the whole matter a great deal of my attention and time. I'll tell you what I would do. First, study my opponent, study his mentality: vital to know what he is thinking, whether he is an old fogey or a modernist. If he is a modernist, then, of course, he will know about mobility, and then one has to be *more* mobile than him. Personally, I'd sacrifice weight of armour for speed. Speed is vital. And then the other thing is to establish real contact with the men. Absolutely vital! The common soldier has to be led, he mustn't be given the impression he's unimportant: cannon fodder. If he believes that the casualties have been calculated, that he's been written off, the common soldier won't fight, or he won't fight with belief, which amounts to the same thing. Leadership, of course, is vital. Men are the same on both sides, more or less. It's the quality of leadership that is the unknown factor and it is decisive. If all your generals are old men sclerotic with age your chances are: zero. I haven't finally decided yet, and it will depend on several factors whether I do or don't, I won't go into the various considerations now, since they are not relevant to what I am saying, except in so far as they affect me personally: but if I do decide, and as I say I haven't finally made up my mind yet, to take up a military career, then I shall only do so if I feel fairly sure I can get my own command – a division – by the time I'm thirty. I have no intention of waiting until I am senescent. By the time you are fifty, you have expended your originality. People don't realize that war, today, is like anything else: a matter of original thinking, invention, imagination, quality of thought, etcetera. What interests me is the opportunity of translating thought into action. War *is* highly interesting, Kazakh. I have a good head for it, I think. As I say, I have been devoting a lot of my time to it and I have worked out some very interesting actions, hypothetical, of course, which' – he giggled – 'I invariably win. I give the enemy all the opportunities commensurate with their resources and abilities, and it always works out, and I assure you I am meticulously honest in the way I work it out, it would be pointless not to be – as, for instance, in playing oneself at chess, which I sometimes do: pointless not to make the best moves, whichever side one is moving for – and it just so happens that I always seem to be able to win these hypothetical actions. The other vital quality in war, Kazakh, and this will surprise you, because it may seem to contradict what I have just been saying about tactics etcetera, is to be able to make the common soldier believe in your good fortune. The common soldier demands of his leaders not only that they should be able men, but also that they should be lucky. If the troops believe they have good fortune on their side their effectiveness is much increased, and so the leader of men must also be endowed with luck and the knowledge of its cultivation –'

It was in '31 that the Bodenkreditanstalt failed; yes; there was a great deal of unemployment; revolution, plots, showdowns, strong actions were in the air, but they were Austrian – more specifically *Viennese* – plots, showdowns, strong actions, which meant that they tended to remain in the air, that plotters turned up late (or forgot to turn up altogether) at their favourite Kaffeehaus to conspire against the state, or against each other, and usually managed to postpone decisions until a more opportune moment: the time was not right, something had to be done but the moment must be carefully chosen, perhaps after Weihnachten, after Carnival – (the balls continued unabated).

Every time a group of demonstrators marched here or there (where they marched was irrelevant), a fearful hope stirred in me: perhaps this time something would happen. The longed-for, and dreaded, explosion would occur, and what a smash up there would be then, what a crashing of edifices: something in me yearned for such a disaster – what a collapse of stout parties. My own world might crash too, but the prospect of such total disorder was not unappealing. I dreamt of calamities.

And my father was planning the seizure of Vienna – with men mounted on a fleet of mobile incinerators, the rubbish disposal vehicles of the municipality. Who'd have thought it?

How they dawdled at every brink! How they all marched – hither and thither – not I though, to march was not in my nature.

I was occupied with other things. At the university I had heard Professor Blumenfeld, whose sphere was the human mind, its deepest recesses, its peculiarities, its lusts, and how many of those there were, and what lusts! Who could think of marching.

Short and neckless, Professor Blumenfeld resembled a snowman, in that he seemed to be made of three contiguous spheres; a massive head, with thick white hair overhanging his collar, rested on rounded shoulders, like a boulder on a promontory, and seemed in moments of high excitement (to which he was prone) in imminent danger of becoming dislodged; the shoulders, round and narrow, were like a bell that has slithered some of the way down an incline and then become unnaturally arrested in a position of imbalance; his paunch, swelling waistcoated out of his open frockcoat, formed the third sphere, and in its solid massiveness provided the counterweight to head and shoulders. Taken as a whole, this elaborate structure looked of doubtful equilibrium, cannon balls spinning on the tip of a conjuror's cane, and yet he had surprising agility of movement, which made one tremble lest the whole precarious pile might topple over as a consequence of some reckless shifting of its centre of gravity.

He'd give us case histories to illustrate his theories.

'The case of the patient H. is illuminating in this context. Father a musician, apparently normal, mother somewhat neurasthenic. In childhood the patient was deficient in natural affection towards his parents, to their considerable distress. His mental development proceeded satisfactorily until fourteenth year. Masturbation commenced at the fifteenth year. Much preoccupied with suicide, considering life absurd. Suffered from *horror feminae*, which took the form of decrying marriage. From the age of nineteen *coitus rarissimus*, *actus quasi masturbatorius*, *in corpore feminae*, *sine ulla voluptate*. But gave this up as desire, gratification, and ultimately even erection were wanting. His *Weltschmerz* attained the level of melancholia, and he made several attempts at suicide, on the grounds that life was absurd. Once, by mistake, he took a cathartic instead of a poison, which sent him not to the other world, as he had hoped, but to the water closet. Everything fatigued him, and he was prone to onomatomania, feeling compelled to solve quite irrelevant problems which entirely dominated his mind. The need to calculate the volume of the leg of a chair, for instance. No sooner had one such problem been solved than another, equally compelling, presented itself to him. In this way he wasted away his days. At the age of twenty-two in an attempt to overcome his *anaesthesia sexualis* he visited a brothel where he experienced attraction towards a *puella* wearing high heels and short jacket ("Hungarian fashion"); coitus did not ensue; but he suddenly conceived the wish that she would make him perform menial tasks, wait upon her, and oblige him to attend her *et inter mictionem*. This masochistic inclination reminded him of the excitement he had felt – in puberty – on reading *Uncle Tom's Cabin*. The idea of slavery, both from the standpoint of master or slave, was so thrilling to him as to cause erection, and he had frequently masturbated with concomitant thoughts of being either the master or the slave, sometimes the one fantasy and sometimes the other gave him the greatest satisfaction. At the age of eighteen he had had a liaison of brief duration with a young lady of good family. This had proceeded normally until in the course of some horseplay in which his inamorata actually sustained injury –'

According to Professor Blumenfeld sexual perversion arose when the normal sexual aims were impeded or denied, in the same way that a river when blocked would form circuitous tributaries. Perversion was a detour from the natural sexual aim of impregnation and procreation. It was only when the impulse to coitus was replaced by lesser aims that we entered the territory of the abnormal. Thus *fellatio* as a preliminary, a stepping stone, to coitus was absolutely normal, but as an end to itself it was a perversion. The same could be said of heterosexual anal intercourse, if it preceded vaginal intercourse it was not perverse, but if it superseded vaginal intercourse it was a perversion. 'The anus,' he declared in ringing evangelical tones, 'must be restored to its right and proper place in the erogenous system alongside' – of course he did not mean anatomically but figuratively – 'the breasts and genitalia. For too long a faecal shame has attached to this important nerve centre of the human body and' – he tended to get carried away sometimes in his reforming zeal – 'many individuals have been deprived of their legitimate sexual rights by the unfortunate associations of this part of the body. I say to you, esteemed *Kollegen*, that provided the spermatozoa are implanted in the vagina, no preceding act can be regarded as perverse.' We felt like cheering. Naturally we warmed to Professor Blumenfeld. 'I speak, of course, of the vagina of a living human female,' Professor Blumenfeld added for the sake of scientific exactitude, 'and the implanting agency must be that of a human male. As to the vexing question of self-masturbation: in masturbation the spermatozoa are not implanted in the vagina, is this therefore a perversion? The answer must be that masturbation represents the expression of a frustrated rather than deflected aim, in so far as the impulse behind this activity is the impregnation of the female, which for external reasons has been frustrated, no perversion is implied; only when self-masturbation is chosen in preference to coitus can it be regarded as perverse. In females, among whom a greater degree of inhibition attaches –' He had a beautiful rich voice, which he used to great effect, and eyes that saw all around at one and the same time. His style was interrogatory and intimate. Supposing I said to you such and such, he would say, fixing his challenging gaze on one of us, you would reply so and so. A dramatic pause, followed by – 'You would be wrong, *Herr Kollege*. Completely, utterly wrong.' Devastated in this way, our assumed answers demolished before we could even think of them, he went on to prove to us why we would be so completely and utterly wrong.

'Esteemed *Kollegen*, I ask you to think of the unconscious as a vault, a strongroom, impenetrable, burglar-proof, impervious to the batterings of vulgar intruders, a repository of the treasures of the mind that we are unable to enjoy because we do not have the means of entry to these depths, we lack the key that will open them to us. But whereas conventional psychology seeks to batter down the door only to discover another and another, the hypnotist, *meine Herren*, slips in under the crack. Aha, you say: how does he do it? An unnecessary, an unworthy question for empiricists. He does it. It is fact. The unconscious, which will not yield to frontal assault, succumbs, yields up its multifarious powers to the gentle voice of persuasion that slips under the crack of the door.'

After a preamble of this sort came the demonstrations, which were the highlights of his lectures. Volunteers were asked for, three or four at a time, and bidden in turn to approach the master who, standing on the tips of his toes, grasped his subject's face as if about to implant a passionate kiss, until they were nose to nose, eyeballs practically touching, breath intermingling – his breath reeked so strongly of schnapps that some students claimed his technique depended on partially anaesthetizing his subjects with alcoholic fumes – and then intoned his instructions. 'Relax, completely relaxed, please. Relax all your muscles. Look into my eyes, and don't blink, under no circumstances to blink. It is essential not to blink. Relax. Relax all your muscles, in sequence. Relax your eye muscles, relax your pectoral muscle, relax your trapezius, relax your latissimus dorsi, relax your rectus abdominis, relax your sartorius, relax your quadriceps. Relax. Don't blink. Relax your gluteal muscles. Relax your gastrocnemius. You are very tired, your eyelids are very heavy.'

By this time the poor student frantically endeavouring to remember what and where was his latissimus dorsi so that he could relax it, and embarrassed lest in his ignorance he should be relaxing his quadriceps instead of his latissimus dorsi, had realized that even if he did manage to remember where all these muscles were situated, by the time he had established their whereabouts and started to relax them, Blumenfeld was already three or four muscles ahead of him in his rapid course along the muscular system. Those who conscientiously attempted to follow the master's instructions were soon twitching and jerking about in a seemingly mesmerized way, long before anything like a trance had been achieved. At the same time Blumenfeld's heavy breathing into their nostrils, his intense peering into their eyes while they were forbidden to blink, and his firm grip of their heads, led to a state in which to fall into a hypnotic trance was an enormous relief.

He never failed with the subjects he chose, though once or twice he rejected a volunteer, after a brief examination of his eyes, as 'unsuitable'; what indicated suitability or the converse he did not explain. To be a good subject for hypnosis, Blumenfeld told us, one must have a capacity for obedience: the abnormally uncompliant, the rebel, the criminal psychopath who rejected all authority, could not be hypnotized, unless one could find in him those few remaining chords of obedience, the remnants of his ties to parents, and utilize them. But it was very hard with someone of this type, for there must be a memory of trust; in the absence of that the subject would not yield up authority over his mind to some outsider.

I studied Blumenfeld's method with great concentration, noting his stance, the position of his hands on the subject's face – his fingers below the temples drew the skin back tight, narrowing the eyes and inducing a slight blurring of vision – the modulations of voice, the phraseology employed. I asked him questions. What type of ailments did he believe could be cured or alleviated by hypnosis? He replied that many disturbances in the functioning of the alimentary tract responded well to hypnosis: he had had remarkable success with constipated patients, he could claim several successful cures of colitis, he had successfully treated dozens of pregnant women with a history of aborting in the first three months of pregnancy, and they were now mothers, to mention only those maladies of non-nervous origin that responded to hypnosis. As for the many distressing symptoms of neurasthenia – palpitations, giddiness, chronic headaches, sweating, premature ejaculation, impotence, *horror feminae*, blushing, stammering, masturbation, spots before the eyes, *anaesthesia sexualis*, vomiting, *hyperaesthesia sexualis*, fear of enclosed spaces, stagefright, bed-wetting in infants and incontinence in the clergy – these had all proved remarkably conducive to treatment by hypnosis.

So persuasive was Blumenfeld that I decided my true vocation might very well lie in this field of the mind, into whose unplumbed depths Blumenfeld and his hypnotism promised to give me passage. Hypnotism fascinated me, it seemed to me a technique absolutely suited to my capacities. It was not, as engineering clearly was, merely a matter of applying known facts and theories in accordance with well-tested methods; no, it was an art unfettered by too many rules and regulations, mysterious, inexplicable, lending itself to improvisation and those gigantic imaginative leaps that lead to fresh discoveries. It was, moreover, a technique that depended on personality, on inherent gifts, on capacities not easily definable, it had attached to it an aura derived from the legendary practices of its great exponents: Paracelsus, Mesmer, the Marquis de Puységar, Cagliostro, Bertrand, Richet, Charcot, Leibault, Bernheim, Preyer, Heidenhain, Blumenfeld. And shortly the name Kazakh would be added to that list. Already it looked as though it belonged there, it had an aural affinity with those great names. I tried it on myself – Kazakh, the hypnotherapist, the *eminent* hypnotherapist. Yes, it sounded fine. I stood before my mirror, examining myself, peering into my own eyes. Eyes were fantastic things, what gave them their infinite variety of expressions? I hunched my shoulders in the Blumenfeld manner, sank my head down into my collar, stuck out my belly, I did not yet have a particularly distinguished belly (indeed I was thin), but that would come, or possibly one could be a thin hypnotherapist.

I thought about how Blumenfeld had made five hypnotized subjects lie on the floor, and how he had then played them like a xylophone, issuing commands that made one kick up a leg, another an arm, the third sit up, the fourth roll over, the fifth stand up and sit down; he had given each a number code which would make him perform his particular function, and by varying the order in which he called out the numbers – 3-1-5-2-4 or 5-3-4-2-1 or 4-3-2-1-5, and so on – Blumenfeld could obtain complex patterns of movements. Not one of the subjects failed to respond to a command. It might appear, he told us afterwards, that such an experiment was more theatrical than scientific, but this was not the case: what he was demonstrating was how a group could be co-ordinated, how all its movements could be controlled just as the hammer movements in a piano are controlled and varied by the pianist striking the keyboard. The ramifications were infinite.

Continuing the demonstration, he retired to the back of the lecture hall and asked one of the students to step on the platform and call out the numbers, and the subjects responded to him as they had done to Blumenfeld. This demonstrated, said Blumenfeld, the nature of a group entity and the mechanism of all group actions in society. Co-ordinated group action was produced when a given number of people, whether five or five thousand or fifty million, had individually accepted a common control source; they would then act not individually but as a group: various phenomena such as patriotic fervour, mass hysteria, mass 'possession' could be explained on this basis. He then went on to show what happened when this group unity was broken. He released two of the group from their obligation of obedience to him, saying that when their numbers were called out they could act exactly as they wished. Again the sequence of numbers was gone through, and the result was a mild form of chaos. Whereas the three who still were under orders behaved exactly in accordance with their instructions, the two who had been 'released' got up, stretched their legs, stumbled against the others, walked about in a dazed way. There was no longer any unity in the group.

'From this we can perceive', declared Blumenfeld, 'that the efficiency – i.e. the unity – of a group as a group depends on the extent to which its constituent members are willing to accept a common control source into their individual egos. Conflict in a group arises when different factions have taken in opposed control sources, something which happens for instance in civil wars. And social chaos and disintegration occur when, for whatever reasons, there is no common control source. The efficiency of a group therefore is in direct relation to the efficacy and the acceptability of its common control source.'

Acceptability was an important factor, for – and this he would demonstrate in later lectures – no individual would accept commands that went contrary to his nature. This was a very difficult question, he emphasized, because there were few actions that were truly contrary to nature, since every individual contained within him the possibility of all actions, and what limited or repressed those actions was usually convention rather than anything in his make-up. Thus one could venture to say that the extent to which an individual, or group, could be induced to act contrary to his or its ostensible nature was dependent on the degree to which the control source could penetrate the upper layers of restraint and inhibition, manifestations of the more recently acquired characteristics, and reach down into earlier and more primitive strains in the individual. It could be expressed in this way: the greater the strength of suggestion, the deeper it would reach into the primitive. What gave one individual rather than another great power of suggestion was not fully understood – this, again, was something that had to be treated empirically – but there was reason to believe that someone who by virtue of personality was best able to utilize the original channels of command of the parent-infant situation was likely to have the greatest success.

Until I had seen Blumenfeld lecture, I had been all set to become a heart specialist, but now I was again in the throes of a crisis of indecision. Why should the heart – this mere pump – be my life's work when everything was in fact controlled by the mind? A fortuitous accident had brought me to one of Blumenfeld's lectures, and it seemed had just saved me from once again setting off in the wrong direction.

I decided I would seek his advice. A man with his knowledge of the inner workings of the mind would be able to see through my confusion and be able to advise me, and to advise me objectively. With his extraordinary gifts he would be able to look beyond mere scholastic achievement, and see into my essence, he could tell me whether that essence was cut out to follow in his footsteps. A man of such demonstrable brain-power, of such magnitude, could give me the guidance I desperately needed: perhaps he would even take a personal interest in me if I revealed to him my hopes, my admiration for him; what a wonderful thing that would be, to develop under the tutelage of such a man, what confidence that must give one, what a sense of purpose and direction in place of this feckless meandering to which I was liable to fall victim on my own. As soon as this idea of consulting Blumenfeld came to me, I found in myself a sudden contentment, from which I was shaken only by the thought that perhaps he would not see me, perhaps he would refuse me a private interview. Impossible! Had he not shown me definite encouragement in the way he looked at me when I asked him questions? He was impressed by my intelligence, and perhaps even a little flattered by the intensity of my interest. It was impossible that he would not see me. And again, having decided on this, a peacefulness came over me – I went so far as to cut two lectures, one in physics, one in microscopy, and spent the free hours wandering through the streets indulging in the pleasurable anticipation of my interview with Blumenfeld, which so far I had not even requested let alone obtained. But, as with all important encounters, I felt the need to rehearse this meeting in advance, enacting it to myself in its worst and most favourable aspects, and also in all the varying gradations between these extremes, so that when it actually occurred I would not be taken by surprise.

I pictured the sequence of events that would be set in motion by my interview, I traced the course of my future career right up till the final years of my life, and only when I had become dizzy from a surfeit of imaginings did I put a stop to such wild surmise. Enough of this dreaming! I must seek my interview, obtain the advice I needed, and act accordingly, instead of speculating about imponderables. At the very next Blumenfeld lecture I would ask him. But when I got there, and though the opportunity presented itself, I could not bring myself to make this simple request. Too much depended on his answer for me to be calm. My heart beat uncontrollably, my voice could not be relied upon to blurt out even the one-sentence request. I was paralysed with exactly the sort of fears – and blanching and blushing alternately – that hypnotism was supposed to be so effective in curing, and the irony of this added to my feelings of humiliation. A fine hypnotist I'd make, not even able to stammer out a simple request. Defeated and shamed by this attack of timidity, I suffered several days of depression during which it seemed to me that I had no prospects, that my future was without hope, that I would be better off dead. I could not understand how it had happened that I should be so intensely nervous of this man, it made no kind of sense; but, presently, following previous practice, I ran through, in my mind, the kind of situations in which I would not be nervous of Blumenfeld, and it became clear that – to take an extreme example – if I were the eminent physician and he were the student I would not be nervous of him, so my nervousness had something to do with my feeling dependent on his favours. That was my mistake. I must tell myself – and wasn't it true? – that I was not dependent on him. He was of the utmost unimportance. Whatever he said, or did not say, would have no effect on me if I chose to disregard his advice. I must think of it in this way: here was a brilliant young student – myself – approaching a great but ageing physician to ask his advice: why, it was paying him a remarkable compliment, almost one could say I was doing him the favour, in as much as I was demonstrating my regard and respect for him by seeking his advice. Besides, there was a kind of fraternity in the world of thought that made it obligatory for one thinker to give another thinker (albeit a junior one) the benefit of his thoughts: just as a man of God could not deny you his blessings, if you were worthy of them, so a thinker could not deny you his advice: I was entitled to it, it was my right, I need not ask meekly or humbly for what was my due. I was fast becoming indignant at the fact that he had not offered of his own accord that which was owed to me, his advice, his interest, his concern for my future, my welfare, my intellectual development. It was his concern, it was his duty to advise me: I would demand it. Having attained this frame of mind, I confronted Blumenfeld at the next lecture, and announced, 'Herr Professor, I should be obliged if you would give me a private interview. There are some matters on which I wish to consult you. They are of the utmost importance and urgency.' He looked astonished. 'What are these matters? What matters?'

'I would like your advice about the possibility of – of –' I gulped, my artificial self-assurance already wilting before his blunt gaze, 'of specializing in hypnotism.'

'The proper person with whom to discuss that is your tutor.'

'Herr Professor, what does my tutor know of hypnotism? You are the only person who can advise me, you must.' I spoke harshly, arrogantly – almost spat out the words; my heart was beating so fast and my mouth was so dry that I knew it was the last sentence

I could manage just then, and so I had put everything into it. He gave me a peculiar look, not sure what to make of my brusque assertiveness.

'Very well. I will see you after the lecture. I can only give you a few minutes, however.'

I didn't hear a word of that lecture, nor did I feel that I needed to ask any questions: I already had a personal relationship with the lecturer, it was not necessary for me to resort to questions in public, where I would have to share my answers with everyone else, when I could receive exclusive answers in private. The lecture could not end soon enough for me, and when the students eventually began to file out I was impatient of their slowness and resentful of those who paused briefly to ask Blumenfeld a supplementary question – cutting into *my* time. Blumenfeld had gathered up his papers and was about to leave when he noticed me standing close by, and for a moment it seemed he might have forgotten about our interview, that only my demanding presence reminded him, 'Come with me,' he said beckoning for me to follow, and marched out. He walked at a surprisingly rapid pace for someone of his bulk, along corridors and through halls and down steps, and only when we were outside the university building did he half turn to address me. 'You will take a coffee with me, Herr . . . ?'

'Kazakh. Thank you, Herr Professor.'

'Good. Good.'

I fell in step with him as he continued rapidly along the Eben-dorferstrasse and into the Universitätstrasse. He said nothing while we walked. I had not had time to fetch my overcoat and was shivering with cold on this mid-December day. Several men we passed raised their hats to Blumenfeld, and he acknowledged their greetings with perfunctory courtesy, his hand starting up towards his wide-brimmed black hat but never getting far enough to touch it let alone lift it. At the café he jammed himself tightly into a segment of the revolving door only just large enough to take him and immediately began to thrust with such force that I, in the compartment behind him, was almost knocked off my feet and then virtually catapulted inside. A girl, smiling and rosy red, was waiting to take his hat and coat, and he gave her a little pat on the cheek in passing, and the Herr Obers escorted us to a table in an alcove. Blumenfeld sank his great weight into the blue velvet upholstery, took a worked-gold watch out of his waistcoat pocket, sprang the lid, clicked it shut again and replaced the watch and gave his order to a waiter he assumed was on his left, without looking to see if he was in fact there. Perhaps his eyes had a wider than normal breadth of vision and he could see more than other people. In the lecture room, he could see what was going on all around while looking straight ahead, and the fact that he did not feel obliged to look in the direction of the person he was addressing, or listening to, gave one the feeling that he saw everything.

'You are a *landsman*?' he said, fixing me with his powerful gaze, his thick black eyebrows (though the hair on his head was white) going up with the action of a roll-top desk, compressing his brow into tight folds.

'Yes,' I said.

'It is not a good profession for us,' he declared with an intimate smile. 'Hypnotism – meddling with the mind – not a good profession for us Jews. However scientific you are, to *them*, the others, the goyim, it is always black magic, if you're a Jew. You're in your first year?'

'Yes.'

'You have plenty of time. Choose another speciality. The liver, the heart, the urinary system, the stomach, plenty to choose from. They, the others, will entrust to you their livers, their stomachs, their rectums, and even credit you with some superior understanding of these organs because you are a Jew. Start meddling with their minds, however – ah! I do not advise it. Already there are too many of us. They are suspicious. We want to take over their minds and souls, get them in our power, pervert their reason, destroy their beliefs. When everything goes well, we are those clever Jews; but when something goes wrong – ah – we are a bunch of charlatans and quacks, practitioners of the dark arts.'

His dampening attitude dismayed me, I didn't know what to say. 'But, Herr Professor, I was hoping . . . you see, I had the feeling, hearing your lectures . . . I mean to say, I was greatly impressed . . . I feel that this is the most revolutionary sphere . . .'

'Yes, yes. But it is not necessary to work in revolutionary spheres. You will do better with the lower abdomen. The Viennese eat too much, they are too fat. They all suffer from malfunctioning of the bowels. They eat the wrong foods. Too many creamy pastries, too much rich food. They *know* that there is something wrong with their stomachs, because they have belly-ache. But they do not believe that there is anything wrong with their minds. In any case, hypnotism is not a profession – unless, that is, you want to go on the stage: it is a technique. The technique anyone can learn in half an hour. The skill is not in the technique.'

'You mean I could learn it, the technique?'

'If you have the right personality for it. Try it one day, if it interests you. You will soon see if you can do it. Try it.'

'But isn't that dangerous?'

'Not if you observe reasonable safeguards – always remember to tell your subject, beforehand, that when he wakes up such and such will be the case, or will happen. The unconscious is legalistic in this respect: to speak of what will happen *when* he wakes up implies that he will wake up at some point, which of course it is desirable that he should. I do not normally encourage students to experiment with hypnotism, but they do it anyway: you seem serious about it, no harm will come if you take reasonable care and do not practise on someone who is obviously unbalanced. Read my book, *The Principles and Techniques of Hypnotic Suggestion*, it is all in that. It works by tiring the optic nerve, that is why I ask the subject not to blink. A bright light will have a similar effect. One uses the technique most suited to oneself. And now, Herr Kazakh, you will excuse me – I see my guests arriving.' My time was up and I had not really broached any of my problems.

'Herr Professor,' I blurted out, 'I feel uncertain of what direction to take, I hoped you would advise me, with your great understanding...'

'Yes, yes, yes. I understand.' He paused, and I waited, dizzy with expectation. 'You are a clever young man, I can tell from the questions you ask at my lectures. You are ambitious, want to get on, to do important work, win recognition, it is very creditable. This is my advice to you. If you want to have rapid success, you should become an anaesthetist. It's a minor speciality, and therefore not overcrowded. So few outstanding men are interested in it that anybody who comes along and has any ability at all will go to the top straight away. It's well paid, very well paid. There is no great prestige attached to it, but it is well thought of. The hours are regular, and easy. And it is more respectable than hypnotism. Moreover, if you should happen to kill somebody as an anaesthetist nothing very serious will befall you, but if you should be so unfortunate as to have a patient die under hypnosis your career could well be at an end. That is my advice to you.' And he gave me his podgy hand across the narrow table, as if he were handing me my gloves, by way of dismissing me.

I never talked to my father about Professor Blumenfeld, I was sure he would not understand; if I told him of my ambition to become a hypnotist he would frown sadly, and bring to bear on me the full force of all his irksome misgivings. And so I did not broach the matter with him. Our former closeness had suffered lately, I no longer saw so much of him – his absences grew longer and more frequent, and, of course, I assumed he had a woman somewhere who was taking up his time. It never occurred to me that the Kaffeehaus plots and the revolutions that could wait until after Carnival were serious matters to him and that he was actually planning the seizure of Vienna – with men mounted on mobile incinerators! He kept all that secret from me.

Did I believe in them, these whisperers with their exaggerated air of secrecy? Peeping through the keyhole of his door, he several times caught a glimpse of thick lenses and of a fawn coloured raincoat, always on the arm, never worn. Once, he got a good view of Thick Lenses, round-faced, the bridge of his nose deeply indented from his tight-fitting steel spectacles; he smiled at Stefan as if he knew him well. Who he was, Stefan knew he must not ask, or try to find out, and curiosity tormented him. How could he be sure that these men were worthy of his father, that they could be trusted? Those nights when his father was out were the worst.

My father's death – which, historically, occurred on February 13th, 1934 – is not something that I can fit into a chronology of my life, and leave there: Feb. '34 – death of K.'s father; March '34 – K. leaves University of Vienna to go into business. And so on. My mind is not calibrated to measure in this way. If I am to describe the way in which my mind perceives the fact of my father's death, I have to say that it has little interest in chronology, that chronology is merely its somewhat defective filing system, and that to say my father died on February 13th amounts to no more than saying that I file my unpaid bills under U; the fact that today I am concerned with the contents of Q and tomorrow with those of O and the day after with those of R and a week ago was concerned with those of M does not mean that my unpaid bills have been paid – there they are still. And they would be no less unpaid bills if I dumped them into the folder ø, or burnt them. They remain, becoming dog-eared and mysterious and increasingly inexplicable: final accounts, gentle reminders, fulsome appeals (your valued custom, your esteemed order), uncertain inquiries (if in any way we have failed), threatening demands (within seven days, by return of post, the days of grace have now expired), and brutal statements of fact (deficit). Does it matter when I incurred these debts, or in what sequence? There they are. Ah – but are they correct? Is my indebtedness really so great? Surely this bill I have paid, and that one is too high. What services were rendered me that I have forgotten, what goods received does this sum in red represent? What could these bills be for? Did I eat so much at the Caprice? I search through the files P Q R S T – perhaps V W X will contain the clue, the elucidation. But they are concerned with other matters and events – which may very well have been happening as I was running up these bills, but have only the most fortuitous relevance to my debts – ah yes, it was while I was arranging the deal with Toto that my car broke down and I used the car-hire firm, yes, yes, so that bill is correct. Did I do so many miles? But all these others! P Q R S T and V W X are useless, tell me nothing, or take me off on a tangent. I must, dreadful prospect, look at the bills themselves, and reconstruct the circumstances in which they were incurred, deduce the chain of disparates from the locus.

In my mind (which, indeed, may not be very sound, but who is to say that its reality is a lesser reality than the external one of physical fact) there are no finite events, which may explain a certain reluctance on my part to pay bills, since if nothing is finite what the hell do they mean sending me a final statement, and couldn't we leave it over, couldn't I be given a sort of space-time continuum of credit? As I am perfectly able to pay – notwithstanding my fear of bankruptcy – whether I do or not is merely academic, surely; what does it matter if the amount in question is in red on my ledgers rather than in black on theirs; the fact that I owe them the money does not, since I have it, make it any less theirs: a line of reasoning that few of my creditors appreciate. Anyway, if there are no finite events (only final bills) and if the mind is not calibrated chronologically, and everything is contemporaneous, and therefore everything that has happened is happening, and vice versa, if you can vice versa such a proposition, then, yesterday, in the snowfall, in Vienna, my father died. Died: and I held his body, felt the heat of his life leaving it. And, to complicate matters, it was not I in my Persian lamb hat (I never wear hats, never), aged fifty-two, a man with affairs to attend to, who lost his father yesterday in the snowfall, crossing the Aspernbrücke, the Riesenrad not turning, but the nineteen-year-old Stefan, ice crackling in the playground.

Why should I concern myself with his losses, why should I have to suffer them? I am not responsible for his debts. Do your own mourning. Suffer your own pain yourself. But my mind, which, as I say, may not be the soundest example of its kind, not the most economical structure, not as adept as it once was at sloughing off its burdensome accretions, what I presumptuously call 'my' mind, for I am not always in it entirely, this mind of 'mine', indifferent to chronology and age differential, chooses to place me in the position of this nineteen-year-old youth and to saddle me, a man with affairs to attend to, with *his* undischarged debts. Ridiculous. Nobody with the slightest particle of common sense would expect any man to have to take on such burdens – how do I know what debts this spendthrift youth incurred (in my name)? I hereby give notice that I am not responsible for the debts or the actions or the life or death of Stefan Kazakh. He is no kith or kin of mine. The fact that he is me (was me?) is neither here nor there, a downright solecism.

Staszek Kazakh was killed in the abortive Socialist coup of February 1934. What else is to be said of that? Why do you return to it like a homing pigeon? However you conjugate the verbs of death, you cannot get away from the fact that the Don dies, a sweet fool's smile of accomplishment on his face.

The fact of the matter is that Wirthof and I used to go to *louche* places together: not to put too fine a point on it, we frequented whores, a practice to which everything in the life of the Viennese student or subaltern inclined one, not only was it inclination, the social climate dictated it, virtually made it obligatory.

This has nothing to do with my father's death (I am glad to say), and preceded it by several weeks; in fact, this particular train of thought goes nowhere at all (I suspect), it has no terminal, but just goes round and round, stopping here and there: future stops would include, if I could stand to make them, which I can't, my three wives.

My whoring, which preceded my father's death, and continued after it, and never really ended (i.e. my three wives), was more a matter of show than of desire; my three wives come in this category too.

Wirthof in uniform was something to behold, he had the swagger and glittering air which have been Austria's most conspicuous contributions to militancy. Coming into the café, where Stefan sat immersed in universal equations, and lust (– something odd used to happen at all those *louche* places: I kept seeing Professor Blumenfeld. It is not clear to me now whether in fact I saw him, or if in the inevitable darkness of those places any man who just happened to look like a snowman, three contiguous spheres precariously balanced on the end of a conjuror's cane, suggested to me the ubiquitous professor; anyway, we made a joke of it; if we saw the 'professor' in a place it was the surest recommendation it could have, and wherever we went we'd look around and say, oh the professor doesn't seem to have arrived yet, or ask the madame if she had seen the professor today, or demand of the girls how, with his three contiguous spheres, the professor managed, and once when we saw a man being carried out of one of those places on a stretcher, his face covered, we said with coarse lack of respect for the dead, well, it was bound to happen, overdoing it at his age, poor old professor).

Coming into the café, where Stefan sat immersed in universal equations, and lust, Wirthof took off his cap, shook the snow off it, stamped his feet to rid them of snow, and took off his cape and shook the snow off that. The smile on his pale face had a faintly derisory quality as he came insinuating his way between tables; smooth his skin was, as if no beard would ever grow on it. He was smoking an oval Turkish cigarette with a black tip, sucking tasty puffs from it, holding it between the forefingers of his rigidly extended left hand and moving it to and from his mouth with stiff sweeping motions.

'Kazakh!' he commanded. 'Ka-*zakh*! And what are you doing here?'

'I'm sitting here, as you can see. And you?'

As always, he managed to make Stefan feel ill at ease and somehow in the wrong, as if he shouldn't have been sitting there; he felt he ought to have been able to make some devastating retort to this vaguely belligerent question: drinking the blood of Christian children, as you can see, Wirthof.

'Women are impossible!' he explained, pulling up a chair. 'Don't you agree?' Wirthof's uniform was without epaulettes or belt, with just some silver braid work on the stand-up collar that clasped his neck in a tight band. 'Kazakh,' he said again, as if he couldn't get over it, 'isn't that amazing. How's life treating you? What are you doing? No fish – I see – this time.' He would have to bring up the fish – the faint thread of mockery ran through everything he said, weaving labyrinthine patterns through his words.

'I'm at the university.'

'At the university!'

'Yes.'

'Good God! What are you taking?'

'I'm in the medical faculty.'

'You intend to be a doctor?'

'That is usually why one attends the medical faculty.'

'Good God!'

'And you? So you did go in the army.'

'Oh yes, oh yes. I'm at Wiener Neustadt, at the Academy.' He looked around him. 'God, this is an awful place.'

'I like it.'

'How can you like it? It's – dirty.' He blew out a disdainful puff of Turkish smoke.

'Oh it's not bad, you know.'

'Not *bad*. If this isn't bad, I dread to think what you *would* consider bad. Do you know, the ridiculous creature, the young lady with whom I had the appointment – a little seamstress, charming, sweet – didn't turn up. Women are absurd. And to cap it all, just been virtually thrown out of the Sacher. Can you imagine! I hate Christmas, don't you? Ah well, I don't suppose it troubles you. You and your co-religionists don't celebrate the birth of our Saviour, do you? I shall have to become a Jew. The waiters take

73

their time here, don't they? Herr Obers! Look here, I ordered a beer ...'

'It's coming, Herr Leutnant. It's on its way.'

'From the Tyrol?'

'We are a little short-staffed today. Because of ...'

'Yes, yes, I know.'

He sat there shivering with a generalized disdain, which took in Stefan, the place, the waiters, the day, Jesus Christ, Austria, the future, life itself. How inadequate it all was; how unfortunate that he, Konrad Wirthof, should have to put up with such an inept configuration. The transition from child to youth had taken the form of some minute adjustment within him, making him that number of years older, adding height to him, adding time rings to his personality, and yet just as the child had seemed already to contain the old man so, now, conversely, the youth embodied the child, who peered out of him mockingly, with knowledge of the privileges and exemptions and immunities of childhood, all of which he had no hesitation in claiming for himself now, at this moment, notwithstanding that he was no longer a child. Stefan, as always, felt awkward with him, shy, unsure of the basis of their relationship. Wirthof seemed enviably uncircumscribed, possessing (by right of what?) carte blanche, unimpeded by those petty restrictions to which others were subject. He could do anything – that was the impression he gave – without having to consult anyone or defer to anyone or take anyone else into consideration.

'I tell you what,' he said suddenly, 'let's get out of here. We'll go somewhere else.'

'Where else is there? Christmas Eve –'

'I'm glad I ran into you, Kazakh. I was bored. One thing I can't tolerate is boredom: it depresses me. Boredom is the very devil, isn't it? I really am awfully glad to see you, Kazakh. We've known each other for years and years. When was the first time? In the Prater – that's right. In the magician's booth. The fellow swallowing razor blades, and you believed he really did swallow them.'

'And I beat you at running.'

'Oh did you? Did you? Is that so?'

It was a dreadful café, Stefan decided, why did he like it? Because, in its shabbiness, he felt at home there? He began to feel suddenly self-conscious of his appearance, tried to hide his frayed cuffs, he was always trying to hide something when he was with Wirthof, if it wasn't fish it was the wretched state of his clothing. He was trying to tidy himself a little without Wirthof noticing, but of course he saw, gave his fastidious though not altogether unfriendly smile, and said, 'God, you look a mess, Kazakh.' Stefan reddened and shrugged and said with a weak smile, 'I'm not in the army.'

'I tell you what,' Wirthof proposed, 'we can go back to my flat first and you can tidy up. I may be able to lend you a decent jacket. You agree?'

'Everything will be closed.'

'Something must be open. The whole town can't be dead.'

Darkly snowing outside; thick flakes swirled around their faces, they bent forward into the wind, in a moment Wirthof was covered with polka dots; he searched slit-eyed for a taxi, shoulders hunched under his cape, the peak of his cap becoming white rimmed. His lips were so pale as to have no distinguishing texture, making him seem lipless. There were no cabs to be seen, and he was furiously cursing. Could there be greater ineptness than this, on the part of whatever providence was responsible for cabs? They pushed on through the snowfall. The buildings shuddered like water reflections; the city was slipping quietly into its holiday death; streets almost empty, shop windows glittering with unbought presents, holly and laurel wreaths hanging over entrances. The few people who passed them were clearly hurrying towards the family dinner, the Christmas tree, the warming conviviality of home and hearth, a Santa Claus in a store window regarded them with sickening benignity: all at once they were strongly linked, avid, both, for some act. Joined by this burgeoning impulse they were like kids with catapults looking for windows to smash. God, how he hated all this ceremonial – the ritual of obeisance, the hypocritical grovelling of the frightened before God, the *Hochstapler* – yes, if ever there was a *Hochstapler* it was Christ. Son of God: even by Viennese standards that was going far. Stefan turned to Wirthof and said, 'Trust a Jew to think he is the Son of God – hmmm?'

'Oh that's capital,' Wirthof spluttered, 'that's very good. I must remember that. Trust a Jew to think he is the Son of God. Kazakh, that's really first rate, you're not as humourless as I thought.'

They kept on through the snow, warmed by their developing mood, vaguely lost in these dead white streets without contrast, but not caring now: an incongruous pair undoubtedly, he so immaculate, white against white, featureless, Stefan so shabby, making their chortling progress through the still city; almost anything could set off their rampageous mirth: the unsold Christmas trees in a square, so supine: the twin spires of the Votivkirche – that made them roar for some reason: an obese coal-eyed snowman with a carrot nose whom they summarily executed (Adieu, Professor Blumenfeld!), decapitating him with a twig and then crushing his coal eyes underfoot, grinding them into a fine black dust: children singing hymns, unseen, pure-voiced: passers-by laden with parcels: tinselly decorations glimpsed through windows. Their mood made all this funny. They had given up looking for a cab and then one came cruising along and they clambered into it, giggling, and the driver gave his indulgent Viennese smile, assuming they were drunk. Through the evacuated city they rattled – it was an old and leaking cab with a rotting leather hood – and everyone had fled, they were the scourge of Vienna, the conquistadors, Wirthof and Kazakh, the horsemen of the carousel. The Riesenrad was away on their right, illuminated, unmoving, densely veiled. The dead city lurched around them. Empress Maria Theresa sat stoutly in the snow above her attendant generals; the skyline was full of petrified angels and action-frozen heroes, immobilized in marble and lead. Climbing the stone steps at Wirthof's house, they left a melting trail. Stefan was ready to remove his boots, as on the previous occasion, but evidently it was not necessary this time, for Wirthof let the door slam noisily and clattered across the tiled floor, shedding snow everywhere like confetti, threw open the first of the double doors and bawled, 'Katty, where are you? Where are you, little? A visitor. A visitor for you.' And he clapped his hands together loudly, and then listened for some response, which came faintly out of the deep interior of the apartment.

'Come on,' he said, and strode rapidly across the polished parquet, unfastening his cape and throwing it on a tapestried chair, creating a momentary festive flurry of snowflakes. In the next room his cap was discarded in the same way, more doors were thrown open and left open, the melting snow on their boots made trickles on carpets and polished wood. 'Where are you, little? What *are* you doing?' They were in a part of the flat Stefan had not seen the previous time, and after the fifth or sixth set of double doors had been thrown open they were confronted by the sight of

Katty, Wirthof's little sister, though not so little now, in a large lace-pillowed bed, the bedclothing of which was very disarrayed.

Upon their bursting in, Katty had quickly pulled up around her chin a huge white eiderdown, but she regarded them unperturbed as a goldfish.

'What are you doing in bed?' Wirthof demanded.

'I had a headache.'

'A headache! You never have headaches.'

'I had a headache. Where have you been?'

'That's none of your business, little.'

'Oh tell me, tell me, *tell me*, tell me, tell me, tell me.' Her voice slid from the demanding to the appealing, like something going down a bob sleigh run with gathering momentum.

'You remember my friend Kazakh?'

She looked at him blankly. 'Oh yes.'

'Go on, get dressed,' he ordered her. And added to Stefan, 'She's always in bed, this one.'

'I like my bed.'

'It's not *your* bed. It's M'mma's bed, you shouldn't even be in it. Go on; out, out, *out*. You want a spanking? You think I won't do it? I'll spank you right in front of Kazakh. Go on, out you get, lazy.' And he made to pull the large eiderdown off her.

'No,' she protested, 'no, I haven't got anything on.'

'Why haven't you anything on?'

'I was hot.'

'It's freezing.'

'It's hot in here, I was hot.'

'You've been looking at yourself in the mirror again?' She went a deep red. 'Oh she loves to look at herself in the mirror, this one. Always admiring her nakedness.' He began to tug at the eiderdown. She hung on to it, protesting. He was succeeding in pulling it slowly down her body, exposing her small childish breasts; in response to her pleas, which were not altogether serious, he did finally desist. 'We'll go out,' he announced, abruptly tiring of this game, 'so that Madame can perform her toilette.'

As soon as the door was closed, the incident in the bedroom was over and not alluded to again, and his mind had turned to the next question. 'Now, what do we find for you to wear?'

Back they marched in their heavy boots, back through the dining-room, the card room, then into his father's study. He pulled open the drawer of a large bureau, the top part of which contained heavily bound volumes behind glass doors. His fingers searched through the junk in the drawer – dice, some carved wood chess men (several pawns, a knight, a king), a cigarette holder, pencils, a monocle, boxes of pills, two medals, one in the form of the Maltese cross, whose ribbons had become soiled and dusty, a bottle of ink, various loose papers, a bunch of letters held together with elastic, and other objects relegated to disuse. Not finding what he was looking for, he slammed the drawer shut and search-ed in several of the pigeon-holes above the green leather writing top. 'Ah here it is. Come on, Kazakh.' Again Stefan followed him, through this chain of interlinked rooms, which were still darkly curtained but no longer smelled of lavender furniture polish, from the dust on all the surfaces it was evident that little polishing of any sort had been done for some time. Back in the entrance hall again, where their initial deposit of snow had turned into a small puddle, Wirthof went to a closet, unlocked it with the key he had taken from the bureau and opened the wide doors, exposing to view a serried line of uniforms and suits.

'I can't wear your father's things,' Stefan protested.

'My father!' he laughed. 'He won't object.' He put two fore-fingers to his temple in a callous mime. 'Didn't you know? Two years ago.'

'You mean he – ? Oh that's dreadful. Your mother –'

'M'mma,' he said vaguely, 'is away – you don't need to worry about her. In any case, all this is mine, such as it is, all this junk. It's my inheritance, you see, I was left it all. I'm the heir. Now then, Kazakh,' and he poked at the uniforms and fingered the materials, 'do you see yourself as a general? No? Something more in keeping? My father had *some* civilian clothes. How about this?' He pulled out a suit and hung it against Stefan. 'Oh yes. Elegant.' He said it with a slightly mocking inflection, hinting at the essential absurdity of someone like Stefan aspiring to elegance.

'I'm sure it will be too large,' Stefan said, reddening.

'Yes, yes, you're right. I'll have to lend you something of mine. Pity. You could have kept it. It's just rotting here, gathering dust and moths.' It did in fact smell of dust: an unpleasant musty smell.

Again Stefan followed him, and after going through an ante-room they came to the principal bedroom, which must have been his father's bedroom once. Like all the other rooms in the flat, it was crammed full of dark heavy furniture. An enormous carved oak bed; its roof supported by two bulbous pillars at the foot and, at the other end, by a headboard in which a design of swords and banners was rendered in high relief. There were no hangings, but at each of the four corners of the cornice rose plumed military helmets, shaped out of fumed oak, the kind of decoration sometimes found on the tombs of soldiers, less frequently on their beds. Unlike Katty's room, which had left in Stefan's mind an impression of disorder, this one was as meticulously tidy as Wirthof himself. All the pieces in it were large and a murky dark brown and elaborately carved. Opposite the bed there was a maroon settee with banner-type designs cut in the velvet pile and eagles and crowns surmounting the frame of the back rest.

When Wirthof sat down on the bed its vastness made him seem minute, and its negroid darkness emphasized his pallor, and he said, 'This was where he did it.' Again he pressed descriptive fingers to his temple. 'I can tell you, Kazakh, it was a mess. You want to see the gun?'

'No, I don't think so.'

'I'll show it you.' He was insistent. He went to a wardrobe, opened it, felt under a stack of shirts and produced a Mauser pistol, which he held out on the flat of his hand, an object to be venerated. Stefan looked at it to satisfy him, and Wirthof moved his hand about to make the sombre object glitter. 'I think it was best,' he concluded solemnly. 'I don't believe in clinging to life. If I'd been him, I'd have done it. Wouldn't you, Kazakh?'

'I probably wouldn't have had the courage.'

'It's easy. You don't feel a thing. I hate pain, I can't stand pain, but I have no fear of death. Are you frightened of death, Kazakh?'

'I don't like the idea of it.'

'You think the world can't go on without you?'

'On the contrary. I know that it can, and I'm furious.'

'I tell you, Kazakh, I have a theory I subscribe to, which is that what doesn't actually kill you strengthens you.'

'But that's the opposite of what you've just been saying.'

'Is it? Oh! Surely not. Not necessarily. That is to say, I don't maintain that *pain* strengthens me, because for one thing, I don't have pain, I avoid it – I've trained myself to do that – like those Yogis who can lie on a bed of nails without feeling anything – oh you *can* avoid pain; no, I don't say that *pain* strengthens me. What strengthens me is what doesn't kill me, if you see what I mean; coming close to death, which I *have* done, I have actually done that, you see, without flinching, *that* is strengthening, because if you've done that, crept up on death, tweaked its long nose, it gives you a most extraordinary feeling. Are you a gambler, Kazakh? I am, you see. Have you ever played Russian roulette? I don't suppose you have, I suppose that wouldn't appeal to you. It's a most extraordinary sensation. What most people don't appreciate is that the odds in Russian roulette are actually favourable: five to one in your favour, you don't often get such good odds in other circumstances. I've only played it twice. It's the most exhilarating sensation – of course, in certain moods I wouldn't play. I know when I'm in a losing position, but I also know when I'm in a winning position. You never gamble, Kazakh? I adore conventional roulette too. I have a good instinct – a presentiment – about when I'm going to win. I don't use any system: in the right mood, I *know* what numbers are going to come up, you may not believe that, but ask any true gambler – he *knows*. I do believe that there is such a thing as luck, and that you can sense when it's turning against you, if you're receptive to those sort of waves. Sometimes I know I shall lose, a strong presentiment tells me, and other times (and that's where the strengthening part comes in, because after every victory you're stronger and better able to win the next time – it works that way), other times I am convinced I will win, and I do. Real losers, you must have noticed, go on losing, you never see a true loser make a recovery, he goes on losing, that's his pattern, he falls into it, and he keeps on: losers lose and winners win. The trick is not to lose your nerve, ask any experienced gambler; sometimes by not losing your nerve you can force your luck to change. You double up –'

'How d'you double up at Russian roulette?'

'Well, that's rather an extreme example.'

'You don't let anything limit the type of things that you draw strength from, by managing not to let them kill you?'

'Only my sense of honour.'

'Your honour!'

'Yes.'

'That's a deterrant I wouldn't like to have to depend on for my life.'

'You don't have a high opinion of my sense of honour? Had you said that in public I should have had to challenge you to a duel, you realize. But don't worry, I shan't demand satisfaction. I accept your statement in the context of our discussion. In philosophy all questions are debatable – even my honour. Isn't that so? Yes, my honour. I believe in it, whether you do or not; that is to say, I am quite ready to die for it, as I've said I have no fear of death, *per se*, whereas to live in a state of dishonour would be extremely painful to me, and, as I've also said, pain is something I abhor.'

'The question, then is – what you would consider honourable and what you would consider dishonourable.'

'Precisely. I've never actually sought to define honour, it's an interesting problem. What would I consider dishonourable? Well, obviously any form of unnatural subservience, to submit to indignity ... . Yes, all that is obvious of course. You've raised an interesting question, Kazakh. Quite simply I would say – how shall I put it? – that the only morality, the only *valid* morality, is a personal sense of honour.'

'Which you can vary to suit your convenience?'

'No, no, not at all; on the contrary – conventional morality is a matter of fashions, this must not be done at one time but may be done at another time, it is only one's intrinsic sense of honour that remains constant. I find it hard to define because the situations in which it can be tested are, at this moment, hypothetical, and what I am talking of is not capable of theoretical application. In theory one may say one would do this or that in a given situation, but it would be guesswork; what I call honour is something that operates in action, irrespective of preconceived notions.'

'You keep begging the question, Wirthof. What is this honour?'

'It is – it is, it's like luck, Kazakh; you either have it or you don't. When the occasion arises you know whether you have it or not from the outcome. It is a set of instinctive principles, if you like, from which, notwithstanding personal considerations and changing fashions, you absolutely cannot depart, even at the cost of your life. There you are. I think that's rather a good definition. It is something of which only a few people are capable; the majority, the *Lumpenproletariat*, have no honour, all they have are appetites, and the occasional denial of their appetites they call their virtue. But honour is not concerned with such bourgeois playing at self-denial, that is the prerogative of the weak and the timid, of those who are terrified of their passions and of retribution and all that kind of nonsense. The man who has honour, who truly has it, has no need of such artificial self-restriction, he does not need to fear his appetites and desires the way the bourgeoisie does, he does not have to refer all his actions to laid down rules and regulations of what is right and wrong, because his sense of honour will save him – like a sudden flood of adrenalin will save him from danger – from baseness and vulgarity. In the end, I have to say: *I* know what honour is, and because I know, I cannot depart from it, whereas someone who has merely been *told* what it is can, because what you have been told, you can misunderstand when it suits you to, but what you know in your bones, in the way I have described, you know with absolute certainty.'

He was persuasive in his theorizing, but at these last words a warning bell began to sound in Stefan and he remembered his father saying to him to beware of people who profess certainty; there was in Wirthof's whole manner as he spoke the peculiar– and seductive – arrogance of the initiate, of someone with access to a private fount of knowledge unavailable to others, and there was in him, too, an impatient disdain for all those unfortunate fools who could not see what to him was self-evident.

'I suppose, Wirthof, you could say that someone who has honour will behave honourably. But it is begging the question, isn't it? For it all depends, doesn't it? on whether what you *call* honour is in fact honour, and whether the person truly has it, whatever it is. In the end, it all comes down to what you mean by a particular word, and since you can't define honour we are talking in the dark.'

Wirthof was not someone with whom one could argue in a rational way. In a corner, he would simply assert that he 'knew' he was right, give his superior all-knowing smile, and dismiss as bourgeois, semantical, or old-fashioned, any objections he couldn't answer off hand. How could one say to him there was no way of being certain that when he pressed the trigger the pistol's hammer would fall on an empty chamber? That his certainty was delusionary? He would – did – retort that he was still alive, *that* was the proof: only proof of his good luck, surely: precisely, he exults: but luck, by definition, cannot be counted on; but he *has* counted on it, he answers, and he has been right, because he is still here. His illogic was impenetrable – how often I argued with him in this way. What was worse, it was also seductive, something in me wished to believe in it. So much was unknown, there were so many imponderables, supposing there was some as yet undiscovered law that governed chance, and that some people had a natural capacity to harness it to their will.

For Wirthof this particular discussion, the forerunner of many on the subject of his honour, was over, and won by him, and he felt generously disposed towards the loser.

'I enjoyed our discussion, Kazakh. But I'm forgetting, I promised you something decent to wear.' He went to the cupboard from which he had taken the pistol (now lying on the bed) and opened the second door, offering Stefan free choice. 'Take whichever you like.'

He selected a dark-blue suit; Wirthof stood watching as Stefan tried it on: the jacket and sleeves were too short, but it would do, and even if the trouser cuffs only came to his ankles, what did that matter, considering what an elegant suit it was. 'The shirt is unimaginable,' Wirthof declared. 'Take one of mine. And you'll want a tie. And – my God – your shoes, they are appalling! I hope mine fit, what size do you take? You can't possibly venture out in yours. They look as if you've taken part in the retreat from Moscow. And before you change, I suggest you take a bath. Use my bathroom. It's through there.' He pointed to a door, Stefan accepted the implied insult as entirely justified, he hadn't bathed in weeks. The bathroom was opulent, tiled from floor to ceiling, and the size of a bedroom, and the bath itself! It was an invention, with an intricate system of convoluted pipes supplying the hot water. There were so many knobs and jets and taps that to fill the bath was like performing some elaborate laboratory experiment. After some unsuccessful experimentation – Stefan felt it would involve great loss of face to have to ask how the mechanism worked – he eventually succeeded in producing the necessary explosion of gas jets and a violent flow of scalding water. The bathroom was heated by an enormous central heating radiator, which made it pleasurable to wait naked for the tub to fill up. At home, there was no bath in the flat itself, but a room on the landing of the floor below had been fitted up as a bathroom (it was used communally by the occupants of four flats, for hanging out laundry as well as for bathing); whenever I wanted to take a bath I had to clothe myself in a heavy overcoat as if for going out – the landings and stairs were colder than the street – and then wait, muffled and shivering, for the bath to fill up, which it did with maddening slowness, the tap spurting and spluttering, the water coming out in fits and starts, sometimes clear, sometimes cloudy, and sometimes a dirty brown colour. And sometimes, for no particular reason, no water at all came out. The water which did come out was occasionally warm, but more often tepid, and once sufficient had been collected one immersed oneself in it with great haste, knowing that the plug, a mechanical contraption, was not a good fit, and the water was liable to run out in a matter of a few minutes. But Wirthof's bath was magnificent, colossal, sinful. The bathroom began to fill up with steam. Everything he touched was of a seductive texture: feet cosseted in the deep pile of carpeting, hands touching marble and porcelain and chrome and glass and turtle soap – he felt his pores opening: exoticism.

For some minutes he was in a state of blissful reverie; he was pulled out of it by Wirthof's calling, 'How long are you proposing to be in there?' In due course he re-emerged, fully dressed, smelling of toilet water and turtle soap; powdered, steamed, toenails cut, nails filed. Wirthof had gone.

He sat on the edge of the velvet settee, stiffly, careful not to crease his new suit, hot after his bath, smelling unfamiliar to himself. Perspiration tickled the side of his face; all the rooms in this flat were overheated. He went across to the windows, he pressed his palm against the glass, which was like a block of ice, and then placed his forehead against the pane: it made him shiver. Where was Wirthof? He went to the door and through into the ante-room; it was fully curtained and dark, and he couldn't find the light switch; beyond was the hall – he felt his way towards it. The flat was silent, the only sound that of the clocks. Had everyone gone? 'Wirthof,' he called out in a low voice. 'Wirthof?' No answer. Damn him. The layout of the flat was very confusing. He tried one door and found it locked, then another that was also locked – ah yes, the double doors, these were the ones they had come through. He pressed down the handle, opened the door a fraction and slipped like a cat into the first of the reception rooms. A wide, half-curtained room, the music room; a piano and a harp on a pillared platform, girandoles around the walls, dark pictures in gold frames, in niches bronze figures holding torches, and there was Wirthof's cape on a chair. For some reason he felt nervous of penetrating deeper into this apartment. 'Wirthof,' he called again, in a whisper, to have shouted would have been offensive. The next room was even darker, he nearly knocked over a bronze vase or urn containing something feathery – he struck a match: peacock's feathers. And the clinking sound? Seashells, dozens of them of varying sizes, laid out on a side table. Another set of double doors, very high, with pediments above – heavy, no sound penetrated them, each room was locked in its own characteristic silence, a silence derived from the objects it encompassed; the silence of the first of the reception rooms was quite different from the silence of the room he was in now. 'Wirthof,' he called a little louder this time, but the darkness, the Turkish rugs on tables, the carpets, the velvet pile, the heavy hangings of silk, of damask, of satin, of brocaded silk, the dark foliage of silken thread, the dense undergrowth of woven patterns and designs, and the silence itself (as if it were itself a tangible thing like these others) absorbed his voice, soaked it up instantly, stole its resonance and made it feeble. More doors. Now he was in some kind of a corridor, his fingers found a door handle, a key, I turned it; and stepped into eyes, frosted old woman's eyes. She must have been sitting almost on top of the door, staring at it, so that he was upon her before he could make out what she was, for she was as still and dark as those bronzes in niches and as silent as a stopped clock. She reacted not at all to his intrusion but continued to stare at him out of a putty-soft face, exquisitely handsome, in which the lines were intricate needlework. He knew the room she was sitting in – this was the old nursery, with the double-tiered bunk, and the drawings on the walls, the child's geometric designs making a frieze around this old woman, who – he now saw – for all the exquisiteness of her features had not combed her hair recently, it was grey and thick and stiff, standing away from her head, her robe was old and stained, and the quilted bed jacket she wore over it was frayed: the veins on the back of her hand stood out like an asp-bracelet. Behind her, on what had been a washstand, and later Wirthof's desk, stood a tray of food, and several rows of medicine bottles. The strong smell of formaldehyde, which he remembered from his first visit, was confined now to this room, concentrated here. The lower bunk was made up as a bed, the upper one empty. Between the inner and an outer window there was an iron grille.

He muttered some kind of apology; the old woman merely nodded her head in the manner of someone who does not speak your language but understands that you do not mean any harm and wishes to indicate that she knows this: she said nothing, but continued to nod her head like a doll capable of only one action at a time, either a squeak or a nod, but not both. He withdrew quickly, and when he had shut the door hesitated about turning the key on the outside, a terrible qualm in him. He tried to do it as noiselessly as possible, but the massive lock would not forgo its brutal clanking action. The sound made harsh ripples in the silence of the flat, evoking the response that his feeble cries had not been able to: voices – Wirthof's, Katty's, movements, a door being opened. 'Wirthof – where on earth are you?' A moment later he appeared, withdrawing a cigarette from his mouth.

'What is it, Kazakh?' he said, frowning.

'You disappeared.'

'I was only next door, in Katty's room. You were a devil of a time in the bath. Have you been in there?' He indicated the locked door with his cigarette.

'I was trying to find you.'

'My mother has not been well,' he explained. 'You understand? You're as white as chalk, Kazakh – she's quite harmless, you know.' He brushed past and unlocked the door. His body in the doorway obscured the old woman from view. 'M'mma,' he said, 'how are you, my darling one? Hmm? Hmm? Did you get a fright? There, there. It's all right. Nobody is going to hurt you.' Stefan could hear the sound of the old woman's whimpering – it seemed to come out of the poised, elegant frame of her son, bending over her, clasping her now in his arms. 'There, there,' he was murmuring to her, 'there, there. You're all right, my beauty. How's my madonna – hmm? How's my lovely?' He was rocking her in his arms. 'That was my friend, Kazakh. Say good evening to my friend, come on now. Come on now, my little darling madonna.' He moved his body aside so that she could see Stefan, he was wiping tears from her eyes with her tiny dirty lace handkerchief. The old woman seemed to be composing herself. She looked at Stefan, and then gave a gracious bow like a duenna at a ball. 'Now be good,' he told her firmly, 'take your medicine, and go to sleep. Have a good sleep – hmm? You want me to give you your medicine?' The old woman nodded her head silently, and he crossed to the wash stand and selected one of the boxes of pills, shook two on to the palm of his hand, filled a glass from a jug of water, and then held the pills out to her. She seemed to be expressing distaste for the proffered pills, and he had to coax her. 'Look how pretty they are. Look how they shine, look how pretty. Look. You can have a chocolate afterwards. Come, now, one swallow and they're down.' Talking to her in this way, he got her to take the pills, and after a great many more endearments succeeded in making his exit. He locked the door with a swift flick of his wrist, and Stefan heard her whimpering response to the brutal sound. No further reference was made to his mother, or to Stefan's blundering intrusion. With that facility of his for putting something out of his mind the moment he chose to, he turned his attention to the next matter.

'We'll leave in a minute,' he said. 'There are just one or two things I have to get. We can't call empty-handed – at Christmas.' He gave a peculiar smile, enjoying a private joke, and led Stefan back into Katty's room, where he stood, one hand on hip, one at his mouth with Turkish cigarette, looking around. 'Hmm, that's very pleasant,' he said, his eyes lighting on a perfume sprayer with a fancy bulb on the dressing table. 'That will be appreciated.' He went to pick it up, pressed the bulb and sniffed the air. 'Yes, that will be appreciated.' He put it to one side on the mirrored dressing-table top, and continued his searching examination of the room. Katty was watching him with perplexed and suspicious eyes. He opened a wardrobe door, his eyes going up and down the shelves, a finger playing thoughtfully at his lips. 'Handkerchiefs,' he announced. 'Yes, handkerchiefs. Where are the handkerchiefs, Katty?'

'You're not to take handkerchiefs,' she protested. 'They're mine. You're not to take them.'

'They're not yours, they're Mutti's,' he said.

'You're not to take them.'

'No?' He did not deign to argue with her, but stuck a fist into one of the shelves and brought it out clasping a bunch of lace handkerchiefs, which he placed neatly next to the perfume spray.

'Where are you going?' Katty demanded, her wide eyes communicating with him in their private language.

'None of your business, little. Is it, Kazakh? It's none of her business, is it? Now what else? That's a very pleasant pillow case Very pleasant.' Katty was actually resting against the pillow, on the unmade bed. 'Come on, move, move . . .'

'No, no, you can't take that,' she cried plaintively. 'You can't.'

'Get off, little,' he ordered, and pulled the pillow out from behind her, and quickly, violently, stripped it of its beautifully embroidered tick, which he folded carefully and also placed on the dressing table. 'Now then – what else?' His marauding eyes, in which there was a hard glint of enjoyment, searched the room, taking in his sister in their traversing sweeps, and every time they fell on her she seemed to shrink back further with fearful excitement, trembling, as if he might select her too for his pile of disposable goods. 'What else is there – in all this junk?' he pondered. He saw mauve marabou feathers, hat trimmings, and added them, and then catching sight of himself in a cheval glass, which gave him at the angle at which it was fixed a full length view of himself, his eyes lit up, he slapped his hands together in a motion of delighted self-congratulation at having thought of the idea, and exclaimed, 'Ah – capital – the very thing, perfect.'

'You're not going to take *that*,' Katty protested, deeply shocked. 'Oh no, not *that*. Mutti has always had that. Not the mirror, Konrad. That's the mirror she always used for dressing, when we were going out. When she got dressed up in all her lovely clothes.'

'Mutti doesn't go out any more,' he declared, and gave the cheval glass a slight kick, altering its angle to give him a reflection of his shoes. 'It's just the thing.'

'You can't take Mutti's mirror,' Katty declared. 'You can't do that, Konrad.'

'Of course I can, little.'

'You're wicked, you're wicked.'

'She won't notice it's gone. *You* don't want me to take it because that's the mirror in which you're always looking at yourself. That's the reason, isn't it?' Again he gave it a slight kick, changing its angle so that now it contained a reflection of Katty pressed up against the headboard of the bed. 'It'll make a very acceptable gift, this mirror. I am sure it will be greatly appreciated. You're selfish to want to keep it. Selfish Katty.'

'Where are you going?' Katty asked again, in a lower voice this time, appealingly rather than demandingly.

'I told you, little – none of your business.'

'Will you tell me afterwards? When you come back, will you tell me where you've been?'

'I'll tell you when I come back.'

'Promise.'

'We shall see.'

'No, you must promise.'

'All right. If you're good – if you find some of that paper for wrapping, some of that decorative paper, and wrap up these things for me, in nice neat parcels. Put a big sheet of paper round the mirror too. I want it to be a surprise.'

Half an hour later they descended, laden, to the street, Wirthof carrying the cheval glass, its base protruding from the wrapping paper, Stefan holding the neat little packages. Though the trousers, pleated at the belt, came only to his ankles and no shoes had been found large enough to fit him (to replace those that had seen the retreat from Moscow), Stefan, in six-button double-breasted brown serge, in spotted bow tie, in fitted overcoat with flair in the skirt stopping short of his knees, and with coffee-coloured Mocha gloves to complete the ensemble, felt decidedly elegant. 'Smart,' Wirthof said, 'smart,' and grinned mysteriously. He was looking around for a cab, snapping his fingers at every passing vehicle.

'Where are we going?'

'We're going to pay a call on some acquaintances of mine. It'll interest you, Kazakh, I promise you.'

When a cab eventually came along, they piled into it with all their parcels and packages and Wirthof gave an address to the driver. They headed in a southerly direction, along the Parkring, the Stadtpark on their left, past the bandstand, the conical hedges, the Kursalon, and then turned into Schwarzenbergplatz, past the Schwarzenberg palace and along Prinz Eugen-Strasse, and they were in the dismal long street that is the beginning of the southern suburbs and the gloomy approach of the Belvedere palace and the Sudbahnhof. Where were they going? The few cafés in the vicinity of the Belvedere were all closed and shuttered. No one about. A tram clattered past, empty except for two girls with suitcases, presumably off some late train. The cab skirted the railway station itself, and took a street Stefan did not know, and then made various complicated turns causing him to lose all sense of direction. Where on earth were they going? He suspected Wirthof's prankishness. The streets became darker, and he thought, with some relief, it's going to be a boring evening, and indulged himself in a moment of self-pity for having been left to his own devices tonight by his father.

They stopped in a poorly lit street, white and empty; no sign of any kind of activity: it could have been anywhere, any dreary city suburb in the world. They got out, Stefan with his small parcels first, then Wirthof with the cheval glass, the driver watching curiously; Stefan's clumsiness returned, his parcels dropped out of his hands into the snow, causing Wirthof to utter his superior laugh. 'Kazakh! Ka-zakh!' When Stefan had retrieved the packages and brushed the snow off them, he ran after Wirthof who had gone on ahead without waiting – through a dark doorway and up some badly lit stairs, several flights of them. Stefan was quite out of breath by the time he caught up at the very top of the building, from which he looked down a narrow stair well, as deep and dark as a fall in a dream. Wirthof had already rung the bell and was waiting impatiently, he rang it again, in an urgent rhythm. No answer. He grinned. 'After all: we are not exactly expected.'

'What is this place ... ?'

'You will see.'

'I mean, we can't very well just burst in on people, on Christmas Eve ...' The lid of a spy-hole in the door was being slid open, and Wirthof was smiling into it and a moment later the door was unchained, unlocked and unbolted and then opened, a fraction only, by a woman holding a table napkin in one hand. Wirthof beamed at her.

'Herr Leutnant!' It was not exactly a welcoming voice, but at least she had shown recognition, whoever she was she had not slammed the door in their face. 'Herr Leutnant, this is an unexpected pleasure ... tonight ...'

'Madame,' he said, giving an elegant bow, 'I took the liberty of bringing you a little token,' and he indicated the large wrapped object and the smaller parcels that Stefan was holding.

'How kind of you. Ah – won't you come in?'

'We are not inopportune in our call?'

'Not at all, no, no, please,' she said without conviction.

She was a woman of about forty, fair-haired, tall, large-boned, with the build of a farm girl. She wore a black satin dress, ornamented at the high square neck with a silk bow at one side and artificial flowers at the other, the hem of her dress had three rows of lace flounces, the last of which came to a little below her knees. Her flesh was confined, noticeably restricted, within this dress; she bulged at the hips. Her eyes also bulged. Gold bangles jingled at her wrists, and a heavy perfume came off her. The entrance hall was dim, the bead-dripping maroon lampshade having been decorated with so much holly and other green foliage as to drastically limit the amount of light it gave out. What light it did give showed they were in the right angle of two corridors, one long and dark, the other shorter and leading to a room whose door was open, and from which came lights and the sound of talk. Along the walls of this shorter corridor crêpe paper festoons hung from the picture rail, and the electric candles of the wall candelabra were garlanded with flowers. Sprigs of heather and bulrushes lodged in the wrought-iron curlicues of the wall lamps.

'Madame, this is my friend,' Wirthof said.

'Enchantée, Herr Doktor.' She took Stefan's hand in a formal high grip, and shook it with a pumping motion.

'Please, you will join us,' she said, and added in a lower more intimate voice, 'you understand, Herr Leutnant, we are having a private evening – Christmas, you understand.' And she gave a rather self-conscious, apologetic laugh that brought out a certain girlishness in her.

In the doorway of the room from which the sounds were coming, Stefan hesitated, feeling intrusive: he had an impression of open mouths, greasy fingers and cheeks, flushed faces, partially loosened dresses. Abrupt silence. Everyone stared at them.

'Our good friend, the Herr Leutnant, has paid us a call,' Madame announced, and added, 'I think he has brought us all something.'

'Oh – presents! Presents!' the girls called out, delighted.

'Most thoughtful, most thoughtful,' muttered the solitary man at the table, heavily getting to his feet, one hand on the table for steadiness. 'May we offer you a little refreshment. Please . . .' He indicated the laden table, where the remains of a dismembered goose lay on a serving plate, surrounded by mounds of greasy potatoes; the sweep of his hand included bottles of wine, beer, the variegated stains – orange from carrots, green from spinach, dark red from wine – on the tablecloth, the vinaigrette bottle, the bread baskets, the toothpicks, the Bols bottle and the schnapps bottle.

'Presents, presents, presents,' the girls chorused.

'Later,' Madame ruled. 'Presents are later. We will put them with the others.' Folding doors, a quarter open, connected this room with another, and through the aperture a Christmas tree, its branches giving bud to wrapped packages, could be seen. Stefan was told to place his parcels by the tree. Room was made for them at the table, and Wirthof having assured their hostess that they had already eaten, glasses were placed before them. Stefan poured himself a large schnapps, and then slid the bottle across to

Wirthof. Wirthof was seated between Madame and the man, and
Stefan had been put on the other side of the table between two
plump girls who looked like sisters (though they were not) and
were apparently known as Putzi and Fritzi. They sat close to him,
their thighs touching his, the smell of raw onions which they
breathed into his face alleviated only slightly by their heavy perfume, the same as Madame's. It was a small room, full of objects.
Facing him was a large dresser with a porringer as its centre-
piece, porcelain figurines representing waltzing couples in period
costume on either side, and in the foreground a dense array of
framed photographs, so personal in nature as to be disconcerting.
One did not really care to see Madame's baby bottom, or the
stern bearded features of her father, or the frightened eyes of
her mother as a bride, or, for that matter, Madame herself on
her wedding day, white-veiled, a posy of flowers limply held at
her waist, her bridegroom, a younger, thinner version of the man
at the table, outstaring the slow camera eye. One did not care to
see Madame at nursery school, coquettish and plump, or Madame
and Herr Madame stiffly posed with pigeons on their arms in the
Piazza San Marco, and for that matter one did not care to see
Madame's five sisters and three brothers, nor her framed matri-
culation certificate.

The sporadic waves of lust that Putzi and Fritzi were starting
in Stefan slapped against the insurmountable barrier of these
photographs. He kept refilling his glass with schnapps. Next to
Wirthof, on the other side of Madame, sat a girl younger than the
others, less jolly, with a daguerreotype face, hair long and dark,
parted in the middle, not a whore's face at all. She had a long
neck, pale skin, dull eyes and a prominent nose, her nose was not
her best feature; she had a certain gawkiness, and did not smile
well; when she smiled she showed very long gums, which gave
her mouth an unattractive appearance, and perhaps for this reason
she smiled reluctantly, with a clumsy hoisting of her lips, as if the
cheek muscles weren't strong enough to keep the smile aloft for
long. But when her mouth dropped and her nose wasn't in profile
she seemed quite beautiful.

'You like Elisabeth?' Putzi (or maybe it was Fritzi) asked,
following the direction of his gaze.

'She is very quiet.'

Putzi (or Fritzi) laughed. 'Oh yes, she is quiet. You like her? I
like her. She is my friend.'

'Yes?'

'She is very thin?'

'She is a little thin.'

'I like her very much. You like her?'

'Oh yes, yes. Yes, I do.'

'You take Elisabeth?'

'I don't know . . . I uh . . .'

'Holiday,' she said, giggling. 'Christmas. Nobody work. No work. No love. Nothing.'

'Oh.'

'Elisabeth is very nice, no?'

'Yes.'

'You take Elisabeth?'

'Well, if nobody is working . . .'

'Christmas, nobody is working. No love for the gentlemens.' She went into a convulsion of giggles. 'No love on holy days. Only love Jesus. No love from girls on holy days.' Her thighs, despite her words to the contrary, were pressing insistently against Stefan. She had a chubby, stupid face, which might have looked more attractive heavily made up and in dimmer lighting, but with her chin greasy from goose fat and her onion breath blowing at him, and the spray of her saliva tickling his face, she was less enticing than she might have been. He concentrated his attention on Elisabeth's locket face, oval, perched awkwardly on a stalk neck. 'You have nice present for me?' Putzi (or Fritzi) was asking, squeezing her thigh hard against his.

'Perhaps.'

'I make good love.'

'I'm sure you do.'

'You don't believe? You think Elisabeth make better? Very skinny, Elisabeth. Skinny – too skinny. I have plenty.' And she placed his hand on her thigh.

'Yes, you have plenty,' he agreed.

'Too much? You don't like so much plump girl? Very good for love. Skinny girl not so good for love.' She did a deep inhalation, by way of denoting passion. 'I make it good. You ask Elisabeth, Elisabeth is my friend.'

'I thought you don't work on holy days.'

'No work on holy days,' she agreed, giving vent to a bout of giggles. 'No love for gentlemens on holy days. You are from Vienna?'

'Yes.'

'Not me.'

'No, you are not from Vienna?'

'Helsinki. Me and Putzi.' (So she was Fritzi.) 'From Helsinki. Finnish girls very good for love. Elisabeth also not from Vienna, from Germany. You are tall? How tall?'

'I don't know really.'

'You are tall, Elisabeth like very much, like very much big mens that it hurted her, but she like.'

'But not on holy days.'

'No,' she chortled, 'no work on holy days.'

At the head of the table, Madame's husband, his face flushed, his voice rising to draw the entire company into his net of listeners, was expounding something or other. '. . . profiteers, leeches,' he said, 'who suck the lifeblood from our nation, Herr Leutnant, I speak without prejudice . . .'

'Leo, please,' Madame protested laughingly, 'these gentlemen, I am sure, do not wish to discuss politics . . .'

'You see, you see, Herr Leutnant. Can you imagine? The nation staggers towards the precipice, and they call it politics to be concerned with such matters. Herr Leutnant, I am an artist, I am not a politician, I am concerned with the beauty of form, a beauty little enough appreciated in these times. We live in decadent times. You know what goes by the name art? You have seen. You have seen Rinkmann's women? That is called art. And to paint beauty, what is that? That is considered shameful. But I assure you, Herr Leutnant, I am not ashamed to paint beauty, I do not expect recognition – you know as well as I in whose hands is the art world, like everything. They look after their own, the Chosen. I tell you, Herr Leutnant, I am an artist, I am without prejudice, I piss on the Chosen. Without prejudice I piss on them. Herr Leutnant, I will tell you something about myself . . .'

'Leo, I am sure the Herr Leutnant does not . . .'

'Carla, what you are sure of I wouldn't wipe my arse with, forgive me, Herr Leutnant. If you will allow me to continue, Carla, if you will have the courtesy not to interrupt me when I am talking, I will continue. Herr Leutnant, I have three beliefs: beauty, justice and the Germanic people. For those beliefs I am ready to die. It does not distress me that my work is not recognized, to be recognized by such people I would consider an insult, I spit on their recognition. Was Van Gogh recognized?

Was Mozart? The artist who is truly an artist is indifferent. The artist must be true only to his inspiration, he must live as he can. As you see, Herr Leutnant. As you see. The artist, as the great English poet Bernard Shaw has said, must lie, steal, cheat, kill if necessary, to preserve the holy flame of his artistry. He is not like other people. Except the soldier. Except the soldier, Herr Leutnant, for he too must be ready to kill and die in defence of what is sacred and true. What the soldier defends with his strength and courage, the artist proclaims with his genius. The soldier is the true ally of the artist . . .' He did a fierce flourish with his arm, which knocked over a bottle of beer, adding an amber rivulet to the other stains on the tablecloth. 'I am convinced, Herr Leutnant, that there will have to be blood, when the body is rife with corruption, the foul blood must be let out, there will be need of blood. Dollfuss is an old woman. A man like Fey would put an end to all this dilly-dallying. After all, Herr Leutnant, we are a great nation, we have a heritage of culture and artistry . . .'

'I couldn't agree with you more,' said Wirthof, his hand going to Madame's thigh.

'Please, Herr Leutnant,' she scolded, 'please.' Elisabeth had a smirk on her angular face. Putzi and Fritzi were giggling, watching Madame straining unsuccessfully to remove Wirthof's hand.

'With Madame,' Putzi whispered to Stefan, 'no love, never. Madame very stuck up, she never make with the gentlemens. Also is holy day. Madame observe holy days always.' Wirthof was tugging at Madame's dress, ignoring her muttered protests. 'Presents,' she called out in a strained voice, 'it is time for presents.' As she pushed her chair back and began to rise, Wirthof took the opportunity of slapping her behind. She escaped from him amid the laughter of the girls, and smoothing her dress over rotund hips moved with a faster than normal gait into the room with the Christmas tree.

'Elisabeth,' she called, 'Elisabeth, help me with the presents . . .' But Elisabeth was otherwise occupied, sitting absolutely still and submitting to Wirthof's dexterous unbuttoning of the tiny mother-of-pearl buttons down the front of her bodice. Madame, seeing what was happening, an agitated note creeping into her voice, called out, 'Please, Herr Leutnant. It is Christmas.' But he paid no attention to her, and continuing to unbutton exposed Elisa-beth's little lemon breasts. Madame's husband had a sudden twitch around the mouth, a series of abortive smiles. Wirthof said, 'There is not very much choice tonight.'

'It is Christmas,' Madame's husband replied apologetically, 'the other girls have gone home. Tonight is, you understand, in the nature of a family occasion, we were not anticipating – that is to say Madame was not anticipating, for I have no hand in such business matters, I am an artist, I do not concern myself, but Madame was not anticipating clientele, you understand, being Christmas.'

'Herr Leo, I consider myself more of a friend than a client. Almost you could say – one of the family.'

'That is so, that is so.'

'Elisabeth has a great appeal.'

'Yes, I agree. Personally, I am not interested, you understand, a certain degree of abstemiousness befits the artist, the lusts of the flesh – ah! in my younger days I was as prone to them as anyone. But today: one's appetites diminish, Herr Leutnant. As an artist one is concerned, also, with the more ethereal, the flesh diminishes . . .'

'I'm glad to say it seems not to have done in Madame's case,' said Wirthof; she was in the process of unwrapping the cheval glass and had been joined by Putzi and Fritzi who were excitedly undoing some of the other packages.

'The rump,' said Wirthof, 'is formidable. I congratulate you, Herr Leo.'

'Indeed, indeed, she is a handsome creature. When she was nineteen, Herr Leutnant, ah! – she was exquisite, slim, delicate, the very fragrance of lovely young womanhood. At once, at once I was head over heels in love.'

'Her arse,' said Wirthof, 'is of excellent proportions.'

Herr Leo's mouth was twitching, one of his eyebrows began to move as if involved in a tug-of-war with the other.

'What a splendid present,' Madame cried out, having un-wrapped the cheval glass. 'Leo, isn't it magnificent? It is for me, Herr Leutnant?'

'It is for you, Madame. To admire your nakedness in.' He winked at Herr Leo, who coughed and refilled his glass from the schnapps bottle.

'As long as it is only *I* who admires my nakedness in it,' she responded with a hint of coquetry.

'You would deny the rest of us?'

96

these resolved themselves into the scratching of a gramophone record – Kursalon music floated through the aperture of the not quite meeting doors, and overlaid the other sounds, splutterings, gurglings, murmurings, sighs – sobs? Non-specific sounds. Equivocal sounds. Herr Leo closed his eyes, with the corner of his serviette he dabbed at his tears, leaving green and orange markings on his cheeks (from the spinach purée and the sweet and sour carrots); righteous rage was building up in him, but slowly, very slowly; the record had almost come to an end by the time he had enraged himself sufficiently to wrench open the folding doors. There was Wirthof, fully clothed, and Madame naked, her breasts swaying pendulously, dancing delicately; it took him several moments to appreciate the significance of this, and then his face broke into a laugh and he began to clap his hands to the music, as did the girls, and he called scoldingly to Wirthof – 'Ah, the Herr Leutnant was playing a game, a game. A wicked game, Herr Leutnant. Oh a wicked game! A prank, you might say. Oh yes, a very wicked prank. And he wagged his finger at the dancing couple, and Madame stuck out her tongue at him, and said pig several times.

Which is not to say that all our escapades were quite so lacking in accomplishment. Herr Leo: a couple of years later he divorced Madame and married Elisabeth, a better whore, oh an infinitely better whore, who was to achieve a measure of fame as the mistress of Heydrich, and under the name of Bella became the proprietress of the house in the Albertinagasse with the yellow louvred shutters: Salon Bella, whose girls were known, affectionately it is claimed, as the belladonnas. Madame: her career declined, and she was eventually reduced to walking the Kärntnerstrasse, and would reminisce tearfully with her clients of the days when she had her own little establishment until she was betrayed by her pig of a husband.

Ah – Kazakh! I'm very glad to see you. I have the most awful headache. Nothing seems to shift it. Headaches are hell, aren't they? I prefer any other kind of pain to headache. A headache is so inescapable. It just sits there on top of you, immovable as the pyramids, nothing will shift it. Not my headache. He was sitting up in the carved oak bed, wearing a voile night shirt, an icepack on his head, a moustache net – this was something new – over his upper lip, his features puffed out by soap lather, being shaved by his barber.

'Have you had a doctor?'

'Oh they're useless, quite useless. What do they know? I've never come across one who was the slightest use. Winkler!' he yelled at the sombre-faced barber. 'Good God, Winkler, watch what you are doing, you are cutting me to pieces, man.'

'I beg the Herr Leutnant's pardon, but if the Herr Leutnant could possibly remain still for a few moments . . .'

'How can I remain still, idiot, when I have this ton of bricks crushing my skull?'

'The Herr Leutnant has my deepest sympathies, I will endeavour . . .'

'You must endeavour harder, Winkler. Mirror! Look, there's a bit there you've missed. With this head, Winkler, every bristle is like a barb in my flesh. There, Winkler, there. You're not shaving me, man, you're scraping me. Can't you sharpen that razor?' He turned wearily to Stefan while the barber stropped his razor. 'I seem to be surrounded by fools and nincompoops. I can't seem to get a competent barber even. Ah yes, I'd like your opinion.' And he reached behind his head and untied the tapes of the moustache net, which he removed with a flourish. 'There! What d'you think of it? You don't care for it? Don't hesitate to say. I want your frank opinion.' He picked up an oval hand mirror and examined himself in it. 'As a matter of fact, I have been somewhat discouraged. I have gone to all this trouble to grow these few miserable hairs, nurturing every damned hair with care and devotion, guarding them against the barbarities of this idiot barber of mine, Winkler – you know, Kazakh, for some reason my face does not grow hair easily, it is really quite ridiculous, and now I have come across a description, a most unsympathetic description, in a novel I am reading, of a young man, a miserable, weak, conceited young man of utter uselessness who, as it happens, has a moustache identical, according to this author's description, and he is a well-thought-of author – Zierer: have you read anything by him? an excellent author though a little pompous and moralizing, but quite excellent – as I was saying, this miserable character turns out to have a moustache, and one what is more very similar to the type I am growing. I thought I must ask Kazakh whether there is any psychological basis for connecting moustaches with weakness of character. What does Blumenfeld say about that?'

'Well, I suppose it depends on the moustache. My father has a moustache.'

'Is he a weak character?'

'Not at all, the contrary. But his is a very thick moustache, long, Russian . . .'

'How d'you feel about Mexican moustaches?'

'I have no opinion of them, one way or the other.'

'You think a Mexican moustache might be less weak-looking? In your opinion, would it suit my face? You need have no fear of offending me. Would it make me look Mexican? I don't think I would mind having a Mexican moustache, but I think you would agree it would be going too far to *look* Mexican.'

'I think you are absolutely right.'

'About what?'

'About what you just said.'

'The undesirability of looking Mexican?'

'Yes.'

'Can you recall if Julien Sorel had a moustache?'

'Ah – no – I don't recall.'

'And Werther? What about Werther?'

'I can't remember Werther having a moustache.'

'Raskolnikov I am sure did have a moustache.'

'I think you are mistaken.'

'I have always pictured him with a moustache. I can see him, smashing the old woman's skull – with a moustache.'

'Surely it was with an axe.'

'Yes, yes – I mean that he had a moustache when he was doing it. What do you think of Dostoyevsky? Would you put him in the front rank? God! this headache of mine.' The barber Winkler had resumed shaving Wirthof.

'Professor Blumenfeld has had remarkable results with hypnotism.'

'Hypnotism. For headaches?'

'Amongst other things.'

'I'd be willing to try anything to cure this headache, including allowing this idiot here to cut my throat. Which might be the simplest remedy.'

'I could get rid of it for you,' said Stefan.

'What?'

'Your headache, Wirthof.'

'You? How?'

'By hypnotism.'

'Well, you're at liberty to try. Now you cannot deny that Strindberg had a moustache.'

'Yes, I believe you are right.'

'You see. And was Strindberg a weak character?'

'I believe he was mad.'

'That's another matter. Quite another matter entirely. I am sure, Kazakh, that this connection between moustaches and weakness of character is totally unscientific, whatever Zierer says. In any case, he's a rather second-rate author, don't you agree? I have never thought very highly of him. His attitude is basically bourgeois. That he writes well is beyond dispute, but his philosophy is the philosophy of shopkeepers; for the pleasures of life you must pay, usually with syphilis or suicide or madness. What is the import of what he says? To follow the dictates of passion brings disaster. And all – Winkler, this is enough. Quite enough. While I still have a head left. Go on – out, out! Tomorrow again, at the same time. I shall need a haircut too, if I feel well enough.'

'I trust the Herr Leutnant will be feeling better by tomorrow,' the barber said, gathering up his equipment.

'I trust so too, Winkler, but I doubt it. On your way out will you tell the maid I need another icepack, this one is melting, I probably have a raging fever, you see how I'm burning up the ice.' He removed the icepack disgustedly from his head and dropped it into a basin by the bed.

'Don't tell the maid anything,' Stefan countermanded. 'Herr Wirthof will not be needing any more icepacks.'

'Is that so, is that so?' Wirthof said, spraying talcum powder on his neck and jowl. 'Well, get out, Winkler. Get out, man. Now – where was I? Yes, Zierer. The dictates of passion. The miserably timid souls who read him can find consolation in the thought that freedom of the senses brings disaster – isn't that so? Really, Kazakh, it is appalling the way the intellectuals have got us in the position where timidity, cowardice, indecisiveness and sheer apathy are celebrated as qualities of sensitivity. Frankly, Kazakh, I am bored. I am bored with the inertia of this city, its pomposity, its antiquity. Where is there a truly modern spirit, tell me that, Kazakh? Where is there a voice of today? Blumenfeld, possibly. His views on sexuality are certainly modern. And his ideas on madness – that the mad are explorers of the unknown, casualties of a terrible journey. Very interesting. Don't you find it so?'

'His views on insanity are very speculative. He makes a distinction between those of his ideas which have to a greater or lesser extent been substantiated by evidence and those, such as his ideas on insanity, which are largely hypothetical and await proof.'

'Yes, yes. But these scientists are so cautious, so frightened of being proved wrong, they wrap up everything in qualifications. I judge ideas by their sound. How can you prove a piece of music? You must go by the sound of it. The sound of something, if you have the ear, will tell you if it's right or not.'

'That's a very dangerous precept, surely.'

'Only if you don't trust your ear. We've discussed this before. If one has a sense of honour, Kazakh, then the ear will judge everything in reference to that. If you enter a gas-filled room you are in danger of being overcome, but your sense of smell will warn you of the danger.'

'There are gases that have no smell.'

'And poisons that have no taste. True. But, of course, the gas-filled room is an analogy; I am postulating a sense of honour considerably more complex and sensitive than the sense of smell, and an ear more sensitive than the ear itself.'

'If such a thing exists, and there is no proof for it, you may be right. But you are suggesting, and this is where we differ, that this sense of honour, this super ear, cannot be deluded, deceived, perverted. What evidence is there for that? All the evidence shows that the people who have been most convinced of possessing such an ear have been the most deluded, it is almost a definition of madness to believe that one possesses such an infallible instrument of measurement and assessment, and the purpose of science has been to replace this reliance on vague and indefinable "belief" with the rational consideration and assessment of evidence. What you are proposing is retrogressive, a return to the thinking of the Middle Ages and a belief in such things as possession by good or bad spirits. That is, in fact, what your theory amounts to.'

'Are there no mysteries unsolvable by science?'

Stefan hesitated. 'I don't know,' he said. 'This becomes a religious question now, doesn't it? I would hate to think there are no mysteries, but science must take the view that, in theory, everything can be explained eventually.'

'And yet this hypnotism you propose to practise on me cannot be understood. Even Blumenfeld cannot explain how it works.'

'At the moment. There are many experiences which come in this category. They undoubtedly occur. We have evidence for that – madness, inspiration, religious exaltation, faith healing. We must admit that such things happen, but as yet we have a very poor understanding of them. That doesn't mean they are eternal mysteries.'

'Very well – excellent. Consider what you have said. There are experiences we do not understand – madness, inspiration, etcetera – and at the same time you declare that only science can throw light on them. But – consider this – supposing madness/ inspiration (and I equate the two because there is a well-known empirical connection between them) is the light. Supposing it is the light in which understanding occurs. Supposing madness/ inspiration is not so much that which is to be understood as the light in which other things are understandable, then the mad, and I think Blumenfeld half suggests this, may have greater understanding than we have, they may be *lost* travellers, but *travellers*, whereas we remain in our tight little circles, snug – and smug – in our closed systems that allow of no break out.'

'But isn't that standing everything on its head? It is a semantic confusion. Madness must be madness, it cannot be reason. Something can be falsely described as madness, when it is in fact reason. That is a mistake. That can occur. Even if the whole world were mad and only the mad were sane, the confusion would still be one of semantics, of false labelling. It would not mean that madness *is* sanity, only that we have made a mistake about what we have *called* madness or sanity.'

'I don't agree with that at all.'

'It is no answer to say you don't agree with it.'

'Take hypnotism.'

'What does hypnotism have to do with it?'

'Everything. You cannot explain it, yet you propose to use it on me. You assert that this headache, which responds to no known medication and baffles medical science, is curable by your Professor Blumenfeld's hypnotism. Is that what you assert?'

'Yes, yes; I am saying that I believe I can cure your headache.'

'Then you believe in the unknown. Then you believe in magic.'

'It is not magic, it is absolutely scientific. We just don't know how it works, but we know that it does.'

'Surely it depends on some kind of superiority on the part of the hypnotist, on his being able to impose his will . . .'

'Not at all, not in the least. It works by tiring the optic nerve. If you are willing, I will demonstrate to you . . .'

'If you forgive my saying so, Kazakh, your eyes are not suitable. Too uncompelling.'

'It has nothing to do with the eyes.'

'Oh I disagree, I am sure it has to do with the eyes.'

'Really, Wirthof, what you are sure of is irrelevant. You know nothing about it.'

'I have read Blumenfeld's book.'

'Then you have misunderstood it.'

'Perhaps it is you who have misunderstood it.'

'Possibly, possibly. But we can soon find out. If you will co-operate, I can show you that I am able to do it.'

'You are serious about it? No, no. I'm afraid I'd ruin it by laughing.'

'That is my problem.'

'On the whole, this time, I will suffer the headache, it always goes in the end. I would not feel comfortable being hypnotized by you, Kazakh.'

Arguing with Wirthof was like outrunning him; he would start off at a great pace, throwing in everything he had, expending his ideas recklessly in the first few minutes, and then he'd begin to pant and slow down and presently come to an abrupt halt. It wasn't that one had won – he never conceded that; at this point he just called off the race, and a look came into his eyes, the look Stefan had seen in the magician's booth, which told of the possession of occult knowledge. There were things he knew, perceived with the inner ear, that could not be explained in words, and Stefan felt himself in an impasse, and deeply irritated by Wirthof's imperviousness to logic. However long Stefan went on, however conclusively he demonstrated the faulty logic of the other's reasoning, Wirthof remained firmly entrenched in his untenable position, hanging head down from his feet and maintaining he was standing upright. Stefan was always exhausted after such discussions which might go on, with intervals of less weighty talk, for hours, far into the night. Wirthof's stubborn clinging to his curious ideas maddened Stefan. The time Wirthof had asserted that as nobody knew for certain what the core of the earth was made of, there was no way of proving that it wasn't made of jam. It might just as well be made of jam as of solid gold. No, no, you protested; it was unlikely that it was made of gold, but gold being a natural product this was not a logical impossibility, whereas jam being a man-made product could not constitute the core of the earth. Ah, but that was just a theory, you couldn't prove it, and so the race was never won, or even finished.

'On the whole, I don't think it's such a good idea, after all.'

'Are you afraid, Wirthof?'

'Of course not.'

'Why refuse in that case?'

'I don't believe it would work.'

'Then you have nothing to lose.'

'And if it did work . . .?'

'Only your headache, that is all you would lose.'

'I would feel absurd, Kazakh.'

'Is that such a high price for losing your headache?'

'Perhaps not, perhaps not, but the headache I know . . .'

'You don't trust me. What do you imagine I will do to you? All I will do is take your headache away.'

'You really believe in this nonsense?'

'I know I can cure you of your headache, but if you'd rather keep it . . .'

'Oh very well,' Wirthof sighingly agreed. 'You're at liberty to try. Go ahead. But don't blame me if I have a fit of laughter. You are serious?'

'I'm quite serious.'

'I'm not very prone to suggestion, you know. And really you don't have the eyes for it, Kazakh. They're too – too uncompelling, if you'll forgive me saying so.'

'It has nothing to do with my eyes. You don't even have to look into my eyes. All you have to do is relax, relax completely and find a spot on the ceiling to look at.'

'I can't think of anyone less likely to be capable of hypnotizing me.'

'Just relax. Relax, and fix your eyes on a spot on the ceiling. And don't blink your eyes, let them get blurry but don't blink, just give in to that feeling of drowsiness . . .'

'I don't feel a bit drowsy . . .'

'You will. Just try to co-operate. You must co-operate or it won't work. Just give yourself up to that spot on the ceiling and don't fight my voice, listen to it, let it reach you, give in to it, relax, don't fight, just give up fighting me and entrust yourself entirely, entirely, soon you'll experience a pleasant sensation of languor, allow it, don't resist it, there is time, give yourself over to me, you must let me control your mind for a little while so that I can take your headache away, give it to me, I will take it away, give me your headache.'

'Kazakh, I'm not the least bit hypnotized.'

'You may not think so, but you are. Give up trying to judge whether you are or not, let me do that.' Indeed, though Wirthof was still fully awake, his eyes open, a deeply relaxed expression had come over his face, and he was responding to Stefan's lulling voice, and he was not blinking as he stared at the spot on the ceiling. His face, released from tension, had become child-like and vulnerable. 'Soon,' Stefan continued softly, 'a pleasant drowsiness will come over you, don't struggle against it, it's a relief, it's a relief to hand over your headache to me, I will take care of it, just let go of it. It's agreeable to feel so nicely sleepy, why smile? It's very nice. Listen to my voice and watch the spot on the ceiling, and allow yourself to be completely relaxed. Relax all your muscles. Relax all those tight muscles. You are feeling quite sleepy now, why fight it? Let yourself sleep, yes, sleep. Soon you will be fast asleep, but you will still be able to hear me, and when I tell you that your headache is gone it will be gone, and when I say wake up you will wake up. I think you're very drowsy now, I'm going to let you sleep, I'm going to count five, and on the count of five your eyelids will close, they will be so heavy they will close of their own accord and you will be in a deep sleep in which you will do exactly what I tell you, and when I tell you that your headache is gone it will be gone. One: relax, nicely relaxed. Two. Three – Four. Five.' At the count of five, Wirthof's eyes closed, and the last remnants of resistance became smoothed out of his face. 'Good,' Stefan said, 'now you're in a deep sleep, and when you wake up you won't remember anything I've said to you, but your headache will be gone. Quite gone. No trace of it will remain. You will feel fine. Your headache is going now, it's leaving your head, it's leaving all the corners and crevices, diminishing, I am taking it away, it's leaving the periphery of your skull, there's only a bit of it left in the centre of your head and that is going too, dissolving in my words, my words are dissolving it and in a moment there will be nothing whatsoever left of it. It's all going now. You have no need for this headache, you will not be troubled by headaches in the future. Now the headache is completely gone. In a moment I am going to wake you up, and when I do the headache will be entirely gone, and you will remember nothing of what I said to you while you were asleep. All right: Now wake up, Wirthof.'

Wirthof's eyes blinked open, and immediately that faintly derisory expression which moulded his features returned. 'You see,' he began, about to point out that the experiment had failed, that he had not even closed his eyes, when suddenly a perplexed frown superseded whatever he had been about to say. He screwed up his eyes uncertainly, he swivelled his head this way and that, he touched his skull as if to make sure it was still there. He closed and opened his eyes several times, 'My God,' he said at last, 'my God, it's gone, Kazakh, the headache has gone.'

'Of course.'

'It's impossible.'

'I told you it would be gone.'

'But I wasn't even asleep.'

'You don't remember having been asleep?'

'You were counting up to five, and then my eyes were supposed to close, but I knew they wouldn't because I wasn't in the least hypnotized. You haven't done it, and yet my headache has gone.'

'You closed your eyes, and went into a deep trance. I told you you wouldn't remember anything, and you haven't. But the headache has gone?'

'Absolutely. It's fantastic. You're a magician, Kazakh.'

'There's nothing magical about it,' Stefan said, a thin smile of satisfaction edging on to his lips.

Part Two

Some days after the death of his father at Floridsdorf Stefan was
questioned by two men of the Austrian State Security Police who
called on him in the Obere Donaustrasse. They were very much
incognito, these secret police. The elder of the two was incognito
in Alpine hat with feather and cord to one side, and in two-tone
shoes, the younger in sock-suspender supporting colourful socks.
They smiled sternly, and the older man – who was totally bald
under the Alpine hat with the gay little feather, and only removed
the hat in moments of emotion, replacing it again immediately
afterwards – began by expressing his condolences in somewhat
flowery terms: he had a thick moustache and a sententious
manner. The other man, with the colourful socks tightly suspended from the calf, throughout the interview confined himself
to vigorously assenting to whatever his companion said. Having
apologized for the intrusion, and expressed the appropriate sympathies, they reminded Stefan of their duty, and his. They understood, of course, that he was bound to feel loyalty to the memory
of his dead father, that was entirely commendable, but, they added
craftily, whereas Staszek Kazakh had given his life for his beliefs,
misguided as they were, other men, motivated only by **greed and**
the desire for personal power, had escaped. These men **had fled**
the country or gone into hiding, absconded with funds **provided**
by their misguided followers; they had not stayed to fight, but had
abandoned their cause the moment they saw it was lost. Why else
had the revolution collapsed on the first night? The workers had
been left to die. Stefan need feel no loyalty to men who could so
callously desert their own cause, leaving their followers in the
lurch to die like rats, if he would pardon the expression. Therefore Stefan, as a student and sensible fellow, not a dumb ox as
some of these Bolsheviks were who could so easily be deluded,
must see that it was entirely honourable to help in bringing these
traitors to justice. They were traitors not only to the legal government of the day, but also to their own cause. For hadn't they
abandoned it at the critical moment? The government, true to its
word, was not interested in punishing the rank and file of the
workers' movement; only the ringleaders, the machinators, the
criminal instigators of the February putsch were sought. Some,

like Bauer and Deutsch, were already beyond reach, in Czechoslovakia; but others were still in Austria. These men were the murderers of his father. Had one prominent Socialist died in the uprising? Not one. The leaders sat in their comfortable homes and talked revolution, having first provided themselves with escape routes and Swiss bank accounts, and when it came to it they left the fighting and the dying to the workers they secretly despised. For they were not even true Socialists. How many had ever toiled with their hands? How many had ever done *any* honourable work? How many had died?

The two secret police questioning Stefan had brought with them a large buff envelope full of photographs. The man in the Alpine hat with cord and feather to the side, and the two-tone shoes, emptied the envelope, shuffled the photographs like playing cards and laid them back upwards on the table. Turning up one after the other, he demanded sternly, 'Stefan, do you know this man? Do you know this man? And this man?'

There were about fifteen photographs altogether – some were formal portraits, others grainy snapshots, in which the figures were blurred, ill-defined shapes in a street or tram or café.

'Do you recognize any of these men, Stefan?'

'Yes.'

The man in the Alpine hat and two-tone shoes was quite taken aback. 'Whom do you recognize, please?'

'I recognize Brimmer.'

'Ah yes, yes; good; that *is* Brimmer.' The two State Security policemen looked at each other briefly. 'Anyone else you recognize, Stefan?'

'This man, but I don't know his name.'

'Please, which man?'

'This man.'

'This man?'

'It is a familiar face, I cannot quite place it at the moment. Let me try and remember. Ah yes – I think he must be the man I used to see with my father sometimes. I think he must be quite important, a leader, definitely a leader. Yes, I'm sure this was the man. A rather loathsome character. You can tell from the eyes, can't you? I could swear this was the man who used to come and see my father, I think he must have been the one who was in charge of supplying arms . . .'

'Stefan,' the man in the two-tone shoes cut him short, emotionally taking off his Alpine hat, 'this is a picture of the Assistant Secretary of State Security.'

'Oh! How extraordinary! You don't think, surely not the Assistant Secretary. How extraordinary! Of course, I might be mistaken, as I said I have a poor memory for faces. Ah I see, I see, I understand, gentlemen, I see, you were *testing* me. How foolish of me not to have realized it. You are cunning, I see you know your business. I apologize if I seemed offensive in my remarks. I have an appalling memory for faces, and I get confused, you know. What a stupid mistake to confuse the Assistant Secretary for State Security for one of the workers' leaders. Still, perhaps my memory will be better for some of the others. The extraordinary thing is, *all* the faces look familiar to me. Now this man here – I hesitate to say it after my previous blunder – looks definitely familiar.'

'But you cannot see his face, Herr Kazakh,' the younger secret policeman, the one with the colourful socks, protested.

'His stance is familiar.'

'But he is sitting.'

'Yes, you know the way some men have of sitting. Highly individualistic. As a matter of fact, this other man here, this one with the fedora hat, is also known to me. The hat. I am sure I have seen the hat – hanging in this very hall.'

'It is a very ordinary hat.'

'That is true. But I could swear it was that hat. You know how one has an instinct about certain things. On the other hand, this man here, with the thick-lensed glasses, now this time you don't catch me, gentlemen, I know who this man is – this is the conductor, Fichter. I have seen him many times at the Opera.'

'Fichter, Stefan, is a much older man, and totally bald, whereas this man . . .'

'You are right, you are right, of course you are right. I could have sworn this man was Fichter, but you are right, Fichter *is* a much older man. I regret I seem not to be helping you very much, gentlemen. It is my absurd forgetfulness. It is really appalling – makes me feel so stupid. You know, I forget telephone numbers that I have dialled a hundred times. One day I have them, the next they are gone. 73849 – or is it 93784? Numbers are the worst – and faces. Sometimes I go up to someone in the street, convinced that I know him intimately, and it turns out to be somebody else entirely. It is highly embarrassing. Numbers are such arbitrary things. Why should the laundry be 33541 and not 14576? There is no rhyme or reason to it. One does not forget that a cigar is a C-I-G-A-R, because after all it *is* a cigar. Or that a policeman is P-O-L-I-C-E-M-A-N because he so indubitably *is* a P-O-L-I-C-E-M-A-N. On the other hand, I can see you are going to say, and I concede the point, that there is no reason why a policeman should be called a policeman except that that particular arrangement of letters has come to denote what he is. No reason at all why R-O-S-E should not denote policeman, except, of course, for the difference in smell. Yes, yes, I see what you are going to say; a rose does not look like a policeman, and there I agree with you. These semantic questions are very interesting, don't you think? For example, there is no reason, except usage, why a tram should be known as a tram, it describes only one aspect of it, just as 33541 describes only one aspect of the launderer, not for instance his relationship with his wife or his politics, the tram could just as well be called an electric or a mobile or a long or a red or a green or whatever other aspect of it we choose to know it by. My difficulty with faces – and this must seem strange to you gentlemen, because obviously you do not suffer from this disability, in your profession – is that I cannot establish any indisputable connection between a Schmidt and the face of Schmidt. Why isn't he a Braun? Or a Schmerler. Hence – my stupid confusion. But, if you would like me to go on, I will try and identify some of these photographs for you. It is no trouble, I assure you.'

'May I walk with you?' (This was in the Universitätstrasse.)
'— —'
'I should have contacted you sooner, Stefan. But it wasn't possible. You were being watched.'
'— —'
'They called off their hounds a few days ago. We have been watching you too, you see.'
'— —'
'That displeases you, Stefan?'
'I don't care to be watched.'
'I apologize. It was necessary. No, don't walk too close. Then if there is anyone, they cannot connect us. Don't look at me. All right? I want to express my deep sorrow, Stefan. Your father was not only a comrade but a dear, dear friend.'
'There was no need to take such a risk to tell me that.'

'There is something else. It was agreed, in advance, that if anything happened to any one of us, the others would assume responsibility for that person's dependents.'

'I'm nobody's dependent.'

'Your education, Stefan. It was your father's wish that you should continue with it. And that requires money . . .'

'— —'

'Stefan, we look after our own. It was agreed.'

'— —'

'How will you continue with your studies?'

'— —'

'Your father wanted you to study. An account will be opened for you and a fixed amount paid into it monthly . . .'

'— —'

'Stefan, please, it was your father's wish. You must not regard this as charity, but as your right. A sort of insurance benefit, you understand. Your father gave everything to the movement. In return it was agreed, amongst us, that you would be looked after. Had I died, your father, with others, would have assumed responsibility for my sons. So you see, it is your right.'

'I am not one of you.'

'That does not matter. You gave no information to the police . . .'

'— —'

'We have our sources.'

'— —'

'What I am saying to you is not a political matter at all.'

'— —'

'I don't understand, surely – without going into the political pros and cons, your sympathies . . . Broadly speaking . . .'

'— —'

'That is very harsh. Understandable, in view of your tragic experience, but harsh none the less . . .'

'— —'

'It pains me to hear you speak like this, Stefan. It offends against the memory of your father . . .'

'— —'

'All right, Stefan. I see that in the mood you are in it is useless for me to try and persuade you. But I want you to know that, as far as I am concerned, my obligation to you remains. If you should need to get in touch with me, leave a note addressed to Orsha at the Café Kostroma in the Schwarzenbergplatz. That will find me, and a meeting will be arranged. The phrasing, I suggest . . .' he gave a coy smile, 'should be . . . romantic. "Orsha, beloved, I must see you soon." Something of that sort. You understand?'

'I'd appreciate it if you would stop having your people follow me.'

'I will see to it. I cannot tell you how much it hurts me to find you taking this attitude, Stefan. Always remember, please, we are your friends.'

'__ __'

'I – and the others. All of your father's many friends.'

'__ __'.

'Yes, his comrades.'

'I hope to be spared such allies, Orsha. Beloved Orsha.'

'Your bitterness is understandable, Stefan. But when you have had time to get over the immediate shock and grief, you will realize that what was done had to be done. Whether you are with us or not, now, you will one day come to realize that it had to be.'

'__ __'

'Such considerations were at the heart of our indecisiveness, our bungling. Yes, it was a consideration. It was a risk. But some of us believed it should be taken. Perhaps, if we had captured Vienna. It is impossible to predict what would have happened. There are no crystal balls, Stefan. One can only weigh the risk and use one's judgment.'

'They know about you, Orsha. They showed me a photograph of you.' Stefan heard him chuckle.

'What did you say?'

'I said of course I recognized the face. It was the conductor Fichter.'

'Excellent. I am said to bear a certain resemblance to Fichter. Of course Fichter is a much older man and he has no hair at all.'

'That is what they said.'

'I catch a tram at the bottom, Stefan. Remember – Café Kostroma. Whatever happens to me, you will have an answer from Orsha.'

'Aren't you afraid? Don't you shiver in your boots sometimes?'

'No, Stefan, I don't shiver in my boots. Nor did your father. He took the risk cheerfully. Goodbye, Stefan. God bless you.'

Five days later, in Melk, Thick Lenses, whose name was Heinrich Bimelmann, was arrested. He was tried in the latter part of March, and hanged on April fool's day.

Yesterday in Vienna I walked along the Universitätstrasse, and suddenly in my mind I saw the face of Thick Lenses, beloved Orsha, or was it Fichter's face? The two have become indistinguishable to me, whenever I used to see the conductor's photograph in a newspaper I would think – Orsha, but you are a hanged man, how can you be conducting the Vienna Philharmonic. What beautiful music you make for a hanged man. I have no love for you, beloved Orsha, yet you are an inhabitant of my mind. I did not know you even, yet I think of you rushing to catch your tram; and sometimes I have thought of you saying, 'I do not shiver in my boots.' My mind is populated with fools and dead men. Yesterday, wandering through Vienna in that peculiar state I was in, I found myself at one stage outside the Café Kostroma, and without taking in the name of the place went in and ordered a coffee, and as I drank it I realized where I was, and – I never did take up Thick Lenses's offer. Supposing I left a note – now – for Orsha, what would happen? 'Beloved Orsha, must see you, need you.' Probably a whore would meet me in the Schwarzenbergplatz.

Yesterday. What kind of day was yesterday? A bad day. A good day, too. What was the matter with me yesterday? Something was going on in me? I can't seem to put my finger on it. I had an experience of some sort, walking through the streets of Vienna. What is the opposite of a religious experience? I am better now (you are better?); well, more, more . . . contained, calmer. Yesterday I was beset by – tormentors. The thing is: it didn't seem to have any connection, this experience of mine, whatever it was, with anything that actually happened to me yesterday. Nothing happened yesterday. What did happen to me? Nothing. Nothing.

My mind seemed to be straining in all directions at once; memories rushing. Panic – you must have panicked. You should have taken a drink. If I could have slept. That dream about the wrecked flat. Not such a horrific dream, have had worse: I've *lived* worse nightmares than that. I? Yes, you Kazakh. Was it me? Up in the Karavanke, on the dying mule, forty below zero, maybe only twenty, how d'you know? Still, you survived it, did I though, did I? Well, you are here, in this cold hotel room – which *they* claim is heated, miserable liars! – shivering, shivering with an eiderdown around your shoulders. Then why don't you change hotels? There must be some hotels in Vienna that are heated. You, who survived forty below zero (all right, twenty). No heating here. Comes out of the ceiling, does it? Heat rises. Heat *rises*. How can it come down from above? Needs pressure. No pressure. Fans not working probably, or something. God, it's cold. Remember that time you were ill (I am never ill, never); I used to slap my face, to collect myself, not something to be seen doing in public. Stefan Kazakh, company director, seen walking along the Embankment slapping his face, his own face, yes, poor fellow! Most of the time perfectly reasonable. His wits about him. Oh, he's smart. Quick. Quick. Even when he's sitting still his wagging foot is off somewhere. Wouldn't imagine he was the same fellow who . . . No, you wouldn't imagine it; nor would I. Hah-hah! Nor would I. Play squash with him and he'll hammer you into the ground. Can't bear to lose. Thin as a rake, and tough! Oh God, yes. Except that sometimes, for no reason at all, I faint, collapse of thin party, oh very funny. The death occurred suddenly yesterday of Mr. Stefan Kazakh at a hotel in Vienna. Mr. Kazakh, who was fifty-two. They say extreme cold can bring on heart failure – well, it's not that cold in here, though it's pretty cold. Why d'you go on, Kazakh? You could retire. Devote yourself to your interests, whatever they are, what are they? And supposing? And supposing? And supposing? Kazakh, you have no financial worries, even with all the back taxes they could conceivably catch you for. Then why do I shiver? You shiver because it's cold in here, because those smiling Viennese bastards have given you an unheated room in mid-winter, because you've got accustomed to American central heating, except you can't stand American central heating, and in New York are always going around opening windows. What is the matter with me? The trouble is I hate my whole world of deals, despise it. Liar! No, that's the truth, that's the God's truth, I hate it. Then why don't you get out? That's quite another matter, will you stop persecuting me with your mocking voice and your lousy innuendoes. One does not give up because of a moment of shivering apprehension. Giving up things doesn't solve anything. Remember Leonie used to say that – ah yes, Leonie. She used to say, 'If I thought it would bring me happiness I'd give up everything without a moment's hesitation'; she didn't, of course.

All the same, I wish I had continued with my education. I was in such a hurry, there was no time. Years of study, followed by years of struggle to establish oneself – in a profession where progress is determined by seniority. Oh no, that wasn't for me. My quickness could not wait on seniority. What I had to do would have to be quickly done, in a flash of effort, all or nothing. Bathroom fitments, solid gold or, for the hard-up rich, gold-plated; lavatory paper holders, towel rails, taps, showers, who wanted such things in Vienna 1934–5? I sold a few, oh I could have sold fire to the devil; selling space in the telephone directories was easier though, a more remunerative line. You told firm A that firm B had taken top of the page and if firm A didn't take bottom of the page then anyone opening the directory to find a plumber –

Within a year I had an office with four employees, and was selling advertising space in newspapers, on hoardings, in trams, in theatre programmes, and even on pencils. Hundreds of thousands of pencils were sold every year, why not put an advertising slogan on them? I was developing the idea of putting advertisements on toothbrush mugs, on the backs of playing cards, on deck chairs and in the sky. Why not? I was in a hurry. I wanted to light up the whole city with my slogans. That was all in the year after my father's death, the year Dollfuss was assassinated and the Nazi take-over bid failed.

Everything was getting out of hand, the whole rotten edifice was crumbling, and I was racing the falling masonry, determined to make my big killing before the final collapse. By contrast with the others, whose attitude to every fresh crisis was that it would blow over, I had a continual sense of impending disaster, it was so real to me that I was amazed by the equanimity with which others went about their daily business. How could I have had such prophetic insight, such certain foreknowledge? I *knew* what was coming, and perhaps I was good at business because to me it was a life or death matter. Always has been; even later, when patently what was at stake was only money, every deal was for me a matter of life or death, whereas to my competitors it was merely business, which gave me the advantage. I had a taut and rushed expression as I dashed from hotel lobby to hotel lobby on my business deals, my precipitant manner was wholly un-Viennese and perhaps impressive for that reason. 'My dear Stefan,' Baron Koeppler would say, 'why are you always in such a rush? You must take a little time to enjoy yourself.' I gave my quick smile, and told him he was probably right (I was not giving away what I knew), but it was in my nature to rush. 'It is not good for your health,' they said. What fools they were – advocating relaxation while hanging over a precipice. In my frantic dashing hither and thither I was like a man raising the ransom on his own life –

Ah! fortunate is the man without money, having no financial anxieties. Once, I thought it was the other way round, but now I know what a burdensome thing it can be, money. My chosen burden! Then give it away: that's the impossibility. You will go under one of these days, Kazakh, mark my words, if you don't keep your wits about you. At fifty-two you are in no position to slow down, to indulge yourself in memorabilia. It's days now since you've been in touch with your office: anything could have happened: you haven't looked at an English paper, you could be ruined. Now wouldn't that be funny. Suddenly the prospect of being ruined seemed almost appealing to Stefan Kazakh. He was smiling to himself, and he had allowed the eiderdown to slip from his shoulders. Remember Leonie? Now I wonder what happened to her, the Baroness Koeppler. Wirthof's (amongst others') Leonie. I didn't have time to fall in love with her, a woman like her, married too, though that wasn't a deterrent in itself for me, or anyone else for that matter, but I didn't have time for an elaborate intrigue.

Leonie – that was 1936, the very edge of the abyss, who in his right mind had time for the leisurely seduction of Leonie, Baroness Koeppler, not I with my quick grin and premature ejaculations. You couldn't cuckold the Herr Baron in a hurry, it demanded patience, and a capacity for tolerating uncertainty and rivals.

Leonie! Not a great beauty, but exciting as first snow. Cool and white and sparkling, with the flesh so tight over her bold bone structure: her face had flow, cheekbones high, curving in an elegant slope to narrow chin, and then that long stalk neck, a Modigliani neck, running with speed, with exhilarating speed, into a body smooth as a sleigh run. You could whizz along her from head to toe, carried by the line of her structure, and make the return journey as easily, without loss of momentum. And many did. And many did. Not I though. My love was pure. A sensual woman, and a snob. With her the two were not incompatible. The exercise of her snobbery somehow seemed to complement the indulgence of her sensuality. Theories! Theories! She is not some dead empress to theorize about. Remember the pleasure of seeing her, and her warmth: it was hardly snobbery to show such warmth to me. Nor was it sensuality – alas. I had the better part of her, she'd say; I would have preferred the worse, but she never saw me as a lover. That role was given to Wirthof. Still, I had something. She used to read to me from *Les Fleurs du Mal*, in French, which I did not understand. A great poetry reader was Leonie, Baroness Koeppler: sitting behind her long Renaissance table, on her nose the half oval gold-framed glasses, the kind you peer over, her big round eyes of changeable colour, sometimes grey-green, sometimes auburn-grey, dramatically charged as she raised them above the tiny lenses to fix on her rapt audience, me, her voice ringing with recitative fervour – the Viennese *recited* poetry. What did it matter that I didn't understand a word of what she was saying, the sounds she made were thrilling. She wore white silk blouses with a black cravat, long narrow skirts, trouser suits sometimes. And those slouch hats with the brim pulled down over one eye. Never did she wear anything loose or flouncy, thin-looking clothes she wore to enhance her thinness. And she smoked either a pipe, a delicate long-stemmed one, or long cigarillos, which she puffed vehemently between her words to give them extra force. Curiously, the effect was not unfeminine, and though her clothes made her seem hipless and breastless she wasn't either, by any means. (She had two delightful children, and adored them.)

Reciting, she could become quite carried away (Racine she used to read to me too); her arms waved; her voice quivered, rose, fell, did all sorts of passionate, lovely, dramatic things; excitement lit her eyes, passion coloured her cheeks – all this for Racine or Baudelaire or Grillparzer or Rilke or Hugo von Hofmannsthal or Goethe. It relaxed her, she said, reading to me, though with the energy she used somebody else could have felled a tree. More true, probably, that it was a way of expending some of that burdensome vitality of hers, which gave her no repose, made her life a continual urgency. Everything she did she did urgently: she read poetry that way: she took lovers that way; she collected celebrities (she was a great one for that), organized her *jours*, bought paintings, went on trips, had her clothes made, redesigned her various homes, wrote letters – and she was a prolific and voluminous letter writer – all with tremendous urgency, as if each activity was absolutely unpostponable. As if the whole, involved, intricate, interacting, interdependent structure of her life would crumble if she left out one of these activities. It never occurred to her that if she just stopped – stopped everything – stopped writing letters, giving *jours*, taking lovers, going to dressmakers, buying pictures, talking, reciting, nothing terrible would happen, no calamity would occur. The moments she devoted to me were snatched from this complex schedule of activities; and ah! what reorganization, what telephoning by secretaries and running of messages by personal maids then ensued so that a n unscheduled hour could be made up without disrupting the entire timetable. I too was in a rush, and so we met panting, exhausted by our respective pursuits, and in some way found rest in each other: she was kind to me, very kind. And so was the Baron, my mentor.

Those letters of hers. All those letters. Pages and pages of almost illegible scrawl. Took hours to decipher. She wrote to friends, to artists, philosophers, politicians, writers, scientists, lovers, a great outpouring of gossip, opinions, theories, confessions, art and literary criticisms; a flood of words as regular as the tides. Why? Why did she do it? For posterity? No, it was a necessity for her. Without the constant passage of letters between her and these various men, selected for whatever reasons, she felt lost. 'I want to have around me all the people I love. All the time. It's so sad when people go away, so sad. I can't bear such sadness.' Many of her correspondents were famous in one sphere or another – yes, I hated that. From her talk you'd have thought she knew nobody except the famous. There was something really quite desperate in her letter-writing; as if love denied sight, touch, contact, communication, will instantly die, is not preservable in isolation. You are gone, then you are dead, then you have abandoned me. She wanted her loves around her all the time. But there were too many for that. It wasn't that she feared the times, like all the others she took little heed of the actual dangers –

Leonie: who came out of a maze of Polish princes, margraves

of German border provinces, dictators of Milan, the odd cardinal, soldiers, ambassadors – and the occasional upstart adventurer. (It gave me courage that there had been the like of me in her family history.) 'Baroness,' I demanded, 'let me be the student of Leonie, I want to study you, to know everything about you. May I? May I?' 'No, you may not.' 'Why not, Leonie?' 'Because I do not wish you to know everything about me. Because I do not wish anyone to know everything about me, least of all myself.' All the same, she told me some things, or I found them out.

She had been educated entirely by governesses, private tutors – one was an abbé – and lovers: not necessarily the most disinterested teachers. Her personality reflected the non-objective nature of her education. Her strong point was taste, with which she believed she was naturally endowed; the infallibility of her taste was one thing nobody was allowed to question. Her artistic and literary judgments were all made, in the first instance, on the basis of this almost mystical 'taste' of hers, and, indeed, it was better than most people's, though by no means as infallible as she thought.

The two main articles of her artistic faith were simplicity and modernity. 'Oh it's so simple, it's beautiful,' she'd say of a poem, or a picture, or a hat, or of an advertising slogan that I had invented. Or: 'It's so modern, it's beautiful.' By modern she did not necessarily mean up-to-date, but something much more mysterious: the Etruscans, for instance, were fantastically modern, whereas Mussolini's fascist architecture was a vulgar abomination, something she referred to with utter contempt as quasi-modern, than which there was no worse crime, or else it was neo-paganism, or neo-modernism.

These qualities of modernity and simplicity (and Leonie's 'simplicity' was something of enormous complexity, almost undefinable) could be applied also to people, so that a particular person was 'entirely modern' or had 'a wonderful simplicity', whereas somebody else was '1903 modern' which, for some reason, was to her a date connotative of the moribund. When Leonie made her pronouncements of taste, there was no appeal; you could not argue with her; if something was hideous to her, it *was* hideous, and no amount of persuasion could reinstate the condemned object in her favour. On the other hand, if she admired something or somebody not generally appreciated, she could be a passionate advocate, undeterred by all objections. –

'But can't you see, it's *beautiful*, look at it, look at it, it's so simple, it has such line, it's strong, it's got balls . . .' Her advocacy never went much beyond such generalized approbation. For something, or someone, to have balls was a high praise indeed, even if the person spoken of was a woman, and to say this of her did not in any way malign her femininity: to have balls simply was a very praiseworthy state of affairs. Rotundity on a larger scale, however, was boring: those opalescent globes which were so much seen then were out of the question, pendant lamps had to be octahedral to be to her liking, and generally speaking she preferred 'clean, strong lines', angular creations, to the softness and effeteness of curves. She dressed in accordance with these dicta and redesigned her various homes to conform to them.

Her mother, evidently, had been a woman of great taste, and great simplicity: not, however, very modern. ('Leonie, don't cross your legs' – 'Leonie, you forgot to bow to His Reverence' – 'Leonie, why did you not kneel down at the Sanctus during Mass this morning?' – 'Leonie, you are not to wander off on your own.')

Leonie's mother was a great traveller.

'Four compartments were usually booked for us in the trains of the Compagnie Internationale des Wagons-Lits et des Grands Express Européens to accommodate M'mma, her maid, my French governess, and my German tutor. The governess and I shared a compartment. The international trains in those prewar days adhered strictly to the segregation of the classes, and the second and third classes were absolutely forbidden to me as we, in our rosewood panelled compartments, were, only more so, to them. Inevitably, I was irresistibly attracted to the third class. What unimaginable iniquities must go on there; if the governess let me out of her sight, I'd be off, exploring. Everything was different in those other carriages. The smell, for one thing. How the third classes smelled! And how dirty they were! Inexpressibly fascinating to a child of eight with fine guimpe at neck, ruffles at the wrist and flounced drawers to the knees. If spotted by a Wagon-Lit attendant, I was of course promptly escorted back, but I learned to give them the slip. Once – we were travelling to Constantinople, and at Trieste the train had emptied, M'mma was resting, the governess had momentarily vanished – and off I went, along the littered, uncarpeted corridors, swaying, and with great excitement made my way from carriage to carriage, my heart in my mouth every time I stepped over the shaking steel footplates in those concertina-like connections between the wagons, fearful of being thrown right through the concertinas as the train shuddered on turns. Most of the compartments were empty, evidence of their recent occupation on their dusty seats – apple cores and bits of bread and orange peel and empty bottles. I was throwing open door after door like a ticket collector, and in the fifth or sixth carriage I did at last see something to justify the expedition: a girl sitting on the lap of a soldier, though sitting is perhaps not strictly accurate, she straddled him actually, and what was going on was very quickly apparent – starched petticoats, black hose, brilliant black shoes, with heels, very chic – I remember those details. I was tremendously excited by what I saw: the coarseness of the posture, the violence of the movements.'

Before she was thirteen, Leonie had been twice round the world.

'M'mma had insisted that we must stop in Udine to see Tiepolo's frescoes in the Archbishop's palace –' 'In the gardens of Strà we lost our way in the maze –' 'In Venice we had a little mezzanino on the Grand Canal, and we'd have breakfast at Café Florian.' 'As a girl M'mma had seen Wagner walking under the arcades in the Piazza San Marco on the day before his death, and she never forgave herself for not having had the courage to talk to him, she was a great admirer of Wagner.'

'The greatest disillusionment of my life was when I grew old enough to realize that my father, my wonderful father, of whom I saw all too little, didn't run the world. Shattering discovery that *my* father – who ran my world, even though much of the time he was not actually with us – was not all-powerful, wasn't even influential, that some people took absolutely no notice of what he said, including, I regret to say, my mother. Oh it seemed such a cruel injustice to me. I was heartbroken when he died. I think I blamed my mother, she had not been a good wife to him, she had not cared for him. Only much later did I discover that my father, who was so kind and considerate in his dealings with me, had been a cruel husband to my mother, bringing his mistresses into our own homes, and as a result driving my mother to taking those interminable trips. My mother was a woman of absolute moral rectitude, she never so much as hinted at my father's infidelities, and as far as I know never had a lover herself. But her suffering, which she concealed, made her cruel to him on those occasions when they were together, and it hurt me to see her being so cold to my wonderful father, who would affect a hangdog expression under the weight of her scolding looks. He was, of course, an old hypocrite.'

Having been initiated to travel in infancy, Leonie never lost the taste for this kind of life. Her mind was constantly occupied with the planning of trips. 'I do so want to go to Toledo to see the El Grecos.' Or: 'Next year I have promised myself a trip to the Far East.'

The only time she stayed put for any length of time was immediately after the war when as a young woman she became involved with Maz Engert in Paris, becoming his pupil as well as his mistress. He was already over fifty then, and she was not yet twenty. She had decided she wanted to be a painter. Her difficulty was that she could not bear solitude, and to spend more than two hours working alone, with no one to react to her work, was unbearable to her. Ideally, she would have liked to paint all the time under the eye of Engert, with him supervising every brush stroke. As this wasn't possible, she'd work in fits and starts, become bored, and go off to seek the company of other artists and writers in the cafés. She discovered that she much preferred to talk about painting than to do it.

'In Paris I met Rilke who though he was over fifty looked thirty. We talked excitedly of Cézanne, and he was delighted that I shared his enthusiasm. Not everyone did. The poet's great friend, Princess Marie von Thurn und Taxis, for example, didn't. He told me of his desire to study Egyptology at the Sorbonne. He seemed a very haunted man to me. There was something beautiful, he said to me once, which I remember because it was so inexpressibly sad. He said, "I ask myself whether God ever permits a bird's heart to become so heavy that it can no longer raise it with its wings."

'Rilke spoke often of mysterious moments of compulsion that he had experienced, and I understood him entirely for I had had similar experiences – when something forces one to walk along a certain street, to take a particular turning, past a particular house that one has never seen before but knows to be the particular house that one must go past, to follow this turning to its end, to turn yet again, all the time as if guided, and then the extraordinary sensation of standing before a house of many windows, all of them dark, and to feel observed. This compulsion – my truancy in trains, along those swaying corridors – cannot be described in rational terms, it seems to transcend rationality, to draw on some unknown force that makes one quite impervious to the dangers attendant on such actions, indeed seems almost to make it necessary that one should expose oneself to possible harm, as a test perhaps, sometimes I have walked along a street in some strange city and felt: here I will be murdered, but have gone on, you see, have gone on –'

Maz Engert was the great influence of her years in Paris. He was apparently hard on her as a teacher.

'Maz Engert opened my eyes, literally I had not seen before. My beloved Venice for instance, where I had lived, which was my home at one time, which I thought I knew so intimately – I did not know it at all, had not *seen* it. The first time I saw one of Maz's Venice paintings I was shocked. What place was this? It had none of the pomp and the stateliness and the solidity of the Canalettos, the Guardis, the Bellinis, the Tintorettos, all of which I knew so well. And then I realized that I had never seen Venice in a modern way. Maz showed me that the pomp of permanence which is present in the great Venetian masters is entirely inappropriate today. And then I understood *his* Venice: turbulent with the imminence of upheaval, a temporary, precarious beauty, threatened, dying even. In Maz's work everything is in a state of flux, one thing changing into another – change, growth, upheaval, metamorphosis. Nothing is static. Nothing is permanent. And see – see, Stefan – the way the paint is put on, moulded on with fingers and knife – the paint is the surface convulsed by the force and complexity of underneath. The first important thing that Maz taught me is that in art everything must contain its otherness. An artist, whatever he is painting, must always be aware – not necessarily consciously – of the obverse side, or else his work is superficial. Maz talks of the indestructibility of good and evil – meaning that the total quantity of each in the universe is fixed and permanent, and that all life depends on that basic state of balance. The perceivable world is an ever changing configuration, utilizing these unvarying quantities of good and evil in differing patterns, of which history is the reflection. Art must be equivocal, art must always be concerned with otherness, and it must testify to the experience of our time in the knowledge that our time is part of other times and not an entity.

'When I first went to Maz and begged him to take me as a pupil, he told me that he could not teach me to be an artist. Yes, he could teach me draughtsmanship, the use of colour, but that I could be taught anywhere. What he could teach me had very little to do with painting, but a lot to do with seeing, for it was the quality of seeing that distinguishes a painting. And he said that he could only teach me to see as he saw, and if I painted as *he* saw I would not be an artist, only a copyist. I could only be an artist if I learned to see for myself, and then only if I could attain humility, which he doubted, and, of course, he was right. What Maz means by humility is something quite different from what is normally understood by the word – he doesn't want you to be self-effacing, he wants you to be in a state of awe. Unless one is awed by the experience of life one cannot represent it without diminishing it. Maz says that art is a function of living – it is as necessary to make art as it is to make love, and that the making of art is the reconstruction of shattered worlds, in that lies its power to move. What moves the spectator in a work of art is identification with the artist's struggle to recreate some part of his inner world that has become shattered. Maz says that whereas in the external world things are governed by chance and very little that happens is just, our inner world is governed by absolute mathematical justice, and it is the intermittent awareness of this that men have called God. Therefore, says Maz, many theological concepts have been correct, and it is basically only the geographical location of God with which he would quarrel. I wanted so much to have Maz's "Christ Amid Mirthful Men" – an American dealer got it, I was away when it came up for sale – it is a painting that expresses perfectly the economics of pain –'

In a man like Maz Engert, for Leonie, the dual role of lover and teacher was indivisible, the love act was for her an essential prerequisite of learning, and there were several such men whom she loved and from whom she learned. With these, after the physical affair had ended for one reason or another, she maintained friendships of many years' duration, in this way these love affairs did not end but were merely in a condition of non-consummation, and these men continued to exercise their influence over her. But there were others, young men of varying degrees of worthlessness, some of them actually gigolos, with whom she had brief 'infatuations' of great intensity. 'Ah – do you see that young man, at the table by the door, he was my infatuation last autumn after the disastrous Spanish trip with R. We had both come back, our nerves exhausted, emptied and drained by the Spanish heat – you know the legend that God placed the sun directly above Toledo on the fourth day of Creation, and I can well believe it. We loved Toledo despite the heat, though it was a test of endurance and too much for us in August – so stupid to have gone in August – and then Seville was an anticlimax and R. had one of his terrible spells of melancholia, which infected me also, and he became ill on top of it, so that in September we cut short the trip and went to a little spa in the Black Forest for recuperation. And there I met this young gentleman you see by the door – what need he had of recuperation I don't know. I suspect he was on the lookout for prey. He was, as it turned out, entirely commercially motivated, and indifferent as to whether his patron was male or female, but a very beautiful young man, wouldn't you agree, with a fine body and a good head. For ten days I was totally infatuated with him. Always, when I am in a low state, I seem to need some such adventure, which for a few days or weeks dominates me entirely, I think it must be rather like the fever that grips a gambler, that terrible fever which Dostoyevsky describes with such horrifying exactitude. It is like that. The need to return again and again – to lose more and more of pride, of self-respect, of dignity, there seems to grow a momentum of losing which is irresistible, first to submit to such a man, then to beg him, then to tolerate and gradually relish his cruelty, and then losing all dignity to offer him money and more money. He looks charming, doesn't he? You would not imagine him vicious? Of course not: that is the essence of such young gentlemen. These ridiculous passions – which in the actual moment seem to be so much more intense than the loves one approves of with heart and mind –'

Leonie's marriage, at the age of twenty-eight, to Baron Koeppler amazed everyone; his background – the Jewish merchant classes – was totally alien to everything she had known, and his tastes and interests were remote from hers. True, he was very rich, but it was generally believed that she had sufficient money of her own not to be unduly interested in the admittedly far greater wealth of the Baron. After her marriage, her life did not change in any fundamental respect; friends and lovers came and went as before; only now her interests extended also to politics, or rather to politicians, for she was never much interested in ideas as such, only in the people who propounded them. And of course, with the financial resources of the Koepplers to draw on, her patronage of young artists and poets, her sponsorship of cultural projects, could become much more ambitious in scope and scale.

'You know, Stefan, I always knew how to make money, but Leonie has taught me how to spend it.' The Baron said it smilingly, he was genuinely pleased.

It was through him that I got to know Leonie. I think he wanted to show her that he, too, had the capacity to find clever and promising young men; the truth of the matter is that my cleverness was not the sort that could be easily substantiated or refuted; and as he had no understanding of poetry or art he had to make his find in his own somewhat limited sphere, and the fact that Leonie liked me flattered his judgment. In this way, I became established with both of them. I had a sufficient smattering of ideas to have some conversation, and Leonie would say, 'My God, a friend of Felix's with whom one can talk about something other than the making of money! Fantastic!' Actually, though her knowledge was wide it was not deep, and there were astonishing gaps in it.

She was in the throes of redesigning the Vienna flat, which occupied the whole top floor of a building known as the Palais Koeppler, 'palais' being merely the somewhat grandiose term for a large house of which the owner occupied a substantial part, the remainder consisting of apartments for rent. The Palais Koeppler was situated in the Parkring, overlooking the Stadtpark. Built circa 1870 in imitation Italian Renaissance style, it was of five storeys, each floor having three four-room flats, except for the top floor which consisted of one large flat occupied by the Koepplers. In the main entrance hall there were two lifts, one of which was for the exclusive use of the Baron's household.

The Baron had been married twice before, and his flat showed evidence of the differing tastes of his previous wives. When Leonie moved in the first task she set herself was the radical redesigning of the whole place, and this continued to occupy her, compulsively, for the whole of the eight or nine years that she lived there. She was never entirely satisfied with the result. The first thing she did on moving in was to arrange for herself a suite of three rooms – bedroom, study and drawing-room – to house her modern art collection, which consisted mainly of the work of Expressionist painters such as Maz Engert, Nolde, Kadinsky, August Macke, Kokoschka, Max Ernst, Lovis Corinth, Franz Marc, Paula Modersohn-Becker, and Max Pechstein. As it was, the flat was not at all suited to display these paintings – the Baron's own taste ran to copies of Bonifazio and Bellini – and the decorations and furnishings were all appropriately rococo, with extensive friezes and mouldings, and a great deal of gilt work everywhere. Leonie hated the flat, which she considered in the worst possible taste. She started by throwing out the most objectionable furniture ('weeding it out to create some breathing space'), just keeping the better Empire pieces. Then she took over three connecting drawing-rooms, which she denuded, stripped the walls of the Chinese bamboo wallpaper and the crimson figured damask, had the friezes and ceiling mouldings chipped off, and the whole lot painted a muddy beige-grey. Then she hung her paintings, densely, over one or two walls in each room, lit them with theatrical spotlamps, concealed inside the false ceilings that she had constructed in such a way as to allow the beams to emerge from glassed-in recesses, and then furnished the rooms with the minimum number of Italian Renaissance pieces, which she complemented with modern tables of plate glass and steel, made to her specification. Her bedroom consisted of a seven-foot-square low bed covered, like the floor, in white angora furs. This was the only visible piece of furniture in the room. Three of the walls were hung from ceiling to floor with white silk curtains, behind which there were extensive built-in cupboards. On the wall opposite the windows hung the more lyrical paintings from her collection, including several nudes and a great number of small, plainly framed drawings, and also a painting of horses – yellow horses, with green manes, against a blue-violet background.

Though she was reasonably pleased with what she had achieved in her suite of rooms, she was depressed by the fact that there were still something like twelve other rooms which were by no means to her taste, and each year she promised herself that as soon as she was less busy she would attack this larger problem. She never got further than changing two or three of these other rooms to her satisfaction. The three large reception rooms (which with their connecting doors open formed the 'ballroom' for when they were entertaining on a large scale) she left just as they were, the Corinthian columns were load-bearing and could not be removed, the fake Bonifazios could not be replaced by modern works unless the entire decor was changed, and so they, too, remained, and the Baron's study did not progress beyond getting a new ceiling (in place of the elaborately ornamented one) of polished copper panels.

Much of the time only the three modern rooms – and the Baron's study – were in use, but none the less it disturbed Leonie that there were all these other 'unfinished rooms' in the flat, and she talked always of 'when the flat is in order'. Meanwhile, she entertained every Wednesday in the old reception rooms, explaining that they were going to be re-done soon in a 'simple and modern way'. As they were going to be re-done entirely, she could not bring herself to carry out piecemeal repairs and renovations (pointless to repair ghastly draperies that had become sunfaded in places) which became increasingly necessary though Leonie, in other respects so fastidious, failed to see this. 'Oh it will do for the time being,' she'd say to the Baron whenever he pleaded for some urgently necessary renovation, 'as it's all going to be changed anyway next year.' The result was that the flat, with the exception of Leonie's suite, looked faintly shabby, the plasterwork was full of cracks, the stucco had crumbled badly in parts, escutcheons were missing from some of the doors, the parquet was chipped in places, and the silk or damask or wallpapered walls showed the marks of the big central heating radiators. This faint, but increasing, shabbiness which overlaid the evident wealth gave a strange feeling of temporariness.

Strangest of all was the sensation of going from the rococo-shabby reception rooms with their fake Bonifazios and Florentine-style friezes into the sparsely furnished modern rooms where you found yourself in the presence of coarse, yellow-bodied women, a green-eyed Christ with red hair, yellow horses, angular girls with umbrellas, silk-hatted gangsters, a head like a knot of muscles, men with owl faces, enormous eyes mounted on pedestals, fossilized faces, anthropomorphic vegetation, moon creatures –

All the time Leonie fretted about the unfinished flat, the exhausted nerves of her 'poets of death', the appalling taste of the public in failing to recognize someone or other she had sponsored, the inundation of bad taste that was defacing Vienna, and her own moments of 'demonic passion'; I don't think she gave a prolonged thought to the fact of Adolf Hitler. It was inconceivable that he could actually mean what he said. And the fat Field Marshal, and the *Sieg Heils*, and the Kleig lights, and the half million raised arms and Mythus of the Twentieth Century, and the *Weltanschauung* of the opaque-eyed one, and the blond heads against the cornfields? It was all in the worst possible taste.

How is it *I* knew? I have an ear for disaster, I can hear it at night, it chatters to me; I have a nose, too, for such things.

The following question arises, Kazakh: was your awareness of the imminence of disaster any more rationally founded than their denial of it? Was it the writing on the wall you read, or in yourself? If it was the times, the *Zeitgeist*, why did you not shiver then, and why do you shiver now? You did not shiver then, you knew what was coming, your nose and your ear told you, your father had taught you to read such signs; but for all your foreknowledge, what did you do? To the banks, to the banks – the vandals are coming! You did what they all did, those who could, and you had no excuse because you knew, or purported to. Must I now consider the possibility that I knew nothing? Then your life is founded on a fallacy, Kazakh, then your smartness is a delusion and your quickness mere sleight of hand. But I survived, didn't I? Survived the holocaust and the whores. I did? You did? Did you have to? I mean, why did you have to? Why do you shiver, Kazakh? When you come down to it – tell me this – why was it so vitally necessary for you to survive? Why? Many didn't, and you did. What grandiosity in you made it so imperative for you to survive? What could I have done? You could have died. If I start to think like that I will get into a state again, like yesterday. That is no way to think. The instinct of survival is a basic instinct of man. And what about the other one? Not proven. No? Yesterday, for a moment, crossing the Aspernbrücke, seeing the Riesenrad, still, unmoving, I thought – remember? – I thought I know why I have survived (but I seem to have forgotten now what reason I gave myself): I was calm. Can you think this through? Can you? How can I find myself when I am deposited all over the place, spread thin? So much in I.C.I., so much in F.M.C., so much in Deco, so much in Xerox, so much in Xanadau, so much in Rolinco, so much in Singe r and Friedlander, so much in Brevitt, so much in Crittal-Hope, so much in the Commercial Bank of Australia, so much in Rea Brothers, so much in

Toronto Dominion, so much in B.H.D., so much in Bellis and Morcom, so much in Kundencredit, so much in Thyssen-Huette, so much in Siemssen Hunter, so much in Sisalkraft, so much in Hitachi, so much in British Cocoa, so much in Hambros, so much in Hellenic and General: scattered, spread thin; irretrievable. How much in Kazakh? Nothing. There is nothing in me. You're no fool, Kazakh. You know a straw man when you have lived in him for fifty-two years. You know a bankrupt. A stuffed man. A scattered man. You know whom not to trust. But yesterday, for a moment, crossing the Aspernbrücke, you were calm. I was calm. Stefan Kazakh was calm. Can you think it through? Do I dare? What was that thing Maz Engert said? Leonie's teacher, that lovely old man. 'Every discovery of truth is a journey to the edge.' Do you dare approach the edge? And if I go over it? Too bad, too bad. One survivor less. Stefan Kazakh was calm. That time in the Karavanke, I gave up my life, entrusted myself – to what, to whom? To a dying mule. Never mind. To the very edge, and over if necessary.

Wirthof – whose hair was the colour of dead leaves, and who loved Leonie with a wholly surprising passion. More than I did, anyway. Why him and not me? I came very close to Wirthof, closer than close. He could keep nothing to himself. Had to tell me everything. His boastfulness: I had the feeling – often – of knowing him completely; I had this sense of knowing every twist and turn and feint of his mind, it was like, say, looking at a bottle and being convinced one sees every aspect of it, its roundness, its straightness, its glacial quality, its colour, its size, its proportions, its transparency, its hollowness, its diameter, its fragility, its toughness, its emptiness, its many possible uses; it is inconceivable, looking at it, that any aspect of that bottle is unknown, unrevealed – for there it stands, a simple object, a bottle. Inconceivable that there might be something unknown, mysterious, about a bottle. I know it will break if I strike it with something hard; I know the velocity at which it will fall if I drop it, I know how much it will hold if I fill it, I know what colours I need to paint it, I know everything there is to be known about it, I know you, Wirthof, as I know this bottle, but can I get inside a bottle? Definitely; I can do anything, I can fold up like a sailing ship and slip down the narrow neck, and spread myself again in the voluminous interior, there is plenty of room for me there. I have been in tighter spots – my father's ear, my mother's belly. There is nowhere I cannot go. Wirthof, I am in your dark room now, I have slipped down your narrow neck, if I cannot see clearly yet my fingertips tell me where I am, I am learning the topography of this room – ah, here is a table, here a chair, a chest, a framed picture, a bed, Leonie, the images from my fingertips tell me where I am, they give me confidence in your dark room, and already I begin to see, with your eyes, with my eyes in your eyes, it is not difficult, no more difficult than slipping down the narrow neck of a bottle, and there is an incentive – Leonie.

Awakening in noon blackness, priapic (a regular occurrence that persuaded him he had extraordinary potency; actually it was due to the fullness of his bladder), he did not immediately remove the eye-pads – must have been a curious sight asleep: eye-padded, moustache-netted, and priapic – if there was the slightest chink of light he couldn't sleep: I will stay a little longer inside this dark hood, he felt powerful. And then I killed the old man. Curious – I killed the old man: why? And then I dropped dustbin lids on him, buried him in dustbin lids. I winked, and all the dustbin lids fell on him. Just a wink, a blink of the eye, and he was crushed. Must ask Kazakh what dreams mean, he'll know: Jew's knowledge. The way the old man lay there, under the pile of dustbin lids, all twisted up, crushed, flattened. Like a crushed beetle. Not much blood. Why think of that? Swinish beetle man, why didn't he have more blood? Leonie – ah! She can't intend – why not? The Baroness, spread, outspread, spreadeagled, spread like butter. She will receive me, the Baroness. Oh yes. His bedroom was shuttered and heavily curtained. He despised people who slept deeply and easily. Oafish. He refused to surrender his autonomy to the night. To sleep with a woman was impossible. His bed was too private: besides, I don't care for their post-coital smell. The way her face was so blank, lips pale. Sign of passion. It is well known. All the blood elsewhere, Her and the Baron. Wonder if they. The old oaf. I shall have her, I shall have her. How can one commit *fellatio* on oneself? It's anatomically impossible, unless. Impossible, only a freak. At that age said to be the most passionate. In their late thirties, early forties. Last fling before the *climacterium menopause*. Ravenous. Less coquetry. Her hands – the gloves worn at the fingertips, sweat-saturated there: her sweat. Everybody'd be mad, if that were true. Wouldn't they? Leonie, the Baroness. Oh yes, oh yes, oh yes. Leonie so thin, ravenous, long-necked: liquid. Taking off her . . . her; no, keeping it on, holding it tight, the slip, silky, silky tight, tight against her thighs, naked underneath, little stiff bud naked against the taut, damp silk, damp, damp, her little erection, fantastic. In some respects, he preferred this to the more vaunted sins. Its practice was not dependent on the cooperation of others. Up round her thighs, the silk. Up. Yes. Liquid. Buttocks spread. The dark entrance, the snake pit. When they crave it there. In with my black. It drives them mad. Have them in a vice, there and in front. All those dustbin lids. Blink, blink, blink. Who would have thought an old man. Leonie, my Baroness. I bestride you like a colossus, colossally I – ahh! You can go mad. It is well known. And the spinal cord can be damaged: he turned on his back, ridiculous to waste. Imagine: there are millions – I could sire a race. A million die on the bedsheet, slaughtered under the tap. A brutish business, life. Imagine her from head to toe in black velvet, fantastic, against her whiteness. The great arena, silk draped, half a million people arranged like an Italian garden; with that precision, with that order. Order: absolute. Behind the podium, the golden sign, ancient and new. He comes on in breeches and brown shirt, cross belted. Head high. He is not only himself, but also the instrument of a purpose: that is his strength. The audience knows this, it is united with him in this heroic purpose, tied to him, he to them, my men, he calls them, and they – my Führer. He sees everyone. When he walks through the great avenue, he sees each individual man; there is a blood bond between him and each man. Who else is there with heroic stature? Chamberlain, that old aunt? The cripple Roosevelt? The buffoon Mussolini? To be part of that great throng. It is a choir. A great music comes from it. Magnificence can come of this. He has touched the spring of heroism in each man, and it flows into a great river. (How can one commit *fellatio* on oneself – inconceivable!) These young men with their strong clear faces: there is a profound force in them, a terrible force. The play of muscles in their backs, their buttocks. Those marvellous strong male buttocks. Vaulting, running – leaping like young satyrs. Magnificent. You feel the power in their fresh sturdy young loins. Washing the good male sweat off their bodies – hosing each other: naked: soaping themselves, each other: their glistening bodies: and lying against the strong spray of the water: becoming erect – the super abundance in their fine hard loins. Young stallions. They are unselfconscious in their erect state: they know they will sire a new race. I was eighteen, nineteen? Under the showers. Glistening wet bodies steaming. All wedged together under the showers – sometimes, sometimes. It is not abnormal. It is natural. All that energy; the life energy in their strong young loins: when there is an excess in the body, it finds release. I too. It just happens. The sudden strong flow, like sometimes in dreams. It is quite natural. A purely animal response. The proximity of bodies, it would be surprising if it didn't happen. What is natural is not ugly. A man is not unclean as a woman is. Men produce less sewage. A woman, often, is unclean. Messy. Women are messy in their habits. With that internal structure of theirs, not surprising. A messy arrangement. All that so they can bear children. A messy arrangement. Externally they're fine, *externally*; it's inside, beyond . . . one can have pleasure from the outside of a woman, the pubis, the buttocks, the thighs, the face, lips, all good places, why should it be necessary. It's been known for a woman to have a spasm, in orgasm, that keeps the man trapped in there, humiliating. Ambulance has to be called. Need a doctor to separate you, comical. It has been known. To be trapped like that, inside a woman. That claw grip. Oh dreadful. Women are messy creatures. Katty's room, always in such a state. Soiled underwear. Blood-stained cotton wool. Stains. Of course, their bodies are secreting all the time, it all flows out of them, nothing to keep it in, since they're open down there. A man is more contained. Women always secreting all over the place. They get excited and they secrete. Katty. The smell of her underwear. Of course she's always. Like a rash she has to keep scratching. With a man it's more natural, a clean strong flow. Women have no capacity for nobility. The warrior's rest. Fine for that. Someone like Leonie of course is different. Quite different. Magnificent. Perhaps a few rare women have the capacity for nobility too; must be so; Leonie has nobility of spirit – one can tell. A nation to be strong must banish its womanliness, that is the undoing of great nations. That is something Hitler understands. It is right that he is not married. A great leader cannot be encumbered with the weight of domesticity, which lessens men, diminishes them, saps their strength. A great leader must be free. His love must be a spontaneous overflow of the spirit, flowing out to the entire nation, not secretly channelled into the belly of a woman, mixing with her unclean blood. A great man, a leader, is above such weakness. He must guard his precious essence against such contamination from unclean blood. Self-evident. Only Hitler has grasped it fully. (It is surely anatomically impossible to commit *fellatio* on oneself.) Leonie is magnificent. Stupendous. To take her from the Jew Baron will be a great act. How could she? It will be a liberation of her spirit. Such women as her are rare indeed, a man's nobility and a woman's softness, one can rest in such a woman and not be demeaned, pour seed into her without wastage. Such a woman flows like a river, always drawing refreshment: she is not a stagnant pool, but fresh flowing. Leonie, the Baroness. The heyday of the blood, at that age. Like an overripe fig there. The Jew Baron. Does she give him his conjugal rights? She can't enjoy it, with him. What joy can she have from that old oaf penetrating her? They had children. When he was younger. A woman can conceive without having felt pleasure, that is well known. You can see from her lips that she is passionate, the way her mouth hangs open at moments, like a child looking in a sweet shop. Greedy. Greedy. Baroness, I will feed your greed. Prolonged erotic deprivation makes them greedy, and yet they say she. Underclothes always a little damp. She had that look. The way she walks you know where the apex of her body is situated. Such women have superabundant flow. Unsatisfied. See them in trains pressing their thighs together, the motion of the train does it. I was thirteen. Oh she was definitely. Did she know I had seen. Muscular. When they sit crosslegged. And the train causes vibrations. The Baroness: I shall take her from the Jew: the idea of him kneading her, they're all sensualists: sickening! She has to submit. No such thing as rape between husband and wife in law. Horrible to think that this magnificent elegant woman has to put up with the Baron's money-greasy touches. She should be adored, her body should be venerated: I shall – stupendously. Something colossal. This town is boring, inert. Where is there anyone with heroic vision? Pettiness and bureaucracy and bourgeois . . . standards. What opportunity for heroism and magnificence? One is reduced to the ordinary. The ordinary man, contemptible. This town is a corpse, and the worms are at the feast. The many: *too* many. The worms. Chop them up and they grow a new head. Such are they, the grey ones. Where is there heroism? Tell me that, Kazakh, you have an answer for everything. Tell me where do you find a hero? In Germany? Yes, there is heroism there. Nowhere else. The English? They suffer from constipation. The French are cynical, without honour. The Italians are cowards. The Americans are without culture. The only worthwhile people are the Spaniards. How they have torn themselves! There is heroism. Hitler could make the Germanic people heroic, he has the inspiration. Father used to say a soldier must have honour, courage, self-discipline. My inheritance.

Stirred to action by his inheritance, he leapt out of bed and made a quick dash to the bathroom to take a cold shower, but modified this intention – since there was nothing noble in needless stoicism: just a small turn of the hot tap to take the chill off. Under the shower he pondered the practicalities of getting to see the Baroness Koeppler again, I must have her, he decided, she's superb. He was sure she had been interested in him, though they had not exchanged more than a few words. But her remarkable eyes cut right through social pleasantries and established an immediate intimacy. He was considering various schemes for her seduction; the first problem was to get to see her again – and there Kazakh could be of help, for he knew the Baron, another of the brethren (though the Baroness was not, he was sure *she* was not), and had some business dealings with him. The way the Jews stuck together. But he had to admit, soaping himself, that Kazakh was useful with all his contacts, and with that gift of his for hypnotism, only way of curing those awful headaches. Kazakh would just get him to lie down and close his eyes, none of that business any longer about watching a spot on the ceiling and tiring the optic nerve, and then Kazakh would place his hands on Konrad's temples, and murmur something, and Konrad would get to feel very drowsy and relaxed and then, a few minutes later, without even being aware of having dropped off, he was alert again and his headache was gone. Well, there was no doubt about it, if anyone knew the dark arts it was the Yids. The alienists were all Jews. He'd heard that they could so control the minds of their patients, even respectable women were quite incapable of resisting their assaults. Those circumcised sensual-ists. They could commit rape with impunity, since they controlled the minds of their victims how could they ever be exposed! A clever race. Undoubtedly they were clever; Kazakh had a keen intelligence, but limited, limited by his materialism, by his pedan-try, his logicality. If one stuck to logic, one never took flight. Was it logical that a feather and a man fell at the same velocity? The Jews were a very logical people. Their shortcomings. There wasn't time to test the validity of that hypothesis in the sounding chamber of his inner ear; Dr Schilder was coming at one; there was something else too, some other reason why the Jews were . . . How agreeable it would be to cuckold the Baron (a bought title, of course); one had qualms, surmountable ones, about doing that sort of thing to a brother officer, but there was no dishonour in doing it to a Jew with a bought title. While he was drying himself, he heard the maid come into the bedroom with his coffee, mail and newspapers. He returned to the room, wrapped in his towel, continuing to dry himself, it got the girl very flustered seeing him like that, he enjoyed having this effect on her, one day he'd have to have her, it would make Katty furious; under the towel he was priapic again, something he made no attempt to conceal from the servant girl as she set down her tray on the bed, reddening. 'What's in the newspapers, Tilly?' 'I don't know, Herr Leut-nant . . .' 'What do you know, Tilly? Hmm?' 'What, sir?' 'No, don't put the tray there. Put it next to me. Here.' He obliged her to brush against him in carrying out this order. 'Ah yes,' he said picking up his paper. 'Herr Hitler has been making speeches again. What is your opinion of Herr Hitler, Tilly?' 'Herr Hit-ler?' 'There is no need, Tilly, to repeat everything I say to you. Yes, Herr Hitler.' 'I don't understand, sir.' 'What is your opinion of him? Everybody has an opinion about Herr Hitler. The man who is going to save the soul of the Germanic peoples.' 'Oh I see, sir.' 'You don't want to have your Germanic soul saved by Herr Hitler, Tilly?' She giggled, embarrassed, then frowned. 'Never mind, Tilly. Is my mother up?' 'She's resting, sir.' 'And my little sister?' 'She's awake, sir, but not yet up.' 'An active household,' he said. 'All right, Tilly, you can go. When Dr Schilder comes, show him into the study.' Konrad went to his wardrobe and took out one of his tailor-made uniforms. As he dressed before a long mirror, always an enjoyable function for him, he continued his thoughts about the seduction of Baroness Koeppler, how it might best be achieved. An *affair* with a woman of her age – she must be thirty-nine, forty – and of her position was something he had never undertaken before. Indisputably, she had made the initial move: remarking, challengingly, that young men were too much preoccupied with themselves to be truly interesting, adding how unfortunate it was that a man was in his prime physically when mentally he was scarcely out of knee pants. To which Konrad had replied, 'Baroness, I relinquished knee pants at five.' 'I knew you were exceptional,' she had responded, laughing, equivocating. In white silk trouser suit and short bronze hair, high-buttoned tunic, her womanliness was sly, so sly. Catching it, you were immediately her confidant, a privileged role: exciting. 'Leutnant, you must let me introduce you to Princess Gradiczek, she is a great beauty, a charming child, but I warn you she will fall in love with you, she follows my taste in everything and has none of her own . . .' 'Then, please don't introduce me.' 'She's adorable, very rich, and doesn't have a serious thought in her head.' 'She interests me less every moment.' 'Then I will have to keep you all to myself.' 'I wish you would.' 'It is not rewarding – I am totally unreliable. I make extraordinary demands of friendship . . .' 'I am at your disposal, Baroness.' She laughed. 'And I give nothing in return.' 'That is disappointing, but presumably rectifiable.' 'With me it is inadvisable to presume anything,' she laughed. 'I would not be so presumptuous, where you are concerned, Baroness.' 'In that case, you may come to one of my *jours*.' At this point she had been snatched away, before the invitation could be put on a more definite basis, and Konrad calculated it would be a tactical mistake to press her for a confirmation. Buttoning on his tunic, and approving of the effect, he wondered if she would remember him if he should turn up at her *jour*. There had been half a dozen young men that she had talked to; possibly she had the same conversation with each of them. But all the same, he felt confident of his chances, it was all a matter of playing his cards correctly. Immersed in the tactics of seduction, he finished dressing and went into the study to meet Dr. Schilder. The meeting with the lawyer was routine – Dr Schilder was proposing that because of the worsening political situation –

If Wirthof had something on his mind, it was always a matter of the utmost urgency, and he had come to look on me, since I had cured him of his headaches, as his spiritual adviser, confessor and counsellor.

In point of fact, though he perpetually sought my advice he never took it; if he had any sort of problem, it became my role to state the case against whatever action he was contemplating, and he could then obtain the relief of demolishing my case, at least to his own satisfaction, and as a result feel free to do what he had been proposing to do in the first place. In some curious way, it never worked out that we were in agreement about the resolution of anything and invariably it happened that when he postulated one line of action, I mustered the arguments against it. At the end of what seemed to me a futile discussion, he'd say, 'As always, Kazakh, you have been most helpful. You have clarified my thoughts.' And he'd go off and do exactly what he had been proposing to do in the first place, but, as a result of our discussion, with a feeling of certainty that he had previously lacked.

He had no compunction about interrupting me in the middle of a busy afternoon with a problem that I might possibly have considered trivial; his problems never seemed trivial to him. This particular afternoon, he bounded into my office ahead of four other people waiting to see me, and it would not have occurred to him to apologize for interrupting me at my work, it was assumed by him that he had priority over anyone else where I was concerned.

'Kazakh,' he cried, 'I must have your opinion. I've been considering this question all morning. Baroness Koeppler's *jour*. Everybody knows it's Wednesdays, and she did ask me last night. It is true it was a casual invitation, and it was not confirmed. But would a woman like her expect to have to confirm the invitation, or would she expect me to come without a formal invitation?'

'Leonie's *jours* are formal affairs.'

'Yes, yes, I know. But I must see her. Kazakh, I'm quite infatuated with her. I resolved this morning to have an affair with her. Excessive punctiliousness can be a mistake, don't you think? She is hardly likely to respond to someone who hesitates because he hasn't had a formal invitation. On the other hand, perhaps if I turn up tomorrow – tomorrow is Wednesday, isn't it? – perhaps it will seem too eager. Perhaps I should wait until the following Wednesday, and say I assumed it was that one she meant.'

'How exactly did she phrase the invitation?'

'Oh you know how such things are said. I forget what preceded it exactly. But she definitely said, "You must come to one of my *jours*".'

'It sounds vague.'

'I assure you it wasn't intended to be. I am convinced she wants to see me. She can hardly be any more explicit, in her position, surely.'

'I don't know. If Leonie is interested in someone, she can be very explicit.'

'She was, oh she was explicit. You must not assume that she wasn't explicit, she was. She was only not *specific* about when.'

'She asks a lot of young men to her *jours*. As a matter of fact, I am going tomorrow.'

'You are! She asked you?'

'No, the Baron asked me.'

'Perfect. Then we can go together. Even if I have not been specifically invited, you have been, and you are permitted to bring a guest.'

'Yes, I suppose so.'

'Well, that solves the problem.'

'Wirthof, I am going as the Baron's guest, and you ask me to take *you*. Considering your avowed intention –'

'Oh rubbish,' he declared. 'You know perfectly well that Leonie is unfaithful to him all the time. He must know it too. They have an understanding. I'm sure at his age, anyway, he's past caring. Really, Kazakh, you must not start imposing your bourgeois moral prohibitions on me. I've told you: I'm infatuated with her, it is serious. If you refuse to take me, I shall go anyway. She can hardly have me turned away. I would make a scene – I tell you, I would. Kazakh, that woman is extraordinary. Not beautiful – her mouth is too large, have you noticed? But she has incredible style. To imagine such a woman in a frenzy of passion, it's more than the mind can bear. I absolutely must have her. You know that when I set my mind on something, nothing can deflect me.'

'Say she refuses you?'

'Impossible. I saw it in her eyes. Believe me, I know about such things. I have never been more convinced of anything in my life. She can't refuse me.'

He was so pale and demanding, his needs, however outrageous, were so compelling, and his assumption that they would be met so unshakable, that, indeed, it seemed to me he could not be refused.

I don't think it ever entered his mind that any of his demands were excessive or unreasonable, or that his needs were capable of modification. Whatever he demanded was the absolute minimum life could afford him; to be satisfied with less was inconceivable; he would rather die. He had no fear of death, as he often asserted, and he absolutely refused to live squalidly. (Anything that meant the abandonment of his essential needs – and everything he desired was an essential need – meant living squalidly.) If others chose to live like that, it was their concern; they lacked the courage to gamble, and such people, wretches, had to accept their miserable lot; but not he; either life conformed to his requirements, or he washed his hands of it. How could he lose, since he held the ultimate weapon – that he could abdicate. The gambler in him felt he was entitled to win because he was prepared to lose. And Leonie Koeppler, since he'd set his heart on having her, *must* fall to him because otherwise he would quite likely kill himself: to him this was an absolutely logical proposition.

Leonie's *jours* began at eight but it was permissible to arrive at any time up to midnight. There were those who habitually came early, and others who usually came late, and it was the late-comers who gave to these gatherings their characteristic out-spokenness. At Leonie's you could say absolutely anything after ten p.m. Before then, certain formalities were observed. Subjects of a controversial nature were not brought up, and the conversa-tions, by tacit consent, were confined to innocuous matters – domestic scandals, and such like.

Wirthof and Kazakh, arriving at nine, were shown through high, pedimented white and gold doors into the connecting recep-tion rooms: buffet tables with long damask tablecloths were arranged all along one side, and gilt chairs supplemented the brocaded sofas around the remaining walls. On a small dais the musicians were resting during a short break. About half of the chairs and sofas were occupied, mostly by middle-aged and elderly women and very young girls, while the men, heaped plates in their hands, wandered between these immobile clusters of femininity, stopping here and there to bow and to talk, invariably addressing their initial remarks to the most senior of the seated ladies. Often one of these peripatetic men was invited to draw up a chair, and the conversation continued with the young girls as attentive listeners, but rarely contributing more than the occasional remark; or else, after the exchange of courtesies, the man bowed, once for each woman in the group, and walked on.

Kazakh and Wirthof were welcomed first by the Baron, and some moments later by Leonie. 'I took the liberty of bringing a friend,' Kazakh said. 'Allow me to present Leutnant Wirthof. Baron Koeppler. Oh – and here is Leonie.' She embraced him delightedly, hugging him close for a long moment, and said, 'Stefan, but you are getting thinner all the time. You're not eating. God, you are so thin. I wish I burned up the calories as you do. But you must eat, my pet, or there'll be nothing left of you.'

'It all goes into him lengthways,' said the Baron. 'He is fortunate.' And he patted the swell of flesh above his trouser waist, with disdain. 'Just wait until you're my age, Stefan. Then women stop wanting to feed you – then they're always pestering you to go away for a "cure", by which they mean starvation.'

'You are much too fat, Felix,' Leonie declared firmly, 'and you know it. It is not elegant. I shall not love you if you are fat.'

'You see,' the Baron declared good-naturedly. 'You see.'

Leonie turned to Wirthof: 'Leutnant Wirthof, how very nice of you to come – we met the other night, didn't we? I offered to introduce him to Princess Gradiczek,' she told her husband, 'but he wouldn't hear of it. Are you like Stefan? With Stefan,' Leonie said, 'I have had to give up, he completely refuses to meet decent girls.'

'Leave him be, Leonie. He's a good-looking young fellow. He wants to enjoy himself. One's bachelor days are precious, and brief enough – eh? My own . . .'

'Your own, Felix, have been revived at regular intervals between marriages, so of all people you are in no position to indulge in sentimental nostalgia over their loss.'

The Baron, a boyish expression of having been justly reprimanded on his face, gave Leonie a loving pinch on the cheek. 'Isn't she adorable?' he demanded proudly, and added by way of imparting confidential information, 'Half the young men in this room are in love with her. Any young man who didn't fall in love with her instantly, Leonie would consider beyond the pale for evincing such lack of taste,' he said teasingly to her, making her frown. 'Wouldn't you, chérie?'

'You are not qualified to talk of taste, Felix. The only good taste you ever showed,' Leonie said to her husband, 'was marrying me. Look at this place – like an Inca's tomb. All that gold. All those fake Bonifazios. It's depressing.'

'Yes, yes,' he sighed, 'she is right. I have no taste – no aesthetic judgment. I admit it.'

'You have excellent taste in people,' she said in softer tones. 'Felix has an infallible instinct where people are concerned, and I'm the opposite. You will never take me in with a second-rate work of art, but where people are concerned I am an amateur. I can't bear to think that someone beautiful on the surface should be anything less than beautiful inside.'

'It is a common and excusable failing in women,' said the Baron indulgently. He had a rather ugly face that was by no means unpleasant to look at; the skull was domed and totally bald, and the flesh on his face had formed in disproportionate bulges and declivities and crevices, as if ill-moulded lumps of plasticine had been haphazardly stuck on an undefined substructure. The cheeks, high and rosy as a clown's, plunged in to the round sad hollows of his eyes; the nose, fleshier on one side than the other, was asymmetrically placed in the face, it seemed to jut slightly sideways. The eyes, despite their unhealthy surrounds, were lively, mischievous, with a relish for the paradoxical.

While the husband-wife exchanges were going on, Wirthof, in common with the others in the immediate vicinity, had been smiling non-committally, a courteous spectator. But Kazakh noticed that he had begun to glitter with the iridescence of an animal of prey that must announce itself with some characteristic symbol before it strikes: with Wirthof it was a progressive glitter, like raw steel being scoured until the dull dark grey substance has been brought to a hard blue brilliance. His hair, like dying yellow leaves re-invested with sunlight, glowed a rich golden colour, his eyes shone with concentrated intensity on Leonie, as if by sheer will-power, by some magical demonstration of mind over matter, he could achieve this seduction he had set his heart on. His face was mystical; Stefan could guess at the religious chant going on inside him: I will have her, I will have her, I will, I will, I will, I will. Leonie was not looking at him, and this was the evidence of his effect on her, for she looked at everyone else, only his eyes she quickly passed by, like someone stepping quickly over unsafe ground. His stiff, military posture seemed to affect her like the proximity of a young Priap. When, unwittingly, she looked up at him – for a moment only – his eyes explored all the orifices of her body so unequivocally that she grew pale – joining him in pallor, in bloodlessness of the upper regions – and shivered slightly. I have her, Wirthof exulted, I have her, glee in him, feeling the grip of hook and eye between them, feeling himself, in the making of this pact, so erotically moved that Leonie seeing this, her social sense reasserted itself – the young Leutnant didn't look himself, anything might happen – and she said, 'Stefan, let me introduce you to someone – there is someone dying to meet you. Come.' And taking Stefan's arm she extricated herself from the group and strolled with him across the ballroom, tête à tête, nodding to some of her guests in a manner that was cordial but – for the moment – discouraging of approaches.

'Stefan, who is this Leutnant Wirthof?' she asked after allowing sufficient time to elapse to give her inquiry the right casualness. 'Is he your friend?'

'He is someone I have known for some time,' Stefan said.

'He is striking.'

'Yes? You'll find him pompous. He tends to go on about his honour.'

'What is his background?'

'He interests you, Leonie?'

'Yes,' she said with her characteristic frankness. 'He is so direct. Did you see how he was looking at me?'

'Of course. He's in love with you.'

'He told you that?'

'He indicated it.'

'Who is he?'

'His father was General Wirthof. Dead now. Badly wounded in the war. Lost both his legs. Shot himself. Mother – not quite right. Broke up under pressure of events, I would think. Wirthof himself? – well, seems to have money, not much sense, gambles. Something of a fool.'

'You don't like him?'

'It's hard to *like* him. But, as you say, he's striking. The question is – do you like him, Leonie?'

'Oh don't be silly, Stefan.'

'He's curious. Has the capacity of drawing people to him, even those who don't like him particularly.'

Wirthof, feeling content with the response he had evoked from Leonie in the first minutes of his arrival, was moving easily through the large room, glitter hooded. He knew no one here. It was not his milieu, and yet he was unperturbed. So this is where the power is, he thought, the power-house of the Jews, the dark-haired ones, the magicians of commerce. He was like an explorer in strange lands. The men had animated faces, and fingers flashing jewels, and he could sense their suspicious assessment of him, an outsider, not one of them, a *goy*; the women, with their fast-moving mouths and their quick nervous glances – he felt raked by their quick nervous glances as he sauntered on – were all the time talking in undertones to sturdy daughters with plump arms and prematurely matronly bosoms and dark daunting intelligence in their eyes. The young men, the sons, with their profound noses, long sideburns, and grave, melancholy expressions, stood apprentice-like on the fringes of the adult male groups, listening, learning, contributing an occasional shrug in response to an interrogatory hand gesture. And the older men, with their gold teeth and their gold-rimmed eyeglasses and their conspiratorial closeness and their sudden laughter – he could smell money on them, like whores' scent. It was not money such as he had, unseen, moving from dim vault to dim vault, money that he rarely needed to touch with his own hands, money commanded by his signature, by his word on a phone; the money which he smelled on these elderly Jews was not the same, but glittering coinage, a sensuous commodity, fruit of hard bargains, of the bazaars, and he despised it. Not that all of the guests, or even the majority of them, were Jews, but it was they who first attracted Wirthof's attention. As he continued through the room, his faintly derisory expression announcing a detachment from the entire mercantile class, his pedigree in his steps, his bearing soldierly, he began to appreciate the constantly changing composition of the company: more guests were arriving, others leaving, or moving on from the ballroom to rooms beyond. This area he now proceeded to explore, having supplied himself with a plate of caviar and sour cream and blinets and a glass of vodka. Leaving the ballroom, he found himself in a wide passage with red damask walls and a long line of marble busts on tall plinths, separated by gilt-framed sofas and little side tables. Long windows gave on to a terrace above quadrangled gardens with lawns, statues and conical hedges. The other side of the passage had a series of double doors, and through these many of the guests were now passing – to the card room, to a small music room, to the Baron's library, or to Leonie's own rooms, dependent on their interests. The Jewesses with their plump-armed, plump-bosomed daughters, Wirthof gladly noted, remained in the ballroom, on their gilt chairs, close to the buffet tables, smiling appreciatively as the band struck up a fox-trot and the grave-eyed young men detached themselves from the fringes of their elders and presented themselves, obediently, as dancing partners. In the broad passage and on the terrace the company was not so predominantly Semitic, and Wirthof felt himself moving closer to his objective. He recognized the actress and comedienne, Lili Poll, accompanied by her protector, Prince Yashin, he recognized the Minister of Commerce, Binder, and the Assistant Chief of the General Staff, General Kloster, and Prince Starhemberg, handsomely scowling. A very mixed company, certainly. Between the Baron's library and Leonie's sitting-room there was a crush of people, slowing down movement to a trickle. Wirthof found himself wedged between an elderly woman with permanently waved hair, and a very red-faced young man who was holding heaped plates high above his head and trying to make his way in the opposite direction to everyone else.

When, eventually, Wirthof succeeded in reaching Leonie's sitting-room, there was, disappointingly, no sight of Leonie; still holding his caviar and vodka, he wandered amid the anthropomorphic vegetation, the fossilized faces, the owl men and the moon creatures and the great eyes on pedestals: amazing, he thought, quite amazing.

'Ah, Dr Roder. How kind of you to come. Do you know Stefan Kazakh? You should, Dr Roder, you should. Stefan will help you sell more toys than you have ever sold.'

'How will he do that, dear lady?'

'Because he is brilliant.'

'Is that so? Might one inquire in what particular respect his brilliance is manifest?' Dr Roder, his large, civilized face attentive as a gallant's, was lifting Leonie's hand to his lips, at the same time taking heed of this young man at her side.

'I make up slogans,' Stefan said.

'Ah but what slogans, Dr Roder. The other day he wrote in the sky – you may have seen it, Dr Roder – STEEL IS NOT LIKE THIS –

IT LASTS. All over the sky. The sky was full of those slowly fading signs. STEEL IS NOT LIKE THIS – IT LASTS. Gigantic lettering, and the little, sparkling plane zooming in and out of the fading lettering.'

'A clever idea,' Dr Roder granted. 'And how would you sell more toys for me, Herr Kazakh?'

'I would have to think about that. But – for a start – I would put a free carousel in your store, suitably attended, somewhere for mothers to leave their children, briefly, while they shop elsewhere.'

'Yes, yes – will you come and see me, Herr Kazakh. One day?'

'Gladly. When? Tomorrow?'

'By all means, by all means. Baroness, I am indebted to you for bringing me together with Herr Kazakh.'

'Not at all, Dr Roder.'

'How very agreeable these occasions of yours always are. I am enjoying myself tremendously.'

'I'm so glad. Ah – here is Lili Poll. Lili – how lovely you look. I adored your performance, and so did Felix. Darling, do you know Dr Roder, who makes those beautiful toys, such good taste, they really are such pretty things, I would like to have them for myself. It is such a shame that one's children grow up, and one is denied the pleasure of playing with their toys.'

'Enchanté, madame,' Dr Roder said, lifting the actress's hand to his mouth. 'I am one of your most ardent admirers.'

'And I – one of your constant customers. My children will only play with Roder toys.'

'That shows they have been well brought up,' Leonie declared.

'You are too kind,' Dr Roder asserted, gratified.

He has never seen Lili Poll on the stage, Stefan concluded, and she has never been inside his store, and they both know this; yet they delightedly accept each other's falsehoods as compliments. Ah my Vienna, what a cocotte you are. How could my slogans miss with a nation so devoted to the elegant lie? They could read my pretty smoke signs in the sky, but they refused to see the writing on the wall. Fools, all of them. And you, Leonie, you know what pretty things Dr Roder made later on, when there was less demand for toys? With your exquisite good taste, how were you so blind? Or was all your capacity for horror expended long ago, elsewhere? Your sensibility could not tolerate the sight of imitation leopard skin on my bathroom floor. 'Horrific,' you declared. 'It must go.' And it went, my pathetic aspiration to luxury and beauty. 'Rather a bare wooden floor than this monstrosity,' you commanded, and I obeyed. And yet, dear Leonie, you could look into Wirthof's eyes and see no ghastly clash of colours there, how could you, with your taste and your awareness, have been so blind? That you gave your body to his ransacking I can forgive, but not that you loved him. How could you love him, Leonie?

Inside Leonie's study, Wirthof was continuing to look around. This room was smaller than the others. The walls were a pale beige-grey, the ceiling white and without mouldings. The wall opposite the french windows was closely covered with modern paintings and drawings in plain frames, some of them were no more than fragments of a larger work, preliminary sketches, a few pencil strokes representing a woman's breasts, a hand, the muscular play of a leg; other pictures, in which vivid violent shapes were arranged in what seemed to him arbitrary and perverse juxtapositions, irritated him, like any form of disorder. There was one painting that had some affinity with mosaic tiling, except that the artist did not differentiate between floor, walls, ceiling, windows and view beyond; a childish sun, ray-emitting, lay like a discarded rubber ball in the confusion of tiles, which began with some kind of pattern, but then went berserk, spread like proliferating germ cells in all directions, encompassing static and realistic objects such as a sliced apple, revealing its pips, and a flower whose pistil had come, curiously, to resemble a gun. Such paintings – in which recognizable objects were mixed up with shapes and patterns with no more meaning than spittle – caused him discomfort. He wanted to tidy them. He did not in the least mind storks carrying monsters in their talons or abstracts that looked like the intestines of a chicken; it was when these fantastical images were placed in a context of reality that his sense of the rightness of things was offended. But there were also some paintings that pleased him; shimmering girls in blue with satin ruffs, dancing figures in a Paris café; a view of a bullring; a peasant's face; a man eating bread; green rooftops going down to a green sea; a plump girl, bodice open, lying on a dishevelled bed.

The furniture in the room consisted largely of sofas and armchairs, and there was a magnificent old table, of impressive length, arrayed with books, magazines, newspapers and various writing accoutrements, and behind it a wide, high chair, its gilt chipped and faded. Leonie's chair. As it was unoccupied, Wirthof sat in it.

The people in this room, seven or eight men and one woman, were seated in the form of an unfinished circle, listening to one of their numbers, a man with a massive head and a quivering, attention compelling voice, its authority and sheer volume sweeping aside such muttered interjections and protestations as his words from time to time were eliciting from the others. Wirthof pulled his chair closer to this group so that he could hear what was being said.

'... no, no ... I cannot accept that ... that is ...' somebody had managed to interject in one of those rare moments when the massive-headed man paused, momentarily, to refill his bellow-like chest with air.

'You cannot accept it, my good sir,' came the thunderous reply. '*You* cannot accept it? Are you, then, propounding a concept of passive aggression, are you suggesting that?'

'It depends, does it not, on how we define aggression?'

'Surely, sir, you can be in no doubt about what aggression is and that it is active, and that someone in a passive role, whatever else he may be, cannot be an aggressor. To slam the door in the face of an intruder can never be categorized as aggression.'

'It can be highly provocative,' the objector persisted.

'You are saying, if I understand you correctly, that if a man is attacked, to defend himself can constitute a provocation. What arrant nonsense! If I steal your wallet, and you forcefully retrieve it, that does not make *you* a thief. Or are you suggesting that it does?'

'Forgive me, Professor Blumenfeld, I was not saying that. I was making the point that, as Jews, we must not make the mistake of *provoking* aggression. Pacifism is an honourable attitude. My point is: Render unto Caesar that which is Caesar's ...'

'So we are told, so we are told,' Blumenfeld said quietly, reasonably. 'And you propose, therefore, that the Jews of Germany should render unto Hitler that which is Hitler's? Is that what you propose, my friend? What should they render unto Hitler that is Hitler's – their property, is that Hitler's? Their rights, are they Hitler's? Their liberty, is that Hitler's? Their children's future, is that Hitler's? Come now, my friend, that was not what Christ meant. Christ was not advocating compliance with tyranny. Whatever else he can be accused of, it is not cynicism. He was not advocating a miserable and self-defeating policy of serving two masters. He spoke of that too, if you remember. What Christ meant, and this is quite clear in the light of his other sayings, and yet for its own reasons the world has always chosen to misunderstand what Christ meant,' – and now his voice which had been unnaturally quiet, lulling almost in its sweet reasonableness, swelled – 'what Christ meant was: *If* you can find anything that is Caesar's, then render it unto him. *In that unlikely eventuality.*'

'It is *an* ingenious interpretation,' another member of the group put in, 'but it is not necessarily correct. There is such a thing as duty to the state.'

'To an iniquitous state, no. There is no duty that compels obedience to iniquity. Not even filial duty compels submission to a tyrannical father.'

The sole woman in the group, a dark, slim beauty in a tailored suit, Eton collar and tie, aged about fifty, interposed in a low and elegant voice, 'Professor Blumenfeld, what you leave out is that all governments are iniquitous. Come now, Professor, admit it is so. Some are more iniquitous than others. Some are less iniquitous today than they were yesterday. Some will be more iniquitous tomorrow than they are today. If one took your attitude, one would be in a constant state of rebellion. Hitler's attitude to the Jews is monstrous, it goes without saying. No civilized person would dispute that. But Hitler is a politician, and an astute one. He will denounce the Jews to the masses – as he has denounced the capitalists – because it is what the masses want to hear, but of course he knows he cannot do without the Jews. Who can?' She laughed. 'They hold too many of the purse-strings. That is what infuriates him so. Come, Professor, you must admit there is some basis for Hitler's rage. He knows that the Jewish bankers can break him, that is what makes him so furious. Even if their power in Germany has been curtailed, do you imagine they do not still pull the strings from their offices in Zurich, Paris and New York? Really, I think you have too little faith in the cleverness of your own people, Professor. They have more sublety than you credit them with. I myself take care that in the really important choices of life – in choosing a banker, a lawyer, a doctor, a lover – I choose a Jew. Ah – Baron, tell me you approve.'

'As lovers, madame, we have, I trust, retained our effectiveness,' Baron Koeppler said from the doorway, 'but as bankers we are perhaps a riskier proposition these days.'

'Do you share the Professor's pessimism?' somebody else in the group wanted to know.

The Baron came slowly forward, into the circle, like someone in a strange house not entirely at ease.

'I am familiar with Professor Blumenfeld's view, of course,' he said, remaining standing, hands clasped behind back. 'And I do not deny the validity of much of what he says. But, of course, Professor Blumenfeld is a thinker and a scientist, one who deals in absolutes that do not exist, necessarily, in the world of everyday reality. For example – absolute alcohol, a useful concept in mathematics, but something that cannot in practice be made. While I agree with the professor that compliance with iniquity can never be justified, I, as a practical man, not a theoretician tend to see things in a less cut-and-dried way. It is suggested, for instance, that as Hitler is an evil man, a persecutor of the Jews, I, as a Jew, should have no dealings with Germany. In principle that sounds indisputable, does it not? But in practice, it works out differently. Because I continue to have dealings with Germany, I still retain a measure – a diminishing measure, it is true – of influence. There are still one or two people I can approach who can be relied upon to do something, if pressed, on behalf of those unfortunate people who are being so cruelly victimized. Some influence is better than no influence, some power better than none. In a sense, it is important that we should continue to be useful to Hitler, for while we have our uses – we have a bargaining counter. At least the worst excesses that he threatens can be prevented. If, on the other hand, we make no conciliatory gestures to Hitler, oppose and resist him at every point, then we will simply bring harsher measures upon ourselves, and having shot our bolt will have no room for manoeuvre.'

'Manoeuvre! Manoeuvre!' Blumenfeld cried in disgust. 'You are like a man who seeks to placate a mad dog by letting him bite your arm off, hoping that will keep him from your neck. A man like Hitler cannot be placated. You must oppose him by every means at your disposal. Mad dogs do not become less mad when they have gobbled up your arms, they want more. But if you take a stick to it, if you beat it off, it may stay clear of you. Even madness understands a stick.'

'Such analogies,' the Baron replied patiently, 'are colourful but clarify nothing. Hitler is not a mad dog. He is an asute politician and leader. He understands that his own position is dependent on being able to do certain things for the German people. If the people have no work and go hungry, all his rousing words will serve for nothing. His success is due to the fact that he has created full employment. He will not risk that by precipitant acts that endanger the economy. Of that I am convinced. I do not wish to produce a situation where Hitler can say that we, the Jewish bankers, by devious means, by some international conspiracy, have brought Germany down. That would give him the excuse he is waiting for.'

'You people are always worried about not giving him an excuse; when he wants one he finds one easily enough. You don't imagine he wants for you to give him one,' Blumenfeld said disgustedly.

The knot of muscles representing a human head – what a very curious, and disagreeable, representation of a human head, Wirthof thought.

'We went for the Biennale last summer, it was *so* good, Felix wanted to have all the Carpaccios copied, it was a battle dissuading him, Felix feels that if he can't have the originals he'd rather have copies than what he calls modern junk. Fickert, who came with us, is good, if any copyist can be said to be good, charges the earth too, fortunately I was able to talk Felix out of it, Fickert was furious of course, but our places are full of Fickert copies, and I really would rather spend the money on some absolute unknown who needs encouragement. We hardly went to the Lido, Felix does not care for it. I just hope Mussolini is not going to ruin Italy with his passion for railway stations. Of course it is magnificent architecture when confined to railway stations, but he's building everything in the same style, all those massive structures outside Rome. I hate them, I don't just dislike them – I hate them, they have an aesthetic brutality that I find terribly dispiriting. My precious, darling Venice, fortunately he can't touch that, it's so sad that it's sinking, every year a little deeper, all those motor-boats on the canal wrecking the foundations of those beautiful old palazzos – so sad.'

Wirthof, having become bored with the discussion about the Jews, got up and went to look for Leonie. He went into the adjoining drawing-room. The fact that the paintings on the walls were of her choice made him look at them with interest. The distortions of the human body. Face half crescent moon, half mask, hair like corrugated iron, breasts misshapen, cumbersome bloated arms – a genetic catastrophe. Hips and thighs like parts of an octopus. Toes, monstrous toes. What kind of reality was this? The reality of dementia. Unbalanced: no sense of symmetry or perspective. An affront to the eye. And that, yes, between the octopus thighs, an unblinking eye. A vulgar joke. This was called art. He exonerated Leonie – it was the influence of the Jews. Scribbles. That was all. And that one: limbs like a dog's bone. And that – faces within faces, multiples of the same face. And the large one – God! – what a mess, vomit; what was it meant to represent!

Wirthof saw Leonie, alone for a moment, in the long passage leading to the ballroom; there was a sufficient distance between them for her to have pretended not to see him without being impolite, but she chose to see him, and she chose to wait for him. She waited for him heavy-eyed, not smiling, and when he had come close to her she said nothing, giving him the opportunity to speak first. He said, 'I've been looking for you.'

'Yes?'

'I went to – the room with the modern paintings. It is your room, isn't it?'

'Yes.'

'I sat in your chair. They – the others – were talking about the Jewish question.'

'My chair?'

'The one behind the large table. I got bored – with the Jewish question.'

'Oh yes, that chair.' For some reason she shuddered.

'Are you cold?' Her neck, shoulders, upper breasts were bare, but it was a warm, September night.

'No, I'm not cold,' she said.

'Shall we go on the terrace?'

'Yes.' But the terrace was packed, and having strolled the length of it without speaking they left by one of the french windows and returned to the corridor.

'Isn't there somewhere to be alone?' he said.

'Not here, not now,' she said, scolding him for his effrontery.

154

'When?'

People were passing them all the time, and she had to acknowledge their bows and to appear to be having a casual conversation with the young officer. 'It is very difficult.'

'I want to see you.'

'You can come next week again, next Wednesday.'

'That's too long.'

'I have engagements every night.'

'Cancel them.'

'Impossible.'

'During the day then?'

'I'm at my studio.'

'I will come there.'

'No, you can't.'

'Why not?'

'It's not possible. You must accept what I tell you, if I tell you it is impossible, it is.'

'When can I see you in that case?'

'I don't know. I will have to think.'

'Well?'

'I can't tell you now – I . . . Tomorrow we are going to the Opera, to see *Tannhäuser*. Do you like Wagner?' He shrugged. 'If you like Wagner, come. You can usually get a standing place at the last minute.'

'Five hours of *Tannhäuser*, standing . . .'

'Yes, it is also too much for Felix. He usually becomes hungry in the first interval, and leaves. Felix goes to eat with one of his business cronies at the Sacher, and then comes back a few minutes before the end to fetch me. We have Loge B.'

'Loge B?'

'Yes. Now be discreet and don't talk to me again for the rest of the evening, spend a little time talking to one of the nice young girls, dance, be sociable, and when we're not alone don't look at me the way you are looking at me now. You understand, if you want to see me there are conditions that have to be observed.'

'Well, Stefan,' Baron Koeppler said.

'Well, Felix.'

The Baron gently massaged his eyelids, blinked open his eyes, linked his arm with Stefan's and began to walk him across the open spaces of the ballroom.

'Tired, Felix?'

'A little, a little. These evenings of Leonie's' – he smiled indulgently – 'are for people who don't have to get up in the morning. Leonie is inexhaustible. Fantastic energy. Stefan, I want to have a talk with you, there is something you could do for me . . .'

'Yes, gladly.'

'It's a very full week for me, but I tell you – if you are free – why not come to the Opera with us tomorrow night. *Tannhäuser*. We'll see the first act and then go to Sacher's, that'll give us time.'

'I'd be glad to do that, Felix.'

'Good, good. Five hours of *Tannhäuser* is too much. That Professor Blumenfeld is a peculiar character, isn't he?'

'Oh highly peculiar, but impressive, don't you think?'

'Yes. Is he good? Is he highly regarded?'

'Oh yes.'

'Talks very big.'

'Oh he's a big talker.'

'These thinkers, these philosophers, what do they know of practical matters, of life?' The Baron gave an indulgent smile – a kind of weary tolerance permeated all his attitudes. 'Everything seems so simple to them, so straightforward and clear-cut, what do they know of the complexities of the world's affairs? Hmm? Hmm? What a luxury – to be a thinker. All you have to do is think, and give the world the benefit of your conclusions. What a luxury! No need to concern yourself with the question of whether the ideas work, as long as they are arrived at scientifically, by scrupulous reasoning. Ah yes. But is the world logical, is the world rational? Is it even reasonable?'

'Unfortunately not,' Stefan agreed.

'I'm a practical man,' the Baron said. 'I have to be. What I can't do anything about – I can't do anything about. When I met Hitler in '33, before he was Chancellor, he said to me, "Koeppler, we are going to cleanse Germany of people like you." Charming fellow! Somebody offered him a drink, but he doesn't drink, as you know. They gave him a lemonade. I said to him, "Herr Hitler, I know how you feel on this question, but you're a politician and I'm a banker, we're both practical men, it's in both our interests to try and find some modus vivendi." "The only modus vivendi acceptable to me", he said, "is that you cease, that you absolutely cease." He speaks in that way. Doesn't have any sort of social compunctions about using that kind of language. I laughed, and I said, "Well, I respect your directness, Herr Hitler. But you would hardly expect me to concur with such an extreme viewpoint." "Your concurrence is of no interest to me, Koeppler," he said. "You will see that we do not require your concurrence. Either the Jewish question is solved on my terms, or I will solve it myself." Afterwards, I talked to Hess, who said, "The thing to remember about the Führer is that he is a man of unwavering principles. He does not go around handing out sops to people. The fact that he talked to you is a good sign. It establishes a basis of discussion between you." It's important to understand the way the mind of such a man works, Stefan. It would have been easy to become outraged, what good would that have done? He has to talk like that, that is what one must understand about him. It is his nature. But when it comes to action, he is more practical. Always it's the same. First he talks loud and threatens and uses wild language and waves his arms about, that is when one must keep calm, it is a mistake to rise to that. Then he goes away and says to one of his minions: "Settle the question." Then one can talk. You see, it is his bargaining technique. The bigger he talks at the start, the less he will have to give away later, he hopes. The point is one must not let oneself be intimidated by his language and his manner, that is the mistake. The way to deal with him is to take no notice of all that wild talk – he'd like you to take notice, to be intimidated, to tremble, because then, when you sit down to talk hard terms, you are psychologically at a disadvantage. That is his technique: bluff, big words, intimidation. How do you deal with that? You ignore it. You don't let it influence you. Let him think he has intimidated you, and when you sit down to talk, you get the best deal you can. That's where you have to be clever. If he thinks you're thoroughly intimidated, he, or rather his stooges and advisers, because in economic matters he is an ignoramus, will believe that whatever you accept in the end is an absolute defeat for you and an absolute triumph for him, which, of course, if you are clever, it isn't, it isn't quite. Believe me, there is little enough that can be salvaged, no matter how clever you are, but there is *something*, and in business you have to be content with the best terms you can get.'

'But can you tolerate such a state of affairs permanently?'

'What is permanent? I will tell you one thing, Stefan: one does not put all one's eggs in one basket, not if that basket is Germany, one has to protect one's interests. But how long is a madman like that going to last? How long will the German people put up with him? He will make his mistake. One must be patient, and take everything on a day by day basis. Sooner or later he will either have to see reason, or be made to see reason, or the German people will send him packing. I'm an optimist, Stefan. I think the man who keeps his head, doesn't allow himself to be panicked into precipitant action, is the man who wins in the end. When that *gunif* discovers he can't do without us dirty Jews he'll be more reasonable. You will come to the Opera with us then, tomorrow?'

'Yes, gladly.'

'I have a proposition to put to you. Leonie is such an opera lover, she won't mind that we leave her after the first act. She loves Wagner' – again he gave his tolerant shrug – 'that woman has a wonderful appreciation – of everything. Vitality, taste. You know, Stefan, I'm a very lucky man, a very lucky man.'

Arriving at the Opera shortly after six, Wirthof found that every seat and all the standing places for that night's performance were sold. There was a group of students outside the ticket office, pleased with themselves at having obtained the last of the standing places; Wirthof said he'd pay one of them three times what he'd paid for his place. They shook their heads, worriedly. All right, Wirthof said, ten times. They looked quite angry with him for having made the offer, and they all shook their heads, but one of them suddenly stuck out his hand with the ticket and took the money. The others protested, but the one who'd sold his ticket shrugged and said he could see *Tannhäuser* another time, and walked off with a defiant grin wavering on his face. The students hurried inside to find the best remaining places; Wirthof did not go in straight away – it did not matter to him whether he had a good place or not – but walked round to the main staircase leading up to the loges.

The performance was due to start at six thirty, at six fifteen people started to arrive. Flunkeys in dark-brown knee breeches and long, gold-braided tailcoats scrutinized tickets and directed people to the right staircase, the right door, and to the nearest of several cloakrooms.

It was unusually warm for late September.

I wore tails (one dressed up in those days; one adhered to the formalities). And patent leather shoes, what's more. I who used always to have dirt under my fingernails: manicured that night, and Cologned. Ah! – you were a glitterer too, it wasn't only Wirthof who could glitter warningly; driven to it, you could also put on that dark sheen. To cuckold the Baron! What fantasy. Am I responsible for my thoughts? If not you, who? Who? What kind of love is that? She had the tenderest smile. She never knew, so what did it matter? I am not responsible for my thoughts. It is the nature of a man to think such thoughts. Frankly, Kazakh, you appall me sometimes. I sat between Leonie and the Baron in their black Mercedes, with the light-grey upholstery; what intimacy there was in the smell of her perfume, as if it was her most secret body scent I was breathing – this is how she will smell for you, Wirthof, tonight, tomorrow, whenever. Take her, Stefan thought, take her, she belongs to the vandals, she is made for pillaging. Loot is what you are.

'You really don't mind, Leonie, if we leave you after the first interval?' Stefan asked.

'I think it's unforgivable,' Leonie said, 'but if you must have your boring business talk. This is your bad influence, Felix. You're going to make a philistine of Stefan.'

How well you dissimulated, Leonie, your breasts so white, (how could you have had two children and kept those small, tight, tasteful breasts?); with what chic duplicity you conducted your little private masque, you deserved to be loot. But how could you have loved him? What expectancy was rife in your body? Were you already moist then? What grossness had you planned for the second act of *Tannhäuser*, in Loge B? What fumbling pleasure? Is it surprising I thought of you when I lay with whores? You hadn't even the excuse of sudden impulse, for you planned it minutely.

He will be there, my soldier, in the standing section, down below by the worn velvet handrail, standing. Standing. My soldier. Oh Maz, oh Maz. He has such a pale and terrible beauty. I am not careless of my body, I pamper it with sun and creams and aromatic salts and steam baths and cures in alkaline springs and in sulphate waters and in brine baths and in mud baths and in iodine springs and in iron and arsenic springs, at Ischl, at Badgastein, at Fischau, I diet, I fast to purge this body of its impurities, its excesses. Oh Maz, dear Maz. Why do I do it, this, tonight? A soldier, a lieutenant. Who is he? Is he anyone? Do I have choice? You would say I have, but I don't feel I have. The pull of my otherness is too strong. To risk everything – for nothing. Isn't that the essence of the gambler? Maz, dear Maz, you have the better part of me, you always have had; this other with its cravings and its greeds, it is not even simple sensuality. What is it? I lack pleasure, Maz; I have so much of what is called pleasure, and I lack it, it is my deficiency. In what do I take pleasure? My children. Yes – they are my joy, yes. My only joy. The rest? My life, my possessions, my – For all that I have, Maz, there is a lack in me, a need for something extraordinary, to feel miraculous again, as I did when I was pregnant with Lea, as I did when you first taught me and for a few months I believed I had talent. The other day I noticed some broken blood vessels on my face, the little twisting red lines. Shall I be a raddled old lady? Oh Maz, I want to be miraculous again. It is not that I am bored: the women who do these things out of boredom I find contemptible, no, I am not bored, it is more serious, I am – impoverished. Oh you laugh, I can hear you laugh. It is true. How can you know? You have such riches. I love Felix, our life together, all my friends, you; so much that I love and cherish; but – Maz – if I cannot risk it, it is nothing. Do you understand? My otherness demands the risk. What did you see when you drew me?

> À la très-bonne, à la très-belle
> Qui fait ma joie et ma santé
> Que m'importe que tu sois sage?
> Sois belle! et sois triste!

What did you mean? What did you see when you drew me? A pampered dilettante, a bored rich woman, her head stuffed with theories. Be beautiful and be sad, you said to me. You said to me: I offer you treasures, but you must pay. What did you mean?

Have I not paid? I asked you that then, and you laughed, and you said, 'You have not even begun to pay.' Am I not generous, Maz? Do I not give of my time, my enthusiasm, my feelings, my love, my thoughts? Oh how I hear you laugh. You are right. What do I ever give that I value? What can I give, when so little has true value for me? And of that little how little I have! Can one be generous with something one does not value? Could I have been an artist, had I been prepared to pay? Did I have talent? You said: one does not have to have talent. Forget about your happiness, you said, it is not necessary to be happy. Be beautiful, be sad, you said. But I wanted to be happy. I wanted to be an artist. I wanted. And you said, want less and follow your inclinations and take great risks. Oh Maz. This pale lieutenant who will be waiting for me, he can make me feel miraculous again. You told me, take great risks. Maz, how else can I feel I have something valuable unless I risk it; don't you see – only then does it become valuable to me. How else can I assess it except on those particular scales? Against the great weight of my otherness, what have I? If it weighs only a little it is something and I will be less poor. Maz, he has such a terrible pale beauty for me, he will make me feel miraculous, he will start a heat in me, he will commence flows in me. Oh Maz, it *is* the worse part of me, what can I say? It is all I have freely to give, it is my only surplus, and he will make me feel I give him treasure.

Did you think I didn't know, did you think Wirthof would be discreet – he boasted of the assignation. 'But if you're dining with the Baron, it's perfect, Kazakh. I can rely on you to make sure he doesn't come back. It's perfect.' And did you think, Leonie, there was anything he would omit to tell me; in the black limousine when your eyes shone, you must have known that I knew about the evening's arrangement, after all I had brought Wirthof to you, I had told you of his feelings for you, you could hardly have expected me not to know – oh how you dissimulated. Surprising, that you had no fear I might tell the Baron something, drop a hint, you were sure of me.

'Will you have some supper, afterwards, chérie, at Sacher's?' Felix asked her.

'I don't mind cutting out a meal, I've been putting on weight.' You, with Modigliani neck and hips!

'You could have something at Sacher's, during the first interval. There is enough time. I can get them to have something ready. A few escargots . . .'

'No, it's not necessary, chérie, I prefer not to eat tonight.'

No – one greed at a time; Wirthof had promised you food more substantial, more filling, Wirthof had promised to fill you at the other entrance to your belly, were you already salivating for him that you could not think of escargots? What can he give you in Loge B during the second act of *Tannhäuser*, be practical, the merest morsel, the merest hors d'oeuvre. Or do you plan *fellatio* in Loge B? Or perhaps you think you can take this Priapus in your grotto. In Loge B? In what position? Do you plan to straddle him in Loge B? And say I return with the Baron? What a superb scandal. The Baroness Koeppler caught *flagrante delicto* in Loge B during the third act of *Tannhäuser*, a lieutenant of cavalry plunged in her hairy diadem. Delicious scandal, delicious prospect for a lieutenant of cavalry. While I talk business with the Baron.

'I think,' said Stefan, 'Leonie prefers to show herself off during the interval. That is what the interval is for.'

'She can show herself off in the second interval,' Felix said.

'The second interval isn't the same as the first interval,' said Stefan. 'The initial impact is made in the first interval – that is the important one; the second interval is in the nature of a reprise.' Leonie's eyes flashed a warning not to take the *double entendre* too far; so she did know, or guess, that he knew; so she was not entirely unafraid, it made him feel quite powerful to realize how completely she was at his mercy. Your pleasure awaits my pleasure; supposing I deprive you of your pleasure, supposing I deprive you of his pinches, of his tweaking of your flesh, of his rummaging in your channel, between those small tight boy's buttocks of yours, supposing I deny you him? And if I permit it? Will you let him penetrate you with all his implements, will you let him make a hunchback of you, will you be a twin-backed monster with him, will you bend for him, will you sit on him, will you lie with him? Leonie, you are a woman of sensibility and style, incapable of coarse actions or thoughts, your body is impervious to gross acts and thoughts alike, you have shown me only kindness: you are too precious for him. Refrain. Refrain.

Stefan said, 'Leonie actually doesn't mind five hours of *Tannhäuser*. To us, you see, Felix, it is only an opera by Wagner, but to Leonie it is an intense experience, a passionate involvement, there are women so stirred by music they actually have been known to achieve a climax in the more rousing moments . . .'

'I didn't know it had any rousing moments.'

'That is because you have always been asleep, or at the Sacher.'

'Climaxes,' said the Baron. 'Really? Climaxes? Is that so? Is it feasible? It is not a story?'

'Oh yes,' said Stefan. 'It is quite feasible, I speak as a former medical student.'

'The music alone! You don't think it's helped along by some young buck . . .'

'But of course, Felix,' Leonie said dangerously. 'Of course . . . Don't you know the loges are practically chambres particulières, and the whole of the Opera is an enormous maison de rendezvous. Come now, don't pretend such innocence.'

'The Opera was never my field of activity,' the Baron said, 'so I wouldn't know about that. In my time, we took a girl in the Prater, found some thick bushes, or else got the fiacre driver to close the hood and drive around the Belvedere a couple of times. So that sort of thing goes on at the Opera? Well, I've learned something tonight, I shall bring my opera glasses next time.'

'Felix, Leonie is deceiving you.'

Her composure was perfect; she could not have failed to feel a moment of trepidation, but she said quite easily, 'Of course I am, Felix. Of course things like that don't go on at the Opera, perhaps in some of the cheaper music halls, but can you imagine, at the Opera! I was teasing you, Felix.'

'Oh I see. And the spontaneous climaxes?'

'That is not unheard of,' Stefan said. 'I read it in some book by Stekel.'

'Among the abnormal? As a manifestation of abnormality?'

'Yes, I suppose so.'

'Normal women,' said the Baron authoritatively, 'don't experience such things.' He gave a bawdy chuckle. 'I can remember at times one had quite a hard job relying on the orthodox method.'

How little he knows you, Leonie, how ignorant he is of your fine mechanism. He does not know you, and so on any scale of absolute justice he has no right to you – yes, cuckold the Baron! cuckold the Baron! I give you permission, Wirthof.

At the back of the auditorium Wirthof stood behind the velvet handrail separating the standing spectators, an excited mass of young people (students, shop girls, subalterns), from the rest of the audience. The five tiers of maroon loges, rising in a deep curve, were filling, the loge holders becoming framed as they entered and took their places, until the whole of the vast concave was a gallery of family portraits, everyone formally posed, while down below, in the railed off portion, the closely packed and clamorous young pushed and strained and twisted their necks and gaped and laughed, their unrestrained excitement contrasting with the rigid postures of the family groups, docile daughters, sombre sons, in the loges. At six twenty the great central circular chandelier became illuminated, an explosion of coruscating light that caused a deep ahhhhhh! of expectancy to run through the entire audience, and immediately afterwards the crystal candelabra outside each loge came on and the whole of this vast space flashed and sparkled.

The orchestra was tuning up now, in the loges opera glasses were being focused, and Wirthof saw Leonie, the Baron and Kazakh make their entrance, take their seats. Long white gloves and programmes lay on velvet ledges, a thunderous round of applause greeted the arrival of the conductor, and Leonie's eyes were sweeping the auditorium, they did not linger – I was watching her – when she saw Wirthof, but went on until she had made a full circle. The very young captain had a shattered collar-bone, a casing of plaster of Paris was on his left shoulder and upper arm, he had to rest his weight on his good shoulder, the right one, and she – since his other arm was useless – formed herself for him, he was a grave young captain, it was 1917, she was fifteen, he said nothing, he was in pain; it was not easy, she loved him for the way he was so patient, she let him lie, pillowed, inside her apex, working with mouth and lips at producing the liquidity that rose up in her so plentifully and that seemed to excite him so greatly. Squatting over the captain, who now was half supported on his good arm, she bent forward and placed her hands on the ground on either side of his face – his mouth was open – oh my beauty, oh my love – and thrusting, felt herself tear, and he was heaving up, pulling at her hips, and she was entered, she contained the prize, and it was he who lay like a lovely ravished girl, chest bare, thighs apart, while she could control her pleasure, could bring herself on, could sheath him and unsheath him, until the ownership of this prized object that joined them was no longer certain, supposing it was hers, and she was penetrating this wondrous wounded youth, and with that image she began (or was it him? was hers the heavier flow?) and he to rear below her like a wild pony.

Wirthof, seeing Leonie, feeling himself seen, smirked – I saw him smirk, how sure he was of himself. The lights dimmed, the opera functionaries closed the velvet doors, the last few people admitted dashed to their seats, muttering apologies, and in total darkness the prelude began. Wirthof allowed the music to roll over him, he felt himself become stirred to a passion that was virtually patriotic, and like a man moved by drums and bugles to give up his life for his country, Wirthof committed himself in this confluence of emotions to Leonie, to what was for him a decisive departure, a passionate affair, a full-scale romance, involving heart and body, he was due for such an affair, he wished to taste strong emotion, to abandon himself to an all-consuming passion, to be a Werther, to suffer for or over a woman. What was it Goethe had said?

Naiads dancing in a bluish lake in the far background where the cave curved away into indefinitely prolonged space. Sirens reclining on the rising banks of this lake, and in the foreground – Venus on a couch, Tannhäuser at her feet. Nymphs danced. Glorious, glorious: something gigantic must happen to me, Wirthof vowed. I am sick of trivia, of inconsequential liaisons; I will be gigantically involved, I will make a sacrifice for her, perhaps I shall give up all other women. Anyway, he would think of an appropriate sacrifice. He felt rather pleased with himself for having had such a noble impulse. What can I deny myself – for her? The combination of the music, the resounding words expressing so magnificently his own burgeoning passion, and the immediate prospect awaiting him, after the interval, in Loge B, made him feel almost mythical, predestined, swayed by great forces. One must pursue one's destiny. Anyway, what an adventure! What a game! My soul cries out for her, he decided; it was only your penis in erection, Wirthof, easily confused in the circumstances for the soul's yearnings. Your soul is a tiny thing, a mere irritation on the surface of your ego, a momentary discomfort of your bowels, you confuse flatus with soul, Wirthof. And yet, you did love her, didn't you? It is overrated, love, if you could feel it, in one of those little boxes of your mind. And who are you, Kazakh, to say what love is? Are you an expert?

Even before the middle of the first act, the Baron began to yawn and to shift restlessly in his chair. These Germanic myths do not engage our soul. But Leonie was moved, her stillness was perfect. How can a woman of your taste descend to the vulgarity of loving Wirthof? That posturing fool. Are you so devoid of judgment? Cannot you see how empty he is, nothing but conceit and narcissism and ill-digested ideas.

As soon as the curtain started to descend for the end of the first act, before the lights came on, Felix got up. 'Come, Stefan. I'm ravenous. We will wait for you in the automobile afterwards, chérie.'

'All right, Felix. Enjoy your business talk.'

'And you, Leonie,' Stefan said, 'enjoy the opera.'

'I am enjoying it, very much,' she said.

'Good. Good.' The Baron stooped to kiss her on the cheek, and Stefan also kissed her, his lips brushing the side of her mouth as she turned up her face to him.

Wirthof left the auditorium together with the other standing spectators. It was a relief to exercise his legs, to get out of that stifling hot crush of excited youngsters; under other circumstances he would not have dreamt of taking a standing place – you see what sacrifices he made for you, Leonie – but now he felt noble, having put up with the discomfort for the whole first act. A little fresh air to revive me, he decided, and then I shall have a glass of champagne and a little caviar in the Marmorsaal, he was feeling decidedly peckish and, moreover, caviar was known to be an aphrodisiac. Outside the Opera others, too, were taking the air. It was an agreeably warm evening, and his head was full of music as he strolled. I'm deeply in love, he decided, surprised: what an extraordinary emotion for me. Absurd! He smiled at the enormity of his folly. Who would have thought it felt like this? What did it feel like? Well, for one thing, all activities not connected with Leonie now seemed so dull and unrewarding that it was depressing to contemplate them. How could he have occupied himself with such irrelevancies, even to the extent of having, at times, become quite absorbed in some of them. I shall devote myself to being in love, everything else must wait. I shall resign my commission so that I can remain near her all the time. And if she refuses to leave the Jew Baron, I shall possibly shoot myself. I shall tell her as much, then it will be on her head. Yes, that's what I shall do. He congratulated himself for having thought of such an effective scheme. Or else, as an alternative to shooting himself, he would gamble away his fortune, get drunk every night, sleep with diseased whores, and die horribly. It seemed like an excellent alternative to shooting himself, one that had the merit of being more protracted. A very young and pretty girl student was looking at him, and he revelled in his masculine power; all his movements, the way he walked and sat, were subtly expressive of his state of love: perhaps not evident to the eye (for he had a sense of decorum) but communicable to anyone receptive enough – like this delicious little virgin student. Ah, she can't take her eyes off me, she looks again, she is besotted with me, how delightful; he walked on, glittering, and gave her a faint, soldier's smile with the edges of his moustache. Dream of me, little virgin. Ah – if only I were free, but you would soon bore me, your range is too limited: my soul demands something on a larger scale, a thirst like mine cannot be slaked with apple-juice. Alas, little virgin student, you are not for me. He felt compassion for her in her loss, but he could not bestow himself on everyone, and hadn't he only a few moments ago made a vow of faithfulness to Leonie? He went back inside the opera house and climbed the stairs up to the Marmorsaal.

Leonie did not leave the box during the interval. She read the programme notes more than once, and then used the programme to fan herself with. She would have liked to go out, but she felt uncertain of her ability to conduct a casual conversation if – as was more than likely – she ran into someone she knew. Am I really going to do this? Or will I send him away? If he came to her in the dark, she would not send him away. But if he comes now, in full view of everyone, my social sense will intervene, and then the mood will be broken, nothing will happen. But if he comes in the dark, unequivocally – Will he have the courage to do that? As the end of the interval approached and the auditorium and the loges began to fill up again, she thought – he will come in the dark.

He entered stealthily in the dark, cautious as a thief; out of breath, he flattened himself against the velvet wall to pause. She did not turn, though she must have heard him come in. Her long white gloves lay on the ledge before her, and he saw the movement of white breasts. He crept forward, on his toes, and as the curtain rose, giving light, lowered himself on to a chair a little behind her and to her left. She turned to him, without pretence, and when he reached out for her hand she gave it to him, a fragile smile on her face, a very breakable smile, she gave her hand as a gift, renouncing ownership, and he took it and spread out her fingers, causing a tremor to pass through her, his fingers touched the flesh of the interstices and she, in defence, clenched her fist, taking back her gift, and he had to unclench her fingers, one by one, to which she submitted. When her hand was open again, loose, a disputed object between them, of uncertain ownership, he placed his hand on hers, making her fingers go rigid, and slowly slid the finger that lay on her first finger down into the soft cleft, which she widened. He raised her hand, which was slightly moist, to his mouth and, looking into her eyes, pressed his lips to the delicate groove, the silky fold between finger and thumb. She shuddered all along the length of her arm; a journeying sensation that grew in intensity, its progress charted on her face, and, munificently, she gave him the naked sight of her response. Moving closer, he touched her neck with his fingertips, her shoulders, the sides of her breasts, the breasts fully, and into her ear he said, 'I want . . .'

'Yes, what? What? What is it you want, my soldier?' His hand went to her face, he squeezed her mouth into an oval: he thought I want you to love me desperately, I want you to sacrifice yourself for me, because I am gold, good as gold; he giggled.

'Oh yes,' she said, 'oh yes, I want that too, with all my heart.'

At this, he rose from his chair and seated himself next to her on the two-seater sofa, and kissed her sideways, open-thighed, in full peacock display.

'Gently,' she cautioned him, 'gently. I have to leave here, I have to be seen leaving, and you will have me in rags.'

Ignoring the protest, he pulled her into his side, kissed her, swung one leg across her, so that he was half straddling her.

'It is not possible,' she protested, 'it is not possible.' The music overrode all objections.

'You can't refuse,' he insisted. Take her here and now, she can't refuse.

'It will not be good like this,' she said. 'I want to be alone with you, to have time.'

'Now,' he insisted.

'Oh what a little boy you are.'

'It will be a sign between us,' he said.

'What sort of sign, my rough soldier.'

'A sign.' He was afraid that she might be too fragile after all to contain all his dark hard love.

'That I give myself to you, like this? Why like this?'

'Because I ask it. To give yourself, like this, will be – a – sign.'

Truly, the music was glorious – glorious, it was part of him, he of it, notwithstanding that he could not sustain the simplest tune, was in fact tone deaf.

'And if it were to be tomorrow, or next week?'

'At your convenience? When you choose? No. It must be now.'

'You are very demanding.'

'Yes.' (I can love you only if you are magnificent, if you can submit to the tides, not if you are petty, make reservations, urge restraint, consider propriety, practise caution: you must be ready to sacrifice yourself for me, to stake everything on me: or else I cannot love you. I refuse to love a trivial woman.) He realized that she was not going to refuse, that something in his unreasonableness, in the insistence of his demand, made contact, mysteriously, with the essence of her womanliness. Oh powerful: who can refuse such a man? The act, the sign, now that it was imminent, was almost secondary to the elation of this triumph; the act was ceremonial, she must carry it out in accordance with his requirements of her, that was its importance and its meaning.

'We must move the sofa across the door,' she said. She helped him with it. While he was ensuring that it was firmly placed, she did something small and slight and practical under her dress, her back to him, unfastening, and there was a chortle of delight in him: Madame the Baroness makes ready for me.

'Come then, come.'

He became docile with astonishment at the dimensions of her generosity.

Eyes half-closing, lips cooling, hands holding his face: what a relief that she did not shatter, her fragile smile did not break, a relief to be so easily rid of all his dark gold. At the actual moment, he felt like giggling – with relief.

Watching him buttoning himself, a half grin complementing his moustache, outdoing it in self-congratulation, she said, 'Oh what a boy you are, my rough soldier.'

'You know,' the Baron said, 'with Leonie I have something I have never had before with a woman, Stefan. Peace of mind. Mind you, I do not say that Leonie is incapable of being unfaithful; the man who says that of any woman is a fool; but what I do say is – Leonie is incapable of lying. She cannot lie. If she has to tell the smallest lie, a dramaturgic event takes place on her face, she has no talent for concealment, absolutely none. If you want to be happy with a woman, Stefan, pick one who is a bad actress. I can tell everything that goes on in Leonie. Nothing she feels or does can she keep from me. Of course, perhaps, too, I have the experience to be capable of understanding a woman like Leonie, that is important, if a woman is understood she will keep nothing from you, the desire to be understood – it is a passion, Stefan, strong as any other. A woman's deepest need is to be understood by a man. You know, I am considerably older than Leonie, but we have a good marriage. I don't say we haven't had difficulties – what marriage hasn't? – but we overcome them because we are able to discuss them, openly, like civilized beings. There is nothing that cannot be discussed between reasonable people. That is my belief in all matters.'

'I quite agree, Felix.'

Shortly after midnight, when Stefan had just fallen asleep, there was a loud banging on the door. Opening it, he found Wirthof slowly sliding towards the ground from his leaning position against the doorpost, an expression of concentrated inanity on his face.

'Ah –' he said, 'you were a devilish long time, Kazakh.'

'I was in bed.'

'I got you out of bed?' It was not, by the most generous interpretation, in the nature of an apology, but rather an expression of astonishment, as if he had fully expected Stefan to be waiting up for him to hear his news. He was quite drunk, red-eyed, a faint line of contempt for the entire sleeping population of Vienna on his lips.

'Well, what d'you want, Wirthof?'

'What do I want!' He was immediately deeply hurt by this tone of voice, but, with the magnanimity of the triumphant, forgave Stefan. 'Ah – Kazakh, you have no idea. She is the most fantastic woman. Truly, she is incredible. She is . . . she is . . .' he shook his head and smiled, the possessor of incommunicable knowledge. Recovering his composure, shaking himself slightly, and assuming his most philosophical attitude, he said, 'What is so extraordinary, Kazakh, is that I love her. Consider what an extraordinary statement that is for me to make. Had you suggested the possibility a week ago I would have dismissed it out of hand. That I should desire Leonie Koeppler, that, yes; that she should desire me – that she should give herself to me, in a loge at the Opera, during a performance of *Tannhäuser*, in the second act, is improbable but not unfeasible, you will agree? That she should be, magnificently, everything one could have wished – Kazakh! – ahh – Kazakh, she came while I kissed her, before even I entered her she came, I tell you I brought her on with a kiss. She has cold lips, but between her thighs she burns. What a heat that woman has. A melting pot. You know – you know these young girls, they give out a thin, viscous fluid, pleasant enough, sufficient, but with Leonie it is an inundation, a rich foam, the heat comes out of her as from an oven. She told me she has been for days like this, ever since she first saw me, in this liquid, heated state, when she undressed at night the material of her clothing, her underwear brushing her pubis, brushing against her little swollen bud, the silky touch, was almost enough. She told me that, Kazakh; she told me that she – she – no, no, it is too personal – that she – oh I must tell you – it's fabulous – she thought of me, you see – was it any surprise I should be able to make her come with a kiss, when she was so ready for me. Kazakh, I put it to you – is it not a sign of great passion when a woman tells you such things? She had been longing for me, for days, putting on her nightdress, parting her thighs and holding the silk taut between them, pressing against the taut silk, holding the silk tight over her thighs and pressing her little swollen bud against it, moving, can you imagine, Kazakh, just the slight back and forth, back and forth –'

He was in a state of erotic stupefaction: impossible to tell how much of this was imagining and how much true –

'Wirthof, if you can possibly contain yourself, I would point out that it's after midnight and I have to sleep.'

That thin line of contempt formed on his face at the idea of people who have to sleep at night and keep regular hours and impregnate their wives in the marital bed; how superior he was to all that, he who had had Leonie, Baroness Koeppler, in Loge B at the Opera, during *Tannhäuser*, magnificent coup.

Unperturbed by Stefan's protestations, he slumped into a chair, a drunken, happy, bemused expression on his face, as if intending to go to sleep right there, and then sat up rigid. 'Yes, I know what I came to ask. Kazakh, you are seeing the Baron tomorrow, you are dining with them. She will give you a message for me. She will give you a message where we can meet.'

'Am I to be your messenger?'

'Oh but you must.' He was suddenly deeply concerned. 'We depend on you, you are our link, our contact, without you we have no contact. If I have said anything, anything that was coarse, or disrespectful to her, I assure you it was not meant. If I speak of what happened between us it is not from lack of feeling – on the contrary – on the contrary – it is – it is – that I regard no topic as being beyond the scope of discussion, even Leonie, between . . . between men of honour.' He gave a slight hiccup, slid further down in the armchair, and went fast asleep.

I did not envy him his affair; he paid for his moment of triumph, not that she was unkind to him, it was not in her nature to be, but nor was it in her nature to be reliable or consistent.

Wirthof in love was, if anything, more insufferable than Wirthof on the rampage. He could not stop talking about Leonie, her actual or imagined attributes. 'It is true, Kazakh, it is true: only by going through the pit of carnality can one attain to true spirituality. The paradox is true. No, no, spare me, please, your logical rebuttals. Kazakh, I know, I *know*. You do not understand such things, Kazakh, you are too logical. It is what I have always maintained, if one acts in honour there is no degradation, there is no degradation when there is honour.'

'That is just a way of saying it is not dark when it is light. With that proposition I quite agree.'

Wirthof's adulation of Leonie was accompanied by an enormous increase in his self-esteem, which had not ever been small; to be loved by such a woman confirmed him in his conceit; and as his estimation of himself rose in proportion to her remarkableness, he made her very remarkable indeed, he deified her almost, attributing to her ever more fantastical qualities.

'You cannot understand a woman like Leonie with logic,' he asserted. 'There are people who are not subject to it. Your mundane little theories of causality are completely shattered by a woman like Leonie, who has true mystery. I can only tell you, Kazakh, that when I fuck Leonie, I understand the universal equation.'

'Yes, what is it?'

'It is not the sort of understanding you can communicate.'

'You mean it is only when *you* fuck Leonie that it happens. It wouldn't happen to anyone else fucking Leonie. Because if that were the case then a rather large number of people ought to understand the universal equation.'

'You are a mocker, Kazakh. And I'd rather you didn't use that sort of language in relation to Leonie.'

'But you use it.'

'It's different when I use it. I use it reverentially, not coarsely.'

'Well, I am sure I have as much respect for Leonie as you have.'

'You only respect her position, the external trappings. You do not respect her essence.'

'What on earth is that?'

'You see – and you pretend to know her.'

His euphoria did not last; knowing Leonie, Stefan realized that the let-down would have to come, she could not continue to be totally absorbed with someone like Wirthof. Whatever he had meant to her in the box at the Opera, this was not sufficient basis for a long relationship, and more and more frequently she made excuses for not being able to see him. Usually it was Stefan who had to relay these excuses to Wirthof, who, at first, pretended to see nothing disturbing in her inability to meet him as arranged; she was a married woman, her life was complex, she longed to see him but clearly it wasn't always possible; his conceit did not allow him to realize that he was being dropped, discarded, as other dazzling young men had been taken up and discarded. It took him some time to catch on. When for perhaps the fifth time in a row she had cancelled their meeting, he suddenly said, 'Do you think, Kazakh, that she's trying to get rid of me? No, it's not possible!'

'It *is* a possibility.'

The collapse of his self-esteem was as quick and spectacular as a great marquee coming down when the tension of the supporting ropes is relaxed.

'What could I have done? What on earth could it be? In what way have I failed her? Can one really love, and be over it so soon? No, she could never have loved me, that is the only explanation.'

With stiff dignity, fatalistically, he accepted her decision; his pride would not allow him to protest or to plead; if – he told Stefan – she did not ask to see him he would not seek to see her. That was the end of it. Every day he called on Stefan and asked, 'Well, did you see Leonie, did she say anything? Is there a message?' And every time, Stefan replied, 'She says nothing, Wirthof.

Her children are in Vienna just now. She *is* very busy. Of course, I didn't see her alone, it would have been difficult for her to give me a message for you.'

'She always used to manage.'

'Yes, that's true. But her children weren't here. There was always a moment when she and I could be alone. Now – I only see her when Felix or the children or others are present.'

Poor Wirthof. What did he understand of someone like Leonie. It must have been the first time in his life something had happened to him that he felt he couldn't entirely control. It came as a profound shock. One might have pitied him had he not done it for you. His pale face grew paler; he drank enormously, solemnly, with gathered brow, indulging himself in an orgy of silent suffering. At least he did not talk so much, which was something. With his inclination for posturing before himself, he was conscious all the time, even in moods of deepest dejection, of the impression he created. And – and by this I do not mean that his suffering was not genuine – he derived some satisfaction from the fact that he was going to pieces so convincingly, so classically. He could stand outside himself and watch the signs of disintegration and say yes, yes, this is how it happens, I have seen it on the stage, I have read it in Goethe – ah! the sufferings of young Konrad. He had the ability to put his unhappiness into one of those little boxes of his mind and label it Leonie; it was his fate, its cause was outside himself. If I suggested to him that his unhappiness was disproportionate – that it was irrational of him to have expected happiness of such a situation, that it was illogical to expect consistency of a woman whose act of giving herself to him was itself an expression of her inconsistency – he merely looked at me pityingly, and said, 'You cannot understand such things. It is beyond your understanding. A few weeks ago I could not have understood it myself. She has told me that she loves me, and there are times, Kazakh, when a woman cannot deceive.'

'Perhaps she did love you at that moment, or thought she did, or would have liked to think she did, or would have liked you to think that she did and so convinced herself.'

'You are a terrible cynic, Kazakh.'

'Well, if you are so desperately unhappy, why don't you do something about it? Try to see her.'

'No. If she doesn't want to see me, I would not impose myself. I don't think one can honourably do that.'

'Oh you and your ridiculous honour. In that case, the only thing left for you to do is to shoot yourself.' I had said it flippantly, but he took it seriously.

'I have considered that,' he said.

I burst out laughing, he was so comical in the solemn way he said it; a smile that strove to be sardonic curled up the edges of his moustache, which I noted was still meticulously trimmed; indeed his usual meticulousness of dress had in no way suffered as a result of his despair. He swallowed down another schnapps, emptying the contents of the small glass into his mouth with a simple sharp tilt, jerking his head back to swallow, and immediately refilled the glass from the bottle in front of him.

'At this rate,' I said, 'you won't need to shoot yourself.'

He grinned, gratified that I was giving a measure of credence to his threats.

'As you know, Kazakh, I have never attached much value to life, per se. I do not regard it of supreme importance that I should remain alive. When my life becomes intolerable I shall have not the slightest hesitation in ending it. It has not, as yet, become utterly intolerable – though it might, it might at any time and then I shall know what to do.' He lit one of his oval Turkish cigarettes, took a disdainful puff, got up, screwing up his eyes like a man peering through a sandstorm, and tried to establish the whereabouts of the men's toilet. He managed only three or four steps before, his legs and stomach giving out at the same time, he collapsed into a pool of his own vomit. I had to pick him up, and get him home; somehow he had become my responsibility; I couldn't just leave him there. Not that he ever thanked me for such attentions, he accepted them as his due, the way he accepted that there had always been, and would always be, servants to clean up his messes.

Something else had happened at this time that affected him though he would not have admitted it. His little sister, who was now seventeen or eighteen, had become engaged. The young man's father owned, among other businesses, a number of high-class men's hairdressing establishments, and though the son was studying to be an industrial chemist to Wirthof he was always 'that barber of yours'.

'Konrad, he's not a barber, you mustn't call him that, he's a scientist . . .' his sister protested.

'You little idiot, Katty. He comes from a long line of barbers. His father started as a barber. His grandfather was a barber. He has barber's blood flowing in his veins, you think a few years at a university changes that. He will spawn barbers in you. Whatever he does, he will always have the mentality of a barber, because that is what he is. And if that's what you want – you a Wirthof – I'm not your guardian, as it happens, or *I* would never permit it. That fool uncle of mine has said yes, it has nothing to do with me. My mother's brother – not even a Wirthof. I wash my hands of it. But I never thought that my sister – a Wirthof – would marry a barber!'

'Oh Konrad, why are you so nasty to me? I love him. He's sweet and intelligent, and I love him.'

'Will he cut my hair gratis, do you think?'

'Oh Konrad, stop it, stop it, why are you so cruel?'

'Does he do it well, Katty? Does he stroke your fur and make you hot?'

'Konrad, you're horrible. Horrible. I shan't talk to you.'

'Does he get you excited, little? Does he? Does the barber get you worked up? How are you going to explain to him? These tradesmen have conventional minds, you know. He'll expect his bride to be *virgo intacta*. You think he'll believe you if you tell him you did it yourself, with your own tiny little fingers.'

'It happened riding,' she said, straight-faced. 'It is well known that it can happen riding.'

'Oh I see, oh I see! You've told him that? I see. And he believes it. Well, that shows what a fool he is. He thinks that? Doesn't know what a little firebrand he's getting.'

'Konrad, when I was small certain things happened, but now it's different, I'm grown up ...'

'Oh – you're grown up, are you? Is that so? Little Katty hot-fur is grown up, is she? Doesn't want to have her fur stroked any more now she's grown up?'

'My fiancé, Konrad, is a highly passionate man. I shall have babies and I shall be very happy.'

'Oh he's passionate, is he? The barber of Semmering, the simmering barber of Semmering.'

'His father has a place in the Kärntnerstrasse, it's a very nice, high-class place.'

'Oh – is that so? How d'you know he's so passionate, Katty?

176

Have you felt him? Does he give you a shampoo, your simmering barber of Semmering?'

'I won't talk to you, I won't talk to you if you speak like that. Why aren't you nice to me, Konrad? Be nice to me. Please, please. Oh! Konrad, *please* be nice to me, you used to be nice to me. I want you to love me still. I want you to love little Katty, say I can marry him, say you give your permission . . .'

'You don't need my permission, as it happens.'

'But I want your permission. Permission granted – hmm? Hmm? Say permission granted. Oh, Konrad, please. Say permission granted.' She put her arms around him, pressing her head to his chest, looking appealingly into his eyes. He stroked her face, and lightly kissed the side of her nose. 'Very well. Very well. Permission granted,' he said.

'Oh thank you,' she exclaimed, jumping away and doing a little dance of joy. 'Thank you, thank you. Oh, thank you, Konrad.'

All autumn Wirthof made no attempt to see Leonie – his pride would not allow it – and Stefan noticed a change in him, a greater quietness, as if having gone through the noisy show of raging against fate, he had finally realized that it was indifferent both to his threats and to his sufferings. The discovery that he could not order the universe came as a bitter blow to him, but it made him quieter. Such pain as he was feeling (and his capacity for tolerating pain of any sort was minuscule) he kept to himself; perhaps in one of those boxes of his mind he had found some unsuspected reserve of fortitude, or perhaps he had read another book and adopted what seemed to him the more attractive posture of renunciation.

'You know, Kazakh,' he said, drinking his beer, which was all that he drank now in this new mood of self-denial, 'there is something about the desires of the flesh that is undignified. Don't you agree? It is all too desperate. Absurdly so. There are deeper satisfactions, simpler pleasures . . .'

'Oh yes?'

'Yes. Nature – the countryside. Don't laugh – you know I was hardly aware that it existed. Do you know, Kazakh, that there are such things as trees. Do you know, do you realize, what shattering things trees are? They grow. They put out leaf. Quite calmly. The other day, Kazakh, I sat up in bed and looked at the tree outside my window – it has always been there of course, but I never noticed it before – and I thought: what are you so calm about, you have a male part and a female part, the seeds of discontent are in you, but you are quite calm about it. You do not tear yourself up by the roots in a frenzy of longing. Kazakh, there is a great deal to be said for asceticism, I am serious. Renunciation is also a passion, and on a higher plane than those passions of the flesh that can be so irksome. Do you know that Gandhi demonstrates his asceticism by having two beautiful naked girls share his bed every night. Virgins – *intactae*! Such self-denial has a definite appeal. Don't you agree?'

'I think you are getting over Leonie.'

'There you are wrong. I shall never be "over" her, as you put it. But there can be great love in denial.' He frowned solemnly. 'I wouldn't mind seeing her again. Even if only on the Gandhi principle, you know.'

Wirthof would occasionally drop in at Gerstner's to treat himself to their delicious chocolate-filled cakes with Schlagobers. He liked this place where the air was heavy with the sweetness of confectionery of every kind; the waiters had a special servitude, they understood the nature of the weakness they were catering to, knew exactly with what indulgent smiles and conspiratorial nods the cake-eater's greed could be promoted and her (for as a generic type the cake-eater is female) guilt alleviated. Wirthof sometimes had three or four cakes, a deepening smile passing between himself and the waiters, those white-haired, collusive waiters. He normally ate very little, sometimes for days taking no more nourishment than scrambled eggs and coffee, but pastries were his weakness. If he found himself near the Kärntnerstrasse in the late afternoon, he'd stop, stroke his chin, smile to himself, and ponder whether he should go to Gerstner's to have a cake.

It was mid-December, and though there was no snow on the ground Wirthof wore his snow boots and his fur-lined greatcoat; the street was busy with Christmas shoppers, and the window at Gerstner's was taken up by a scene of confectionery snowmen, with almond noses, having a snowball battle with marzipan, chocolate-capped children. He went inside and took a small table for one by the window, and the waiter who came to serve him gave him a smile of complete understanding. Most of the others in the place were women – hatted, nose-veiled, fast chattering, fast eating: they were constantly dabbing the crumbs and the cream from their mouths and chins with exquisite little embroidered napkins. And their eyes, in which the saga of their losing struggle against temptation was being chronicled, kept wandering up and down the different tiers of the silver cake stands and the pastry trolleys.

Wirthof was finishing his second cake when he saw Leonie in the street below; for a moment he thought she was going to come up; she had paused to look at Gerstner's window, but she smiled and went on. Putting money down on the table, he quickly got up and rushed down to the street, fearful that he might lose her in the crush of Christmas shoppers. She had paused at a shop window only two or three doors further on, and as he came towards her he was hoping that she would look up and see him; he wanted the sign of recognition – the first word – to come from her. She did look up but only when he was almost bumping into her; for a moment she looked startled, then quickly recovering she offered him her hand to kiss.

'Konrad,' she said, 'how pale you look. Are you ill?'

'Not especially.' His greater than normal pallor, on this occasion, was from the excitement of seeing her. Her face, fresh, cool, many faceted, crystalline, was an aggregate of unspecifiable things. Her first words, about his pallor, pleased him: they indicated concern. Nothing had been formally broken off between them, but it was weeks since they had been together and they did not immediately know how to deal with each other. Her curious examination of him told her nothing, for he had that ballroom mask of the smiling gallant.

'Why haven't I seen you?' he inquired lightly, formally.

'I have been very busy. My children have been staying with me . . .' She gave him a quick glance, wondering if this was the way to handle it, stick to generalities, explain nothing . . .

'You are looking wonderfully well,' he said.

'We are going to spend Christmas in Paris,' she said. 'I think Paris is lovely at Christmas time. And there are some exhibitions I want to see.'

'Won't you have a coffee with me?' he asked.

'I don't think I can, I'm in a terrible hurry.'

'Yes,' he said, 'you looked it, stopping at each window.'

'You've been following me?'

'Only since Gerstner's. I was upstairs eating a cake when I saw you "dash" by. Where is it you are dashing off to? I will get a cab and drop you wherever you want to go.'

She laughed. 'I am not going anywhere this minute. I was looking for presents for the children.'

'Then walk with me.'

Leonie saw that his clamorous greedy need of her (which would accept no denial and no holding back) had become modified: that he was accepting her position, her refusals, her separateness from him. She thought he had progressed. She looked at him with renewed interest. She had left something of herself in him, something that she had thought lost and terribly damaged, and it was a great surprise and relief to see from his attitude that, on the contrary, he had cherished and preserved what she had left him, and that it was intact. At the top of the Kärntnerstrasse, by the Stephansdom, he bought a bag of roast chestnuts from a street vendor, and as she did not want to dirty her gloves he shelled the chestnuts for her and placed them, with formal gallantry, at her mouth. He did not attempt to touch her, he was going out of his way to be meticulously correct; if they had been observed there was nothing in his attitude to indicate any kind of intimacy between them. The business of the chestnuts was perhaps a little playful, a little flirtatious, but so open, and such a formalized flirtation, as to be innocuous. Secret liaisons were not conducted in the open Kärntnerstrasse.

Unexpectedly, Leonie was enjoying his company, and the walk – a thin frost had given a patchy glitter to things: it highlighted parts of roofs, the shoulders and helmets of black lead forms, the grass, the sides of tree trunks, the shaped hedges, the intricate ironwork of street lamps. The air was sharp and clear, very cold, invigorating on the cheeks and in the nostrils. The wintry atmosphere of Vienna – the men in broad double-breasted, wide-collared overcoats and otter or Persian lamb hats, the delicate tracery of bare trees: she was pleased with Vienna, with herself, with her soldier. The fact that she was stealing half an hour, perhaps longer, from her schedule, that appointments would have to be rearranged, apologies and excuses made, gave her the feeling that these moments she was having with him were precious and limited. She was amazed, and pleased, to discover in herself a new emotion: is it possible that I am really in love with him? That he can make me feel romantic? Someone like me? Oh what nonsense, Leonie Koeppler. He has kept me with him in a good way, without rage: he has preserved me.

They walked along the Graben, and turned into Dorotheergasse, and Leonie paused to look in the windows of small art galleries and silverware shops. They took the Stallburggasse to the Michaelerplatz and walked through the wrought-iron arch of the Hofburg, out into the Heldenplatz. They walked among the skeletal trees, by the frozen grass, in the grounds of the old Imperial winter palace. She kept looking at him with surprised and pleased eyes, detecting qualities of charm and attractiveness in him that she had quite discounted. Perhaps there were even qualities of tenderness in him: inside himself he had cherished her, when she had behaved so badly to him. And he had behaved with honourableness. Never bothering her, never pestering her with demands and protests: he had accepted the termination of the affair with soldierly fortitude. My soldier. She took his arm gladly.

'You haven't asked me – why?' she declared.

He smiled. 'Why, Baroness?' That smirk of his, however, was intolerable.

'I did not mean you to ask, you mustn't ask, I only meant to comment on the fact that you hadn't asked, and that impresses me.'

'I am glad I impress you in some way, Baroness.'

'How handsome you are, Konrad. I had hardly noticed previously. You make me think of the young Raphael. But pale, so pale. Why so pale, my soldier?'

'Pining,' he said lightly, smiling, making a gallantry of it.

'But you were always so pale.'

'I suppose previously because I hadn't met you, and then I pined because I might lose you, and then because I had lost you.'

'Oh such silly talk.'

'You look wonderfully well, Leonie.'

'I am *quite* well. I am always *quite* well. My life, you know, is an endless series of minor catastrophes, all very occupying and annoying and depressing. Nothing major however. I am glad to say. You do not really see me like that, do you, Konrad?'

'Isn't it time you allowed something major to happen to you, Baroness?'

'Oh no. For that I am much too clever. I am a very pampered woman, you know, Konrad. Such things you wouldn't know about. But I am finicky about the temperature of my bath, the number of minutes my soft-boiled egg is cooked in the morning, the way a dinner table is laid. I cannot stand bad taste. It is an affront to me. There are houses we never go to because the draperies make me feel physically sick.' She laughed at herself. 'That is a slight exaggeration, of course, but only a slight one. It is not that I demand costly and fine things around me. I am perfectly happy with very simple things. But they must be good. If we lend a picture for an exhibition and a blank space is left on the wall, it offends me. I am restless and unhappy until I have found another picture to occupy that space. If the picture comes back slightly damaged, it is a catastrophe for a few hours. Sometimes I think that all the minor catastrophes of my life are a kind of magical offering I make, to ward off the big major catastrophe that I feel might otherwise overwhelm me. My life, Konrad, is too complicated, too intricate, and too pleasant, to be turned inside out. I don't want anything major to happen to me, do you understand?' She laughed. 'I am a coward, of course. The faint whiff of danger is enough for me, an erotic stimulant, yes: it is enough: I do not need the reality, all the awful sordid, squalid emotionalism – jealousy, recrimination, charges and counter-charges. There is no room in my life for that. You see, in a roundabout way I have answered what I forbade you to ask. This is not something I am proud of, Konrad, but I know myself well enough: my passions, like my catastrophes, are minor, and soon over. I don't mean that unkindly to you.'

He paused and made her turn her face to him and look at him directly, and he spoke intently, 'Leonie, you are not this woman you describe. You are not this finicky woman who indulges herself in minor love affairs because she is afraid of anything that might disrupt the agreeable routine of her existence. You pretend to be this person. But the Leonie I know is completely above and beyond such mundane considerations. *She* is magnificent. No, no, you mustn't protest or argue. I will not have it otherwise. I know. I know this Leonie better than you do. You know the other one, the boring one who doesn't interest me, the one who fusses about the temperature of her bath water. That's not my Leonie. My Leonie is magnificent. That other one is the Baroness Koeppler, let her have her lukewarm baths, let the Jew have *her* . . .'

'Konrad . . .'

'. . . the other one, Baroness, is mine. What has once been given cannot be taken away. I have her. I have her more than you have her, because you want to deny her very existence. How can she, my Leonie, breathe in that choking atmosphere? My Leonie is entirely magnificent – she comes when I kiss her.' He was close to her. He made no effort to touch her.

'Oh vain, vain!' she accused him. 'Does that truly thrill you? That you could have had that effect on me.'

'Of course. And you? Doesn't it thrill you – *you, my* Leonie – to remember that? Doesn't it make you tremble a little, doesn't it . . . ?'

He touched her upper lip lightly with the knuckle of his hand, lightly, lightly, frosted lips, white breath clouds like engine steam between them, pluming and hissing, the body engine breathing like a locomotive: warm inside her upper lip, warm, moist, sharp teeth: where, where?

'Shall I kiss *my* Leonie?'

'Yes.'

When she had sufficiently recovered herself to appreciate the stupidity of allowing him to kiss her so publicly, where she might be recognized by anyone, they thought about where to go, and the only place they could think of that would be safe was Stefan's flat.

He was insistent when he burst into my office. 'Kazakh, you can't refuse. I met her purely by chance. I only had to see her – I knew – and it was the same as before. We must be together, Kazakh. You cannot refuse.' When I returned home two and a half hours later the flat was empty, undisturbed, nothing out of place – perhaps they hadn't been there after all. In the bedroom, however, nose twitching, he sensed their recent presence, the grey bachelor room was changed by their passion; he threw himself down on the bed, chest pumping, and then sprang up again immediately because the bed seemed to be heaving, and when he went to the bathroom he froze at the door with a premonition of naked bodies. They had left some aura of themselves in all the rooms they had used, though everything was meticulously tidy, not an object had been moved, they had left no tangible traces. It was always like this, on later occasions when circumstances obliged them to use Stefan's flat. Sometimes when he returned they were still there. He had to have an attitude then, to see him through the ensuing conversation. He found it always an uncomfortable situation, one of the few that he had difficulty in handling. Several times he said to them, 'I don't think you should involve me in your affair. It's very unfair of you to put me in that position. Felix is a friend of mine. It is a terrible betrayal of his friendship for me to be doing this for you. What you do is your concern, Leonie, but you are very unfair to involve me, to make these requests of me.'

'Oh, sometimes you are a bore, Stefan. All right, we won't come here again. If that is how you feel. Oh you are so pompous, Stefan.' She was angry and cold-eyed, in high dudgeon, and immediately he climbed down, feeling impelled to placate her. 'Look Leonie. Don't get in such a huff. You are very unreasonable. You must understand how I feel. What you do is your concern, you are right, it has nothing to do with me. Let us leave it like that.'

Their affair was constantly being broken off and restarted; it was not continuous; there was always the seduction, a repetition of the original seduction, followed by days or weeks of meetings and partings leading up to the final parting, the final parting, the one that she would not go back on. So their affair was a series of breathless seductions, followed by several more and more gloomy meetings when their bodies' fever was an attempt to rid themselves of the heavy weight of their next inevitable parting; then came the crisis of the parting itself, permanent this time as always, and indeed it was sometimes as permanent as three or four months, during which time a tenuous and secret contact was maintained through Stefan, who saw them both. 'Oh, Stefan,' Leonie said, 'you should have stopped me, why did you ever allow me to get so involved in such a ridiculous affair.' And Wirthof would say, 'Yes, I am glad it is over. She is too marvellous to have to suffer. There is a great purity of spirit in her and I cannot bear to see that tarnished by secrecy and lying and deception. She does not have the strength to break free, I pity her for that, but I forgive her.' 'How very magnanimous of you, Wirthof.' 'I feel nothing but magnanimity towards her,' he declared perfectly seriously. 'Whatever she does, she has infinite credit with me. She is one of those people who, whatever she does, will always be able to rely on me implicitly. I feel absolutely responsible for her.' 'Would you marry her?' 'Of course. If she were free. But marriage is not essential. You understand, Kazakh, I do not say that I will be always faithful to her, I am not, even now I am not, after all a man is a man, with a man's appetites. In some way what I have with Leonie is outside all of that, it is on a different level, you understand. This is something you will almost certainly not understand, Kazakh, but Leonie can make great demands on me, whatever happens between us. That *is* permanent, and not dependent on her. You understand? No, of course not, it's not logical, it's not common-sensical.'

It was difficult to tell with Wirthof whether something he said was factually true or only an aspiration; if he experienced a sudden overwhelming longing to attain nobility, he was already – in that instant – noble; if he wished to love Leonie permanently, irrespective of her attitude to him, it was an accomplished fact that he did; in his posturing and attitudinizing it was difficult to tell whether he was deceiving you, or himself, or both you and himself, or pretending, or, or, or: the deception within the deception was endlessly perpetuated in him; trying to come to any definite rational conclusion about his real attitude to anything, or anybody, had the same brain-numbing effect as struggling with some conundrum about mirrors within mirrors and their multiplying images. One stopped coming to conclusions about him, or rather confined one's conclusions to the moment.

Part Three

At the Villa Berghof, in Berchtesgaden, Kurt von Schuschnigg, the gracious, courteous, clerical-fascist Chancellor of Austria looked into the opaque eyes of Adolf Hitler and said – the state of the world looks rather promising, don't you think? Yes, and he said something about Beethoven, about Beethoven having chosen to live in Austria, which did not impress Adolf Hitler. And he remarked on the view from Hitler's study, a gracious compliment. And he was struck by the exceptionally fine Dürer Madonna ('my favourite picture because it is so thoroughly German,' Hitler said). And he thought that the young SS men in snow-white steward's uniforms who served lunch were remarkably handsome. He was dying for a smoke all the time, but Hitler wouldn't allow him to smoke in his presence. Supposing he'd lit a cigarette, during lunch. Excuse me, Herr Reichskanzler, I feel like a smoke. Supposing. Supposing he had. I feel like a smoke. How can you defy a tyrant if you're dying for a smoke? And he was a chain-smoker, Kurt von Schuschnigg. Not one all day. Like asking a man to be brave when his bowels are opening.

'I am carried along by the love of my people,' says Adolf Hitler. 'I am quite willing to believe that,' says Schuschnigg, dying for a smoke. Could I ask him? Do you happen to have such a thing as a cigarette, Herr Reichskanzler? Herr Schuschnigg, people who smoke in my presence are shot, shot instantly. Why do you think I have three generals here? Anyone found smoking in my presence is liquidated – I can quite believe that, Herr Reichskanzler. You are a liar, Schuschnigg. I would point out, Herr Reichskanzler, if you will allow me, that you are right and I will do my utmost. 'After the Army, my SA and Austrian Legion would move in, and nobody can stop their just revenge – not even I,' screams Hitler. I wonder if we might agree, Herr Reichskanzler, that if I give you Austria you will give me a cigarette. Your demands, Schuschnigg, are unreasonable and impertinent. I don't know why I don't have you shot this minute. I will not hear of conditions. Germany is a great nation, I have been chosen by destiny to lead Germany along her historic role. I have made the greatest achievement in the history of Germany, greater than any other German. NO, you cannot have a cigarette. That is most kind of you, Herr Reichskanzler, allow me to express my appreciation.

Schuschnigg was not a coward, but when he looked into the opaque eyes of Adolf Hitler he was lost. How can you talk to a man whose eyes are a dead end. Panic. The eyes are a wall at the end of a maze: you will never find your way back. Panic. O God, if only I had a cigarette. The eyes of Thanatos. You could have died, Schuschnigg. No, it's not as easy as that, dying is the least of it. On your head be it, Adolf Hitler, on your head. You have the eyes of Thanatos. I will not shed Austrian blood. I will not spill the blood of my countrymen. On your head, on your head. And the opaque eyes of Adolf Hitler say yes – his genius! – it is on *my* head, I will spill your blood, Herr Schuschnigg. You are most generous, Herr Reichskanzler – ah! the magnanimity, the greatness, the relief. If only I'd had a cigarette. It is on his head, on his head.

They came soon afterwards, as expected, those clean-looking men with the smell of refuse on their breath. They came in their brown and black uniforms, and in their field grey. I watched them coming. They took over as germs take over an unresistant body. They came with cannons and baggage and trucks and horses and field kitchens, they came unopposed – on their heads it was. The soldiers with their steel helmets low on their foreheads – squat heavy, Germanic, those heavy helmets, obscuring the face, obliterating much of the head, its shape, its flesh, its physiognomy, their young heads bearing the sombre weight. Adolf Hitler re-entering his birthplace, and seventy thousand had been arrested to make his entry safe. There was jubilation. The flags were out. Where did so many flags come from? Every house along the route of Hitler's triumphal entry of the city was bedecked, every child on the route, it seemed, had a flag. The bowels perceived what the mind did not grasp: a monstrous intrusion, an alien iron in the body, a sodomy. Anschluss, it was called. General Zehner was murdered, the generals were arrested or sacked, reliable officers were exchanged with those in German divisions – it was done with expertise. Seven Austrian divisions were added to Hitler's strength.

One of the first to be arrested was Baron Koeppler, and his flat – in fact, the entire building – was taken over by the SS.

When the Baron was arrested there came into force an arrangement he had made with me long before in anticipation of such an eventuality; this arrangement gave me power of attorney to use certain funds, and to utilize the facilities of the Koeppler network of interests, for the purpose of obtaining his release. In effect, I was his nominee in the negotiations with the Nazis. He had appointed me to this position the night of *Tannhäuser*, when I had dinner with him at the Sacher. He had said then that he needed someone he could trust implicitly to act on his behalf in the event that he was arrested by the Nazis on one of his trips to Germany. (He had not then specifically anticipated a Nazi take-over of Austria.) In the event of his arrest, it was essential that someone other than himself should be able to set in motion the mechanism for obtaining his release. It was important that this someone should be (a) completely trustworthy, (b) unconnected with his companies – since it was possible that all the leading members of his companies might be arrested simultaneously, (c) a person who would not easily be intimidated and could negotiate with boldness, (d) someone who should not appear to have too much power, as then he might himself be exposed to torture, intimidation, blackmail, etc. I filled the bill. If, for instance, he had appointed to this role one of his prominent associates, the Nazis would assume they could obtain whatever they wanted by putting sufficient pressure on him. But if I were the negotiator, they would have no way of knowing the precise extent of my power, and would recognize the uselessness of trying to intimidate me. It was the Baron's own plan; we discussed it that night at the Sacher, and worked out the details on subsequent occasions, and as the plan grew and took shape he became excited by its many subtleties and we did not think of the actual circumstance that would bring it into operation. He was very pleased with his plan. It was gone over again and again. It made him feel safe. Having this plan, he felt free to visit Germany whenever he needed to, secure in the knowledge that should he be arrested, immediately a complex mechanism of financial retaliation would be set in motion that only his immediate release could halt. Of course he did not believe that his plan would ever have to be put into force, but it was a wonderful plan all the same, and it seemed almost a pity if it was never used.

When the Nazis came for Felix, he was calm – did he not have a perfect plan? indeed he did – and he seemed even to obtain some sly satisfaction from discomfiting the two Gestapo men by asking them to sit down. In a sitting position it is for some reason more difficult to arrest a man, especially if you are unaccustomed to sitting on a narrow Second Empire settee with winged lion sides. They had both been motioned into the same settee, which proved not really wide enough to accommodate their joint bulk. They looked like overgrown schoolboys waiting in the headmaster's study as Felix with deliberate slowness went through the charade of writing something on sheets of paper in the large red leather portfolio decorated with his crest. When Leonie came into the room, he further disconcerted the two men by introducing her to them; and then he kissed his wife on the cheek, and said, 'Chérie, these gentlemen have asked me to accompany them to the Metropole. "For questioning". It's outrageous, of course' – he smiled at the two men, absolving them, personally, of blame – 'but they have their instructions. Will you telephone Stefan and tell him what has happened.' And then, turning to the two men, he said, 'Shall we take my car, or yours?'

'I think our car, Herr Baron.'

'Very well. Very well.' He looked at his watch. 'I trust this will not take long. I have a luncheon appointment.'

'On that we have no instructions, Herr Baron.'

'Chérie, if I should be late, make my apologies to Dr Schaeling, and explain that I've been – detained.' He seemed amused by his pun, and indicated for the two men to go ahead of him, out through the high cream and gilt doors.

Leonie was not prepared for such a situation; she knew nothing of his plan, or of my part in it; and when she saw Felix in the wrought-iron cage of the lift, a Nazi lout on either side of him, she became hysterical.

When we had worked out the plan, at the Sacher and later, we had assumed that his arrest would be followed immediately by a confrontation with the authorities at which the nature of their demands would become known, and so a basis for bargaining would exist. This did not happen. When the Baron arrived at the Metropole he was subjected to a cursory cross-examination by a minor official, who noted biographical and other particulars on a printed form, and then told Felix that he was being detained until further instructions. He was taken to a small room at the top of the hotel. A sentry was posted inside this room, his rifle with the safety catch unlocked, his pistol holster open. The sentry was changed every hour. Felix was not allowed to talk to him, and was not permitted to go near the window; if he did, the sentry was instructed to shoot. During the night, his room was locked from the outside, and a sentry remained in the corridor. The following morning Felix was woken at six a.m. and told to wash himself: his guard watched; then he was made to clean the room, make his bed, sweep out, and dust the radiator, the window frame, the low table, the legs of the chairs. For this purpose he had to use the small towel with which he had dried himself. When he had finished, he was taken to an adjoining room, the guards' quarters, and made to clean that. He had to empty their washbasins and slop bucket, and to use his towel to wipe them dry. He asked for a fresh towel for himself, but the request was refused. He asked for a newspaper, and was told he could have the *Völkischer Beobachter*, but no other. His request for a radio was denied. He was however allowed to order whatever he wished for breakfast, provided he paid for it in advance, in cash. He had brought very little money with him, not being accustomed to carry large amounts in banknotes, and he calculated that he had enough for perhaps two or three meals at the hotel's scale of charges.

Immediately on hearing from Leonie what had happened, I telephoned the Metropole and asked to speak to someone in authority in connection with the case of Baron Koeppler. I was asked my name, address, telephone number and status; I said I was the Baron's representative; after a few minutes, during which some exchange was going on at the other end, a man came to the phone and said that if I was required I would be sent for. 'It is not a question of my being required,' I said, 'I insist on speaking to someone in authority now. Unless I am immediately connected with someone authorized in this matter, I shall hold you personally responsible. Kindly give me your name and rank.' There was another short consultation at the other end, and then the phone was put down. I spent the afternoon telephoning to government offices, the police department, the SS, Army headquarters – trying to find an official who at least showed some indication of knowing of the Baron's arrest. In the course of the next few days all my requests to be allowed to see him, or to talk to someone in authority in connection with his case, were refused; but at the Metropole I was told I might bring the Baron's pyjamas, toothbrush, a change of underwear, and shaving things, and that these articles would be given to him; also, I was permitted to pay for his meals, in cash, and a receipt was made out to me. Every day I telephoned the office of one of the Baron's companies in Zurich and spoke to an agitated director who demanded why I was not doing anything, what instructions I had for him, what action they should take; I had to tell him there was nothing that could be done for the present; every day the French and Swiss embassies in Vienna made inquiries of the Foreign Ministry for information as to the Baron's whereabouts and well-being, but as he was an Austrian national they had no official backing for their inquiries; they were told that the Baron was being detained pending certain investigations into his business affairs and associations. Throughout all this I remained calm; I might compare my calm to a certain kind of nightmare in which the dreamer is immune to terror because he knows he is dreaming, and has the power – he feels – to control the actual outcome of his dream: can always escape at the last minute, as the axe descends, as the ground gives way.

Leonie's state was worrying; she had always been so composed, never at a loss; the way her life was organized, with that tremendous energy of hers, carried the conviction that nothing could possibly happen that she would not be able to deal with by means of a telephone call, a word in the right ear, a letter to an important friend, a little of her incomparable string-pulling. Why, she knew absolutely everyone, senior ministers, high-ranking officials, statesmen. There was no one she didn't know. Most of us are to some extent accustomed to being at the mercy of bureaucracy, unfeeling officialdom, and know what it means to be passed from department to department, made to wait around, asked ridiculous questions, refused elucidation. This was something she had never experienced. And now these men of influence and power who had always responded to her requests, glad to be of service to her, either no longer had the power and influence, or else were fearful to exercise it on her behalf. She had become haggard, her many-faceted sparkle had dulled to a grey smear; she hardly ate, and the elegant slimness she had always cultivated was quickly transformed into the drawn look of sickness. Where were her reserves? She had none. She had expended herself, given too freely of her vitality, to her poets of death, among others. Maz, her old teacher, had gone with his entire entourage of students and relatives to Switzerland, she felt abandoned by him and everyone else who had left; and those who had stayed were as useless to her as she was to them. Indeed, she had to cope daily with others pestering her to use her influence – surely *she* must have influence – on their behalf, and when she told them she could do nothing, they regarded her suspiciously and bitterly: of course, only concerned with her own welfare!

When she wept, there was no outpouring, nothing to pour out, she was dry and gaunt and without substance inside herself, her sobbing was a scrabbling in a dry well.

As I repeatedly pointed out to her, we had many strong cards to play, once the Nazis got around to negotiating with us, and I told her that when someone with power was appointed to take charge of the case he would be confronted with our plan, and that meant we could step by step raise the cost to the Nazis of keeping the Baron imprisoned, and there must come a point when the cost to them outweighed whatever advantages there were in holding him. 'Look, Leonie, there are already at least four companies in Germany and Austria, of vital importance to the economy, who are finding themselves in difficulties because their credit has been cut off in several foreign countries. That step went into force the day of Felix's arrest. These companies will be putting pressure on the authorities. Besides, we have made other provisions. Funds are available. If necessary, a very large sum of money indeed will be paid in return for the safe release of you and Felix and the children. They're gangsters, and people like that can always be bought off. It isn't as if Felix is identified with any ideological opposition to them and therefore can't be released. It would serve absolutely no purpose for them to continue to hold him. What is going on at the moment is a wearing-down process, intimidation – to raise the level of the opening bid. I'm not worried, I really am not worried about Felix. But, if you like, send the children away, you'll feel better then.'

The presence of the children in Vienna, it seemed to me, gave the Nazis added powers of extortion, and from a purely practical point of view I was keen to have them out of the way: the fewer hostages, the lower the ransom. I was determined not to allow myself to be intimidated into starting the dealing with an excessively high bid. It was, after all, because the Baron relied on my not panicking that he had appointed me his negotiator. I said to Leonie that if she was going to send the children away, it was imperative to act immediately, while people were still allowed to leave, and before the Nazis got around to realizing that the presence of the children in Vienna gave them an additional hold over the Baron. In fact, I urged her to go too, saying there was no useful purpose she could serve by remaining, but of this she would not hear. 'That is out of the question,' she said, 'that I could not think of while they hold Felix. But I will send the children to Venice, with Mara.' Mara, her secretary, a competent and cultivated woman in normal circumstances, had been even more hysterical than Leonie. Mara did not seem to be the most suitable person to accompany the children, but she was fond of them, Leonie trusted her, and she was a one hundred per cent Aryan who would not arouse the suspicion of the border guards unless they had been alerted to watch out for the Koeppler children, which I was gambling that they hadn't. The difficulty was getting Mara sufficiently in possession of herself to undertake such a trip. At first she refused outright, bursting into tears every time it was suggested: she couldn't leave Leonie, she wasn't well, she couldn't accept the responsibility of the children on such a hazardous journey. Eventually we succeeded in calming her sufficiently, by plying her with champagne, to agree tearfully but with a sudden access of determination that she would do it. I noted with relief that the struggle to get Mara in possession of herself had had a beneficial effect on Leonie, who had for this purpose put her own fears aside. The hysteria was still there, in both of them, but it was held down for the moment.

Stefan had insisted that they arrive at the station by taxi, because the Baron's car would have aroused attention, and he had also laid down that the children and Mara must take the absolute minimum of luggage, no more than they would have taken for a long week-end. The luggage, he had ruled, must be plain and cheap, the Koeppler's monogrammed leather suitcases were out of the question. The children must have nothing obviously expensive with them. It was hard making Lea leave the gold wristwatch that her father had bought her for her eighth birthday only a few months ago, she didn't see why she had to give it up and wear the plain chrome watch that Leonie gave her in its stead; Friedrich, two years younger than his sister, was more reasonable about giving up his all-gold fountain pen. He was a slight child, very attached to his mother, he had her long thin face and large eyes, only his were dark with the glowing moistness of incipient tears. He was much quieter than his sister, and it was poignant the way his eyes were so desperately hanging on to his mother, and the way his hand kept reaching for hers. He knew that he had to be brave, that he mustn't cry or make a fuss, or attract attention to himself. He had been told that his parents would join them all very soon, but he knew this wasn't like other trips: this time something was very wrong – he had seen the change come over Vienna during the past weeks, had heard the shrill *Sieg Heils*, the chants of *Ein Volk*, *Ein Reich*, *Ein Führer*, had seen the swastika flags, the men in black and brown, the garlanded portraits of Hitler in shop windows. He had not seen his father during this time, and though he hadn't been told what had happened he knew that something now threatened his world. He'd often before been away from his mother, but parting from her was always hard for him, and this time he sensed that it was an even more serious parting than usual. In the taxi, going to the Sudbahnhof, he stared out of the window as if he couldn't bear to look at his mother, and his hand lay limp in hers. When Stefan tried to cheer him up by saying wasn't it nice to be going to Venice, he'd be able to go on those fast motorboats, and in another month or so he might already be able to swim, he burst out with, 'Why can't Mutti come too, why can't she?'

'I will be coming,' Leonie said. 'Very soon. At the moment I can't.'

'Why do we have to go?'

'Because I say so.' He pulled his hand out of hers, and shrank his small body into the side of the car. But a moment later he was tentatively seeking her hand again, and gave a sudden big smile when he found it, as if he had been dreading it might no longer be there.

Lea, seeing her mother's ill-concealed concern, said, 'Don't worry, Mutti. I will look after the child,' which brought a flash of resentment to Friedrich's eyes, and caused his small face to take on a stubborn look.

When they got into the railway station and saw how densely crowded it was, Stefan felt the dismay in Leonie, her sense of helplessness at being exposed to such conditions. 'It'll be all right,' he said to her quickly, 'it's not a long journey, after all. Pushing forcefully, dragging the children along by the hand, they made their way across the outer lobby and towards the platforms. They were expecting the crowd to thin, but it got denser and their progress became harder, the little boy was whimpering, not able to contain himself, and he kept saying, 'Mutti, I want to wee-wee, I want to wee-wee,' and she said, 'You can't now, you see you can't now, you'll have to wait.' 'But I've got to wee-wee, Mutti, I've *got* to.' It seemed that she might strike him, and there was such reproach in his eyes as he shrank back from her that Leonie began to weep softly, and in the middle of that milling crowd she picked him up in her arms and showered him with little, soothing kisses, his nose, his eyes, his ears, his fingers, until she had kissed the reproach from his face.

'Leonie, come on,' Stefan insisted. 'Come on.'

The crowd moved forward like slow oozing lava, and to stop as Leonie was doing caused added confusion, and angered the people immediately behind who found their progress halted and saw others getting ahead of them.

The fear of not being able to get on the trains was affecting everyone, making women's faces hard and unrelenting as they pushed and elbowed. By the ticket offices stood policemen with swastika armbands on the sleeves of their greatcoats, and there were Storm Troopers too – like faces on posters, the eyes looking in all directions at once.

Even after all this, the sight when they got to the platforms was a shock: between the railway tracks, broad black alleys of people coagulating into a solid mass. 'Oh, it's impossible,' Leonie gasped. 'It's impossible.'

'It's like this every day. They must get on,' Stefan said. 'There's not a hope of getting on an aeroplane, you know that. Besides, for air flights they have to have names.' Mara was looking distraught, and Stefan regretted that he had agreed to the proposal of letting her take the children. The only thinly suppressed hysteria of these two women was beginning to affect him, and he pushed violently. 'Come on, come on, Leonie, come on, come on.'

On the platform, when they succeeded in getting to it, a slow muscular tension could be felt in the body of the crowd, a giant eel beginning to move: the train had been spotted in the distance. They found themselves in a group of dark-skinned men, Turks, who were passing unlabelled bottles around and throwing back their heads to pour down their throats the disagreeable-smelling liquid that, seemingly, they couldn't drink without spilling all over themselves. They had around them piles and bundles and cartons, many coming apart, ineffectively tied with string, and their belongings smelled even more disagreeable than their liquor. Leonie shuddered. They were talking and shouting in their strange language, laughing, calling out to each other, staggering. They had those indentations below the cheek-bones, of hunger and race. The train guard making his way along the edge of the platform pushed them out of his way with a signal stick, calling 'Vermin, vermin' at them. The train was getting closer, and the people nearest to the track had to fight back against the surge of the great eel behind them. Leonie was holding Friedrich in her arms, and his face had become screwed up as a preliminary to tears that did not quite succeed in coming out but threatened to at any moment. Mara was standing rigidly hunched, biting her lower lip hard. As the train got close enough some people tried to jump on, though it was going too fast still, and those who succeeded rushed into compartments, pushed down the windows and called out to wives, daughters, mothers, brothers, grandmothers to hand up children and baggage. However, as the train was still moving quite fast the relatives on the platform were rapidly passed – they fell away, became lost to sight – and the successful boarders, panicking in their agitation, rushed back along the corridors yelling, 'Here. Here.' 'Here, Malshi.' 'Here, Betty.' 'Lena, Lena, I'm here, *here*.' 'Rekusha – here.' The Turks, drunk on their smelly liquor, not agitated as these others, in the midst of all this pandemonium had formed themselves into a sort of football team group, the ones at the back standing, those in front crouched or kneeling, for a photograph, which another of their number, evidently someone staying behind, was taking, manipulating his shiny new box camera with an unconvincing air of expertise. Once the picture had been taken, the man who was staying embraced each of the Turks in turn, strongly, with firm gripping fingers, and kissed each man on the cheek, he might have been a father seeing off his sons, except that one man could not have had so many sons, there must have been twenty of these Turks, at least. The train had finally come to a halt, causing a quiver of movement in the long black eel, a quiver that preceded its sudden break-up, the black mass becoming fragmented into clusters of clawing, reaching, climbing bits and pieces of humanity: now the train looked like some big, supine animal being devoured by ants. Hemmed in, pushing this way and that, thrust aside, and then forward, Leonie, Mara, the children and Stefan were entirely at the mercy of the mass movement, taken close to the train and then away from it, and Leonie was gasping, both the children were crying – and everywhere, now, children were crying, and overwrought strident voices were calling out – and Mara, unable to contain herself, let out a scream, and Friedrich was sobbing, 'Don't leave me, Mutti, don't leave me, don't leave me, I'm frightened,' and the dark-skinned Turks were swarming on to the train, climbing over each other, blocking an entire carriage, passing up their bundles and packages above the heads of the crowds, and taking over empty compartments, filling them with their body heat, their smells, their language, their bottles, their loud voices; in a vacuum-filling rush they piled in, filling the empty spaces in a matter of moments, their possessions tightly packing the luggage racks up to the ceiling, their interwoven limbs occupying the remainder of the space, and then they were at the windows, waving to the companion they were leaving, and singing. In five minutes the train was full, every bit of space occupied, and half of the people who had been waiting on the platform were still there, amongst them Leonie's children and Mara. Now that the maniacal scramble had abated, it was possible to see individual distress: the taut, straining faces of women with children, and of old men rushing up and down the length of the train in search of unoccupied places. Stefan, leaving Leonie and the children and Mara, ran along the platform, looking in one compartment after the other, pushing against resistant bone, ignoring the cries of 'Nothing, nothing. No room here,' wrenching open doors that those inside were attempting to hold shut against those outside. With rage and panic in him he rushed along the platform, encountering at every compartment the hard and unrelenting faces of passengers, as they now were by dint of strength and luck, holding on to what was theirs – a few cubic feet of space – with grim possessiveness. It was not these unfortunate and frightened people who were to blame for these conditions, for the need to get out, but it was against them that his rage was directed, a rage of dispossession that sucked the blood from his brain. He tussled with people determined to keep him out; when at the tenth or twelfth carriage he found a hand thrust out policeman-fashion to stop him, he grasped it in fury and would have torn the man down from his perch had not something else at this moment caught Stefan's attention. What he saw was another section of train, consisting of two carriages, being shunted along the track to join on to the full carriages. Others had seen this too and were rushing along the platform, only to come up against a barrier guarded by policemen and railway officials. Stefan ran towards the barrier, and when he got close enough heard the impassive-faced officials repeat with monotonous disinterest, 'Nothing. There is nothing. All full. All reserved. Everything. All full. Go away. Go away.' Pleas, entreaties, bribes – all were refused with the same hard and contemptuous disdain. There was no point in even trying. Slowly Stefan walked back to where Leonie and the children were waiting. Friedrich was bawling, and Mara's hands were clasped together in frenzied supplication, or perhaps thanksgiving for not now, after all, having to endure this journey. Stefan walked slowly, giving himself time. When he got to Leonie, he saw that the dark-skinned Turks, who stuck out of the window of the train like a many-headed creature, were gesturing and calling, making signs and noises – loud, rough noises, jocular and perhaps even disrespectful signs – but Stefan saw what Leonie had refused to see, or understand: these Turks were being friendly, in their coarse way, trying to be helpful, and what they were attempting to convey was that there was room – that they could make room in this hot fetid swarm of arms and legs for Leonie and the children and Mara and Stefan. They rocked their arms to signify children, they pointed at Leonie – laughing uproariously – they made private signs and gestures to each other, and they pointed at Stefan and at Mara, and with fingers indicating the interior they showed that room could be made.

'I think they are offering room in their compartment,' Stefan said to Leonie. 'Look, they are. They're being friendly. Look.' He smiled at them vigorously, nodding his head to show he understood.

'Oh, my God,' Mara gasped. 'Oh, my God, I'd rather die.'

'You're not suggesting, Stefan . . .'

'Why not. There's no harm in them. They're noisy, that's all. They are offering to share their space. It's only a few hours to Venice. They're going on to Istanbul. That *is* a long journey.'

Stefan's words had broken whatever catch in her was holding back the hysteria, and now it came out in a series of elongated and strung-together deep shaking sobs. She was holding Friedrich to her, pressing his head hurtingly against her, and emitting gasping sounds: trembling, straining, retching expulsions of pain. Stefan realized he could not stand it; quite suddenly he felt, without surprise, that he would do anything to rid himself of the feelings that Leonie's sobs were causing. Coming on top of everything else – the familiarity of the panic all around, the sense of having intimate and deep knowledge of this situation and these people (the dark-skinned Turks, like the old porter in his dream making his impossible offer to take the luggage when he was already bent double) – coming on top of all this, Leonie's state, warning of imminent collapse, made him feel that anything, anything was preferable. He said, 'There is a possibility. I have thought of something. Will you be all right if I leave you for a few minutes while I make a phone call? The train doesn't go for another hour at least.' The assurance in his face startled them all into calm. An easement, as if by the removal of some harshly chafing object, was produced by his words.

He did what he had determined to do and was back within fifteen minutes. Leonie did not ask what he had done, but waited patiently.

Never before had he asked anything of Wirthof.

When he arrived, Leonie did not at first recognize him, and when she had recognized him did not connect his arrival with herself. What was this black uniformed SS man with black peaked cap, silver braid epaulettes, swastika armband, to do with them? As he came closer the children and Mara instinctively shrank back, what connection could this man have with them? Before their group, he stopped, removed his cap which he placed under his arm, and taking Leonie's hand raised it to his mouth. 'Please, Baroness,' he said, 'if you will follow me.' And he went ahead, walking not too fast, palely smiling, and all along the platform people moved aside, making an unimpeded passageway for them. When they reached the barrier, the clutter of people still vainly striving to get through likewise stood aside on becoming aware of this black-uniformed figure, and Wirthof addressed one of the railway officials. 'This woman and the two children require a private compartment as far as Venice.'

'Ah – everything is full. It is all taken. Everything has been reserved, Herr Obersturmführer.'

'Then it will be necessary to requisition a compartment,' Wirthof said. 'Show me your list.'

'But Herr Obersturmführer,' one of the policemen said, 'we have instructions. These reservations are all made by authority.'

'Let me see the list,' Wirthof said. He was handed a sheet of typed paper, which he examined briefly.

'This sleeper,' he said. 'Reserved for M. and Mme Solange, travelling to Zagreb, is requisitioned.'

'By what authority? By what authority? I must have authority,' the railway official protested with consternation, turning imploringly to the Austrian policemen.

'By my authority,' Wirthof said, glittering. 'Be so kind as to show these people to their compartment.'

The policemen looked at each other in perplexity, they shrugged, the railway officials huddled together and pored over their lists, shook their heads, muttered, murmured, and shook their heads again, and when they looked up and found Wirthof's quietly glittering eyes undeflected, regarding them with ominous patience, they, with abrupt speed now, raised the turnpike to allow the group through. Wirthof, arm outstretched, politely indicated for the others to go ahead; the policemen, and then the officials, raised their arms in a tentative Hitler salute.

The railway official, so contemptuous of manner in his treatment of the crowd, had become all bowing obsequiousness as he led the way, unlocked the door of the sleeping compartments, and showed Mara and the children into a wood-panelled sleeper, with red plush seats and crisp white linen antimacassars.

'Is this suitable, Baroness?' Wirthof asked.

'Oh yes,' she said, 'oh yes,' her eyes expressing her gratitude, and a smile uncurled at Wirthof's mouth, unabashedly proud.

'I am so grateful to you,' Leonie said softly, in her wonderful voice, from which all the former hysteria had gone.

'It is entirely my pleasure, Baroness,' Wirthof said, bowing.

He waited on the platform until Mara and the children had been safely installed, chocolates and lemonades bought from a trolley and given to Lea and Friedrich – even Friedrich was smiling quite happily now, no longer frightened or tearful as he took leave of his mother – and as the train began to move off. Wirthof delivered the supreme stroke: he clicked his heels, kissed Leonie's hand again, nodded to Stefan, and left before any more intimate or personal thanks could be expressed to him. And as they watched him go, his triumph and theirs intermingling, they permitted themselves a moment of luxurious sympathy for the hundreds who had not been able to find a place on the train.

With the children safely out of Austria, an improvement occurred in Leonie. Some of her former purposefulness returned. The desperateness had gone from her, and she was able to embark on the delicate business of sounding out former friends and acquaintances to discover where they now stood. Her social talent reasserting itself, her keen ear alert for nuances, she began the slow process of reassessing everyone in the light of what had happened. Who was to be trusted? Who was strong? Who was pliable? Non-committal questions eliciting non-committal answers, she had to be content with the equivocal responses that the situation dictated; this notwithstanding, it was possible, tentatively, to eliminate some people as totally unreliable and untrustworthy and to designate others to varying categories of trustworthiness.

'It's only the pictures I truly miss,' she told Stefan. 'The flat: it's a relief I don't have to keep it up. It is not for these times. It caused me hardly a pang when I received the requisition order. The pictures I *am* sorry about, but I know them all so well. I can keep them with me still. Maz used to have such amusement in his eyes when I talked of my needs, my imperative needs! He was right, I always used to think – how can I give up "my life", what I thought of as "my life", and now all that is gone and it is almost a relief.'

'I'm glad you are in such good spirits.'

'I have recovered my strength. I'm glad you made me send the children away. I miss them terribly, of course, that is the real heartbreak, but the fact that they are safe and being looked after consoles me, and I can bear the pain of being separated from them, only just, but I do bear it, you see, and, you know, Stefan, the fact that I *can* bear it is a consolation to me. It enables me to feel some slight, very slight, degree of respect for myself. I never was able to do anything that was hard to do. I suppose I didn't believe I had the capacity. I have started a thousand things, and abandoned them. But now I am doing something hard – oh that may be useless too – but I don't any longer feel quite useless. I would like . . . I would like to be able to play a role of some sort. I know so many people. If I could put that to some use: there are people in Vienna who oppose all this ghastliness, if only they could be brought together, if only . . .'

'Leonie, you must take care, with your passion for organizing.'

'I am very careful. Anyway, what do I have to lose?'

'You still don't believe that these people are capable of what they say. I tell you they are. They are capable of anything. And it isn't a game, with the loser paying a forfeit.'

'What can they do? Kill me?'

'Yes, they can do that.'

'You are too pessimistic. After all, I am not without some friends. And there is foreign opinion. There are some things the world will not stand by and allow to happen.'

'You believe that? I warn you against such comforting delusions. I am serious, Leonie. You must take great, great care.'

'I do, Stefan, I do. But don't deprive me of my illusions, if that is what they are. If I did nothing, then I would not be able to bear the waiting. I know now what it is to feel the pressure towards action, any action, when one has to say: this I will do, come what may, because to do nothing is worse. Do you understand? If I just sat in my hotel room, waiting, doing nothing, I'd go mad.'

Felix, though he looked much thinner, had kept his nerve and his stubborn belief in the efficacy of 'the plan'. He was tolerably comfortable, he said, and added, smiling, that he had become an accomplished houseworker. He had overcome his initial feelings of humiliation at having to clean out the guards' quarters every day. 'One must not allow them to see that one finds it irksome, that merely makes them gloat. They are ignorant louts, and of course they enjoy seeing me on my hands and knees cleaning up their messes. But, that apart, I am not badly treated. From time to time, someone a bit higher up than the others comes in, reels off a string of abuse about the Jewish financiers, and how we are going to be eliminated – it's a set speech, they learn it parrot fashion. I just let them have their say. I don't answer them. And when they're finished, I ask if I can have a radio, and that is refused, as I know it will be, and then I ask if I can have some books, and that request is refused, and I ask for something else – it was a gramophone last time – and for some reason that is granted. So now I have a gramophone and a few records. Wagner of course, and you know how I feel about Wagner. Stefan, I want to say to you – the way you are handling this is absolutely correct, Stefan. In due course, they will come round to a more reasonable attitude. Just the other day one of them, seeing I was having some digestive discomfort, heartburn actually, insisted on having a doctor examine me. Not a bad fellow. Listened to my heart, said I was in excellent shape. So, you see, they are anxious to keep me alive at least.'

'Excellent. Excellent. You are handling it extremely well.' (His invariable response.) Cheeks, nose, chin were crumbling a little, features beginning to droop, a surreptitious trickling away of the body's vitality: he did not know it yet: he complained of spells of dizziness but was very fit otherwise, he said; had some weakness of the legs, that was all, and his knees hurt, housemaid's knees, he said laughing, from floor scrubbing. Cigarettes, had Stefan brought cigarettes? He was smoking more than ever, when he ran out he was forced to cadge cigarettes from the guards: 'the devices one resorts to – they make me plead – I curse them inside and plead, one becomes desperate – against my will I feel grateful to them when they give me a cigarette.' When Stefan suggested they should drop the plan, no more bargaining, pay them whatever they asked, he wouldn't hear of it.

'I am not making much progress,' Stefan said.

'Nonsense. You are doing very well. With what is at stake, of course the negotiations are drawn out. But you are doing very well.'

'Felix, Felix – pay them what they ask, Felix, and have done with it. You'll be out of here. What does the money matter?'

'I wouldn't hear of it. It is not the money, you understand. I could not lift my head again if I felt I had had to capitulate to those swine. No, if we keep our heads, Stefan, we can outsmart them. They are fools. We can outsmart them. Come, Stefan, you must not lose heart when you are doing so well. I tell you, what keeps me going, what makes me able to bear all their insults and humiliations, is the thought that you, you Stefan, are meanwhile making fools of them. Ah – that gives me a satisfaction here.' He indicated his heart. 'That thought keeps me going, Stefan.'

He asked about Leonie, and what news there was of the children in Venice. Stefan gave him the latest information. 'I'm glad they are in Venice, that was a smart move. I wish you could get Leonie to leave too – she is impulsive you know, easily carried away, she would be better in Venice.'

'She won't hear of it, Felix.'

'Anyway, see that she doesn't lose her head. She is so impulsive, she has so much imagination. Tell her I miss her in every way, but that I am well and in good spirits. I send her kisses and I send her love, and I send kisses to the children. Buy something for them, Stefan, and have it sent from me – hmm?'

'Yes, I will.'

'Good. Good.' He embraced Stefan. 'And take care of yourself too, I don't need to tell you that: I have an impression that you know how to go about things. I have no misgivings. I think it will be another month, and then I shall be out of here.'

Precipitantly the spring came, sickly smelling, smelling of new leather: a flush of warm days through which ran an insidious chill, like the cold shiver of fever. Langour had gone; the sleeper slapped into awakeness saw blurred the hot harsh colours of the New Order, the marching men with vexilla and flags, the garlanded portraits of Adolf Hitler – huge as cinema screens – the proclamatory legends on hoardings above the Nazi-art faces of the conquistadors: the *Hakenkreuz*, a brand stamp of possession. The camouflaged staff cars drove fast and came to abrupt, hard-braking halts. Young warlords who had not yet fought a war, they sat in the cafés wide-thighed at their ease, like men in a bordel, watching with a glass-eye glitter the *süsse Mädchen* of Vienna. Danger, equivocal and many-faced, agitated the air. The former faint shabbiness of the city was covered up by a new hard enamel lacquer.

Wirthof said, 'I will take you somewhere. You'll be interested.'

'Where?'

'You will see, you will see.' He called a taxi.

'Well, Kazakh, you must admit Vienna has come alive. Something is happening at last.'

'Murder and torture, yes.'

'You exaggerate. There has been no bloodshed.'

'What about Zehner?'

'That's one man. And it's not certain who murdered him. How

205

many were killed in the Left uprising of '34? A great many more.'

'Nobody knows how many of all those who have disappeared are still alive . . .'

'The arrests are a precautionary measure. More sensible to arrest potential troublemakers than to have to shoot them down in the street. Surely you would agree with that?'

'It is hardly likely that we are going to agree, Wirthof.'

'That is true.' He laughed. 'We never do seem to agree, do we? I have never known you to agree with anything I say, Kazakh.'

'That's because you're quite incapable of adhering to any rational process of reasoning.'

'What a pity you are a Jew, Kazakh. It limits your whole outlook. You have the *Weltanschauung* of a provincial schoolmaster. You believe you know the answers to *questions* of which you cannot even conceive. I cannot imagine why I bother to argue with you.'

They got out at a café behind the Opera. Stefan was immediately aware of a predominance of uniforms: 'Why are you taking me here?'

'You disapprove?'

'I'm not sure I want to be seen in such a place.'

'Oh! What a pity. I thought it would interest you. You could hardly come here on your own. I thought you would appreciate being taken.'

'You really are absurd, Wirthof.'

'Would you rather we went to one of your places?'

'Not in that uniform of yours.'

'You object to the uniform?'

'What do you think.'

'It was quite useful, at the railway station.'

'Yes. *Yes.*'

'Well, where shall we go?' They were standing on the pavement now, looking indecisively about them.

'All right. Let's go in here,' Stefan said.

Curious eyes upon them – the tall one, could he be a Jew, with the pale young SS officer? – they made their way past the sprawl of tables on the pavement and went in through a revolving door, and inside the Herr Obers led them to a dim alcove, one that was just being vacated by a monocled colonel-general and his woman companion. It was a place rococo and dark, with dim mirrors, pink bizarre veined marble, golden cherubs casting silk-shaded light from niches and pedestals. 'It's a good place, don't you think?' Wirthof demanded. 'Come now, don't be perverse – it's congenial.' In a smiling and confidential undertone, he added, 'This is where they come with their mistresses and their young boys. It is highly discreet. If you had not been with me, I can tell you, you would not have been found a table. Don't you think it's congenial?'

'It is not the word I would have chosen for it.'

The occupants of the alcoves were concealed from those in the adjoining ones by the high backs of the leather bench seats and the masses of greenery above. The columns along the centre of the room, the low-key lighting, the high rubber plants, limited vision, fragmented it, and the innumerable mirrors threw back one's own image wherever one looked. The spying eye kept coming upon itself. Stefan saw a grey gregarious head growing out of a basket of wax blooms, another bisected by the line of a pillar, another multiplied in a bay of mirrors: scarlet striped legs nudging a black-hosed thigh: a black-sleeved arm with silver thread clasping another black-sleeved arm with silver thread: scarlet lapels touched by a woman's hands: and Stefan saw his own face dispersed by mirrors, glowering back at him. He turned to Wirthof for the comfort of his solid presence.

After they had given their order, Wirthof said in a low voice, 'The Baron, are you making any progress? When are you going to get him released? They've held him now for months.'

'Your concern surprises me.'

'It is not him I am concerned about. But he is the father of Leonie's children, and I can't bear to think that she is suffering. Besides,' he added, bringing his mouth close to Stefan, 'I can't see Leonie while *he* is under arrest. Can I? Can I? It wouldn't be honourable.'

'Really, Wirthof, you are absurd.'

'Why do you say that?'

'You sit here, in this room, in that uniform, and you talk of honour.'

'Kazakh, you have no idea what you are talking about. The unit I am in is a military unit. It is an armoured *military* unit. Do you imagine I am part of the Gestapo? I have nothing to do with anything like that. The SS is a vast organization, with innumerable divisions, the unit I am in is a perfectly honourable one. My former commandant at the Academy at Wiener Neustadt is in an

SS unit, and that he is a man of honour is unquestionable. As a matter of fact, it was his influence that got me in. It's a privilege to be admitted to such a unit.'

'If you believe that, Wirthof – that being in the SS is the same as being in the army – then you are even more deluded than I had always thought.'

'Yes, yes, yes, yes. I know all that. But that does not concern me.'

'How can you say it does not concern you?'

'I'm in it, Kazakh, because it's a first rate unit. I tell you – I've done two months' special training – and it's a revelation, after the Austrian army. The Austrian army is an anachronism. It's antediluvian. The SS is modern. It is of our time. You know the training those fellows get – they're lower working class mostly, the men, *Lumpenproletariat*, when they go in, but my God! They come out of the *Ordenburgen* hard as iron, disciplined, self-reliant, in superb physical and mental trim, and capable. They're taught things in those institutes. They're not just boorish soldiers, they can handle themselves, they can handle machines, they have a grounding in every aspect of modern warfare, and they have endurance. If they didn't have endurance, they couldn't survive the training, believe me. To them heroism is automatic: they are machines for heroism. I tell you, if it comes to war, they will go through the French like a knife through butter. Of course they have a lot of mumbo-jumbo drilled into them; they are not expected to think, and the infallibility of the Führer is a useful doctrine that ensures absolute unquestioning obedience, which is what any officer requires of his men.'

'You talk like one of them.'

'Rubbish! I am describing to you what *they* are like, the men. It is quite different for someone like me. I was brought in, because they need officers like me, who *can* think. One can do fantastic things in an outfit like that. You can be a general at thirty. And if it comes to war, I'd rather lead such men than ordinary soldiers. Your ordinary soldier has one ambition in war, and that's to come out of it alive – a boring ambition, unsatisfactory militarily – and perhaps he'll do a bit of looting and raping on the side, given the chance. Not these. They want to win. They're bursting to go, you can accomplish something with such men. What you don't understand, Kazakh, about the new German army is that it is the only truly modern army, it's in the twentieth century, while the rest of the world is still thinking in terms of horse cavalry. You should hear their ideas on armoured warfare. Brilliant. They know in Berlin that what wins a war today is armour, and air power. And their strategy is tied to that. Maginot Line! They will go through it like a knife through butter. You should hear Rommel. You should hear Guderian. Those men know what they are talking about. You don't know what a relief it is to be associated with people who are competent. Concentrations of armour, that's the secret of modern warfare. Nothing can hold back concentrated punches of armour, the way they plan it.'

'They are already planning it then?'

He grinned and stretched back in his seat. 'Oh – there's going to be a showdown. I'm sure of it. It's going to come. I promise you, you will see something. It will be fantastic. Fantastic! It will be something colossal. You have no idea.'

'On the contrary, I have a very good idea.'

'It's a pity you're a Jew, Kazakh. They're getting to be very tough on the Jews. I don't say they're right in that, it seems excessive to me, but, you know, events have a force of their own, it is the force of events, they carry you with them, history must realize itself, you can't quibble with it or alter its direction, it has to go a certain way, and I know the way it's going, Kazakh.'

Reaching into the infinity of possibility, losing himself out there on that distant plane of the all-possible, he was in regions where the friction of reality has been reduced to nil, in a state of superfluidity in which the expanding 'I' knows of no restriction. There one can be lost for ever, in that exile from the self, with no hope of return.

How is it I know you, Wirthof? How is it I always have known you, going back, going back. The crowd is a multiple of the one with opaque eyes: its opacity is the despair of being another: its arms are a burnt forest. Its black arms. Ah yes, it was excitement. You, Wirthof, were not alone in feeling that. I too. Yes, I too.

I felt it. And I stayed. What aberration was that? I could have left. Of course I could have left. There was time. The scent of madness was strong in the air, and all animals have a nose for self-survival, don't they? but I did not leave. What kept me there? The Baron – incarcerated in the servants' quarters of the Hotel Metropole, in the Morzinplatz, just round the corner from the Judengasse? Wipe shoes, the sign said in the entrance, a wholly extraordinary finickiness in the circumstances. Was it the Baron who kept me there? Or Leonie? Or you, Wirthof? I was not afraid. No, that is not entirely true: I was sometimes afraid: but it was a fear that I could put outside myself, observe it with detachment, as if it were somebody else's. And when it threatened to move towards me, this fear, I could watch it coming, I had the capacity to take preventive action, I could overcome the fear by an act of, of – what? It was an exertion of some sort – I had many gambits: my resources were capable of rapid redeployment: I was confident of my quickness. There was a part of me that could overcome anything. I had powers that I could call up in myself, sometimes – sometimes I felt quite magical. If it was delusion, it was efficacious. Wasn't it? There have been other times, too, when I have had this, this – certainty: but not lately, lately I have been losing it, I did not have it yesterday, what was it that happened to me yesterday? It has been a long time coming. I used to have certainty. The certainty my father told me to distrust. He was a quixotic fool. What did he know? I trusted it, and have I been wrong? I survived, didn't I? – the holocaust and the prostitutes. I am rich. Tomorrow I may be ruined. But today I am rich. And yesterday? Yesterday I was sick – the sickness unto death: is despair, says Kierkegaard. Yes, yes, I was in despair yesterday. Over what? *So one might say perhaps that there lives not one single man who after all is not to some extent in despair, in whose inmost parts there does not dwell a disquietude, a pertur- bation, a discord, an anxious dread of an unknown something, or of a something he does not even dare to make acquaintance with, dread of a possibility of life, or dread of himself, so that after all, this man is going about carrying a sickness of the spirit, which only rarely and in glimpses, by and with a dread that to him is inexplicable, gives evidence of its presence within.* Oh I have read books. I am not one of your financiers who only reads the news of the markets. Once, indeed, I might have been an educated man.

I am not that, but I have read books. But of what was I in despair yesterday? Nothing happened yesterday. The time when I had cause for despair, I was not in despair; on the contrary, I was unafraid, impervious, magical – full of gambits. Kierkegaard says: *one form of despair is precisely this of not being in despair, that is, not being aware of it.* In that case my despair yesterday was the other form of despair, that of knowing I have always been in despair, without being aware of it. Is that not the best way of being in despair, not knowing it? Is that not the smartest way, the cleverest? *The dearest and most attractive dwelling place of despair is in the very heart of immediate happiness.* True. I have been happy. have been happy in the body of a woman, and I have been in despair, that is quite true. I have been happy in the realization of ambitions, and have been in despair. But what is the alternative to the sweet despair of not knowing one is in despair? The despair of knowing. Ah – that is the desert. That is the journey to the edge. And if one once has known that despair – and yesterday I think I knew it for a moment – all other despair is frolicsome posturing. But am I ready for the desert? Or is that, too, a posture? A hypothetical heroism? Kierkegaard speaks of the despair of not willing to be oneself; or still lower, the despair of not willing to be a self; or, lowest of all, despair at willing to be another than himself. I have known all these forms of despair, without knowing I was in despair, and should I give up the habit of a lifetime? Despair also is habit: the addiction to one's repeating pattern: the refusal to give up one whorl of my repeating pattern. Can the pattern choose its own mutation? By what force? By the despair at being a pattern, and knowing that I am a pattern to infinitude. But one must go through the desert first. What will make me do that? There are easier routes to despair. To the despair of not knowing I am in despair.

Yesterday, what was the matter with me yesterday? The possibility has to be considered – does it not? – that all this now, is delusion. That once I was capable of action, unafraid, or able at least to put my fears outside myself; that, once, I had a great vitality that comes of certainty, and that this vitality is lost to me now, and that I am in the despair of my lost vitality. That is a possibility, is it not? It is just as possible, is it not, as the other alternative that I was always in despair, and have only now become conscious of it? My common sense tells me that I have lost something, there is evidence for that: I am not so bold, I have less daring, almost no sense of certainty. What, then, is it that tells me, against the evidence of common sense, that I have gained something that outweighs the loss, something of such doubtful weight as – the knowledge of my despair? How much is that worth in the market place? How much could I sell that for? I think I shall have a drink. Yes. Yes. Definitely. Good for you. Softens the arteries. Medical fact. And the brain? Oh yes, a softening of the brain can be congenial.

Stefan Kazakh had three large whiskies, and stopped shivering.

There, that's better. Much better. Always could get a good feeling from three large whiskies. Despair is three large whiskies – ah, yes, the sweet despair of not knowing one is in despair. I opt for that. I thought you were going to think this through, Kazakh. Kindly mind your own business. I shall have another whisky. Am I not thinking it through? A little whisky helps the flow, loosens the mind, frees the memory. Is that what it does? Is that a fact? I shall have another whisky, that will put paid to your quibbles and your mockery. Was I not brave? After four whiskies – five – yes; it is one way of looking at it. Why should I look at it your way, Jeremiah? Will you let me have my story, mocker! Feel much better now. Not so cold any more, have stopped shivering: the whisky. Why didn't I have a whisky yesterday? Stupid of me. Feel much better now. I will have my story, yes, yes. Tell me a story, tell me a story, O. used to say. I love a good story, she'd say. Soothing. Yes, so do I – love a good story. Story of infamy and carnage and horror and magic. Soothing, very soothing. At least I was not afraid.

So you say. So you say. There's proof, mocker, there's proof, for have I not survived? I will believe that when I believe that the centre of the earth is made of raspberry jam. Be that as it may, be that as it may, I will have my story, and damn you and your despair. Now – I have lost the thread, the causal link, the plot. There is no plot. It may be so, but memory abhors a plotless tale, plot is the mesh in which memory is caught, cut the mesh and the memory is gone, memory cannot tolerate the non sequitur, it needs links, cause and effect, chronology, sequence, plot – that led to that, and that to that, even if it didn't. The thread, the thread, yes. Remember those rhymes you used to learn at school to help you remember the solutions of problems. Could always remember the rhymes, but not the problems whose solution they contained. Still, can work backwards. Deduce the problem from the solution in the rhymes. Yes, that's a way. The jingling rhyme. Rhymes I can remember.

When was it I started to feel unafraid? About the time of the Baron's arrest – no, before that: but this unfearfulness of mine came to fruition round about then. Except for the time at the railway station: that was a retrogression. When I met Wirthof and we went to the coffee house, I was not afraid then; and all those meetings at the Metropole, bargaining for the Baron's life, I was not afraid then either; I was not at all afraid then.

Wirthof of course didn't see Leonie: would not have been honourable, you see, while the Baron was under arrest. Very quirky, Wirthof's honour. He loved to look at himself in the SS uniform; black, he said, had always suited him; that must have been when I first became conscious of him dyeing his hair, or rather when I became aware that it was of that unnatural flat yellow colour, like dead leaves. He was only in Vienna a short while, had to go back to finish his training at the Adolf Hitler school in Bad Zoeltz: I think he expected to be a general by the time he came out. His admiration for the men was mixed with a good deal of contempt: they have about as much sensibility as an orang outang, he'd say: he always, of course, considered himself a man of great sensibility, and so he despised these ruffians, but they were good men to command because they were tough, disciplined fighters, absolutely obedient, and Wirthof wanted to be a general. He had set his heart on that. He saw himself as the youngest general in the German armed forces, and when he lay on his bed recovering from one of his headaches, the bedclothing was littered with military manuals and maps and his own sketch plans for crushing the enemy (as yet non-existent) in a pincer, or taking them from the flank, or by whatever military manoeuvre he was that day contemplating.

All that summer I was trudging from office to office ('Wipe shoes'), through all the divisions and sub-divisions of the SS, the police, the civil authority, the Wehrmacht, seeking to obtain the Baron's release. They were all now willing to talk; the talks were endlessly protracted, and on the highest levels, and I was treated with varying degrees of courtesy, after all I was a buyer, I had come to buy the Baron's life, and that entitled me to some consideration. Now I was allowed to see the Baron regularly. He was getting to look very ill, though he strenuously asserted that he was in the best of health, that the exercise – scrubbing the guards' quarters – was doing him good; he was avid for information always, not so much information of his immediate release, because he had come to the conclusion it was going to be a much longer tussle than he had originally supposed, but for details of how I had handled a particular situation, what I had said to this or that official, chief, leader, minister, in reply to their questions, accusations, exploratory soundings, etc. 'It does my heart good to hear it,' he'd say when I told him of some actual or invented counter-thrust of mine to their innumerable attacks and accusations. 'Tell me again, Stefan, what you said when Heydrich said to you . . .' He relived these incidents, and they were all that kept him going between my visits, so I could not deprive him of the pleasure of savouring my audacity and daring, my devastating retorts. In the retelling, my audacity grew, I was all the time administering crushing defeats to them – I came to believe this too, to some extent, the power of my repartee, of my contempt: oddly enough, defeated though they were by me, I was no nearer to securing the Baron's release. But to him I was always doing well. 'It is always like this,' he assured me, 'a successful negotiation is an intricate business, it has its own speed of growth, it cannot be rushed. Only by giving in can one bring it to an immediate solution.' And though he was dying, and this was evident to me (though not to him, presumably, or perhaps it was to him too), he was not going to give in. Or perhaps, possibly, the fact that he was dying was another card that he held, that he proffered, putting a time limit on the negotiations. It amused him that they had a doctor examine him every week. 'You see, you see, they can't afford to let me die.' The imminence of his death would put added pressure on them (loss of ransom, international odium), and so the signs of death were seen by him not as melancholy signs, but rather as weapons in his armoury; yesterday I had another fainting spell – ah! that will make them shiver in their boots, the swines, that will make them shiver!

The negotiations dragged out all that summer of '38 and all winter too, and into the New Year; they were not entirely futile, in one respect; when it became know that I had access to high officials of the regime, others with money who wanted to get out approached me to effect their release, and in some cases I was successful. When I called at the Metropole or at the Palais Rothschild, and later at the Palais Koeppler, I had with me a list of the names of people whose release I was seeking to obtain. Whenever the negotiations for the Baron's release looked like breaking down, I was given the release of the others on my list, as a token; for they were very interested in the Baron's money, and they did not want the negotiations to break down. I think I could have secured the Baron's release, on terms, it is true, that were excessively high, but he forbade me to accept them, saying they would come down in due course. Should I have concluded a deal against the Baron's wishes? I had his power of attorney. He could not have stopped it – though, of course, they, the Nazis, did not know this. I didn't do so because – because I still believed I could outsmart them. I got to know some of these men, these negotiators on the other side, very well; I knew them intimately, I knew how their minds worked, and I was sure I could outsmart them. I got very involved in those negotiations. Did I, perhaps, lose sight of my objective, at times, in the excitement of the bargaining: the Baron too: were we not, then, in the grip of mania, or I should say despair, though it did not feel like despair, for is it not the ultimate despair, which only mania can obscure, to attempt to value a man's life in monetary terms? I can understand the form of this madness as it affected the Baron, to him there was more of his life in his money than there was in himself; but what was my madness? A different madness, to be sure – I was going to outsmart them. Was that why I had stayed? Was that my purpose? To outsmart Thanatos with my quickness?

That was the winter it was so cold, the first winter of the war; there was no coal to be got, and everyone froze. (Not I, though: it did not bother me; yes, I was quite indifferent to the cold, and surprised that others kept complaining about it.) People sat around indoors in their overcoats, with blankets over their knees, I remember that. The parks were deep in snow, and you saw children dragging their sleds along the hard frozen streets, and carrying their skating boots on their backs, and women wheeling old perambulators containing a precious sack of coal, obtained by barter. Already money was of only nominal value. (That did not stop my bargaining.) Almost everything you wanted to buy was on points. I used to buy clothing on my periodic visits to Zurich; as a negotiator I had to be well dressed, I could not afford to look shabby while dealing in millions, could I?

Vienna looked quite beautiful, I remember, that first winter of the war, as it always does when the snow is thick, it is a winter city; it is not like those cities where the snow turns quickly to slush, in Vienna the snow stays hard, and the old snow is covered by new snow, constantly, a constant renewal, white on white, and the whole city undergoes a metamorphosis, becomes indefinite, its outline changes, its character too, everthing acquires a new texture, windows become thickly framed, always as a child I loved the snow, and was sad to see it melt, those beautiful white domes, the streets like womanly white limbs, even the field marshals on their black lead horses were quite jolly fattened by the snow.

I had a girl that winter; yes, that's right, it was a passing thing. Sometimes we went for walks, and I felt like other young men: I was surprised by the potency of quite ordinary pleasures, they were not for me, of course, I knew that. At times – yes, I had forgotten – I though of taking her to Switzerland with me and not coming back. The Baron would have to make his own terms, he was quite capable of doing that, he did not need me; but such thoughts were only a passing fancy, like the girl herself; I had a task. What task was that, Kazakh?

There was talk all the time of a spring offensive; the war had not really got started yet; and it seemed to me that in the spring, when the snows had melted and the tanks began to roll, all sorts of things would emerge clear and sharp out of the indefiniteness of winter. And in March – it was after Hitler and Mussolini had met at the Brenner Pass in a snowstorm, I saw the newsreels of that: Hitler in his long leather coat, waiting on the platform; Mussolini's train coming in in a snow cloud; that short, stiff, bent arm salute of Hitler's; his generals some distance behind him; Mussolini getting out, fierce-eyed – yes, in March, in late March, I got rid of my girl of the winter, whose name I have forgotten, so there would be no entanglements to limit my freedom of action. It was not such a cosy winter as you make out, Kazakh: there was the ninth of November, have you forgotten that? – when they dragged the Jews screaming from their homes and burned the synagogues, and there was Finland, and all those stories filtering through from Poland, not such a cosy winter. But I expected all that, nothing surprised me – except the way my snow girl fitted neatly under my arm and rested there so naturally, serenely, and the gratitude in her eyes when I made love to her, as if I had done some marvellous work within her for which she would be eternally grateful: I was not used to *that*. All the rest I expected with that certain foreknowledge of mine; all the rest I had known was coming, had always known with painless knowledge. Saying goodbye to my snow girl was painful, is the only pain I remember of that savage winter.

All winter I heard nothing of Withorf. I did not even think of him. Whatever the link between us had been, it now was broken, and I was glad of that. The direction he had taken had marked out our respective positions clearly, and I was glad of that too. It meant I didn't have to bother about him any more, I could leave him to his grandiose ambitions. I was finished with you, Wirthof, I had done with you, I thought, *I thought*, I was a man thinking he has done with shadows when the sun reaches its meridian.

In the spring we all heard of Wirthof again. Suddenly he was in all the newsreels, a hero, and famous. He'd blown up some pillboxes in France, or something. A *Lied* was written about him, it had a good tune and became very popular. It was one of the songs invariably sung at youth rallies. One kept seeing him in newsreels of Nazi junketings, looking mystical and noble; the camera angles chosen gave his face a solemn beauty; his eyes, clear and intense, stared unflinchingly, sternly, into the future; he was profiled against fluttering flags and banners, or against corn fields; the directors of these newsreels loved to fade his wind-blown hair into images of corn fields, out of whose horizon came marching children; or they showed him against a montage of Germans labouring for victory, in fields and in factories, at home and at the front.

Lüdenscheid: face damp, damp as a damp handshake, always that thin film of moisture, large pores, a nondescript face, small soft earlobes hairy as gooseberries, small damp eyes, prissy lips, Ernst Lüdenscheid, Gruppenführer SS. He had a peculiar walk, due to the fact that his hips were rather broad and his legs too short and his trunk meagre: a sly walk, like the tiptoeing of a sneak, or like the walk of a shop assistant (which he once was), adept in sidling up unnoticed. His speech was affected by sudden choking fits, when, understandably, he'd have difficulty in getting out his words and his eyes swelled and streamed, and then he'd gulp down water from the flask always on his desk; his words, even when he was not choking, came out in odd rhythms, sometimes in a sudden rush, sometimes in a slow, slow, deliberately slow procession, slow and sombre as a funeral march. He sounded like someone trying to control a stammer (though there is no evidence that he ever had one) by speaking with very deliberate articulation, with the absolute control of someone marshalling his words, arranging them in little assault groups or stringing them out in defensive positions, and an expressionless delivery, except of course when he was choking, gave all his words uniform flatness. His vowels came out quite well, with attendant halitosis, it was on the consonants he sometimes choked, as if in constricting the air stream from the lungs, he went too far and in a sort of revenge – like a baby that stops breathing out of tantrum – cut off all air supplies, ingoing and outgoing. The deliberateness of his speech, from time to time disrupted by these violent choking fits, produced in one the same tension as listening to a stammerer, and it was very tiring being with him any length of time. Despite this speech difficulty, and even when his words were coming out in a funeral march, he was a formidable interrogator.

Posts and Telegraphs (which included Telephones), Occupied Territories, was the SS department in Vienna of which Lüdenscheid had charge. Those who wished to minimize his standing maintained that his responsibilities were confined to ensuring the efficient functioning of the posts, telegraphs (and telephones); but Lüdenscheid was not a man to be limited in this manner, and, for instance, made himself responsible for Speech (clearly a subdivision of Posts, Telegraphs and Telephones) and, as an inevitable extension of Speech, for Singing, too. By such accretions he eventually acquired overall responsibility for Communications, which meant that he also took control of measures to prevent the disruption and/or subversion of communications in the occupied territories. It is not clear whether in fact he had this overall responsibility (the Nazis believed in overlapping functions) but as he did control what went out over the posts, telegraphs and telephones, and also by courier service (another inevitable accretion), his directives on all matters that he chose to interest himself in went far and wide, even if they weren't acted on. He showed considerable cunning in that he never made it clear whether these directives were issued solely on his own authority, or whether he was fulfilling his role as Gruppenführer of Posts, Telegraphs (and Telephones) and relaying directives from higher up.

In practice, his authority was not disputed by commanders in the field (when they wished to disregard what they considered his interference in their affairs, it was simpler to give some technical reason why a particular directive was ignored). In Vienna Lüdenscheid had under his command a small body of highly trained men, about three hundred in all, all graduates of his SS training school at Bad Zoeltz, and so was able to actually implement his orders – make arrests, carry out searches, take over buildings (he had taken over the Palais Koeppler). But beyond Vienna, he had to rely on others implementing his instructions, and this was not always done to his satisfaction or with the speed that he would have wished. He made up for this by sending out an increasing number of directives on a range of subjects ever less and less connected with Posts and Telegraphs. It was by some such extension of his actual function that he came to command a motorized SS unit in France in 1940 (actually he was supposed to be co-ordinating communications and establishing efficient post and telegraph and telephone systems in the conquered areas); and it was by an even less explicable extension of his responsibilities that he came to take over the negotiations for the release of Baron Koeppler. (Perhaps he considered it his responsibility because he occupied the Palais Koeppler.)

Lüdenscheid's men wore the black SS uniform with a flash on the arm consisting of a telegraph pole superimposed on an envelope; I didn't notice this distinguishing insignia when they picked me up in the Franz Josefs-Kai, their manner was no more polite than that of the Death's Head units.

'Stefan Kazakh?'

'What?'

'Is that your name?'

'Yes, why?'

'Never mind. Get in.'

'But I have just come from the Metropole.'

'Get in.'

'On whose instructions?'

'Get in.'

'Where am I being taken?'

'You'll see.'

They shot off, accelerating violently as they always did, and continued along the Franz Josefs-Kai as far as the Aspernbrücke, where they turned into the Ringstrasse, then past the old Imperial War Ministry, which had become the headquarters of the German Forces, and the car went on further. Outside the Palais Koeppler it pulled up, abruptly. There were two sentries by the main entrance. Stefan K. was conducted inside.

The walls of the main entrance hall were bespattered with notices, leaflets, posters, proclamations; above the lift cage an index told of the ramifications throughout five floors of Posts and Telegraphs, SS. There was also a stand on which dozens of type-written, officially embossed announcements were pinned up. Signs conveyed the usual instructions about wiping shoes, and proclaimed a variety of prohibitions: it was forbidden to enter without authorization, equally it was forbidden to leave without a check-out pass, smoking was forbidden, so was spitting, loud conversation in the public corridors was not to be engaged in, nor was it permitted to leave personal possessions such as hats, umbrellas or overcoats in the main cloakroom, except by authority; the leaving of litter in any part of the building was strictly forbidden, and anyone who lacked express authority to ride in the lifts was commanded to use the stairs. Evidently his SS escort lacked express authority to ride in the lifts, for they urged Stefan up the stairs, two going ahead of him, two following behind. They all panted up to the top floor. The door of what had formerly been the Baron's flat was held open by a wooden stand, which said that entry was forbidden without an official pass; two black-uniformed SS men in steel helmets stood on guard just inside the hall of the flat, where an Unterscharführer sat at a desk and scrutinized people's passes as they entered or left; at a nod from him, the two guards opened the high gilt and cream doors, and admitted the visitor to the reception rooms, which now were serving as a long waiting room. When the SS men accompanying Stefan Kazakh had shown their authorization and been given a signature, Stefan was told curtly to go in and wait. Inside, perhaps thirty people were sitting or standing, in silence, waiting. Every time the doors at the far end opened and a young SS man appeared in the doorway all eyes fixed on him while he looked down his list prior to calling out a name, whereupon the person called got up, re-focusing his personality as he rose, and walked self-consciously, his footsteps making a loud sound on the bare parquet, towards the far door. The reception rooms, like the ground-floor hall, contained stands with proclamations and propaganda pictures of German soldiers in action, and also the usual admonition to wipe shoes, to keep silent, not to leave litter; the latest special regulations were pinned up under the boldly printed word WARNING. Citizens were warned that it was an offence, punishable by death, to engage in blackmarket activities. Likewise, to forge a travel pass carried the maximum penalty of death by beheading. To listen to foreign radio broadcasts was forbidden, and the maximum penalty for this crime was – predictably – death. Anyone hearing anyone else engaging in dispiriting talk about the war was urged to report the miscreant to the authorities, and failure to do so constituted an offence. The use of real leather for shoe repairs was forbidden.

One or two of the people waiting around in the reception rooms were studying these regulations gloomily for lack of anything else to read; they all had the stiff and weary look of people who have been waitng for many hours. Occasionally people who were together addressed a whispered remark to each other, but never to a stranger; and even these whisperings were shushed by others holding fingers to lips, and indicating a bold notice which stated that it was forbidden to talk.

The former faint – and somewhat eccentric – shabbiness of the Baron's reception rooms had become the more definite shabbiness of all government-requisitioned premises. There was no heating in these rooms, people sat in their overcoats, windows were closed, and there was a sour stuffy smell in the air. Typewritten notices were attached by drawing pins to the panelled doors, when rococo door handles had come off they had been replaced by bakelite ones, some of the fake Bonifazios and Carpaccios and Correggios had been removed and replaced by portraits of Hitler, and as the Führer did not occupy exactly the same space as 'The Adoration of the Magi', the 'Noah's Ark and the Deluge', or for that matter the 'Road to Calvary,' being on the whole less broad, the outlines of the previous pictures were noticeable. The sofas and settees displayed their horsehair stuffing through tears, and daylight (in which these rooms had hardly ever been used recently) showed up the dust that any strong movement of the heavy draperies tended to produce. The frequent wiping of moist hands on arm rests had left dark markings on silk and damask and velvet.

As he came into these rooms, Stefan felt himself being looked over; when he returned the looks the appraising eyes dropped instantly. He felt in his pocket and took out a packet of cigarettes, extracted one carefully and placed it in his mouth; as he was doing this he became aware of half a dozen wagging fingers silently warning him, pointing to the sign that forbade smoking. He gave a casual shrug, smiled, and lit his cigarette. Immediately everyone was looking at him, and a dozen heads were shaking gravely. He took no notice and continued to smoke, and he felt the people close to him turning away, as if to indicate that they were in no way connected with him.

When the far door opened and the SS man, who was young and easily shocked, appeared in the doorway and saw the blue smoke curling in the air, he could not at first believe his eyes, he looked around to discover the source of this forbidden smoke, encountering averted faces everywhere, until his eyes rested on Stefan, on whose face there was an expression of innocence. 'Smoking is forbidden,' he exclaimed, shocked.

'Oh, is it?'

Stefan looked around for somewhere to stub out his cigarette, and finding nothing suitable, asked, 'Is there an ashtray?'

'There is no ashtray,' the SS man said indignantly, 'since smoking is forbidden.'

'Perhaps, in that case, you'd put it out for me,' Stefan said, offering him the cigarette across the room. The SS man, rendered speechless by this impertinence, indicated the floor with a stabbing forefinger.

'Ah,' said Stefan, 'but it is also forbidden to leave litter. I suppose a cigarette is litter?' There were one or two titters at this, which only served to enrage the SS man more.

'Out of the window, out of the window,' he shouted. And when Stefan had disposed of his cigarette in this manner, demanded, 'Name?'

'Kazakh, Stefan Kazakh.'

The SS man looked down his list until he found Stefan's name; he looked at Stefan, then at his list, then at Stefan again.

'Kazakh,' he declared, 'you will wait until you are called.'

'Evidently, but when will that be?'

'And you will be silent.'

'Who am I here to see?' Stefan asked.

'You will be silent,' the SS man repeated, and called out another name, whereupon the person named got up unhappily, and crossed the room.

There was silence again. Stefan sat down on a ballroom chair and crossed his legs. When he looked down, he felt eyes upon him, but whenever he turned to meet these glances the eyes scurried away like mice into holes, lowered eyelids covering their escape. Stefan examined some of these faces sunk in the solitary stillness of waiting: they were different from the faces he sometimes saw at the Metropole, where fear was overt; here, in this room, nothing was admitted. They kept whatever twinges they were feeling to themselves, showing a disdain for everyone else. They were all reasonably well-dressed, and all men: businessmen or members of the professional classes, he'd have said. Stefan knew three or four of them slightly, but they gave no sign of recognition, indeed were at pains to avoid looking in his direction.

The next time the young SS man with the list came to the door, Stefan stood up. 'Can you tell me whom I am seeing, and how long I have to wait?' he asked. There was a rustling of incredulity from the others at this. The SS man glared at Stefan.

'It is forbidden to ask questions,' he declared.

'In that case,' said Stefan, 'will you inform whoever it is I am seeing that I am here.' The SS man made no reply to this, he called out a name, and the person called rose, gave Stefan a reproving look, and walked heavily to the far door.

Two or three minutes later the SS man reappeared, and called out, 'Herr Kazakh. Please.' Stefan noted the Herr and the please. He got up and walked rapidly through the connecting rooms, following the SS man into the wide corridor and along it, past closed doors. About half way down, a screen had been placed, leaving only a narrow opening between it and the french windows giving on to the terrace. Stefan was shown through this opening. He was now outside the library. 'You may wait here,' the SS man said.

In settees against the wall opposite the tall windows sat four men, each man occupying a separate settee.

Leonie's paintings had been removed from her rooms and stood against the walls, awaiting disposal, partially obscuring each other, producing a strange continuity of images: anthropomorphic vegetation overgrowing a red-bearded Christ who had become the precursor of giant eyes on pedestals which ran into rat-faced men and silk-hatted gangsters and a girl looking into a hat shop, after which came an apocalypse, followed by yellow horses and coarse green-bodied women and fossilized men and Venice sinking, and still farther along there were paintings turned to the wall, and others whose subject matter was not apparent.

Stefan sat down on a chair almost opposite the library door, and took out a cigarette. The people in this corridor also gave the impression of having waited a considerable time, but there was something very different about them; for one thing, they met Stefan's eye, they acknowledged his presence, admitted him to their group. One of them, a bored major, kept glancing at his watch and stretching out his long legs. The three others were curious-looking individuals. One was an Indian, of minute size, with the densely lined face of a crafty old woman; he sat with hands folded on his lap, knees close together, unmoving, a continuous smile on his face; the smile, which perhaps wasn't a smile at all, was not related to anything, it was like the smile on some Eastern stone carving, an uncaused smile, or else caused so long ago that the cause was long forgotten and in any case no longer relevant. The man on the next settee was enormously tall, so tall that in the sitting position he looked like a piece of hopelessly entangled flex, arms, legs, fingers complexly interwoven; he had a long neck, which was shaken periodically by a convulsive tic, as if the neck too was seeking to wind itself up in the way that the rest of his body was wound; he had extremely gloomy eyes, deep-sunken and still sinking – a quite freakish-looking man. He and the Indian could have been a fairground act, except that they did not appear to be together. The third man was somewhat more normal-looking, in his fifties, of large build, with an actorish face, broad, florid, an ageing actor – an opera singer perhaps – still playing youthful roles. Talcum powder on his neck and shirt collar. There was a muscular strength about his large and almost lipless mouth. A very queer-looking trio.

The actorish man turned to the spiral man, and said, 'Ah – always one must wait so long. Always.' It sounded as if it was the fiftieth repetition of this sentiment.

'It is always like this,' the spiral man agreed.

They both looked at Stefan, and included him in their mutual commiseration.

'Whom are we waiting to see?' Stefan asked.

'You don't know?' the spiral man asked.

'No.'

'We are here to see Gruppenführer Lüdenscheid,' the actorish man said.

'Who is he?'

'Ahhhh.'

'Yes?'

'I did not say anything.'

'I though you said – ahhhh.'

'That may be so. It could well be. You are very young.'

'Yes.'

'You are a medical man?'

'No. How long does one have to wait?'

'The Gruppenführer is always very busy,' the spiral man said. The Indian did not speak; he was still smiling though. The major had a disdainful expression, indicating that he was nothing to do with these three odd-looking characters. After this brief exchange, there was again silence.

During the next three hours very little was said; nobody came; periodically they heard a name being called out beyond the screen that cut off their section of the corridor, and then they heard footsteps, doors opening and closing.

It was eight in the evening when the library door opened and a solemn young SS man appeared, and said, 'Major, will you go in now.' He turned to the actorish man and the spiral man. 'The Gruppenführer will not be able to see you today. You will be informed when he can see you. Herr Kazakh, you will wait.' To the Indian, who was still smiling, he said nothing.

The major was inside only five minutes; when he re-emerged, the solemn young SS man said to Stefan, 'You will go in now.'

It was cold in the room, almost as cold as it had been in the unheated reception rooms, a noticeable (and presumably intentional) drop in temperature as compared with the corridor, but the man seated at the Baron's desk had a faint film of moisture over his face, a damp handshake of a face. He sat still and upright in his high-backed chair – an unnatural posture – as Stefan approached. He had a nondescript face. A quite undistinguished face. A banal face. The face of a dustman happy in his work. He blinked several times as Stefan came closer.

'You are the Koeppler negotiator?' he said as Stefan sat down.

'Yes.'

'Then you know this flat well?' He was attempting to be conversational, for which he had no gift at all.

'Yes.'

'As you will have seen, we have made some improvements.'

'I noticed you've made changes.'

'You do not consider them improvements?'

'The pictures in the ballroom weren't particularly good, but I preferred them.'

'I agree it is not a good portrait of the Führer.'

'I wasn't referring to the quality of the photography.'

'I had heard that you are an impertinent fellow.' He smiled with prissy sly lips.

'Is that in my dossier?'

'I do not object. I don't like lickspittles. I have kept you waiting: I apologize. There are many people to see, and many matters to deal with. And I have been in Vienna only a short while. I dislike keeping people waiting, it makes them resentful. Then it is much harder to deal with them. It is foolish to antagonize people unnecessarily.' He choked a little on unnecessarily.

'I did not think that bothered you people.'

'When I asked you to come and see me, I thought I would be able to see you immediately. Unfortunately . . .'

'I was not exactly *asked*.'

'Yes, I have been told. It was a mistake, for which I must ask you to accept my apologies. My instructions were that a car was to be sent for you. One's orders are not always executed in the spirit in which they are given. The men in question will be reprimanded.'

His voice was monotonous, that of a man dictating a letter. He had no gestures. His hands, resting on the desk top, did not move. When he spoke, his mouth movements seemed disproportionately meagre. A ventriloquist's mouth in a dustman's face. The blinking of the eyes was the main movement in his face. A whole intricate system of blinks.

'Now,' he continued. 'The negotiations for the release of Baron Koeppler. What is holding them up? What is the difficulty? You understand, it is not my direct responsibility. But perhaps I can be of some help.'

'The difficulty is in agreeing terms'

'What terms are you proposing, Herr Kazakh?'

226

'The Koeppler organization has agreed to make over to the German Government all of the Baron's property and other assets in Germany and Austria.'

'But that is already accomplished.'

'Illegally.'

'You must accept, Herr Kazakh, that in Germany today the Führer is the law. Also, it appears that the Baron's holdings in Germany have diminished. Large sums have evidently been transferred out of the Reich.'

'I know nothing about any of that. I am acting as the agent for the Swiss company. Any proposal you have will be conveyed to them.'

'I have no authority to state this as a firm offer but I am of the opinion that a million dollars, *in dollars*, payable in Switzerland, is a sum that would meet with a not unfavourable response.'

'I, too, have no firm authority: to accept or decline. I will convey your offer, if you wish. Personally, I think the Swiss company dealing with this matter would have difficulty in finding a million dollars . . .'

'I find that hard to believe, in view of the Baron's exceeding wealth.'

'You have already taken a large part of his wealth. The remainder is not at his disposal; you understand, the transfer of such a large sum – in dollars – to Germany raises political questions.'

'That was why I suggested Switzerland, a numbered account. There is no need for anyone except us to know . . .'

Stefan interrupted him. 'While it is true the Baron's associates abroad are prepared to make a deal with the German Government for his release, I can tell you, in confidence, that there are those in Zurich who would be quite pleased for the deal to fall through, or for the demands of the German Government to be so excessive that they could not be met. You understand, every extra day you hold the Baron, and while you shown no sign of your readiness to release him, these rivals of the Baron's grow in strength, and in influence. At the moment I have instructions to negotiate, to find out the German Government's terms, which I will report back to Zurich. But who is to say that if matters are delayed too long, business being business, it may not be decided to write off the Baron as – an irrecoverable loss. However, if you wish, I will convey your offer.'

'All this to and fro. That is how the stalemate has arisen.

Frankly. Herr Kazakh, I do not believe that you are unable to accept the offer yourself, just as you don't believe that I am unable to make it. There has been altogether too much fencing on both sides.'

'In this matter I am an agent of the Swiss company. I take my instructions from Zurich.'

'Come now, is it likely that Baron Koeppler would place himself in the position of being dependent on the decisions of his business associates in Zurich? You have yourself pointed out the hazards of that, which he would surely have foreseen, a man who has had the foresight to transfer a great deal of his wealth out of Germany; I do not believe that such a man would have failed to provide for the present contingency. And he would have been foolish,' choking a little, he poured himself a glass of water and swallowed gurgling slightly, 'foolish to provide less than a million dollars. My own belief is that the fund contains more than that, a million and a half perhaps, possibly even two millions; in a numbered account; the money to be paid over only on your signature, that would be sensible. It would not be sensible to appoint as his negotiator someone who was dependent on the decisions of business associates in other countries, a cumbersome arrangement, the Baron would have calculated that possibly they might not be as responsive – to his predicament – as he would wish – them to be. He would not, as a sensible man, wish to place himself – so entirely – in their hands. If my reasoning is in any way faulty, please be so good as to indicate where.'

'Your reasoning is sound. I wish ours had been as sound. Unfortunately, we did not think of all the things you think we thought of.'

'The Baron is not a fool, neither are you, of course you would have thought of all this; to have remained in Vienna without providing sufficient funds to secure his release would have been sheer idiocy, which is something of which I would not accuse the Baron, or you. This being the case, I deduce, therefore, that such funds were provided, and are available. Fact: you are not easily intimidated or brow-beaten, you stand your ground, you bargain – I have been through the files. Furthermore, additionally – the Baron is experienced in choosing the right man for a particular task, for what task would he require someone with your qualities? The question is – at what are you most adept, Herr Kazakh? And the answer is: bluffing and bargaining, it would seem – it would seem. Conclusion: that is what you are doing, bluffing and bargaining. To carry messages to and fro calls for a messenger. The Baron's lawyers are a highly respected Gentile firm, eminently suitable as intermediaries, but they were not chosen, you were. If I find a man on that building opposite repairing the roof, and it turns out he is an expert marksman, I assume that, as it is possible to get people who are not expert marksmen to repair roofs, his marksmanship is of relevance to his being on the rooftop. Similarly, when I find that a man with your qualifications has been chosen to act on the Baron's behalf, I refuse to believe he is a messenger; I assume, therefore, that you are in a position to accept my offer – or to ensure that it is accepted.'

'There is something you have left out of your reasoning.'

'What is that?'

'Such reasoning is based on the assumption that people act rationally, always. It may be rational for a wealthy man to value his life more highly than a million dollars, but supposing he doesn't?'

'Accepted. Good. Very good. But the ploy is double-edged. Just as we cannot count on the Baron's rationality, you cannot count on ours. If you offer less than a million, it might be rational for us to accept, if we felt it was the most we could get. Even half a million is after all a good price for one man, but we can be as irrational as he, and refuse.'

'You have overestimated the funds at our disposal.'

'Why such meanness?'

'You know rich men.'

'They are the same as other men, they wish to live, and they do not like to pay, if they don't have to, and they always think they don't have to. Sometimes they miscalculate. I must warn you: to continue with the pretence that you have to obtain authority from Zurich will be expensive. If you tell me, now, that you accept my terms, that is good enough, that is acceptable – you see: I am reasonable. It will take a little time, I realize, to settle the practicalities. But if you do not accept *now*, I shall charge you interest on the million dollars, until such time as you do accept. Every day that you delay will cost you interest. Is that not the method of business? If you agree today, well and good – I will allow ten days free of interest for the completion of the arrangements. But thereafter interest commences. Those are the Jews' methods, are they not? If, in ten days' time, the sum of one million dollars is transferred to a numbered account in Switzerland that I shall give you, the Baron will be free to leave Austria together with the Baroness.'

'I agree to three-quarters of a million. Half to be paid now; the remaining half when the Baron and Baroness are safely in Switzerland.'

'What guarantee do we have for the second half?'

'I would be the guarantee. I will be here.'

'You are not worth anything, Herr Kazakh.'

'No. But you must calculate – would I make such an offer, if I thought it wasn't going to be met?'

Lüdenscheid was silent for a time. His eyes blinked steadily. Then he said, 'I propose that the Baroness remains. Until the second half is paid.'

'That is not acceptable.'

'A pity. It means the negotiations fall through.'

Stefan got up. 'The Baron is a sick man,' he said. 'You will have read that in the file. You have a diminishing asset in him. Today, three-quarters of a million dollars. In ten days, who knows? A dead man?'

'A good point. I accept your proposal. You see – I am reasonable.'

'Fine.'

'One further point.'

'Yes.'

'Any attempt at retaliatory measures by the Conspiracy of the Elders of Zion, as a result of this transaction, would have the most serious consequences.'

'What!' Stefan laughed.

'I know the vengefulness of the Jews.'

'What conspiracy are you talking about?'

'The world Jewish conspiracy.'

'That is sheer fantasy, as you know.'

His expression had not changed. 'I know the Jews,' he said. 'I know how they stick together. I know their cunning. *If I forget thee O Jerusalem may my right hand forget its cunning*. The Jews are a secret society in the world, they infiltrate, they communicate in secret signs, looks, gestures, nudges, I have seen it. Conspiracy is natural to them. When one Jew sees another, he knows him as a fellow conspirator: the bond is in their blood. Nothing need be prearranged, or said. Each Jew knows his role in the world conspiracy, as the hatched crocodile knows to turn towards the river.'

'You know that I am a Jew, that must have been in the file.'

'In the file it says you are a half Jew. Your mother is not Jewish.'

'I thought any amount of Jewish blood, according to Nazi ideology, is enough to make someone a Jew?'

'It is my opinion, Herr Kazakh, that you are not even a half Jew. I have been studying your features. I know what Jews look like. They are small and you are tall, they have oily skins, and yours is clear. Their hair, their hair is coarse and dark, and yours is auburn and soft. They have a characteristic smell, and they do not walk firmly and they cannot look you in the eye. None of which applies to you. Therefore I am satisfied you are not a Jew.'

'I see. Then my father wasn't a Jew either?'

'*He* was. That has been gone into. That is indisputable. But it is my opinion – after having seen you, my conviction – he was not your father. In view of what is known of your mother, it is quite probable. I apologize for casting such aspersions, but to have had a whore for a mother is preferable to having had a Jew for a father. Is that not so? Now – to continue. There are some details we must still settle. It is almost eight thirty, I propose we continue over supper.'

Lüdenscheid, mania rising, no sign of it, nothing changed in his demeanour, you shake yourself – is this the same man talking? He does not say it like a madman, but matter-of-factly, prosaically, without warning: the enamel of his teeth chipped from too vigorous brushing, wherein is a man's mania revealed? – in the too vigorous brushing of teeth?

Lüdenscheid: didn't believe in unnecessary executions, very reasonable man, reasonable man, mad, three lumpish daughters on his hands, and a wife who called him Ernschien, you could do business with him, a closed mind but with ports of entry, you could wheedle your way in, insinuate your way in through the maze, if you knew your way, I did, I knew the way into that mad mind –

Supper was extraordinary: in the Baron's dining-room. Eight blond SS officers around the long table, four blond SS men in spotless white serving, and the little Indian sitting there smiling, eating nothing but dried raisins, while the others gorged themselves on roasted wild boar. Wirthof was there. Lüdenscheid introduced him as his aide – 'Ah, but of course you know each other.'

'Kazakh' -- in a whispered confidence -- 'have I put you on to a good thing?'

'What?'

'Lüdenscheid. *Lüdenscheid*. It was my idea. How did it go?'

'You suggested it?'

'Of course. Listen, Kazakh, he's very interested in' – his voice became even softer – 'hypnotism. I told him about you.'

On the figured oak floor a circle had been drawn in chalk; points on the circumference were numbered from one to seven, and lines joined these points to form a series of inner triangles. Inside the vertices other numbers were written: 785, 333, 48, 99, 12, 24. These numbers were repeated in differing combinations. Alongside this circle there was a series of boxes in the form of ascending steps, and in each box words and numbers were written, and in the highest box there was a circle containing a triangle containing a circle, in the box below there were two concentric circles, and so on, each box containing a different symbol, with the final box containing the symbols O and O minus.

During supper Stefan had Lüdenscheid on his right and Wirthof on his left. The Gruppenführer did not eat what the others were eating. He ate a little wheat germ, two raw eggs, some nuts and raisins, baked potato jackets, leaving the inside of the potato on his plate, and finished up with dried prunes. He drank nothing except buttermilk. The little Indian looked on approvingly, smiling his non-smile.

'A frugal diet,' Lüdenscheid declared as he masticated the meagre flesh of his final prune, 'is essential to good health and clarity of mind. Excessive eating draws the blood from the brain to the stomach, and thus it impairs judgment. Many of the most calamitous decisions in history have been taken after an overlarge meal. The mind is clearest in the morning, after the first bowel motion, when the body has rid itself of its toxins. As the day progresses, more and more toxins are absorbed, in one way or another. Stress, by using up the body's natural restorative properties at an excessive rate, diminishes the capacity to arrive at sound decisions. Bad foods, contaminated by chemical impurities, as most of our food is these days, further reduce the individual's reasoning capacities, because his system is devoting itself entirely to eliminating these poisonous substances, leaving insufficient of the vital fluids needed for sound reasoning. Of course, the average person has sufficient surplus of the vital fluids not to be affected by the average amount of stress he is likely to encounter. But a person in my position, who has to constantly bear the burden of decision, is subjected to infinitely greater stress than the average person, and therefore uses up his vital fluids at a far higher rate. That is the explanation, Herr Kazakh, of this somewhat sparse meal you see me eating. It is not that I do not enjoy food.'

He went on and on in his monotonous voice, choking from time to time. Nature provided its own cures, a man whose ear was attuned to the voice of nature – something that was virtually impossible in our city culture – would find his own remedies. But a man needed help in this, for the busy life of public affairs deafened the ear to the voice of nature. Had Kazakh read Priessnitz? A man of the greatest insight. As a shepherd's boy he had observed how a roebuck, shot in a hunt, cured its lame leg by making daily for a spring and immersing its leg in cold water. Daily an improvement occurred, and eventually the leg was completely cured. That was a true nature cure. And Priessnitz had instituted this form of treatment in the Priessnitz Sanatorium on the Grafenberg, near Freiwaldau. Lüdenscheid had himself tried the water immersions. The knee immersions. The immersion of hip and thigh. The total immersions. Unfortunately, cold water did not have a beneficial effect on him. Alternate hot and cold baths were better, and hot baths best of all. Each man had to find the cure that suited him. His objection to the cold immersion dogma was that it ordained the same treatment for everyone, irrespective of the malady, and he was sure that individual adjustments of the treatment were needed to suit the varying metabolisms of different individuals. Had Kazakh read Hieronymus Bock, the sixteenth-century herbalist? Or Theophrastus of Hohenheim? Did he know of Father Kneipp and his water cures? Always he had felt, instinctively, that by observing the rhythms of natural life – nature's own process of growth and elimination – a man could discover the secret of sound health. 'If you have observed how nature retreats into herself as the winter months approach, in order to rest and repair itself, in order that it may again achieve the yearly miracle of rebirth, then you know, Herr Kazakh, that a man must also withdraw in order to be restored. Man cannot do this on a seasonal basis: therefore a man must set aside time, in the busy routine of daily life, for withdrawal, so that he can return again to his task, renewed.'

And so he went on, choking periodically.

When, finally, he got up and left, Wirthof said, grinning, 'Well, Kazakh, have I put you on to something good?'

The department of Posts and Telegraphs, having only a nominal militia at its disposal, was much concerned with the making of pronouncements. Twice a day, members of the administration and military liaison officers in Vienna were called to the Palais Koeppler to hear the latest directives and to receive 'guidance'. Guidance was given on a great range of matters, from the proper way to celebrate Christmas to the soldier's correct attitude towards executions.

Every day a great mass of new instructions, prohibitions, exhortations, orders, directives and 'guidance' came from Berlin over the telegraphs, through the posts, and on the telephone. It was the function of Lüdenscheid's department to communicate all this material to the appropriate sections of the occupying forces in the conquered territories (for this purpose Austria was considered an occupied territory, though not for others). And on all matters relating to communications, their maintenance or their disruption, he also issued his own directives, and he was inclined to interpret communications as meaning whatever he wanted them to mean.

Wirthof, as his principal aide, often acted as his spokesman.

Twice daily the administrators, the officials, the military liaison officers and the representatives of sectional interests assembled in the third reception room at the Baron's flat for these 'conferences', military in the morning, civil in the early evening. They sat on delicate gilt ballroom chairs, the caning of which was no longer sufficiently resistant to the fidgeting of so many massive posteriors, and sometimes gave way.

Wirthof had a good manner for his role of spokesman. He had a good way with pronunciamentos – he could get his tongue around them, which not everyone could: even those monstrous German portmanteau words which strung together two or three concepts in one long-tailed clanking harangue came seductively off his tongue. He could get out words that choked Lüdenscheid. And to the driest of them, and to the most brutal, he lent his youthfulness and his glitter.

Lüdenscheid was proud of him, you could see that.

You might almost have attributed to him paternal feelings, seeing the way he blinked with satisfaction (you had to know him to realize that those particular blinks signified satisfaction in that immobile face) when Wirthof delivered one of the Gruppenführer's more cumbersome exhortations as if it were pleasantry.

Lüdenscheid felt quite dashing to hear himself so well pronounced. It was a delight to him to hear his directives spoken – so well spoken, so authoritatively and yet so seductively, so Germanically, so culturally – by Wirthof. The clumsiness of the phraseology, the tortuousness of the concepts, the madness of the ideas became in Wirthof's delivery poetical and mystical, at any rate to listener Lüdenscheid.

Wirthof himself, bored, hardly took in what he was saying, and it is likely that his audience was less than enthralled by the ideas of the SS Chief of Posts and Telegraphs on subjects like eugenics, German culture, motherhood, inner health, Yuletide celebrations –

'All armed units of the SS and the Police should celebrate the solstice and yuletide in their quarters, so far as the possibilities of war permit. The significance of these celebrations – the eternal return of the sun and the victory of light – remains always the same. The way in which these celebrations are carred out depends on the possibilities afforded by the position of the troops. But it should be noted that Carnival is not derived from the term "carne vale" (goodbye, meat), which owes its origin to the custom of fasting introduced by the Roman Catholic Church, but from "carrus navalis" meaning "shipping cart". These carts, representing ships, were used in the Shrovetide festivities of the Italian people, in the expression of joy and happiness, and were therefore quite in contrast to the gloomy "carne vale" of the Church. The ship is among seafaring nations the symbol of fertility. Ash is considered by peasants as a most efficient manure. When the Church introduced fasting for forty days, it was destined to drive all the joy of living out of Shrovetide celebrations.'

Quite so, quite so, two dozen drooping heads agreed.

'Proper attention is to be given to the findings of the *National-Sozialistische Korrespondenz* concerning the Jewish origin of Roosevelt. Photographs of Roosevelt that indicate Jewish features can be used to good advantage in this connection. Due attention should also be paid to the fact that he is a cripple, whose physical incapacity has given rise to megalomania.' Quite so, quite so.

Apart from these general pronouncements intended to guide propaganda and press officers primarily, there were announcements of orders and regulations, announcements of death penalties passed on black marketeers, rebuttals of rumours about special privileges conferred on SS and other officials in the sphere of rationing and housing, and exhortations to put up with difficulties and shortages for the cause of German victory.

To the commanders in the field there were instructions about the provision of medically inspected brothel facilities for the troops; and SS men, before going into action, were urged to procreate a child with a female of good Nordic blood. There were instructions for the setting up of special homes for the mothers.

'The Reichsführer SS has decreed that beyond the boundaries of bourgeois laws and customs which may in themselves be necessary, it will now become the great task, even outside the marriage bond, for German women and girls of good blood, not in frivolity but in deep moral earnestness, to become the mothers of the children of soldiers going off to war. Since the men of best blood are the bravest, they are the ones most likely to be killed, and a nation cannot afford to lose its most valuable blood on the battlefield, and so provision for the replenishment of the stock must be made.'

There were announcements of Mother Crosses, for the wives of SS men who gave birth to seven or more children.

When SS men died, their graves should be marked with a Teutonic cross, and not with the insipid symbol of Christianity.

Mothers in *Lebensborn* homes must not entertain male guests, and they must eat fruit and porridge for breakfast, English Lords and Ladies were brought up on porridge, and they had the slenderest figures. German mothers must get used to porridge, and their resultant blood pressures must be taken and statistics compiled.

Wirthof was bored. He wanted to be a general, not a spokesman. When he got too bored he got drunk, and then he did not deliver Lüdenscheid's pronunciamentos quite so trippingly or so seductively or so culturally.

Though Lüdenscheid disapproved of drunkenness, he made allowances for Wirthof who had blown up six pillboxes and been decorated personally by the Führer. A very useful man to have in Posts and Telegraphs to emphasize to its denigrators that it was a fighting force, not just a branch of the Post Office. He arrested Jews on the same principle, to show that the disrupters of the posts and telegraphs and telephones, the sowers of discord on the wires, the spreaders of subversion, the communicators of obscenity through the mails, the speakers of calumny, the singers of perfidy, for all of which the Jews were notorious, had him to reckon with.

Gerstner's window in the Kärntnerstrasse consisted of a pyramid of cardboard cake boxes, which did not, however, contain any cakes, as Wirthof discovered when he tried to buy one. There was a reliable black market in alcohol, but it was exceedingly difficult to obtain real pastries.

'It will be an evil day if the Germanic people do not survive. It will be the end of beauty and Kultur, of the creative power of this earth,' he announced to the drooping heads in the Baron's third reception room.

He was really most upset about the pastries.

'Snapshots of executions are strictly forbidden because of the adverse effect of such snapshots falling into wrong hands and being misinterpreted,' he announced to the liaison officers of the SS Death's Head units who sat close together in the final row of ballroom chairs, the dust-heavy curtains undrawn behind them.

'On the Emerald Tablets of Hermes Trismegistos was inscribed "Learn to separate".'

'The first step is self-realization, and the second is separation.'

'Everything in the universe eats and is eaten: it is the cosmic system of reciprocal maintenance.'

Lüdenscheid loved to hear him speak his injunctions, his

exhortations, his enjoinders, his lessons, his expostulations; woe betide anyone in the Baron's third reception room noticed dropping off by Lüdenscheid.

'Every creature feeds on something lower than itself in the cosmic hierarchical system, and it is in turn fed on by something higher. The average hydrogen of man is 24, he sustains himself on hydrogen 96, and serves as food for something with an average hydrogen of 6. That is the Law of Seven, illustrated by the circle. In accordance with this law, which is the law of the universe, the higher forms of man must feed off the lower forms. In the scale of man there are groups of men designated as food, because they themselves are incapable of higher achievements, lacking as they do the basic minimum of vital hydrogen. The function of such creatures is to serve the higher man, as it is the function of the ox to serve all men.'

Ah! – the heyday of Gerstner's – imagine: ships made of pastry, loaded with marzipan fruit: statues, fountains, castles, soldiers of bitter-sweet chocolate: the *Milchrahmstrudels*, flaky paper-thin crust, filled with sweetened curds, cream and raisins, and the *Sachertorte*, not too sweet, neither too soft nor too dry, nor too granular; it dissolved in the mouth.

The cabarets of Vienna bored Wirthof terribly – mostly acrobats and jugglers and bad comedians. There were no magicians any longer. Together with fortune-tellers, crystal-gazers, soothsayers of every kind, readers of palms, interpreters of cranial bumps, they had all been banned from the variety theatres and cabarets – Wirthof had himself proclaimed the ban, which originated from Dr Goebbels, who was convinced that one of these men had exercised a malign influence on Hess and induced him to make his flight to Scotland.

Sometimes, when he was bored, and the bars that he frequented had run out of their under-counter supplies of Bols gin, Scotch whisky, Polish vodka and French cognac, he went with some of his chums from the Death's Head units to Salon Bella in the Albertinagasse, where rare entertainment was to be had. The girls were known, affectionately it is claimed, as belladonnas. There was always plenty to drink at Salon Bella.

'If you pour gold dust into the sea it is dissipated. A nation with a high average vital hydrogen, like the Germanic nation, must preserve its racial purity and not allow it to become dissipated. A great nation can feed off a lesser nation, and incorporate its vital hydrogen, but it must not merge (that is to say, exchange vital hydrogen) with a lesser nation for in that way it dissipates itself in the sea and in the wind. Ideally, procreation should take place only between people whose vital hydrogen is approximately equal, in this way multiplication of vital hydrogen occurs, but if a person with a vital hydrogen of 19, a high content, procreates with someone whose vital hydrogen is low, say 30, the offspring will have an even lower vital hydrogen than the lower partner's.'

Wirthof definitely had a glassy look at times.

In the winter of 1941, potatoes vanished from the shops, suddenly there wasn't one to be got, first time this had happened: potatoes had always been plentiful up till then – in restaurants you could always get a second helping, free, to supplement the meagre portion of meat. But suddenly there were no potatoes. The summer had been abnormally wet, which had affected the potato crop, and then the autumn was particularly cold, and the cold had started earlier than usual, and the potatoes couldn't be moved from the earth pits, they froze in the cold freight wagons. Eventually, the government had to use heated passenger coaches to transport them, which meant that the passenger services were drastically cut.

Food shops were becoming emptied of their stocks in the first hour of opening, and in other shops those shirts and pyjamas and shoes in the windows were *nur Attrapen*, only for decoration. The liquor shops had shelves of bottles containing coloured water, also for decoration.

What made it so striking, this decline – and the difficulty of getting enough soap for shaving, and the poor latherless stuff that it was, and how you could smell the lack of soap in trams and cinemas and the cafés – what made it so striking was its suddenness, up till the time of the Russian campaign there had been no grave shortage. On the contrary, every minor bureaucrat had his supply of best French champagne, and soldiers returning on leave were laden with silver foxes from Norway, silk stockings from the Boulevard Haussmann, perfumes, cigarettes, bottles of Armagnac: the servant girls of Vienna had never had such gifts. But all at once the cupboards of Europe were bare, totally ransacked, there was no more, and the war began to be felt by Germans at home. And the gloom was particularly severe because the privation they now experienced to a greater or lesser degree followed so close upon the greedy gobbling up of what had seemed like an inexhaustible supply of plunder.

As Posts and Telegraphs had taken over Singing in addition to Speech, the department's responsibilities included the distribution to the proper authorities of officially commissioned songs to celebrate victories. These songs were top secret, because they usually anticipated a campaign which had not yet been launched, and though it was desirable that these songs should be available to accompany the start of the campaign and then the announcement of its victorious conclusion (the one following hard upon the other in the beginning), they must not be known of prematurely, in case they gave away intended military strikes.

In the third reception room of the Baron's flat there was soon a stack of variously broken ballroom chairs, reduced to this condition by the cumulative fidgeting of bureaucrats and Death's Head Hussars with too large posteriors.

'The Jews have the lowest vital hydrogen of all, for they have dissipated it in the wind, for they are the wind, and they have little more average hydrogen than animals and inanimate objects, though, of course, there may be individual exceptions to this. The Jews are the leeches of vital hydrogen. That is the explanation of their greed and their profiteering. Lacking sufficient vital hydrogen themselves, they would feed off those with a high content, as leeches feed off an unconscious man. Germany under the leadership of our Führer has awakened to consciousness of itself, and will no longer allow itself to be sucked dry of its vital fluids. The Führer has aroused the Germanic peoples to consciousness, and thus enabled them to fulfil their role in the cosmic hierarchical system.'

It was Wirthof who read out the official comments on the fighting capability of the enemy. A defeated adversary was sometimes granted 'misguided valour' or 'fanatical courage', but usually he was credited with no more than 'bestial tenacity' or 'sheer animal instinct'. Such qualities had nothing to do with the German understanding of bravery, which was a conscious assertion of faith in the Fatherland and the Führer.

His job did not seem to be taking him any nearer to becoming a general, though he was the SS equivalent of lieutenant-colonel – Obersturmbannführer.

Wirthof was regarded as an excellent spokesman, even when slightly drunk. How, after the best part of a bottle of Armagnac, he could get his tongue around *Aufenthaltserlaubnis* or *Wirtschaftsverwaltungshauptamt* amazed everyone.

He and Lüdenscheid were very intimate. On occasions when some aspect of the department's work was being challenged, and Lüdenscheid was in the process of framing one of his tortuous replies, sweating and choking from the effort, Wirthof would get it out for him quick as a flash, smilingly, disarmingly, knowing exactly what Lüdenscheid had been about to say, and able to say it quicker. When that blank expression of slow deliberation crossed the face of the Gruppenführer, and the questioner knew he was in for a long wait, a faint nod from Lüdenscheid to Wirthof resolved the situation. 'The Gruppenführer is of the opinion . . .' Wirthof would just elaborate on one or other of the Gruppenführer's standard themes with which he was familiar. Lüdenscheid did not expend his breath recklessly.

Wirthof walked with Lüdenscheid in the Stadtpark. They did this quite often – Wirthof, as the favourite, was often required to walk in the Stadtpark with Lüdenscheid, who did it for exercise, in which he was a believer. Lüdenscheid when he walked in the Stadtpark, or anywhere else, did not merely stroll, which was useless as exercise, but walked fast, inhaling and exhaling rhythmically and holding his stomach in and flexing his muscles in sequence. He loved the laburnum anagyroides.

'In certain circumstances, the Reichsführer SS and Chief of Police will order flogging in addition to detention. There is no objection to spreading rumours of this increased punishment to add to the deterrent effect.'

The extent to which advice and directives were acted on depended on individual commanders, on their standing in the hierarchy, and on their personal relationships with the Nazi leaders.

Where instructions had to be conveyed to more senior officials and officers, those who did not normally attend the conferences, Wirthof acted as Lüdenscheid's personal courier, calling on Gauleiters or generals and delivering to them sealed instructions, which, after having been noted, had to be burned in his presence.

'The following offenders, considered agitators, will be hanged:

anyone who makes inciting speeches and holds meetings, forms cliques, loiters around with others; who for the purpose of supplying the enemy with atrocity stories collects true or false information about the activities of the SS.'

'In cases where a person in the occupied territories is endangering German security and is arrested but not executed within eight days, the prisoner is to be transported into Germany in secrecy, the prisoner will vanish without leaving a trace, no information to be given of his whereabouts or fate. This will have a deterrent effect. Such a person will vanish into the Night and Fog.'

'Vital hydrogen is dissipated by miscegenation.'

'The legality of the executions to be explained to the men. They are to be influenced in such a way as to suffer no ill effect in their character or mental attitude. The need for rooting out the delinquent from the common weal to be stressed.'

'This whole people is held together by Nordic-Phalian-Germanic blood.'

In the occupied countries, children who were racially good types but whose parents were politically suspect, should, where possible, be abducted from their parents before the age of five, and brought to Germany for Germanization.

'The moment the law which is the foundation of our race is forgotten, and the law of selection and austerity towards ourselves, we shall have the germ of death in us. Our principle: blood, selection, austerity.'

'No man shall know absolutely who commands him; obedience is to the command, not the commander, to the order not the man.'

There was the hierarchy.

There was the maze.

There was Night and Fog, into which people vanished and out of which came the command not to be questioned.

'Magicians, fortune-tellers, crystal-gazers, soothsayers of every kind, mesmerists, palm-readers, readers of cranial bumps, starers into space – all are proscribed, by order.'

Walking in the Stadtpark, the pale SS man with the violet eyes, shivering with cold, and the peculiar-looking one, who breathed rhythmically, inhaling and exhaling forcefully, always shadowed by his bodyguard. The smaller man's hips were rounded more than is normally the case in men, and his ceremonial dagger, because of the comparative shortness of his thighs, fell unnaturally, inelegantly, suggesting a lack of expertise in the matter of wearing ceremonial daggers, the dagger should not ride up encumbering the legs, but stay ceremonially at the side – that is the whole point of a ceremonial dagger.

The pale one, to whom elegance came easily, eyed the young and youngish women, and even the older women, with the smirk of one who knows their essential weakness, their womanliness, their inescapable, if temporarily denied, need of him, but the other one did not look at the women, and indeed seemed to consider the roving eye of his companion a source of irritation. The peculiar-looking one was definitely senior in rank, evident even to those who could not assess the comparative amounts of silver braiding on their respective shoulders. The one with the some-what too rounded hips and shortish thighs did look once at a woman, her face unseen in widow's weeds, and his eyes sought to penetrate the heavy veils – to see her grief, as some men look at a trim ankle or a pert breast or the protuberance of a suspender clip.

Such men walk with lumpish daughters and dowdy wives in the menopause (who invariably wear brown fur pelts across their costumed bosoms, and brooches from which some stones are missing, and remark in undertones upon the characters of passing acquaintances); such men are called Ernschien by their wives, and perform pleasureless intercourse with them once every two months or so (thinking the while of widows in their weeds and long black veils and grief); such men, called Ernschien, ejaculate noisily, ahead of their wives, who none the less, as a matter of form, make the requisite noises of compliant satisfaction and, possibly, in an ecstasy of self-abnegation experience a flutter of something akin to feeling in their wombs, where they have made lumpish daughters. Such men work in stores in the Kärntner-strasse, selling ostrich feathers, sidling up unnoticed and making jump women with whalebone corsets (such men have peeped discreetly through the known chinks in the changing cubicles), and become store managers after fifteen years, or Gruppenführers in the SS, in charge of posts and telegraphs. Such men, too, called Ernschien by their wives in the menopause, have capacities – for organization, for command – not appreciated by store owners of Jewish descent or affiliation, and are not fully stretched selling ostrich feathers, not really realized in their aberrations peeping into cubicles, nor do their ejaculations every other month, or their three lumpish daughters with female ailments (including phantom pregnancies), satisfy their immortal longings. Such men arouse the contempt of Wirthof when they walk in the Stadtpark inhaling and exhaling rhythmically, and breathing in the fragrance of the flowers, but also command him with the full power of their self-overcoming, which, it follows, such men must have in abundance to have overcome themselves, with all that they have had to over-come, and on the hard stone of the world's contempt such men sharpen themselves into the very essence of knives. Only there lingers in such men the memory of their bluntness – and they crave respect.

Although Wirthof was the favourite and walked with Lüden-scheid in the Stadtpark, he was not sycophantic, on that he absolutely insisted; Wirthof considered sycophancy contemptible. On the contrary, Wirthof maintained he was almost alone in refusing to be a lickspittle, and he spoke his mind to the Gruppen-führer. What was more, Lüdenscheid respected this outspoken-ness. The fact that he sometimes finished Lüdenscheid's sentences for him, or expounded his thoughts, was not to be taken as indicating subservience; quite the contrary, whatever the contrary might be.

'On the other hand, Kazakh, I can quite see why the others are all manoeuvring to win his favour – he has influence, you see, he has the Führer's ear, he is in a very strong position, having been with Hitler from the start. Oh he's a very remarkable man, an organizing genius. And inspires fantastic loyalty. And his military ideas are extraordinary – daring, bold, I would go as far as to say inspired. I know for a fact that he dislikes his present job, and would give anything to be at the front, commanding men in battle, even though his health is poor and he does not have great physical endurance. But his mind is extraordinary, Kazakh, his military thinking and mine correspond entirely. He has absolutely original ideas on the use of armour, things I have been saying for years. It really is absurd to waste such a man in Vienna, though you must not suppose that his sphere of influence is confined to the post and telegraph services, he has very extensive duties. You should have seen him in action – with astrologers and sooth-sayers in attendance, takes them everywhere. Ostensibly his task was to secure the communications, which meant taking over post offices, telegraph offices, radio transmitting stations, etcetera – many a post office was staunchly defended . . . those village postmistresses, formidable women! Gave us a great deal of trouble. After all, one has compunctions. But the lines of communication had to be secured, absolutely vital. Kazakh, you should have seen it.

'Reinhardt's panzer corps was across at Monthermé, and at Sedan Guderian had a good bridgehead for one division established and was blasting the British and French dive bombers out of the sky, and by afternoon he'd got all three panzer divisions across and well established. The French were beginning to crack open wide as a split virgin. They were in full retreat and we were hounding them. It was fantastic. At times we were averaging forty m.p.h., stirring up the most incredible dust clouds. Dust as far as the eye could see. Our own shell craters were the biggest obstacles: had to detour them. The roads were clogged with refugees, horse carts piled high, abandoned French equipment, guns, lorries, burnt-out tanks, and there were French troops scared out of their wits hiding in the ditches and bolting in all directions. It was a spectacle to see. Going through villages we saw kids scattering as if they'd seen the devil, we were trying to be friendly – offered them chocolate, but they were like scared rabbits, you couldn't approach them, those First World War atrocity stories the Belgians put about, you know – about German soldiers chopping off hands of women and children, those atrocity stories stick. Our troops were very decent, I didn't see anyone behave dishonourably. The nights were spectacular, farms were burning around Clairfayts, and our tracer bullets were sending out a deadly rain of fire, the French were surrendering in their hundreds, we had to build prisoner-of-war cages in the fields to hold them. And then we were into the Maginot Line and through it, it was fantastic, not just a beautiful dream but real. It was outside Clairfayts that there was the unpleasantness of the French infantry captain. We'd disarmed a whole lot of French, two or three hundred, and ordered them to start marching, anywhere out of our way, didn't matter where, we didn't have time to take prisoners and couldn't spare the men to act as guards, and this French captain, you see, refused to budge. Just refused. They were clogging up our road, impeding our progress, and while he wasn't marching none of the French was marching, and consequently Lüdenscheid told him that if he didn't obey he would be shot, and he just spat, the French captain, and of course I had to do it – that is to say, shoot him – you see, there was too much at stake. We moved on.

It was fantastic. In extended order, over a front of two thousand yards, depth of twelve miles, we went straight across country, slicing through the high cornfields, tanks, anti-aircraft guns, field guns, all with infantry mounted on them, horse-drawn columns, the attack moved forward, and we could smell the sea. Don't imagine it was easy. The French had more tanks, and their tanks have 40mm. and 60mm. armour whereas our mediums have only 30mm. But where the French make their mistake is that they don't use their tanks purposefully, they use them piecemeal, and as infantry support, whereas we use punches of armour: we kept smashing through their thin lines – we had a great phalanx of armour thrusting across the Meuse.

'Lüdenscheid was remarkable; as I say, his health is not altogether good, but he never lets up. As a matter of fact when I talked to him about you, how you cured my headaches, he was very interested, and wanted to hear more. He's very interested in everything like that. Of course, a lot of the characters he has around him are just quacks, those astrologers and Indians. In my opinion they're complete charlatans, but he has a great interest in any form of natural cure, distrusts medicines and doctors, won't let doctors near him. He's a remarkable man, as you'll discover. His strong point is organization. Can organize anything. He has that sort of mind, and of course he has the unquestioning loyalty of his men. But, then, you see, he's utterly loyal to them. He stands by his own men. I know of cases where he has interceded directly with Himmler, or even the Führer. No question of abandoning someone in trouble. If the person is someone who has served Lüdenscheid well, and of course he asks a great deal of you, he'll stand by you. He'll only do it, naturally, if it's someone in whom he believes, and if that man doesn't let him down. He'll give a man a second chance, never a third. The men respect him. All his most trusted officers come from his own school, having been trained by him they know how he operates, which is a tremendous advantage in action, there's such communication, you know what he's *thinking*, it's automatic, you act, it's you thinking what he is thinking, and you act. It's so integrated that chain of command, every part so linked to the other, there's absolutely no wastage and no time lag. It was unpleasant about the French captain, but the man was a fool disobeying a command, absolutely nothing to gain from it, and of course one can't allow oneself to be soft in such matters. Remorse can be very insidious. If one has acted with honour there is no necessity for remorse, that is to say no necessity for wastful self-recrimination, etcetera –'

Throwing the sticks of dynamite through the firing slit, so cleverly, creeping up beneath the line of fire: in with the dynamite; or climbing up on the roof, immune up there, and lobbing the sticks inside, after that glorious episode there had been the business of the French captain whom Lüdenscheid had ordered him to shoot, quite properly, for disobeying an order, oh absolutely properly, even so it was not easy to shoot the man like that, cold, but he had done it, feeling that Lüdenscheid required it of him, and really the captain was irrelevant, what was important was that Lüdenscheid had demanded this of him, and he had understood the demand, the fullness of it, the meaning of it, had understood all the arguments for the action without Lüdenscheid having to make them, a proof of the perfection of their understanding, the quickness of their communication, which was at the heart of their subsequent closeness, of his ability to finish Lüdenscheid's unfinished sentences, to read his pronouncements so seductively, so culturally, so –

Yes: Wirthof had admired this man, was at times fulsome in his praise of him, but never sycophantic, never that, Wirthof's admiration was a subtle thing; oh yes; its other side was contempt; he was quite incapable of appreciating the extent of his own subtlety: was he not genuinely dismayed when he discovered that the objects of his admiration had proved unworthy of him, as they always had done, in the end they all had proved unworthy. Hadn't he always known they were going to prove unworthy? Oh yes; in retrospect, his foresight appeared acute – of course he had foreseen it all along, in that subtle part of his mind that did not know its own subtlety. How extraordinary that he had had such certain foreknowledge; from the vantage point of the future he congratulated himself on his foresight. Odd, though, that with such certain foreknowledge, as it seemed later, he always gave his admiration to men who would prove unworthy; decidedly odd; almost one might conclude that he, or at any rate that subtle part of him that did not know its own subtlety, had chosen these men for the obloquy that would certainly fall on them in the fullness of time, say the length of time it takes a flame to run the length of a fuse. Whose flame, whose fuse? Why, his flame, his fuse. But that, after all, was his subtlety, and he was not really capable of appreciating it. And when he shot the irrelevant French infantry captain, at Lüdenscheid's behest, but not sycophantically, he felt relieved – in the certain subtle foreknowledge (that, however, was only manifest in retrospect) that he would not long have to give admiration to this man who was his commander, that the duration of the tribute would be short. And when he walked in the Stadtpark with the Gruppenführer, whose favourite he was, he need not feel subservient – oh he was never subservient – knowing what was on the other side of his admiration, and how well-chosen Lüdenscheid was for *that*.

Lüdenscheid: his face a child's scrawl in the dust, with changeable features (always damp), changing with the light – and with other circumstances of which I have no knowledge. A pedantic face, an absolutely ordinary face, a puddle of a face. It could become a terrible face, the way a familiar object, a mop, an old rag, a broom, a raincoat hung on the door hook, can become terrible in uncertain light to a child. I have seen broom-faces and rag-faces and mop-faces, and I have made faces out of old rags and I have scrawled in the dust the image of a Lüdenscheid.

Three days before the Baron was due to be released under the terms of our deal, he died: of a heart attack, while scrubbing out his guards' quarters.

Lüdenscheid summoned me to the Palais Koeppler. At first he made no direct reference to the Baron's death.

'I am informed you have achieved cures by hypnotism.'

'I have dabbled in it, in an amateur way.'

'Such gifts are God-given.'

'On the contrary.'

'The source is immaterial. I have a proposition to put to you. I suffer from a condition. You understand, it is not for myself that I seek a cure, only to enable me to carry out my task.'

What a vision of catastrophe if he could not carry out his task. How the telegraph wires and the telephone wires would hum with subversion, how the mails would explode with treachery, how the word of mouth would spread its contamination!

'You must be aware, Herr Lüdenscheid, how I feel about your task.'

'That is understood, but it should not present an insurmountable difficulty. All relationships are based on mutual usefulness. If you render me a service, you will be entitled to ask something of me in return. You are a businessman. You are not averse to deals.'

I was wrong to think his face nondescript: it was a banal face, yes, neat and boring as a suburban back garden, nothing of the wilder excrescences, but there were mad rhododendrons growing there, his blinking eyes were dustbin lids. The smell of refuse was strong on his breath.

'I doubt that there is anything you could offer me.'

'But we have already concluded one deal, most satisfactorily. Circumstances have prevented its fruition, but the deal as such was satisfactory to both of us. A deal proliferates, spawn deals, Herr Kazakh. There must be something I could offer you. A man has hopes, desires, ambitions, requests: I am in a position to implement them. Make you requests, Herr Kazakh.'

'I have no requests.'

'Even if you have nothing to request for yourself, is there nothing you would ask for anyone else? How selfish of you to turn down such an opportunity. You have a list, I believe, a list of people whose release you are attempting to secure. Would you be so unfeeling as to deny someone on that list a chance?'

'What is it you are proposing?'

'How many people are there on your list?'

'About thirty.'

'The nature of their offences?'

'Perhaps you can tell me that.'

'They are Jews?'

'Is that a question or an answer?'

'I will give you two Jews for each treatment.' Sweat trickled down the side of his face, in the cold room.

'What is the nature of your trouble?'

'I suffer from rectal spasms. I cannot achieve a motion without excruciating pain. It sometimes reaches such intensity that I become unconscious.'

'Perhaps you have cancer.'

'I believe in hypnotism. I believe there are powers in the human mind that can overcome anything.'

'Cancer is not curable by hypnotism.'

'Let us proceed on the assumption that I do not have cancer.'

'Have you had a medical examination?'

'I do not trust doctors.'

'You would trust me?'

'I would trust our deal. Of course there are precautions I would insist on. The presence of observers of my choice. And the presence of one of my officers with instructions to shoot you, should you attempt to exert any undesirable influence on me in the hypnotic state.'

'Apart from other considerations, I cannot imagine that you would be a suitable subject. Hypnotism does not work unless the subject entrusts himself to the hypnotist, accepts his authority.'

'I understand that.'

'I need some information before I can give you an answer.'

'Yes. You may ask me whatever you need to know.'

'Can you eat raw lemons?'

'Raw lemons! I have done so.'

'Do you have any aversions to foods? Do you eat brain, heart, liver, kidneys, pancreas, lungs?'

'I do not care for offal. However, I have eaten liver sausage.'

'Brain would revolt you?'

'I haven't thought about it. Yes.'

'And heart?'

'I don't think I would eat heart.'

'You have no aversion to ordinary meat?'

'It must be well drained. I do not care for meat that contains too much blood.'

'What about snails?'

'I have never eaten them.'

'And frogs' legs?'

'These are not German foods.'

'Are you referring to the nationality of the frogs?'

'I am referring to national traditions.'

'Have you had syphilis?'

'No.'

'Are you impotent?'

'I am not impotent.'

'Do you dream?'

'I never dream.'

'Are you homosexual?'

'I am a normal man, in every respect. I am a married man, I have three daughters.'

'Have you committed incest?'

'Take care, Herr Kazakh. These are very offensive questions.'

'You told me to ask what I need to know. I cannot treat you if you stand on your dignity. Dignity impedes bowel movements.'

'These are not normal questions.'

'If you wish me to undertake your treatment, you must not question my methods. You must accept that from the start.'

'Very well. Please continue.'

'Do you have tooth decay, halitosis, dandruff, excessive flatus? Does the Gruppenführer fart excessively? Is the smell of semen offensive to you? Are you revolted by the sight of your own faeces? Other people's? As a child, did you eat your own stools? Is there madness in your family? Are you colour-blind? Do you have a calcium deficiency? An excessive amount of uric acid in the blood? Do you have hernias, do you suffer from giddiness? Do you vomit blood? Is there blood in your stools? Are you afraid of death?'

'I am not afraid of death,' he choked. 'And the answer to your other questions is negative, except that I do suffer from giddiness.'

'When?'

'Sometimes when I enter an unfamiliar room, I suddenly feel giddy.'

'You have not answered truthfully. You have foul breath.'

'I was not aware of it.'

'Take my word for it – your breath is foul, Lüdenscheid.'

'I find your attitude lacking in respect, Herr Kazakh.'

'I speak medically. Lüdenscheid. You suffer from halitosis – it is not irrelevant to your condition. Do you take drugs?'

'I believe in the curative effect of herbs. I do not take chemicals into my system.'

'Can you touch your toes?'

'Yes.'

'Do so.'

'Is that necessary?'

'You must do what I say . . . Touch your toes. Now remain in that position until I tell you you can rise. Ah yes – yes. As I thought. As I thought. You are mouldering, Lüdenscheid. I speak medically. You are clogged up, Lüdenscheid. The reason you can't shit, Lüdenscheid, is because you are full of hubris. Up now. I will let you know my decision tomorrow.'

Stefan was at the door when Lüdenscheid spoke.

'Herr Kazakh, I have not given you permission to leave.'

'If you wish me to undertake your treatment, you must understand that the hypnotist controls the patient, not vice versa. First you must get cured of hubris. Hubris impedes bowel movements.'

Under the copper-panelled ceiling, Lüdenscheid lay supine, doughy, solemn as a corpse, still as a puddle. I told him he must obey, he must give me authority over his mind. His three freaks chortled with their eyes. The minuscule Indian sat cross-legged on the floor inside the chalk circle; the spiral man was coiling himself against a marble pier, like a strangulating creeper; the actorish man had subsided into a leather settee, charts covered him, pencils, compasses, dividers, rules, magnets, barometers, thermometers protruded from his bulging pockets. Wirthof sat on the edge of the desk, pistol in hand, safety catch off. The slats of the Venetian blinds were closed. The spiral man's Adam's apple moved up and down inside his scrawny neck like a piece of machinery. All except one of the thick-glass octahedral lamps were extinguished, and at the lit one I commanded Lüdenscheid to look without blinking, to concentrate on its eight opaque planes. I told him to relax, not to resist me, to give me dominion over his mind, I told him I could take his pain away. Had he not paid my price? – two Jews. His three freaks were derisive. What sort of hypnotism was this? No metronome. No steel rods. No flashing glass. No dazzling ring, faceted and deep. Who was this amateur among experts? This meddler. The lipless man consulted his orrery, moved the positions of sun and Saturn on the Zodiac calendar scale, and sadly shook his head.

I did my abracadabra – who knows how hypnotism works, what trafficking it involves, what pouring out, what taking in, what deal, what collusion, what rummaging in the tub of eels, what interlocking of cogs, what Orphic descent, what Jewish cheek. I told him – my abracadabra – he must rid himself of hubris, accept my control, relax his muscles, relax his sphincter, I told him I could contain his pain, his faeces, I was his purge, his Jew, the opener of his clogged bowels, his commander. I told him he would have no more pain, but that he must pay the price, I told him to sleep, I entranced him. My magic was quick: almost immediately he was asleep. (Perhaps, indeed, such gifts are God-given, or the contrary, the source is immaterial, isn't it?)

He was loosening, something solid in him was shifting, and with this shift his face changed, its banality had a history, and this, now, came out of him in a fluid motion of the mind. I had not told him to speak, only to release his bowels from their griping, but one cannot know what one will find rummaging in dustbins.

Plumes, I found, and uncurled ostrich feathers, and nose veils with flower patterns, and Merry Widow hats with heron plumes, and veiled hats, the veils draped back over the crown, and marabou muffs, and boas of ostrich feathers, all had the smell of refuse on them, and long hatpins, and shell hairpins, and fancy side combs, and automobile veils to be tied under the chin, and sixteen-button gloves, and silver mesh evening bags and long-handled umbrellas, and neck ruching, and lace cascades, and puffs of chiffon, all had the smell of refuse on them: it was Jewish owned, the shop in the Kärntnerstrasse: Goldberg and Stern, in curvilinear sloping lettering on the marble fascia: opalescent globes suspended from brass chains lit the interior, *cipollino* marble facings on walls and piers, built-in glass drawers in timber frames up to the ceiling, there was a ladder for getting at the upper storeys. Details stuck in his mind like wedges. Fräulein Meltch, the daughter of his landlady: a fine type of girl: her fine hair, looped over one eye, flat at sides, with back hair in a figure of eight; she used a curling iron; he adored her, he would have kissed her feet if she had let him. Sometimes she allowed him to help her off with her high-laced boots, it was the height of intimacy, his hands trembled. He hated the women who came to the shop. Moneyed Jewesses. 'It is most elegant, madame.' 'I don't like it. Show me something else.' 'Certainly, madame. Nose veils are most elegant, madame.' In a long mourning veil, wide-boned girdle under: yes, like that: only a peep, to take in her grief, ah! Eyes filling with moist remembrance, memory unclogging: the rubbish of his mind: he was troubled about his shape, always had been, hips too large, almost matronly, legs short, an odd shape, spent hours trying on different suits of clothing to disguise his odd shape. 'I was a God-believer then.' He repeated that several times: 'I was a God-believer then.'

A good Lutheran. *Let every soul be subject unto the higher powers.*
For there is no power but of God: the powers that he ordained are
ordained by God. Whosoever, therefore, resisteth the power
resisteth the ordinance of God – the Apostle Paul had said. And
Luther had said, 'Burn down their synagogues, take away their
books including their Bible. They should be condemned to
forced labour. If they dare to pronounce the name of God, denounce them to the authorities or pelt them with cow dung.
Moses already said, "Don't suffer an idolator"; were he alive he
would be the first to burn their temples down. May they follow
him and return to Canaan. I would rather be a pig than a Jewish
Messiah.' The *Urvolk*, the inheritors of Luther. *He* had known the
Jews. Fräulein Meltch was so charming. He went walking with
Fräulein Meltch. The sanded walks of the Belvedere, the gardens
sloping down, from there the whole of Vienna was to be seen.
His beloved Vienna. Walking with Fräulein Meltch. He knew the
names of all the flowers, a real naturalist. This impressed her very
much. Those, with the so smooth petals, were pasque flowers,
and those were bee-orchids, and those snake-orchids, and the
sulphur yellow ones were wild roses. In the Prater, the wilder
parts, clumps of silver poplars, and along the Hauptallee, horse
chestnut trees; by the Lusthaus, blue scillas. The parks in which
he walked with Fräulein Meltch were overhung with lilac and
laburnum. He stole from Goldberg and Stern to bring little gifts
for Fräulein Meltch, dress shoes with a silk top once, a little hat
with high crown and drooping brim another time, a sunburst imitation diamond breast pin, a lavallière, ribbons, bows, artificial
flowers, tight-fitting unwashable gloves of white. It was very
satisfying to steal from the Jew merchants for his Fräulein
Meltch; it was not really stealing; they were the thieves, he was
merely retrieving that which was his – and Fräulein Meltch's –
by right of birth. In Munich the café had a curved central cash
desk, from behind which the proprietress-cashier watched everyone. Black bentwood chairs, elliptically curved frames, cane seats.
Captain Goering was always late. Sometimes Hitler came. 'I
always felt tired after seeing Hitler. Had to lie down somewhere.
Hitler was not good with one or two. Nothing ignited. He was
morose He needed a crowd – ah then! But with just one or two
it was always tiring. Beneath the falling weight of his eyes.
Exhausting. Like carrying a trunk up five flights of stairs on your
head. It was disappointing when nothing ignited – Hitler morose,

Captain Goering boastful and loud – but when the spark caught. Ah then, then.' His health had never been good. For several minutes he rambled on about his health. As a child he had been subject to mysterious fevers. His mother used to give him wet-packs to bring down the temperature. First she spread a mackintosh on the bed, and then she wrung out a linen sheet that had been soaked in cold water. She laid the sheet on the mackintosh and little naked Ernst on the sheet. Up came the wet cold linen, first on one side, then on the other, tucked under, tucked under his heels, a blanket over him. Cold, then a glowing feeling. He'd always had constipation. 'I can't make ah-ah, I can't make ah-ah.' Try as he might, he couldn't. It displeased his mother greatly. When he made one for her, a shiny brown one, she was so pleased, proud of him. She gave him that horrible tasting stuff to drink. Supposing he made such a big ah-ah the whole of his inside came out, down the lavatory bowl, flushed away. His feet had always been bad, flat, and there was his hay fever, and his nasal congestion. Once he went to a brothel. The girl was a good type. Washed herself and him before and after. He was especially impressed that she washed him again after, that was thoughtful. He did not enjoy it very much though: she was too coarse and vulgar, he did not care for the familiarity with which she handled his private parts, it was lacking in respect. He had not gone again to prostitutes. Someone called Helmut came up several times. The nature of the relationship was not clear. There was a lot about uniforms. Long involved arguments about braiding, colours, cuts, emblems. It went on and on: a long evacuation.

He awoke in a state of urgency, imperative need roused him from the settee, he tried to hop across the room with some semblance of dignity, his legs going like scissors, but his need growing fast he broke into a waddling run, threw open the doors – out into the corridor. Steel-helmeted guards came to attention. *Heil Hitler! Heil Hitler!* Along the corridor, fast, fast, the inordinate length of this gallery, past the Second Empire settees, the busts on marble plinths, walking, running, the Führer watching from the figured damask wall, mirrors elongating distance; anthropomorphic vegetation engulfed him, eyes on pedestals smirked, Venice sank, the owl-men and the rat-men and the coarse yellow-bodied women and the green horses and apocalypses accompanied him to his destination – ah! there it was. At last! Thank God! He'd made it. Glory Hallelujah, he was shitting!

Glory Hallelujah! *Heil Hitler! Sieg Heil! Ein Volk, Ein Reich, Ein Führer! Lebensraum!* No pain. We are the *Urvolk.* With awe he regarded the fat brown shiny object, proud of himself. Mother would have been so pleased.

And so it came to pass that the magician Kazakh found favour in the eyes of the dust man: for he had cured him of constipation and the dust man was well pleased, and he rewarded the magician Kazakh with the lives of two Jews, and there was rejoicing, and Wirthof and I and the three freaks and Lüdenscheid (who never drank) got drunk together.

Why do you mock me, Kazakh?

Why will you not let me have my story?

Of course the three freaks were furious. The spiral man kept fiddling with his orrery, rearranging the respective positions of earth, moon, sun, Saturn in the Zodiac calendar scale, and consulting his tables. Where had he miscalculated? And the minuscule Indian temperamentally struck out the number 783 from the vertex of one of the inner triangles of the circle of the Law of Seven.

On Lüdenscheid's staff there were four or five young officers who were particularly close to him. Their respective positions tended to fluctuate, there was constant manoeuvring and a good deal of jealousy – the atmosphere was aquiver with all the jealousies of a girls' boarding school – but at this particular time, Wirthof was the undisputed favourite. His spectacular heroism in action (the blowing up of the six pillboxes!) Lüdenscheid relished as if it had been his own. You could see the pleasure he derived from Wirthof's presence, and from every reference to the action. At the regular sporting events in which his men took part, the *Konradlied* was always sung – those piercing sweet young male voices. Lüdenscheid sang it as fervently as any of them, in his rather less than melodious voice, occasionally allowing his eyes to rest on Wirthof with unabashed pride.

All the men on his staff had come from his officer training school, and were selected because of their unwavering loyalty to him; and very special demands were made of them, dating from their earliest training. Their personal conduct had to be beyond criticism. They were expected to comport themselves with dignity, pride, honour, and with deep moral earnestness. For one of his men to get drunk in public was inexcusable. They must not incur debts. It was considered undesirable that they should buy goods on hire purchase. Homosexual acts were criminal, and would result in immediate expulsion from the SS. Involvements with unsuitable women were frowned upon. Any kind of unhealthy activity such as excessive smoking or eating or the taking of patent medicines (rather than herbal remedies) was strongly discouraged. Above all, complete and utter honesty was demanded.

Every morning, as a matter of routine, each man had to report his private activities of the previous day to his immediate superior; the superior reported to his superior; he to his superior; and in their turn the five most senior officers under Lüdenscheid reported to him. These reports were not just soldiers' reports: they were personal and detailed, and were supposed not to exclude anything of significance that the man had done the previous day. Nor was the report to be limited to actions: thoughts, feelings, speculations had also to be reported. In this way, a man could be given help before he had taken some calamitous step. Secrecy was the greatest offence, for in secrecy insidious and dangerous impulses could grow unchecked. If reported, they could be counteracted in good time. A man had to report having had pessimistic thoughts, having made a joke about the Führer, having experienced sexual attraction towards an unsuitable female, having failed to bestow due care on his own body by some failure of hygiene or cleanliness, having harboured disloyal thoughts towards the Gruppenführer, having felt envious of a fellow comrade, having indulged in greedy thoughts of personal acquisition. All these offences against the code of the SS officer were forgivable if confessed, and if a real effort were made not to repeat them. The man who admitted his failings was not treated harshly, but was helped to strengthen his resolve to resist these temptations when they next occurred.

More was expected of the five most privileged officers who reported to Lüdenscheid himself. Of them the very highest standards of honesty were demanded, which gave them a criterion of the standards of honesty they must in turn demand of those who reported to them, and so on all the way down. They had all been doing this for so long, since their earliest training, that none of them any longer found anything extraordinary about these daily confessions, and many actually derived considerable relief from them.

When Wirthof told me of this practice, in doing so committing a breach of the code which he had to report the next day to Lüdenscheid, I saw how naturally it would come to him, for, with me, without any external pressure, he had always been ready to pour out the contents of his mind.

'What sort of things do you tell him?'

'Oh I tell him about women, and that sometimes I have disrespectful visions of Dr Goebbels pissing, and that at ceremonials I sometimes have disloyal impulses to yell – "Fuck the Führer." That sometimes I feel sorry for Jews. Or allow my instinctive humanity to make me feel sympathy for convicted enemies of the Reich. That sort of thing.'

'Have you told him about Leonie?'

'No.' He actually reddened, and quickly passed over the subject. 'You know, I don't tell him *everything*. There are certain things he's obsessed about. There's no point in overdoing it. As long as you tell him *something* that reflects badly on yourself he'll give you credit for honesty.'

'Konrad,' – they were on first-name terms on such occasions – 'I lately have found in you a certain surliness. I find this disturbing. I have the impression that you are withholding from me.'

'You are unjust. It is quite untrue. I withhold nothing from you, Ernst.'

'I find you secretive.'

'I do not have secrets. I report everything to you. Every damn thing.'

'Your manner, your tone of voice – even now – is resentful, querulous.'

'It is my normal tone of voice.'

'Are you sulking?'

'No. But I am bored by the perpetual accusation that I am withholding, when this is untrue.'

'Konrad, if you have some problem. I would expect you, not only as a matter of duty, to your commanding officer, but also as a sign of your trust, in me, personally, to tell me of it. To with-hold, from me, however trivial it may seem to you, indicates a defect in your loyalty, as well as being a failure of your soldierly obligation.' His words goose-stepped.

'I don't see how you can accuse me of disloyalty. I am exceed-ingly loyal.'

'I am not accusing you of disloyalty. You should not twist my words. I am saing that *if* you are withholding something, *if*, *if* you are not totally honest with me, and only you can know that, only you, it would indicate a lack of loyalty and respect. A lack, a grievous lack.'

'Well, as I'm not – not withholding – it shows, doesn't it, that *my* loyalty is not at fault. I think that harping on this all the time isn't very friendly of you, since you want me to be honest about how I feel.'

'I want you to be honest with me at all times. Even if you felt hatred for me, I would expect you to admit it. I have taught you that.'

'I know, I know.'

'Your great shortcoming, Konrad, as I've told you, frequently, is vanity. Even now, after all this time and all our work together, there is a part of you that will not surrender itself to obedience. You do not like to accept that discipline, do you? You want things your way.'

'I have sworn obedience.'

'You have sworn it, but do you feel it? Every so often your disobedience asserts itself.'

'I wish to report to the Gruppenführer: I have talked, illegally, to the Jew Kazakh about the procedure of reporting.'

'It is an offence. But it is not a Grade 1 offence as there is sufficient evidence, of a convincing though circumstantial nature, that Kazakh is not a Jew. However, it is an offence of the second grade to communicate to anyone, even a non-Jew, outside this command anything relating to the work of this command.'

'I wish to report to the Gruppenführer: an officer reporting to me has reported that a non-commissioned officer reporting to him has admitted to a liaison of an emotional nature with a Jewess.'

'The man's name?'

'The offender's name is Hindl. Hauptscharführer Hindl.'

'He must be severely reprimanded, and instructed to break off the liaison immediately.'

'I have so ordered.'

'You must ensure that it is carried out, and that extra special attention is paid in future to the matter of Hindl's honesty in reporting, since clearly he had put this liaison in effect prior to reporting it.'

'I do not follow the Gruppenführer. How could he have reported it before it was effected?'

'He could have reported the desire, the inclination.'

'Such things are sometimes not readily recognizable for what they are, that is to say, an act of a permissible sporting or recreational nature can become, in an unguarded person . . .'

'Yes, yes. But if he had reported correctly, his superior should have detected the danger.'

I had said to him – this was after five or six treatments: when? '42? April? March? it was still cold, March it must have been because it was shortly before we went to Bad Zoeltz – I said to him (it was something I had been intending to bring up for some time, but was waiting for the right moment, when he was reasonably well), I said to him that I had now done as much as I could do for him, and that he should try to find someone more expert to continue his treatment. I wished to leave Vienna, I said. The Baron was dead, which meant I had no further work in Vienna, and I wished to be allowed to leave. Did I really expect him to agree to that? Does a broom-face respond to reasonableness?

'Herr Kazakh, we have – a contract.' His damp eyes made him seem constantly on the verge of great emotion.

'Well, yes, yes, in a way we do, I agree, in a manner of speaking. However, as you will agree, it was merely a tentative arrangement.'

'None the less – a – contract.'

'Not, of course, in any formal sense.'

'It is – a contract. A contract must be honoured.'

'I agree, of course, if an agreement has been entered into it should be observed. But our arrangement is hardly of this sort.'

'I disagree.'

'Then there has been a misunderstanding, and I must put that right. After all. I can hardly be expected to continue indefinitely with this – unusual arrangement.'

'A contract once made cannot be disavowed at will.'

'What I am saying – trying to make clear – is that, in any real or meaningful sense of the word, there is nothing in the nature of a contract between us. This is self-evident from the – the – nature of the transaction. You could hardly expect me to be permanently at your disposal.'

'I expect you – to fulfil your contract.'

'We are just going in circles. I am saying there is no contract for me to fulfil – really this is absurd – and even if there were: this is not the kind of matter that can be the subject of a contractual arrangement. You must agree, nothing was put in writing – how could such an unusual arrangement be expressed in writing, in formal terms?'

'A contract does not necessarily have to be in writing.'

'Let us be clear on this, Lüdenscheid. You are saying that you do not want me to discontinue the treatment – now that is one thing, but to maintain that . . .'

'I must correct you.' He could be quite cryptic, when he was out of breath, for instance, or choking. He was decidedly less verbose when his choking was bad.

'But I have made no such undertaking. This is fantastic. How could I have given such an impossible undertaking? To be indefinitely at your disposal. Whatever you may think, Herr Lüdenscheid. I do not consider myself in any way bound to continue with your treatment.'

'A bond is a bond, whether you consider it one or not.'

'But, surely, you are not suggesting that, without my being aware of doing so, without any formal agreement, I have entered into a binding contract of – of – unspecified duration, involving me in undefined obligations – this is too absurd.'

'My interpretation of our agreement is that you are released from it when it has been satisfactorily concluded.'

'But what does that mean? What do you call satisfactorily concluded? It may never be what you call satisfactorily concluded.

You may be suffering from an incurable disease. I am not a doctor. I have no way of knowing. I advise you, Herr Lüdenscheid, to seek proper medical treatment. There are doctors who undertake hypnotherapy.'

'I do not have much regard for the medical profession, as I have told you. Besides, I don't consider that your gifts have anything to do with knowledge or training. Such gifts are God-given.'

'Are you saying to me that I am bound to continue with your treatment until such time as you regard it satisfactorily concluded? Is that what you are saying?'

'It is in the nature of any deal that all its ramifications are not foreseeable.'

'That makes me a prisoner.'

I don't know why I said it with such shocked amazement, why, indeed, I imagined that a semantical argument about whether or not we had a contract was of any relevance. They didn't exactly depend on legal sanction for their actions, but, in a curious way, they did like everything to be lawful, even if in the final analysis this lawfulness derived from the principle that 'the Führer is the law'. You couldn't question this basic tenet. But Lüdenscheid was in a tricky position with me; having declared me a non-Jew (for his own purposes) he could not invoke anti-Jewish laws against me without admitting to a serious blunder. Besides, his superiors might not have approved of the terms of our deal. I therefore had some cards to play (it is a fact, remarked on by several historians of the period, that on the whole the more recalcitrant you were in your dealings with the Nazis the better, comparatively speaking, were you treated, the greatest brutality was shown to those who were most docile); and in playing these cards I, as gamblers tend to do, became so taken up with temporary advantages that the inherent madness of the game was not apparent to me.

Also, in some respect, the deal was actually satisfying to me: I cannot discount that. It brought me no benefits personally, and to say I did it for the sake of the anonymous Jews whose lives I was saving is a rationalization (a rationalization that, of course, I indulged in then) for there was no way of knowing that every time he released two Jews and arranged for their transportation to Sweden (of this I was given evidence) he did not arrest twelve others, or a hundred others, if there still were a hundred to be arrested in Vienna. In fact, it is quite possible that he balanced his books in some such way, though I have no certain knowledge of his having done so; on balance, I think he probably didn't, because it was essential for him – essential if my theory is right – to honour our agreement, and not to trick me. In his dealings with me he was always scrupulous – the correspondence over the release of the Jews who were my price was shown to me, and I received letters from the Swedish Foreign Ministry confirming their safe arrival. Once, when a Jew died in the course of the journey, I was given another one by way of a replacement, even though the death had occurred beyond the Swedish frontier. It was important to Lüdenscheid to keep to his side of the bargain, and when he protested at my attempts to break it, as he saw it, he genuinely felt he was the injured party, and that I was in the wrong.

His reply to my complaint that it made me a prisoner was the sanctimonious statement, 'Every man is the prisoner of his commitment. I, too, have obligations that I have taken on from which I cannot expect release until they have been fulfilled. All men of principle are the prisoners of their principles.'

But I was not going to argue with him on this level. I was playing cards. 'You cannot compel me to treat you,' Stefan Kazakh said. 'The treatment would not work under duress.'

'It is not a matter of my compelling you. The compulsion is inherent in the contract.'

'And if I break the contract?'

'Our contract places you under my protection. If you should break it you would forfeit that protection.'

'What is that supposed to mean?'

'I do not understand the question.'

'It sounds like a threat, and I have told you I can be of no help to you under duress.'

'It is not a threat. A threat implies punitive measures. I do not say that anything would happen to you if you broke the contract. I only say that you would no longer enjoy my protection.'

'What would be the result of that?'

'I cannot foretell the future, Herr Kazakh. Both of us can make guesses, but that is all they would be.'

In the trance, he rambled on, first, about his trip to Rome. He hated Rome. The sight of all those priests in their women's garb! It was an affront to manhood. It was disgusting to see men so reduced. The Church of Rome was an abomination. There was a great deal about Pope Gregory the Seventh, who was a friend of the Jews. His election was financed by the Jews. His son also became a Pope, and the grandson of this Pope, Jewish again, was also a Pope. That was the state of affairs in the so-called Holy Church. Ribbentrop considered the Italians charming; kept saying how charming they were – but was it the role of a man to be charming? It was for women to be charming, and for men to be manly. The Italians were a nation of Jesuits, could never get a straight answer out of them, always equivocating. Entering a church, always, always, it turned his stomach – the stench of holiness. So-called. For a man to be charming was a contradiction in terms, the one was a negation of the other. A man who was a man had better things to do than to be charming. He was as appreciative as anyone of feminine charm, in a woman; in a man – repellent! Women should cultivate their beauty, a man his manliness. In Italy the men had all the charm and the women all the courage. A hopeless nation. They were not serious. When asked to deal with the Jews, they said they would do so, and did nothing; and when he complained, they said it was difficult to know who was a Jew and who wasn't, as Jewish features were not dissimilar to Italian features. A hopeless nation. Their deviousness was infuriating. The mess they had got into in Greece. They had declared war on the French, and advanced as far as Nice! It took him ten minutes or more to vent his spleen on the subject of the Italians. These men of charm! If they were not homosexual, they were impotent. That was why there were so many priests. The priesthood was a way for a man to conceal his impotence, or his homosexuality. The convents were rife with perversions. It was well known. The reason young girls were able to maintain their virginity was because in any case the men were only interested in buggery, and only resorted to the other act in marriage to produce children. From time to time he became totally incoherent, then a measure of clarity returned. He had seen two disgusting old people, the man fat and old and bald, dripping with fat, dragging his corpulence like a ball and chain, the woman like an old fisher-woman, disgusting, unkempt, dirty, foul-smelling; and these repulsive old people had sat down on a park bench and begun kissing, kissing passionately, tonguing each other; in between kisses they looked deep into each other's eyes with passion and desire; it was obscene, he was revolted. 'My father was a dancing master,' he said suddenly. 'He taught little boys and girls of five or six to dance.' The effete Society dances, of course. The waltz, the polka, the fox-trot, the mazurka, the two-step. There were children's balls – the sight of dozens of children in evening clothes, dancing, while the adults looked on and applauded! He, Ernst, never danced. He was a non-dancer. A smile of crafty superiority crossed his face. The superiority of the non-dancer. His mother was very old, older than his father. She had been over forty when Ernst was born. Her breasts were scrawny. She had no milk in her scrawny breasts. But she was a hard worker. Being a dancing master was not really a serious occupation for a man.

Stefan was anxious to leave, always after a 'treatment' he felt exhausted, and the interminable meanderings of this man reached the point where they were no longer bearable, and then he had to get up and say, 'If you will excuse me, Herr Lüdenscheid, I am feeling rather tired.'

'Yes, yes – you must not tire yourself, Herr Kazakh. I am only too aware of the need for the conservation of energy. I apologize for keeping you. But, always, after your treatment, I feel such a surge, such a superabundance of energy. You must take good care of yourself, Herr Kazakh. My car will take you wherever you wish to go.'

'That is not necessary.'

'As you wish . . . Herr Kazakh, on Friday I am going to Bad Zoeltz, I'd be very happy if you would accompany me and continue with your excellent work there. The air will do you good, and you will see for yourself what can be done with young Germans and Austrians of good blood. It will be a revelation to you, if you have not seen one of our schools before.'

Always, afterwards, there was the exhaustion, my brow ached, my eyes burned, and there was insufficient air for me to breathe, The dust of this man lay on me; it was in my nostrils, in my hair, my eyes, my throat, it clogged my windpipe, it lay on my stomach, it passed through all my deep internal organs, leaving its deposit in pancreas, liver, lungs, coronaries, heart, bowels, accumulating in the linings of joints: I was made entirely of dust, this choking stuff, and the streets I now saw were full of dust men like myself, all walking around in the perilous state of coalescence – a mere gust could blow us apart – that is the natural condition of our sort.

Precise rules governed the method by which the Jews to be released as part of the deal were chosen. They must not know why they had been chosen, Lüdenscheid insisted that the choice must be on an entirely arbitrary basis – by sticking a pin in the list: this method seemed to him the fairest and most satisfactory. The orders for their release gave no explanation: if families were divided this was of no consequence: it was desirable that other prisoners should hear of the release of their compatriots, without being told why they were being released.

The orders were all couched in the same terms: 'By order of SS Gruppenführer Lüdenscheid the Jews X, Y, Z are to be released forthwith. They are to be given such medical attention as they require, and adequate rations and clothing. As soon as they are in a fit state to travel, and in any case not later than ten days hereafter, they are to be conducted to Sweden where they will be received by an official of the Swedish Foreign Ministry from whom a receipt for their safe delivery must be obtained. In the event of any complications, such as death in transit, I am to be immediately informed. The Jews are to be treated with courtesy and respect.'

It was agreed that any individual who did not not wish to be released because it meant separation from husband or wife or other close relative was entitled to decline his freedom, in which case a substitute would be found, by the pin method again. But no information was to be given as to why a particular person was being offered his freedom, and indeed the officials entrusted with carrying out the order did not know why. Lüdenscheid was a great believer in the hand of fate, and he went to some lengths to imitate its arbitrariness. 'It would be intolerable,' he maintained, 'to have to consider individual cases.' Their deal was for the release of two Jews in payment for each treatment, which meant *any* two, not a *particular* two. The deal having been made could not be varied.

Lüdenscheid kept his part of the bargain, and even if the individual selected by the pin method was someone who had actually engaged in activities against the regime, even if he was a resistance leader, or suspected of being one, if he had committed acts of sabotage or murder or espionage, he was none the less released.

If he happened to be a thief or a swindler or a wife killer or a forger or a madman, provided he was also a Jew and had been picked out by the pin, he was released. That was the deal.

It interested him to speculate about the reactions of the people suddenly offered their freedom in this way, saved, as it must seem to them, miraculously; what theories would their minds construct to account for their deliverance? Would they suppose that it was God who had come to their aid? Or would they attribute it to the kindness of an official, or to the poignancy of their appeal, or to the intervention of an unsuspected friend in high places? And how would they explain to themselves why they had been selected, either by God or the unsuspected friend, in preference to all the others? The last thing they would suspect was the actual basis on which they had been granted their liberty, they would never conceive of such a deal as the one between Lüdenscheid and Kazakh, and that the agent of their deliverance was a pin. Lüdenscheid derived a great deal of satisfaction from such speculation.

The pin method's apparent lack of human fairness – to free a man, say, but not his wife and children – was an indication of its justness on the Absolute scale, because Absolute justness must not be influenced by sentimental human considerations.

Some days Stefan Kazakh refused to attend on Lüdenscheid. He used the pretext of being unwell, he had a fever or a racking cough or a sensation of pins and needles in his limbs, he was debilitated and fatigued, his head was bursting, and in such conditions, he said, he could not summon up sufficient hypnotic powers to be of any use. Lüdenscheid never employed duress to make me attend upon him. Sometimes I refused his call for several days, and then a staff car with two SS men in it waited outside my flat night and day until such time as I was well enough to go again to the Palais Koeppler.

I entertained the hope that Lüdenscheid having become dependent on the treatment might suffer a complete breakdown if I could just stay away long enough, or at any rate might be forced to plead with me to come, which would have been an important victory for me, since it would have meant he could not rely solely on our arrangement, but had to fall back on personal appeal. If this happened, then the compelling nature of our deal would have been broken, and it would have been established that

I had some option in the matter. But he never did call me up or plead with me to come, however much pain he was suffering.

After one or two days it was I who became agitated – I cannot imagine why – and it was a struggle to stick to my resolution not to go to him again. Even if I had not been ill to begin with, I became quite ill: it was extraordinary, I actually began to experience some of his symptoms – I burst into sudden sweats, I felt a constriction of my lungs and a grinding in my bowels. My apartment became unbearably oppressive, and the presence of the SS men outside the flat prevented me from going out. I could not keep still but had to walk around continually; my distress was the more terrible for being inexplicable. It was not that I was afraid of what Lüdenscheid might do, or have done, to me: it was not as specific as that. It was a sort of generalized agitation from which nothing could give me relief, except compliance with the arrangement. It felt, indeed, as if this deal into which seemingly I had entered had an inherent force that I was unable to oppose, and when I tried to resist this force it assumed such proportions as to make me feel utterly crushed – annihilated. Desperate ideas occurred to me then, of which the predominant one was that I must kill Lüdenscheid, that seemed to me the only way I could free myself of our deal. And so I told myself that I had better continue to attend upon him, bide my time, and await my opportunity. Whenever I made this resolve, I began to feel better immediately.

Oddly enough, when I was actually with Lüdenscheid – administering the treatment or listening to his rambling dissertations – I felt no fear, certainly not of him, for there was something so nondescript about him, and I felt so sure, then, of my capacity to handle him, had such faith in my ability to negotiate his maze, was so sure of my Daedalian quickness, that I was, temporarily, almost elated. Yes, elated is not too strong a word for what I felt. It was the elation of a falling man who convinces himself he is not falling at all; no, no, it is not a fall, it is a tactical descent, calculated and cunning, and this illusion swelled into an Icarian conceit – falling? I was actually flying. Each stage of the process of falling is holy to the faller, who denies strenuously that he is doing anything of the sort: he invents the most ingenious explanations of his unaccountable topsy-turvy condition (I am merely experimenting with the upside-down position, it is the most natural position to be in, brings the blood to the head, invigorates the mind): oh yes. Anyway, it seemed to me manoeuvring on my pin's head that if I was going to kill Lüdenscheid – and I was going to, wasn't I? – I could not afford to antagonize him unduly. Logical, logical. If I was going to kill him, and assuredly he deserved killing, I had to keep his trust, bide my time, negotiate his maze. Perhaps if I could make him absolutely dependent on me – on the treatment – I could, by choosing the moment when I withheld my services, destroy him utterly. Or else make him so dependent on me he could refuse me nothing. That was surely a useful position to get into, one that could be of incalculable service to my cause. What cause? The cause of my survival, of course.

When, after a lapse of several days, I presented myself again at the Palais Koeppler, Lüdenscheid would express great solicitude for my health. 'I am glad to see that you are better, Herr Kazakh. You must take great care of yourself. You are extremely valuable to me, you know. I could not afford to lose you. It would be most, most unfortunate if, in the course of being so beneficial to me – and there is no question but that you have been most beneficial to me – you should yourself become stricken by illness. We must see that you are well cared for. You should take more exercise, Herr Kazakh. The life of the city is not conducive to good health. We must get you out in the fresh air. Nature is very restorative. I have myself not been in the best of health, but seeing you here I am already much improved.'

At such times he had smiles secreted in all the crevices of his face, like a sly schoolboy who has been up to something and cannot quite conceal the triumph he is feeling. It was no longer necessary to go through all the rigmarole of hypnotism: he had become such a well-trained subject that at a sign from me, the utterance of an agreed formula, he went immediately into an easy trance. In this condition there was no substantial difference in his manner of speech as compared with the non-hypnotic state, except that he spoke more freely, in more of a flow, without that feeling of obstacles between his words, and without choking.

A few hours from Vienna – by Mercedes with out-riders – Lüdenscheid had his school in what had formerly been a prince's shooting lodge. It had been added to, before the war, by an hotelier who had bought the place and turned it into a popular mountain resort. Lüdenscheid had taken it over for his SS officer training school in 1939. It was his pride; for a while he had run it himself; Wirthof and all his other most senior and trusted officers had been trained there.

The curriculum was not exclusively military. There was great emphasis on sport and physical endurance. The deer was hunted. There were lectures on ideology. And, most important, Lüdenscheid's system of 'reporting' was inculcated into the men from the start. Thus it was not only their bodies and ideas that were trained, but also their emotions. They learned to distinguish negative emotions from positive emotions, and how to counteract the former. They learned that to be healthy in body they must also be healthy in mind, which meant they must not harbour unproductive and energy consuming feelings. The hierarchical system of reporting was designed to relieve them of such useless and potentially incapacitating feelings, and to reduce internal conflicts to a minimum. A man had only to follow the procedure of reporting everything he felt and thought in order to obtain the guidance that would give him peace of mind, and the hierarchical system ensured that the ultimate responsibility of decision did not fall on anyone at the school, since even the commandant was required to report, in the laid down manner, to Lüdenscheid.

There were three hundred young men at the school, ranging in age from seventeen to twenty-two; they came from every walk of life, but before being accepted each man had had to undergo a ten-day test, which only one in six passed. (Moreover, before being tested at Bad Zoeltz a man had to have passed through an elaborate sifting process.)

They were fine specimens of Germanic manhood, these young SS officer cadets. They were tall and blond and their family genealogy had been subjected to careful scrutiny to eliminate the possibility of contaminated blood in their ancestry. The shapes of their heads had been studied by experts to remove all vestige of doubt as to their pure Aryan origin. The distance between nose and chin and between eyebrow and the beginning of the hair was measured and compared with the size of the ears – the three sets of measurements were required to correspond. The maximum width of the shoulders was supposed to be a fourth of the height; from the elbow to the tip of the middle finger had to be a fifth of the height; from below the knee to where the penis began must be a fourth part of a man's height. The width of the hips should be equal to the distance from the top of the hip to the bottom of the buttocks, when the man stood equally balanced on both feet. The waist should be halfway between the armpits and the bottom of the buttocks. These were considered the ideal proportions, and though minor departures from the ideal might be overlooked, too many 'disproportions' counted heavily against acceptance by the school.

The first thing required of a would-be cadet was to stand naked in line in the gymnasium, and to take his turn in being measured by a physique expert, who entered the details in a ledger. If passed physically (a medical took place at a much earlier stage of the sifting), the candidate was then required to undergo various tests over the ten-day period. These included a test of his tolerance of extremes of heat and cold (Wirthof had failed the cold test) and, on the psychological level, of his tolerance of uncertainty. Some time each day during the ten-day period the candidate was told how he had made out in his tests so far; he was told to go into a particular room, and to wait. Sometimes he was kept waiting for five minutes, and sometimes for four hours. While he waited, his demeanour was observed. If a candidate revealed a low tolerance of waiting and uncertainty, fidgeted too much, showed signs of strain, it counted against him.

The usual military exercises, with refinements, were supplemented by interrogations in which a man's capacity to stand up to continuous and intensive questioning and brow-beating was tested. He had to be able to go for long periods without food or water and be unimpaired in his judgment; he had to give correct answers to ideological questions and to state with conviction why loyalty to the Führer came even above loyalty to kith and kin. But, above all, he had to demonstrate his 'co-operation', which meant not holding back physically or mentally, and being willing to place himself in all matters in the hands of his superior officer. A secretive man, or a man who cherished privacy in thought and action, was not acceptable.

The cadets lived together and trained together, and they must not withhold. There were no private lockers, no bolts on bathroom or toilet doors, personal possessions were strictly limited, and of course all letters to families or sweethearts had to go through a censor. During the initial intensive training period there was no leave, and a cadet had no opportunity of being with a girl.

First thing on arriving at Bad Zoeltz at the head of his convoy of cars, Lüdenscheid inspected the assembled cadets and training officers. Then he addressed the company. He told them that they were the cream of young German manhood, and that he was proud of them. Around him stood his guests – there were always guests, Wehrmacht generals, Party officials, correspondents of foreign newspapers, scientists, industrialists, ministers. Lüdenscheid told the cream of young German manhood they would be the spearhead of an invincible force, and the guests nodded their admiring agreement. Lüdenscheid told them that the future was theirs. Still and solemn, chin up, eyes damp, bowels griping, he told them that they would be the scourge of the East, the redeemers of Germany's honour, the fighters of total war, of a more total war than had ever been fought before, an even more total total war than this total war had been up till now. He told them that great sacrifices would be asked of them, and that each one of them could ask for no more than to be allowed to give his life for the Führer and the Fatherland. He hardly ever choked when he made these sort of speeches in the open air.

The former shooting lodge of the prince was of timber, with a roof that overhung the walls sufficiently to provide cover for the stacked lumber; there was a clock tower with a clock face on each of its four sides, at different times of day one or other, struck by the sun, was obscured by a golden glitter; the bell tower gallery was sometimes used as an observation post during large-scale exercises.

It was high up, and for the last stage of the journey snow chains had to be used. The surrounding mountains were particularly magnificent. On arriving, everybody always said, 'Ah, but this is beautiful,' and Lüdenscheid beamed with pleasure.

Visitors also invariably remarked on the beauty of the young SS men. 'Ah, what fine-looking young men, what magnificent sturdy bodies'. Women in the party often were moved to sympathize with the plight of these young men so deprived of female company: one high Party official's wife had been quite overcome by the sight of twenty or thirty of these young men prancing naked in a stream, and had to be given smelling salts.

In the dining-hall, everyone ate on scrubbed wood tables; and after meals there was singing: a gruff swell of male voices, the words brutal and proud – 'Unfurl the blood-soaked banners . . .' 'Drums sound throughout the land . . .' – the melodies sweetly nostalgic. Every day there were solemn rituals: the kissing of the blood flag: a minute of silent mourning for fallen comrades: the ceremony of awarding badges for various accomplishments: and – rarely – the stripping of a disgraced cadet of insignia and silver braid.

Lüdenscheid was in his element at Bad Zoeltz; fervently he breathed in the pure mountain air, he could be seen long before sunrise in vest, shorts and plimsolls, strutting around the deserted parade ground vigorously breathing in and out, his normally paste-coloured face suffused by a sort of drinker's flush, his stomach throbbing toad-like above the elastic of his shorts, his bony knees rising and falling, his body putting out sweat, his personal bodyguard trailing him with pistol holster open. (Lüdenscheid went in perpetual fear of assassination, though he was not really sufficiently high up in the Nazi hierarchy for this fear to be justified.)

On the drive from Vienna there had been a noticeable tension between Lüdenscheid and Wirthof; little was said; Lüdenscheid's only remarks were to the effect that it was unusually warm for the time of year, which just caused Wirthof to shrink deeper into his fur-lined greatcoat.

'Are you by any chance cold?' Lüdenscheid inquired of him eventually, tauntingly; as always they travelled with all the car windows open.

'Yes, Ernst, I am,' Wirthof said.

'How extraordinary. Your blood must be thin.'

'Yes.' A hangover darkened Wirthof's face with gloom.

'Herr Kazakh is not cold.'

'I am also cold,' Kazakh said.

'We shall do some hunting,' Lüdenscheid said. 'That will restore the blood circulation.'

Wirthof gave a derisory laugh.

'What is that laugh supposed to mean?' Lüdenscheid asked coldly.

'Nothing.'

'Such a laugh does not mean nothing.'

'Ernst, I don't care to explain absolutely everything. Can I be allowed to laugh without having to explain it? Take it as meaning whatever you want it to mean.'

'It was a decidedly disrespectful laugh, and I insist on an explanation.'

'Very well. If you insist on knowing. I was laughing at the idea of you going hunting.'

'Why is that amusing?'

'Because you can't shoot, Ernst. You can't hit anything.'

'The evidence is that I usually have the largest bag.'

'Yes, because they are lined up for you. Didn't you know that the deer are lined up for you? They are driven past you so close that you can't avoid hitting some of them.'

'Is that true?'

'Of course that is true.'

'I don't believe it.'

'Believe what you like, but it's a fact.'

'If it is true, the culprit will be punished.'

'Everybody is in it, Ernst. The whole school. From the commandant down. They all know that when they go hunting you are to be allowed to have the largest bag. That's the object of the excercise. You'd have to expel the whole damned lot of them. Including me, Ernst. I'm in the plot, too.'

'It was my impression my marksmanship was first class.'

'It's not, Ernst. It's rotten.'

'The matter will be thoroughly investigated.'

Throughout the week-end at Bad Zoeltz the squabbling between Lüdenscheid and Wirthof continued; Wirthof was all the time delivering sly taunts, or smiling in a disrespectful way when Lüdenscheid expounded one of his favourite themes. When called upon to speak on behalf of Lüdenscheid he would sometimes do so with an ironical inflection in his voice. There was nothing really tangible in Wirthof's behaviour to which Lüdenscheid could take exception, it was all a matter of nuances and timing. This irritated the Gruppenführer more than direct insubordination would have done. He rose to every real or imagined taunt, eager to produce a showdown, which Wirthof always neatly evaded. 'But, Ernst, how can you imagine that I would wish to be disrespectful to you, you know me better, you are imagining it. Are you not well? Perhaps you should get Kazakh to give you another treatment.' He did not, of course, know what he said in the trance, or, indeed, that he said anything, for Wirthof hadn't told him, and neither had I, and his three freaks (who still acted as observers) didn't dare to suggest that he sometimes showed himself up in an absurd light. In fact, it would have been difficult to point this out to him, for the light in which he showed himself, and the things he said, differed only in degrees, and in emphasis, from his everyday utterances.

The thread of mockery that ran through Wirthof's words (of this I had ample experience) could be profoundly irritating, but to Lüdenscheid it was worse than irritating, it was a persecution by gnat bites, and he was all the time on the verge of an explosion, which one moment Wirthof seemed quite determined to provoke and the next was adeptly averting.

In the evening, unable to put up with this any longer, Lüdenscheid called Wirthof into his office and accused him, somewhat tearfully, of not showing proper respect, and of verging to the very edge of disobedience.

'I do not like your tone of voice, at times.'

'It is my normal tone of voice. I have not changed it.'

'It is disrespectful.'

'Servility does not come natural to me.'

'I do not ask you to be servile, only obedient to your superior officer.'

'I though you didn't care for lickspittles.'

'I detest them.'

'But you surround yourself with them. I am more honest with you, that's what you don't like.'

'It is a lie to say I surround myself with lickspittles.'

'Really, Ernst, it's pointless to argue with you.'

'You are not required to argue with me, Wirthof. You are required to pay heed to what I say, and to act accordingly.'

'Exactly. To be a lickspittle.'

'I find your attitude offensive.'

'If you want to have a formal discussion with me I will address you formally. If you want to talk to me on a personal basis, I will say what I think. You are always asking me to be absolutely honest.'

'That is correct. I expect of my most trusted officer absolute honesty; nothing less will do. That is what I complain of, that you are not absolutely honest with me. I have the impression that you harbour some grievance against me, and this is expressed in various underhand and secret remarks, gestures, looks.'

'I will tell you one thing – I'm bored.'

'Your reasons?'

'I am bored with the work you give me. I find it dull. I am sick of reading out pronouncements and directives. Vienna bores me. The whole set-up there bores me.'

'Now – at last – you are being honest.'

'I have not made any great effort to conceal my boredom from you.'

'You have not reported it to me in your daily reporting.'

'I thought it was only too evident.'

'I want you always to admit such feelings to me, Konrad. That is how the system works. When such unproductive feelings are admitted – or any others, for that matter – they can be counteracted.'

'How do you propose to counteract my boredom?'

'By enabling you to bear it, Konrad. As a matter of duty.'

'Yes, I was afraid it was going to be some such solution. That's why I didn't bring it up.'

'You should have done – there is your disobedience. There it is. You are bored. I deny you opportunity for heroism. You want to be a hero again. There is your overweening pride. And because of that, you hate me. Isn't it so that you hate me at times for denying you food for your overweening pride, for subjecting you to irksome discipline?' He seemed positively pleased at having found this evidence of Wirthof's hatred of him; he smiled tenderly.

'As always, you exaggerate ridiculously, Ernst.'

'I insist that you refrain from such abuse.'

'I thought I had to be honest.'

'There is a difference between honestly, and co-operatively, admitting to certain feelings, on the basis of wishing to overcome them, between that and resorting to abuse,' he patiently explained, 'there is a difference.'

'All right. If you wish. If you wish. I report to entertaining the feeling that sometimes you make ridiculously exaggerated state-

276

ments. I would like to have this feeling counteracted, but I must also report the suspicion that I don't think it can be.'

'I will not pursue this side issue. We are making progress in that you now can acknowledge your resentment of me for depriving you of opportunities for heroism. Correct?'

'If you like.'

'Please do not sulk. Now – go further, Konrad. Admit that you hate me at times. Admit that sometimes when I ask you to do something that seems unreasonable to you you entertain perfidious thoughts? Admit it, Konrad. Admission is the first step, it clears the air. Admit that, sometimes, you even entertain thoughts of – thoughts of killing me.' For some moments he omitted to blink.

'You want me to admit that? Oh it's absurd.'

'Such feelings are not unusual – in a way they are natural. It is when they are not admitted that they fester and grow dangerous.'

'As you wish. Sometimes, Ernst, I'd like to kill you. How is that? Will that do?'

'Good, good. You see, we have made progress today.'

'I'm glad you think so, Ernst.'

But next day Lüdenscheid had more substantial cause for complaint against Wirthof.

'Obersturmbannführer Wirthof, in December last I sent you to the East with special directives.'

'Yes.'

'They were sealed directives, were they not?'

'Yes.'

'One of them was to be given to General von Blitt.'

'Yes.'

'Please recall the circumstances for me.'

'All the directives were delivered in accordance with my instructions.'

'The exact circumstances, please.'

'I can recall no special circumstances. Except that it was very cold, that there were a lot of casualties, and that, it seemed to me, the winter clothing of the troops was inadequate. All of which I reported to you on my return.'

'I recollect that you did so. Was there not something that you omitted in your report?'

'Not as far as I can recall.'

'Try placing a greater strain on your memory, Obersturmbann-führer.'

'Ernst, will you tell me what you want to know . . .'

'This is formal, this is formal . . .'

'I apologize to the Gruppenführer. I do not know what the Gruppenführer wishes to know. I suggest with respect that if the Gruppenführer will tell me precisely what information the Gruppenführer is seeking I will be better able to provide it than if he merely subjects me to . . .'

'Be silent. Obersturmbannführer. Do not tell me how to conduct myself. When you handed the sealed directive to General von Blitt, what happened? Exactly?'

'As he's here, I suppose he has told you. Well, you tell me. I cannot recall that anything in particular happened. He read it, as far as I can remember. That's all.'

'That is not how the incident has been described to me by General von Blitt.'

'In that case, if you will tell me how General von Blitt recalls the incident I will be able to either confirm or deny his version.'

I will give your memory a slight jog. General von Blitt's recollection is that he opened the envelope, in your presence, read the directive and uttered an obscenity . . .'

'Yes, yes, he's absolutely correct, he did. I apologize for having omitted his obscenity from my report. He informed me what you, and the Führer, could do with the directive, his advice was explicit. I didn't consider it of interest to you, sir.'

'I will not tolerate sarcasm from you, Obersturmbannführer. I am warning you. What else?'

'What else?'

'What else happened?'

'I think it can be said he expressed disapproval of the directive. I told him that he was required to act on it. He became very angry and told me that I was not to tell him what he was to do.'

'All of which you omitted to report to me on your return.'

'It slipped my mind.'

'It slipped your mind. What else slipped your mind, Obersturmbannführer? Did it also slip your mind that he tore up the directive in your presence?'

'It is regulation that these directives are to be destroyed on receipt.'

'By burning. Not by tearing.'

'He had no matches. And mine were lost.'

'You are lying to me, Obersturmbannführer. He tore up the directive in anger.'

'I believe it would be correct to say that the manner of the tearing up expressed an element of disapproval, yes. But this would have been supposition on my part. He could have maintained that he was merely destroying the directive as stipulated.'

'Before he tore it up, did he not offer to show it to you?'

'Yes, I believe he did.'

'What did you do?'

'I reminded him that I was not allowed to see the contents of such dispatches.'

'What did he say to that?'

'I do not recall that he said anything to that. I believe he uttered an obscenity, he frequently does.'

'All of which you omitted to report.'

'I omitted his obscenity, yes. Does he now insist on its reinstatement in the official record?'

'Obersturmbannführer Wirthof, this is a serious matter, though you evidently do not consider it to be. A senior general reacted with contempt and disdain to a directive issued by me on the direction of the General Command, and you failed to report this to me. He tore up the directive in a manner indicative of the fact that he intended to ignore it. You failed to report this to me. Is it not clear that this is a serious lapse?'

'I assume you were testing me, Ernst. That this little scene was enacted for the sole purpose of testing whether I would report it or not. And that the real test was whether I would read the directive when he offered to show it to me. Well, I didn't and I must say, I resent your distrust of me.'

'Your resentment of me is properly expressed, Obersturmbannführer, in your personal reports to me. It is also inappropriate to use my first name. I must caution you that I consider this to have been a serious failure on your part.'

General von Blitt was a fierce-featured man with duelling scars on his cheeks; he was about fifty; his eyes were light grey.

'Our last meeting was not particularly cordial.'

'No, sir, it wasn't.'

'Perhaps this meeting can be more cordial.'

'That seems unlikely, if I may say so, sir.'

'Your father was General Wirthof. I served under him.'

'Yes, sir.'

'You trained here, Wirthof? At this place?'

'Yes, sir.'

'Under Lüdenscheid?'

'Yes, sir.'

'What made you join the SS? You, a regular army officer?'

'It seemed to me that it offered certain opportunities.'

'For sneaking?'

'That is not called for.'

'You are right. It isn't. I was not speaking of you, I was speaking generally. I am surprised, Wirthof, that you didn't report our previous meeting, in full, to Lüdenscheid.'

'However, you have done so.'

'He's been hauling you over the coals, has he?'

'Yes, sir, he has.'

'What a pig that man is.'

'Am I being tested again, sir? You know I am supposed to report conversations such as this.'

'You didn't report our last conversation. Why?'

'But I have now been warned I am being tested.'

'You are being tested, Wirthof. I admit it. But by me. Not by Lüdenscheid.'

'How do I know that?'

'You don't. That is the nature of the test. If you report this conversation to Lüdenscheid, you offend me. If you don't, you offend him. I shall know which you have done. If you trust me, and don't report to Lüdenscheid, you take the risk that I am in league with him and that I am doing this at his instigation.'

'Are you, sir?'

'I thought, Wirthof, that I would tell you the contents of the directive you saw me tear up. Last time, you refused to read it.'

'I am not permitted to know the contents of dispatches.'

'I think you should in this instance. It is not a military secret. And, as a matter of fact, it was rescinded, partly as a result of my protest, which is what irks Lüdenscheid.'

'All the same, sir, I wish to make it clear that I am not allowed to hear what is contained in dispatches.'

'You are going to hear, Wirthof. Unless you choose to walk away. I can't prevent you doing that.'

Wirthof continued to walk at the general's side. The scarred fierce face eased into a downward smile. 'The directive you brought me, Wirthof, was an order concerning Soviet prisoners of war. It said that Soviet prisoners were to be branded with a special, and durable mark. The brand was to consist of an acute angle of about forty-five degrees with a one centimetre length of side, pointing downward on the left buttock, at about a hand's width from the rectum. That is the order I tore up.'

'Yes, sir.'

'Is that your only reaction? Branded, Wirthof. What do they think German soldiers are? Cowboys? What would you have done, Wirthof? Would you have carried it out?'

'Am I still being tested?'

'Don't answer if you don't want to.'

'I find it impossible, sir, to project myself into hypothetical situations. I was not required to act on that order, only to deliver it to you.'

'Have you no imagination, Wirthof? Can you not imagine what you would have felt, and what your reaction would have been? What do you think your father would have done, given an order like that?'

'I don't know what I would have done, sir. I can only say that I hope I would have acted honourably.'

At supper, in the large dining-hall, Lüdenscheid expounded on the eternal return of the sun, the victory of light, man's need to attune himself to the rhythms of nature. 'It should be noted that the derivation of Carnival is not "carne vale" – goodbye meat – a dispiriting prohibition of the Church of Rome, but from "carrus navalis" – ' The ship was among seafaring nations the symbol of fertility, and ash was a well-known manure. He was blinking rapidly, always with him an indication of excitement. The solstice, when the sun, at its furthest from the equator, stood still – But something was impeding this familiar exposition, he could not seem to keep his mind on the eternal return of the sun. 'You are fond of mountain scenery, General?'

'It is most stimulating.'

'And fond of walking? Personally, in my experience, as exercise it is not very effective unless one walks fast enough to bring some sweat to the skin. Unless the skin sweats –'

'For exercise, Lüdenscheid, I have other means. I walk for

pleasure. Solely for pleasure. The pleasure of the air, the pleasure of agreeable company.'

'The air here is excellent, would you not agree?'

'Indeed, indeed, quite excellent. Formidable air.'

'It is one of the defects of our city culture,' Lüdenscheid began, but did not complete the thought, and it was accepted in its unfinished condition, as were many of his thoughts. 'And the company, General, I trust you have found that agreeable too?'

'Indeed.'

'Of course, in time of war, conversation is limited by the exigencies –'

'My experience is that where mutual trust exists –'

'A dangerous premise, General, surely –'

'I have not found it so. But perhaps in your line of activity –'

'Your inference escapes me, General.'

'Then I am sure it was not particularly apposite, since so little escapes the Gruppenführer.'

'I believe a man should cultivate his powers of observation, the majority of men are so defective in their perception that they see nothing.'

'Certainly that could not be said of the Gruppenführer.'

'You are right, General. You are quite right in that observation. One's perceptions are capable of very considerable development. For instance, the art of lip-reading – I find that a very useful exercise in the sharpening of perception.'

The general's duelling scars became prominent as the taut smile inflated his cheeks. 'I can imagine that would be so.'

'It is. It is.'

'At times, however, it must lead to dispiriting discoveries.'

'All discoveries are worthwhile, even dispiriting ones.'

'An admirable sentiment, Lüdenscheid.'

'I am delighted you were able to visit us, General. What do you think of our school?'

'Quite remarkable. The curriculum is perhaps a little unusual. To an old soldier, you understand. In my day we were never taught lip-reading, but I can see it must have its uses.'

'It is useful,' Lüdenscheid agreed.

'The Gruppenführer has many enthusiasms,' Wirthof said. 'Hunting is one of his passions. You will have heard what an accomplished shot he is.'

'Yes, I have heard about that.'

'His lip-reading was a later interest. I think you would agree with me, Ernst, it is, perhaps, not quite up to your shooting. For accuracy.'

'I am relieved to hear,' said General von Blitt, 'that the Gruppenführer has limitations, like the rest of us.'

'I take it,' said Lüdenscheid, 'that your differences with my aide-de-camp were resolved in the course of your agreeable walk this afternoon?'

'Oh entirely. They were based on a misunderstanding.'

'I am glad to hear it. Wirthof is an excellent officer,' Lüdenscheid said. 'He has his limitations, of course . . .'

'As have we all,' said General von Blitt.

'As you so rightly say, General. Wirthof's, for instance, are excessive pride . . .'

'Is that so? A soldierly failing –'

'And he finds obedience irksome.'

'Do you propose to enumerate all my limitations, Ernst? Is there sufficient time?'

'One can summarize.'

'That would hardly do justice to them.'

'We can confine ourselves to disobedience. What is your attitude to disobedience, General?'

'Oh a most serious matter,' said General von Blitt, 'though, personally, I don't mind it as much as sneaking. Can't stand a sneak.'

'I agree that sneaking is reprehensible, but one must differentiate between the sneak, activated by motives of personal self-advancement, and the man who out of duty and love of Fatherland – who out of these duties, with no thought of self – acting with serious moral purpose, you understand – having, as it were, shed – shed – above all –' His voice faltered, his mouth hung open, silence accumulated around him, spreading outwards; the gap between his words widening, he stumbled on, out of breath, like a man who has run a great distance. 'A great nation – this nation of Nordic-Phalian-Germanic blood – weakened – threatened from within – such an eventuality – to counteract such an eventuality – it was written – on the Emerald Tablets of Hermes Trismegistos was written – "Learn to separate" – since vital hydrogen is dissipated by miscegenation – a great nation cannot afford – the waste of essence – the Jews are the wind – and if you pour gold dust into the sea – pollution. Pollution. It is the function of the ox –' He could not go on, had come to the end, had wandered off the track, had become lost in the maze of his mind, was actually panting. At what moment had he become side-tracked, when had he lost the point? Energy had gone out of him like a tide: a choking gurgle had begun in the back of his throat, his mouth hung open like that of a dead fish, his face shone with sweat from the effort at articulation. No one coming to his aid. They were allowing him to sink into this strangulating silence. Wirthof was smirking, making no effort to help – he who knew better than anyone the line of argument, the intricacies of the reasoning, its progression, its flow, its beauty, its culmination. The Jews were the leeches of vital hydrogen. The humiliation! Before the entire school. The worst attack yet. Wirthof and von Blitt were exchanging looks, secret and intimate. The sudden silence of the head table had spread outwards, quieting table after table of men whose penises were precisely at the centre of their bodies, and whose shoulders were a fourth of their height, and the width of whose hips was equal to the distance from top of hip to bottom of buttocks, though in Lüdenscheid's case this was far from being so: his hips were considerably wider across than the distance from the top of the hip to the bottom of the buttocks. These men and youths, whose waists were exactly halfway between the armpit and the bottom of the buttocks, stopped eating, moved in their seats, and turned their correctly proportioned skulls to fix correctly coloured eyes – grey, blue, blue-green: but not brown, not brown, the colour of dog eyes, the colour of ox eyes, the colour of Jew eyes, the colour of betrayal – on the Gruppenführer in his difficulty.

Wirthof held the Gruppenführer upright with his eyes and then – why not, why not? – let him totter over, how very comical! – into the vat of molten lead, where he became encased in black lead, sculpted from life, what a grievous accident to befall the Gruppenführer of Posts and Telegraphs. When he had become solidified in his head-to-toe death mask, in his leaden suit, and was immobilized in perpetuity, and could have been mounted thus outside the main Post Office, only then did Wirthof say something about Lüdenscheid's laryngitis, and finish his thought for him, somewhat perfunctorily.

All this time, ever since the Baron's death, Wirthof had been looking for Leonie. He considered it the height of unfriendliness (he still made the unquestioning assumption of my friendliness towards him) that I wouldn't tell him where she was.

'She doesn't want to see you, Wirthof.'

'But don't you see that I *have* to see her. Supposing she's not well, supposing she needs help.'

'Her health is all right. As all right as anybody's.'

'You wouldn't conceal anything from me?'

'If she were ill, I'd tell you.'

'How does she look, Kazakh?'

'Thin. Thinner than she was, even.'

'I suppose her hands have become rough. A woman like her is not meant to do rough work. Oh it's appalling to have to think of it.'

'Worse things are happening to people than rough hands.'

'You know, I will find her, I promise you I will find her. If she tells me to my face that she doesn't want to see me then I will respect her wishes. But I must hear it from her.'

In his free time, he put on civilian clothes and went from café to café, from food shop to food shop, asking of her. It wasn't easy for him to obtain information: he was often recognized, his face was familiar from the newsreels, and nobody with Leonie's interest at heart was willing to reveal where she was to someone who was in the SS. His search was impeded by the fact that he didn't want the authorities, and through them Lüdenscheid, or one of his minions, to hear about it, for that would have meant explanations of his secrecy, which he did not feel capable of giving. He therefore had to be very discreet in his inquiries.

From the fact that Stefan evidently saw her quite often – this much he gathered from their talks – he deduced that Leonie must be somewhere in the Inner City, since Stefan could not have had enough transport passes to see her that regularly if she were living farther out. Having satisfied himself on this point, it was a matter of inquiring at all the food shops; even if she was using another name somebody was bound to know her. He did this systematically, dividing the city into areas, and covering a different

area each day. That he eventually tracked her down to the Wied-
ner Hauptstrasse was not due to any of her friends: it was an
informer, anxious to curry favour, who gave Wirthof her address,
some miserable sneak, whose motives at best were of self-
interest and at worst of malice. Why did he have to be the one?
It somewhat spoilt Wirthof's joy at having found her at last. He
felt nervous climbing the stairs to her apartment, the lift of
course was out of order. He had never before felt so unsure of
himself. When a small boy passed him, he turned his head to
avoid being recognized. He had an exaggerated sense of his own
fame: he felt, morbidly, that everyone knew him, and for the
first time this was disagreeable to him, even, at this moment,
abhorrent. A few steps below the top landing, he hesitated,
heart thudding – despicable nervousness: oh well, if she won't
see me I'm done with her, finished, it's the end, I will certainly
not plead. Ridiculous that I should be put in this position, who is
she after all? My Leonie, *my* Leonie. It was finding her in this
way that made him feel so – so like an SS man (he sometimes
forgot that that was what he was). He hadn't even brought
flowers. I must bring flowers, that's what I must do, that's what
I must do – but where to get them? – it meant going all the way
back. He had turned to go down again when, to his consternation, for he had not composed his face into a suitable expression
– what was a suitable expression for such an occasion? – the
door opened and Leonie appeared, wearing a grey cloth coat
wrapped around her tightly, belted tightly, carrying a net bag,
and saw him. He was in an awkward posture, half turning, and
seeing her almost threw him off balance. 'Leonie,' he said,
steadying himself against the wall, which was damp from where
rain water had leaked through. 'Leonie.' He tried to do his
glittering smile, but the circumstances were not conducive to it,
and it wouldn't form. She was shocked to see him, and then
recovered herself.

'You look as though you've seen a ghost,' she said. 'Do I look
so terrible? How did you find me?'

'I've been looking for you for months. Nobody would tell me
where you were.'

Collecting himself a little, he came slowly towards her and took
her hand and lifted it to his mouth, formally, very formally, with
that touching formality he sometimes had.

She regarded him in amazement.

'Why did you come?'

'I wanted to see you.'

'You should not have come.'

His hair was like seaweed, his face was running with water, and his body heat made him steam under his clothing.

'I think you should leave.'

'I want to talk to you.'

'Why? What is there to be said?'

'Don't send me away. Let me come in – for a few minutes.'

'All right. For a few minutes.' Why did she agree? He followed her into the flat which smelled of bad fish and some disgusting ersatz cooking fat (at this time ersatz cooking fat was being made by a special process from restaurant refuse); entering this smell he was seized by nausea, a retching began in him, and for a moment he thought he would not be able to control his stomach, but the wave passed, and he continued along the corridor, which was full of suitcases and bundles of personal belongings. 'I have some friends staying just now,' she explained. (In fact, there were always 'friends' staying, anything between four and twelve, whom she somehow managed to accommodate in the three-room flat. If they were not friends, they were friends of friends, people who had nowhere else to go. She fed them, clothed them, looked after them, consoled them, and sometimes with my help succeeded in getting them out of the country.) She took him into the room that she kept for herself. It was fairly small, over-crowded, and furnished in the dingy manner of cheap furnished flats. Suitcases stuck out from curtained recesses, coats and dressing-gowns hung from hooks on the back of the door, cardboard boxes were stacked on top of the wardrobe up to the ceiling. He thought, painfully, that she was, in this room, divested of everything that he had found so hateful in her life, more his Leonie than ever before, he felt responsible for her.

'Why didn't you let me see you? I could have helped.'

He felt envious of those who had been permitted to help her, and resentful that they, whoever they were, Kazakh amongst them, no doubt, should have had this privilege conferred on them in preference to him. 'You must have known you could rely on me. You must have known that there was anything you could have asked of me.' He wanted to outdo these unknown others, these helpers, to outbid them, to prove to her that his help, his capacity to help, was superior to anybody else's, that she could ask enormous things of him. He was almost glad that she found herself in these straits, if it would enable him to do something colossal for her. 'You know I would have moved heaven and earth to spare you pain,' he declared.

'That would have been unnecessarily spectacular,' she said, quietly, 'and useless, it wasn't required. I only needed to have good friends, and I have those.'

He was standing, feeling that to sit down would constitute an assumption of intimacy – there was only the bed to sit on – that he was not entitled to make.

'I'm afraid there is nothing I can offer you. I am out of coffee.' He did not know what to say, and finding him so awkward and tongue-tied caused her to smile; the smile made a ripple of lines in her face, from the corners of her mouth upwards, like fine tissue paper becoming crinkled up, she was not a young girl, her complexion was not flawless, her cosseted beauty had suffered, leaving the stark basic bone structure unsoftened now; it moved him that her beauty had suffered, my Leonie, my Leonie. He saw the tiredness of her eyes, the fragility of her long neck, all the marks of hurried ageing: I will restore her, he vowed, I will be the restorer of her beauty, how she has lacked me, my Leonie, my Leonie, who is not beautiful, but who has need of me. She has no one, he decided with certainty and relief, pride of man-liness giving him back his assurance.

'Couldn't we go somewhere?' he asked.

'Where? Where is there?'

'There are some places.'

'I don't think I would want to go to those places.'

'Nowhere where I am known,' he said. 'I will not take you any-where like that.' (She wanted to get out of the flat – her friends if they saw him and recognized him would take fright.)

'All right. Can I go like this?' She was still wearing her overcoat, the room wasn't very warm. Her expression was dull and non-committal. He was surprised by her matter-of-factness. As always with her, he had the sense of being inside a circle that she could, when she chose, quickly draw around any present situa-tion, putting everything that was incongruous outside. She gave a laugh that was much younger than her face, and threw him a towel with which to dry his hair. He saw her do things neat and precise to her face, using an eyebrow pencil on her eyelids and a little lipstick on her mouth. 'I have an umbrella,' she said when she had finished. 'It's going to be impossible to get a taxi.'

In the darkening street, cold sharp rain driven by the wind spattered their faces, they struggled with the small lady's umbrella – the direction of the wind was changing all the time, sudden gusts filled the canopy, blowing them sideways, or halting them momentarily, and several times turning the umbrella inside out. Dragging back against the strong pull, hands wet and slippery, they suddenly felt the umbrella wrenched away, and it was gone, lifted high, silk tearing, thin metal ribs snapping, and they stood watching it fly: it became right way round again with a change of air currents, a blue floating dome partially collapsed, and then the next gust tore into it, breaking it up, ripping the cloth. 'Oh', Leonie said, 'it was my only umbrella.' They watched it disintegrate in the air, and the stick with its tangled metal ribs fall on the far side of the street. They ran. Hard pellets of sleet stung their faces. Ahead of them a tram was coming to a halt at a stop and they ran harder to catch it. It was very full, but they managed to squeeze in. Pressed close together in the crush of people smelling of rain and after-work, he took out a handkerchief and dried Leonie's face, carefully drying around her nose, chin, eyes, carefully, carefully, she made no attempt to stop him, regarding him with her over-large eyes, over-large because her face had shrunk to a new tightness. Her face was hard and amazed.

'Where are you taking me?'

'We will find somewhere.'

Through the tram's steamed-up windows little was visible except the pattern of raindrops; at the next stop, two seats were vacated, enabling them to sit, and Wirthof wiped a section of the glass clear and peered out to establish where they were exactly. The tram had turned somewhere behind the Kärntner Ring, and after a while he got his bearings. 'There's a bar in the Canovagasse. I've never been there, but we could try it.' They got off at the next stop and made a dash towards the torn striped awning of the Bar Intime. It was closed. The shop next to it was also closed, it had a sign saying 'Closed down for stocktaking', a somewhat mysterious legend since the window was totally bare except for a Mumms champagne placard, and the interior looked just as empty. Equally mysteriously, the bar though closed said open.

Wirthof rattled the door. The torn awning provided only partial shelter, but it was better than being totally exposed in the street. Again he rattled the door. The trees on the other side of the street, already leafless, had acquired a foliage of camouflage netting, blown by the wind from a near-by military installation; in their iron caging, and entangled in this wire netting, the trees looked like captives.

After a long time, slow footsteps were heard beyond the door and an approaching shape was perceived through the frosted arabesques of the glass panes. A waiter, ethereal in his antiquity, opened the door, bowed profoundly, and made a motion of his slightly trembling hand for them to enter, at the same time, with his other hand, surreptitiously switching on lights. He took their coats over his arm, visibly sagging from their weight, and led them with a trembling smile, and after careful consideration, to a small fixed table with shiny brass feet and an octagonal marble top. He asked for their order, and shook his head compassionately as Wirthof mentioned Scotch whisky, gin, vodka. In that case, what could they have? 'Excellent cuck-tell,' the waiter responded unencouragingly. 'Holy-Voot cuck-tell. Razzle-dazzle. Extase.'

'Extase?'

'It is very good,' he said evasively.

'And Razzle-dazzle?'

'It, also, is very good.'

'What are the ingredients?'

'Ah – Holy-Voot cuck-tell, I recommend.'

'They are all the same,' Leonie said. 'You don't really expect to get Scotch whisky?'

'Some of them have a stock.'

'Ah – Scotch whisky,' the ancient waiter declared, reminiscently, 'Scotch whisky, yes, yes.' He was smiling his trembling old smile, and shaking his head.

'All right. Bring us whatever you have.'

Two or three of these concoctions, searing on the palate, searing in the throat, chest, stomach, and sickly sweet from their principal constituent, a thick grenadine syrup, produced a cloying haze.

She was not talkative; he could get no response from her. 'This is a dull place,' she said.

'Yes. These places don't fill up until later. Shall we go somewhere else?'

'They are all the same, aren't they?'

'More or less. *Leonie* . . .'

'Do not talk of personal things, please.'

'What shall we talk of then?'

'The war. What else is there to talk of except the war? Your beautiful war.'

'It will be over by the spring,' he said.

'Yes? You promise it? I hope you are wrong.'

'You want it to go on?'

'Oh yes, oh yes. I want to see Germany defeated.'

'Not so loud . . .'

Her mouth turned down harshly, making her quite ugly. 'Crushed out,' she said, quietly still, grinding her cigarette into an ashtray. 'Like this.' Violence flared up in her face. She shrugged stiffly, savagely. 'It is what they deserve.'

'You shouldn't talk like that. It's dangerous.'

'Dangerous!' She was lighting another cigarette. 'Ehh,' she said inhaling, 'camel dung! Filthy.' She expelled the acrid smoke with disgust, and inhaled again deeply. 'You think I care that it's dangerous. You don't know me. You don't know women, you know only little girls.'

'And the Leonie who had to have her bath water a certain temperature, and her massages and her mud treatment . . .'

She laughed provokingly. Catching a glimpse of herself in a mirror, she said, 'God, I look awful. Still – it's something to see them hungry, it's something to see them drink this muck, smoke this filth. And when their beautiful old city is a pile of rubble – pray God! – I will be singing.'

He gave her a cautionary frown. 'Somebody may hear you.'

'Do I make you nervous?' she asked. 'You?'

'I care about you,' he said.

'Ah!' She dismissed it as unlikely and in any case irrelevant, sweeping away cigarette smoke with a bony hand. 'You are such a child, Konrad. What do you know? You don't even see what goes on, or you couldn't wear their obscene uniform. Or perhaps you do see. God help you. God help you then.'

'What is the point of talking like this?'

'You can leave,' she said, 'if I'm too dangerous for you, but while you're with me you have to put up with my talk.'

'What is the point of it?'

'The point?' Another violent shrug. 'The point is to hear me say it – for you to hear me say it. If you want to see me, that's my price. Not silk stockings. Not Paris perfume. For that you get servant girls. But with me,' she rapped the table top with a forceful forefinger, 'you have to hear me say: I want to see them crushed. I pray for the bombers. When all this is rubble, and I in it – I couldn't care less – then I will have joy here.' (Indicating her heart.) 'What they have done to Warsaw, to Belgrade, I want to see done here. Primitive, yes: an eye for an eye, yes, yes, *yes*.'

'That is the Jews' code.'

There was an elemental streak in Leonie, and she was pared down to that now, it was what she had to fall back on. Very Italian: there *was* some Italian blood in her (from those dictators of Milan, from those cardinals, perhaps from the upstarts too) and there had been lit in her a perpetual rage, low-burning but constant, that hardened her. Rage, also, was what she had to fall back on. Sophistication was only a couple of generations old in her, and she had gone farther back than that. He was astonished to find her so basic, primitive almost. Could the old Baron have meant something to her, after all? When she had been so unfaithful to him? What did Wirthof understand of Leonie? What did he know of the Leonie who had screamed like a peasant woman when told of Felix's death? (Crudeness in women appalled him, except in bed where he found it charming.) She seemed crude to him now, her manner, her attitude, magnanimously he forgave her because of what she had been through. Could she perhaps have loved the old Jew? He could not understand her peculiar passions, nor her patriotism for the dead and gone.

'What has been done to Felix has been done to me,' she said. 'And I don't forgive – *anything*. I don't forgive. The humiliations they put on him, they put on me.'

'All this fury for him? He'd have died anyway quite soon. He was an old man. You deserved better, Leonie.'

'I deserved better? Ha-ha! You, my soldier? *You?*' She swallowed the rest of her Holy-Voot cocktail and banged the table with the empty glass, calling for another. She was fairly drunk, it made her calmer. 'Yes, it so happens there's truth in what you say. I deserve – for what I did to Felix in his lifetime. I deserve – for that alone.' Abruptly her eyes flashed with tears. 'Now I sit here with one of his murderers. Appropriate. Nobody can say it's not appropriate.' Her eyes cleared and became dull again.

'The old Jew's heart gave out.'

'True, it's true. You know what makes the heart give out? – disgust, *disgust*. Disgust attacked the heart of that man. Lies attacked the heart of that man. When I saw you on the stairs, I was shocked, yes, I was – you don't think I can be shocked, I can be. How can he dare to look for me, one who wears their uniform, and has fought for them – how can he bring himself? Is there such arrogance in him that he does now know what a sordidness it is to present himself – outside my door. But after all, it is appropriate, isn't it? Why not? He is a fair claimant, I reminded myself. Why not? It is a sordidness, yes: but why not, when have I shrunk from that before? I was not so finicky before. My otherness, I prefer to call it – oh it is a lovely term, isn't it? isn't it? for sordidness of the heart. It does not sound like depravity. Who would have the indiscreetness – the vulgarity – to call it depravity? My otherness. A delicate euphemism, tasteful. You might say – poetical. That is all you know of me, Konrad. My otherness, for which there are less poetical terms too. To that you are a fair claimant, my soldier. I tell you, between us there can be nothing but that, nothing else: that you can have of me – plunder, yes – nothing else, and you must hear me say my prayers to the bombers – Dear bombers, who art in heaven, grant us this day the blessing of your bombs . . .'

'That is not the kind of love I want of you.'

'Isn't that a shame, isn't that a downright shame, my soldier. My heart cries for you. How sad! How poignant! The soldier loves her, but her heart is already given, to the bombers. But – don't look so downcast, ask Methuselah for another of his poison punches, hmm?' She gave his hand sharp convulsive grips with her bony fingers, smiles flashed recklessly across her face. 'Believe me, I give you nothing of value, nothing, understood – understood? and never have done – whatever you have of me it is an empty house you plunder.'

Passionately, he spoke to her, 'Leonie, you see the iniquity of the Jews, you see their power, even from the grave they hold you. Rid yourself of them finally. You will not be harmed, I promise you. There will be no bombers over Vienna. We blast them out of the sky. Have you seen our guns? Be rid of this old dead Hebrew, who cries eyes for eyes from his grave, and infects you with his

Jew's vengeance. Those Jews are magicians, they know the dark arts, you must let me save you from them. I will save you, Leonie. That's why I looked for you.'

Who can say it was not love, who can say with certainty it was not love: he was going to save her from the Jews, absurd knight of a black cause: none the less, he was committing himself to her. It was going to cost him something, this commitment, did he know that? He who had never paid for anything, for everything he wanted was his by right; but for once, perhaps, he was prepared to pay. Did he know how much? And if he had known, would he have held back? Would he have said: you are not worth it, it is too much. Looking at this woman, made ugly by her rage, he wanted to restore her: could that not be called love? At a pinch? In the dark?

At other bars they drank cocktails with different names, but the same ingredients, and saw juggling acts and acrobats and bad comedians. By early evening these bars and cabarets were all packed; some of them had singers, large, middle-aged women in tailored striped suits, or balding men with operatic gestures, and in the dark alcoves soldiers embraced their girls, and Party men danced with the hostesses, and the waiters sold Osaka, which was said to be good for potency, occasionally somebody fainted, overcome by the smell, the smoke, the cocktails, and by lack of food.

'Leonie.'

'Yes, my soldier, my soldier of the black heart.'

'Love me.'

'I love the bombers.'

'No. *Me*.'

'It is not possible. In any case, it would amount to the same thing.'

'You will love me.' He vowed it; he who could be denied nothing. Why did he want her to love him? Why was that necessary to him?

'Dance with me. You can hold me very close. And pretend – whatever you want to pretend. Only hold me very close and let me feel your body become strong.'

Dancing, her precise body was a filament, light receiving, his light, my Leonie, the receiver of my light, she glows from *me*, my energy in her, I will restore her. Her torsion easing as they moved infinitesimally, he watched her face re-form, this for him was the moment – the catch of hook and eye; the intimate smell of her body undisguised: her expression becoming intense.

'You see,' she said softly, her violence elsewhere now, 'love is not necessary. I feel you strong. That's good, it's good. In that way we were always good together.'

'Yes.'

'Stronger, my soldier. Such a long time.'

'Did you think of me?'

'In that way, yes. Shameful thoughts, my black-hearted soldier, but I thought of you.'

'Tell me your thoughts of me.'

'You are vicious to ask that.'

'Tell me them.'

'You want to humiliate me? They were the usual thoughts, it is not dignified.'

'I would not humiliate you. How can you think such a thing?'

But she told him her thoughts of him, or made them up to please him, or to please herself, or to humiliate herself.

It was a noisome night of wind and continuous rain, and every time they left one place for another they were pummelled by the storm – the sky, strangely illumined in places, was full of camouflage netting and flying umbrellas, and the streets were strewn with wads of green gauze, and hats scurried along the pavements, their owners in pursuit, and flags floated down from upper storeys, and children hung on to their parents, and old women hung on to copings, and men on foot hesitated to cross the bridges of the Donau for fear of being blown away, as had happened. Such a night it was. Out of the smelly body heat (there was not much of any other sort) of the cabarets, into the streets, looking for another place, and another, and another: somewhere deep and suffocating and *louche*, where intimacies openly took place, where Osaka was sold, where the cocktails were less syrupy and more alcoholic, where small cubicles could be rented by the hour at an exorbitant rate; where elderly women sang of soldiers' love. Such a place they were looking for, neither wanting to return to her flat – the feelings between them were too variable to be sustained throughout the tram journey back, the walk, the climb up those stairs, too variable to survive the looks of small boys, the smell of fish in the corridor. They must find a place where soldiers took their girls, though neither had formulated this idea until leaving the sixth or seventh cabaret and standing uncertainly in the doorway, the old doorman, whom Wirthof had tipped over-lavishly, inquired if they were perhaps looking for a private room, because if they were he knew a place, very elegant, tip-top, premier class. No, not a hotel: who could find a hotel room in Vienna? – no, this was a *private* house, a very special private house – officer class – he was assessing them, this old sad tout, he did not want to direct them to an inappropriate place. 'For connoisseur?' he said questioningly. No, Wirthof said, no, they were not interested, but Leonie said why not, as long as it was clean. 'It is de luxe class,' the old sad tout protested. 'Very elegant, madame. Also expensive.'

He took them himself, he was so frail the wind blew him about on a zigzag course, it was not far, he kept saying, not far; they followed him meekly, he kept looking over his shoulder to ensure that they were still behind him, and each time he did this the wind took hold of him and made him perform a little jig. From the direction in which they were going it was becoming apparent to Wirthof where they were being taken, and again he said to Leonie, 'Do you really want to go to this place?' And Leonie said, 'What does it matter, if it's clean.'

Salon Bella, the house in the Albertinagasse with the yellow louvred shutters that were always closed: belladonnas the girls were known as – affectionately, it is claimed.

Rare entertainment was provided at Salon Bella.

Have you ever seen monocled colonel-generals on their hands and knees on a Transylvania rug with floral motifs in red, blue and white on a gold field, playing mouse steeplechase, with mousetraps as the hurdles?

Darling girls the belladonnas were, with infantile sly faces: never coarse.

'Child, child, come here,' the colonel-generals said.

Attentively the belladonnas listened to the requirements of old and young men; they were not tardy either in offering suggestions of their own, always nicely, never coarsely. They knew the resources of Salon Bella.

Whispering of possibilities, eyes bright, lips sly, faces infantile. Look. See. Something new. Have you seen? Greta, Theresa, Mitchen. You must. Yes. Of course. Would you like? You are interested? But of course. Fantastic. Mitchen. Cabaret. Special cabaret. Mitchen. Greta. Exceptional. It is possible. Definitely.

296

No reason why not. Oh yes. It can be arranged. Everything can be arranged. You must speak to Madame. Gladly. Speak to Greta, Greta is the one.

Lingerie could be bought (Madame kept an extensive supply, extortionately priced) as gifts for the darling deadly nightshades; excitedly the gifts were received, with practised gratefulness, and tried on in the presence of the giver in rooms set aside for such purposes. Of course, brassières, corsets, girdles, riding boots, black stockings, silk drawers, suspender belts were all returned to Madame to be resold. (For this reason she did not need to keep a very large stock – only an extensive one.)

The colonel-generals (and also the colonels, and the majors and the Sturmbannführers) loved to bestow these personal gifts on the darling belladonnas, whose gratitude was so touching, whose eyes were so slyly communicative, whose silken (or patent leather) limbs were so nice to stroke: on their hands and knees the colonel-generals fastened hooks and eyes, little buttons, clips, zips. What zips! And if a gift was not received with sufficient gratitude – a carefully calculated lack of sufficient gratitude, I may say – why! then the ungrateful girl was due for chastisement, the other belladonnas insisted on it, the offender herself admitted it; a spanking for the wicked girl. She must be made to remove, or partially remove, the insufficiently appreciated garment, and to receive, with gratitude, the stroke of a cane or a riding crop, which also could be hired, the charge depending on the number of strokes administered with it.

Ah! how grateful were the darling belladonnas – those who had been insufficiently grateful for brassières or corsets or riding boots – for the deserved strokes of a riding crop, how their little buttocks twitched with enjoyment of the just punishment, and how excitedly the others, in their gratefully received gifts, watched, caressing each other, or themselves, and so transported were they by the justness of the punishment that sometimes, in their excitement, unwittingly – so they told the colonel-generals – they came, the darling girls.

There were many games to be played at Salon Bella on Ukrainian pile carpets and on Ladik prayer rugs and on northern Persian carpets: it was a finely appointed house.

Immediately on entering it, a deadly nightshade, pert and pouting, infant eyes bright, sprouted up out of a dark dense undergrowth of foliated ormolu, braided cloths, violet draperies,

convex mirrors, satyr masks, swags of fruit and flowers, gilded
swans' necks, Jove's eagles clasping thunderbolts in their claws,
love birds, twined snakes, gilded tendrils, grape clusters: fresh as
a daisy in May she sprouted, and asked what they might desire,
offering them limitless choice. A private room, if such a thing
was available, Wirthof said. She knew him, but was not so
indelicate as to betray the fact. Madame at the moment was
engaged, but undoubtedly a private room was a possibility. Her
eyes were full of understanding and sympathy: they concentrated
on Leonie, intent on overcoming antagonism, a woman too has
special needs and requirements, though she might lack the
boldness to express them – the belladonnas were expert at overcoming such feminine reserve, if and when encountered, they
were famed for their friendliness. With the utmost discreetness
she mentioned cabaret, supper, champagne – a special entertainment. Eyes engaging Leonie's, she added that it was an entertainment for connoisseurs. No, they merely wished to take a
private room, Wirthof said shortly. Yes, yes, she quite understood; she indicated the curved stairway leading to a gallery. The
cabaret could also be watched from the gallery, or even – if the
door was left open – from the private room itself. Of course it
undoubtedly *was* more private there. If the lights were extinguished, it was impossible to be observed. It was a house of the
utmost discreetness. Where they stood under the gallery, patches
of deep darkness offered immediate purdah, only a step back
was needed. Perhaps, Wirthof said, perhaps they might be shown
to their room, in that case. They did not require supper. But they
would take a bottle of champagne. A price was whispered; it
was open to discussion, but Wirthof did not bargain, he stuck
his fist into his pocket – by the side of the curtained double doors
to the next room a picture light shining on a 'Venus, Ariadne and
Bacchus' was causing some reflection on the glazed canvas
surface, obscuring parts of the painting – and came out with a
fistful of notes which he pressed without counting into the girl's
hand. She must have thought him nervous, his manner was so
precipitant; the ease with which he habitually conducted himself
in such places had deserted him, he moved awkwardly, with a
grating of parts. What a good place, Leonie thought, leaves of
acanthus, gilded swans' necks, crustaceans, oh what a good place:
the very place for my otherness, for my heart's squalor. Leading
them up the curved stairway, the girl kept looking round, eyeing

them alternately; below, in the dim arcades, shadows with monocles and brass paw feet engaged in dealings with necks of alabaster, and Leonie thought, oh it is appropriate, very fitting, and was excited. And on the gallery she saw herself in a surround of silvered fruits, cherubs, leaves, sprays of foliage, saw herself in brittle dark glass that gave her a sequinned appearance, and she thought it was absolutely fitting. The room into which the girl showed them had red quilted walls, somewhat greasy, and a *lit de repos* with blue silk velvet upholstery, amatory themes carved on the panelled sides, and fleurs-de-lis lavishly distributed all over it; eight feet long, occupying an entire wall of the chamber. The room also had a washbasin and a soap dish containing a large slab of unbelievable pink bath soap such as was unobtainable in the whole of Vienna. Delightedly she considered the prospect of washing with real soap, imagined its touch, resolved to steal it. The girl was busying herself, making up the bed, putting pillows into place, flashing her eyes at each of them in turn. She did her work with excessive slowness, smiling at them between each of her actions, tidying up fussily, rearranging ashtrays, rugs, lamps, experimenting – to Wirthof's intense annoyance – with the effect produced by differing combinations of lights.

'You can leave that,' he told her. She would bring the champagne, she said.

The girl was a long time coming with the champagne. It was airless in the room, it smelled disagreeably of women's face powder – the smell of dressing-table drawers. The room was altogether too red, disagreeably so, they heard a woman's voice – 'Meine Damen und Herren . . .' Fitful music; cabaret time; the music becoming dilated with shrill and voluptuous notes. Wirthof sat down on the *lit de repos*, brows darkening with a nascent rage; Leonie had begun to undress, removing blouse, starting to unhook skirt.

'You might wait,' he said, 'the girl will be coming with the champagne.'

'What does it matter? In a whorehouse?' Edgy, her voice: abrasive. She slipped off the skirt, eyes provocative – and mocking, of him, of herself. 'I'm going to wash,' she said, 'isn't that what the girls do, in a high-class place like this? Cleanliness is so important. You wouldn't want to catch a disease. You don't know how many other soldiers have had me.'

She went to the washbasin, turned on the taps, lathered her

hands with soap and then assumed a squatting posture. He watched her with hatred. 'Why are you doing this?' Rage was building up in him.

'You don't consider cleanliness is important?'

'Stop this.'

'Oh – why? Is my body not exciting to you, my soldier?'

'You are vicious. Why? *Why?*'

'You don't find me appealing?' She flashed her eyes at him, a belladonna's love look, a parody. 'I told you all you could have of me.'

'I don't want that.'

She laughed and began to soap herself.

'You are coarse.'

'What is it you expect in a whorehouse?'

He came towards her in fury, seizing her arm to stop her, her arm was strong and rigid; they struggled; the soap slipped out of her hand on to the floor; he had her against the washbasin. 'Like this,' she said, 'take me like this. Oh yes.' She offered her contemptuous lips. He had soap lather all over his trousers. Her hands clawed him. He had to use strength to fight her off.

'Oops,' the belladonna said, coming in with champagne.

Wirthof stood away from Leonie, she was unperturbed, gleeful indeed. The silence of an interrupted act spread out between them. The girl was attuned to this silence, she set down the champagne carefully, she picked up the soap from the floor.

'Perhaps,' she suggested, flashing between them, 'Madame would like me to wash her?' Oh yes, oh yes, they were highly trained in their craft.

Leonie laughed. 'What is your name?'

'Karizza.'

'You wish me to, madame?'

'You must ask the gentleman.'

She asked him with belladonna eyes; she took his silence for assent, dropped on to her knees at Leonie's feet, the soap obscenely held.

'Swinishness,' Wirthof said.

It sounded like approval to her; Leonie laughed, spreading herself, drawing up the sodden slip.

'Out!' Wirthof said.

'What?'

'Out!' He grabbed the whore by her arm, yanked her to her

feet. 'Out! Out!' Violently he pushed her – she was still clutching the soap: it slipped out of her hand, slithered across marble – towards the door. Then, roughly, with hurry and fury, he wiped the soap from Leonie's body, and forcefully dressed her; un-resistant as a child she was as he pulled skirt, stockings, blouse, jacket on to her, not bothering with fasteners, allowing stockings to hang loose, and bundled her into her overcoat. And throwing open the door, he dragged her out into the gallery in this dish-evelled condition – she was sobbing as well as laughing now. 'Swinishness,' he said, dragging her along after him – the cabaret was on, in a cage a girl hung manacled from a post, her body twisting, heaving, seeking purchase from the air, coloured lights played on her – she was bloodstone, corcidolite, malachite, operculum, moss agate, lapis lazuli, black moonstone, rhodo-nite. Arms reached in through the bars of the cage, fingers touching, tweaking, pinching, tearing, pulling, jabbing, scratch-ing, the body turned and became contorted, like an umbrella in the wind turned back on its axis, open to the pillaging fingers. She must have been a contortionist, the way her body turned inside out, reversed itself, so that it no longer resembled the body of a person.

He took Leonie back to her flat. She was shivering and ill. All night she kept vomiting. He sat up with her, holding her head over the basin, dabbing her face with Cologne. Even in the fever her eyes did not lose their amazement. 'Why?' she demanded, continually.

'Because I love you,' he told her furiously.

'Oh, my God,' she said, 'oh God! That's all I need.'

I did not try to understand it; other people's loves are always inexplicable. I did not tell her that I considered Wirthof ridi-culous, not even genuinely frightening, despite his uniform, a bubble of vanities and poses and grandiosities. That such men were the terrors of Europe, it was laughable.

Once, at this time, Wirthof said something to me that abso-lutely confirmed this feeling of mine. He'd had a nightmare. It was really awful, he said, a presentiment. He'd dreamt that he was dying, of some wound he had sustained, but that wasn't the awful part of it. The awful part of it was that, in this dream, he had suddenly thought – what will become of Leonie? and the thought had been so unbearable to him that, dying of this terrible wound, he had begun to weep at the idea of Leonie having to do without him. 'I don't know why you're laughing, it was a deeply tragic dream.'

'I am laughing, Wirthof, at the idea of you considering yourself so indispensable that the thought of your death makes you weep with pity for Leonie.'

Factors in Wirthof's downfall. They were: his drinking; his secrecy; and Leonie. The last two, of course, linked. It was his secrecy about her that was considered most heinous. When Lüdenscheid discovered that his most trusted officer, his aide in whom he had placed such confidence, was conducting a secret affair with the Baroness Koeppler, widow of the Jew Baron, and a woman of very doubtful standing with the regime, he took it as a personal betrayal. It was bad enough Wirthof having become involved with this woman, but that he kept his relationship so secret, never mentioned it in his daily reports, indicated that he was not worthy of the high trust that had been placed in him. Wirthof's drinking was an additional offence. Often, at the early evening conferences, his words were slurred. No longer did the pronunciamentos ring out: sometimes they were actually incomprehensible. Things came to a head in December, by which time Lüdenscheid had known for several months about Leonie, and had been having Wirthof watched.

'Obersturmbannführer, is there nothing else you wish to tell me? I am giving you this opportunity.'

'Oh, that's generous of you, Ernst.'

'This is formal.'

In the Baron's library the Venetian blinds were distorted, bent out of their parallel alignment by the action of someone repeatedly pushing down one or two of the slats to peer out. One of the octahedral thick-glass lamps hanging from the copper-panelled, and riveted, ceiling did not light up, its bulb having burned out and not been replaced. On the Empire *escritoire* stood a large adjustable office table lamp. The arcaded bookshelves were half empty, the subversive and otherwise proscribed literature – I fear unread by the Baron, he was not a great reader – having been removed and consigned to the bonfires.

'What exactly would the Gruppenführer like me to tell him? I will gladly tell the Gruppenführer whatever he wishes to hear. Why should I be the exception?'

'You are insolent, Wirthof.'

He did not deny it, but seated himself in a reclining position on a sofa, determined to make himself comfortable for the dressing down that was evidently in store for him. From under lowered eyelids, and through his headache (not unconnected with the amount of alcohol he had drunk the previous night), he peered biliously at Lüdenscheid.

'I ask of you honesty.'

'No more? A mere trifle. No more than that, Ernst? Ah – I forgot, I apologize: this is formal. Ah yes – what sins can I confess today? Perhaps if the Gruppenführer could tell me his preference in the matter – his personal predilections, so to speak.'

'Take care, Wirthof. You may go too far . . .'

Wirthof jumped up abruptly, with a flash of anger, then smiled again in his mocking way. He went to the window and looked out through the distorted blinds. He spoke quietly, 'I wish to report to the Gruppenführer a mounting resentment of him . . .'

'Continue, please. Have I stopped you? Continue.'

'Further,' said Wirthof turning, swaying a little, eyes closing momentarily, 'I wish to report a diminishing desire to overcome my mounting resentment of the Gruppenführer. As a matter of fact, I would say that the desire has reached zero.'

'Take care, Obersturmbannführer.'

What stupidity to advocate care to one who had thrice played Russian roulette! and survived. 'At times, I further wish to report, taking due care in doing so, that I entertain thoughts of the Gruppenführer meeting with a gruesome accident. A variety of accidents occur to me, all of them rather – bizarre. For instance, I frequently have an image of the Gruppenführer falling into a vat of molten lead, and becoming encased from head to toe in lead – solidified in it like a statue. Furthermore, I regret to say, I find that this spectacle of the Gruppenführer turned into lead – usually in a somewhat undignified position, legs kicking up, etcetera – strikes me as being highly comical. At other times I have indulged in the reprehensible speculation as to what might happen if the Gruppenführer could not perform his natural functions, and I have imagined him becoming so bloated that he –' Wirthof smiled – 'bursts.'

'Wirthof, you will be silent.'

'You no longer wish me to be honest?'

'You are insubordinate.'

'Ah yes – one is either insubordinate or dishonest.'

'You are both. What is more, you are drunk, repeatedly, disgustingly, drunk.'

'Correction. I *was* drunk, disgustingly drunk, as you so rightly say, last night. It is much to be regretted that I am not now, or I wouldn't have this appalling head.'

'You have become a vulgar and insolent drunkard, Wirthof.' It was no surprise to find himself hated, not even dismaying. My task, if necessary to darken the world. The beauty of necessity. He did not mind hatred. But lack of respect was something else. That he would not tolerate. Hatred he could bear, as iron can bear fire: in it his strength was forged. I am iron – but I will not tolerate impertinence. 'Unchecked, Wirthof, such behaviour as yours leads to the decay of nations. Armies rot in the juices of their excesses. In Capua Hannibal's soldiers frittered away their fitness for battle, allowed themselves to be seduced by the pleasures and the beauty of the town . . .'

'Yes, yes, yes,' Wirthof interposed, 'and ash is a well-known manure and the ship among seafaring nations –'

'I warn you against Capua, Wirthof. You disdain my help, you resent it –'

'Your *help*.'

'Yes, my help. Why do you think I insist on the admission of everything – even that which may seem most trivial to you, your most private thoughts, your fluctuating impulses, the drift of your feelings? Readings must be taken. One must take readings, Wirthof. Would you seek to cross the oceans without instruments of navigation? Readings must be taken of the mind. You are like a foolish sailor who resents the mast of his ship because it is higher than him. Without me, Wirthof, you are adrift.

Without me, you are at the mercy of every passing qualm . . .'

'I have no qualms. What makes you think I have qualms? I have done nothing dishonourable.'

'There is your secrecy. You deny your qualms – all men have qualms.'

'Even you, Ernst?'

'Naturally. But I am strong enough to bear them.'

'I have no qualms.'

'There I have found your secrecy.'

'I have no qualms. I have done nothing dishonourable.'

'I have found your secrecy. You fear I may command you to act in a manner that you would consider dishonourable, and you fear that your obedience would not be strong enough to surmount your qualms and meet that demand. Admit it – come, admit it.'

'What are we talking about, Ernst? Be more precise.'

'A woman.'

Wirthof laughed. 'Only a woman. For a moment I thought you might be talking about something serious.'

'A certain Baroness, Wirthof. That liaison is contrary to your duties. It is necessary for you to give her up.'

'It's out of the question, Ernst.' There was a foolish fire in his eyes, someone who did not know him well might have taken it for anger or determination, but not I, I would not have made that mistake – I have seen the flickering ignition of marsh gases, and I know what delusive fire it makes: only phosphorescence.

Next day Wirthof was making some routine announcements in connection with the Winter Aid campaign. It was early evening and he was again somewhat drunk. Speaking without consulting the prepared statement, he told the assembled Party workers that this year, with the terrible conditions obtaining on the Russian front, it was of the utmost importance that an all-out effort should be made in collecting for *Winterhilfe*. Warm clothing was very badly needed – even single gloves, or single shoes. What use were single gloves or single shoes? one of the Party workers asked. Wirthof seemed taken aback by the question. He had got into the habit of rattling off announcements and exhortations without considering their import. Now, jolted by the questioner into considering what he had just said, he seemed perplexed. Indeed, what use were single gloves and single shoes? His face became screwed up with the effort of finding the answer. Even single gloves and single shoes was what Lüdenscheid's directive said. Suddenly a knowing smile began around his mouth and spread outwards.

'I can only suppose,' he said brightly, swaying a little, 'that so many of our men on the Eastern front have lost one arm or one leg that they only require single gloves and single shoes.'

Immediately afterwards, he was called into Lüdenscheid's office.

'Before you say anything, Ernst, I admit I made a stupid mistake just now, a slip of the tongue. I was not aware, as I spoke, of the connotation . . .'

Lüdenscheid cut him short, 'You were not aware of what you said, a condition in which you have frequently found yourself recently, because you were drunk.'

'I had had a little to drink, I've told you – I am bored with this job. I have asked repeatedly to be given duties that are more suited to someone of my capabilities.'

'That is your overweening pride . . .'

'I am not a ventriloquist's doll, which is what you use me as.'

'The first test of an officer's capability is to be able to accept the role assigned to him and to perform it diligently.'

'I did not join the SS to be an announcer. If you wanted someone of that sort you should have applied to the railway station.'

'You are insolent again.'

'I have certain rights, and I insist . . .'

'You stupid man: you have no rights, and you will not insist with me.'

'I beg to correct the Gruppenführer. As an officer of the Austrian army, whose father . . .'

'The Austrian army does not exist, and it does not interest me who your father was . . .'

'I would remind the Gruppenführer: I hold the Knight's Cross – I was decorated.'

'At my behest, at my behest, Wirthof.'

'Perhaps it was also at your behest that I blew up those French pillboxes.'

'You are under *my* command.'

'This is becoming more and more absurd. You deny me everything.'

'I warn you, by taking this arrogant attitude you are making matters worse for yourself.'

306

'Look here: what I did this afternoon was an indiscretion, I don't consider it any worse than that.'

'*You* don't consider – you! It is evident that your attitude, Wirthof, is impervious to reason. It is not compatible with the high trust that I have in the past placed in you.'

'What is that supposed to mean?'

'It means that I cannot accept in one of my officers – contempt. You have increasingly displayed contempt. I cannot use a man who has such contempt of everything. Your secrecy and your arrogance –'

'Then transfer me out. Transfer me to another unit.'

'It is my intention – '

'Good. I welcome it. In fact, it has been my intention to request it. I will immediately and formally place before you my request for transfer . . .'

'It is not a question of request. I am having you dismissed from the SS. You will revert to your former rank of lieutenant in the army, and you will be stripped of your decorations.'

'What! Revert to lieutenant?' Wirthof was outraged. 'You mean – I have wasted my time.'

'You are concerned only about the wastage of *your* time.'

'Naturally. My time is of the greatest importance to me.'

'You are not concerned about all the time that has been wasted on you, on your training and development. All the time I have wasted on you.'

'Lüdenscheid, I was given promises. Promises were made to me.'

'You are not suited for a position of high command.'

'I have wasted five years of my time. *My* time. I was given promises. I have submitted to your absurd rules, I have reported to you my thoughts – all on the basis of promises I was given.'

'You are not the material of commanders. You lack the qualities of –'

'Lüdenscheid, my father was a general when you were selling ostrich feathers . . .'

'You dare to address me in this arrogant and familiar way! Without respect! You lack respect, Wirthof.'

'You are perceptive to notice it.'

'Wirthof, you are making matters worse for yourself every minute. You would do better to show contrition.'

'Contrition? You are absurd.'

'You see how your pride contaminates everything you say and do. I should have seen this sooner. I have nothing further to say to you, Wirthof, except this. In the next few days, after your formal expulsion, you will be informed of your new posting. If you can find in yourself contrition, if you can succeed in overcoming pride, you may some day be given another chance by me, but you must earn it. Bear in mind what I say to you now, reflect on it. That is all now.'

'I wish to place on record . . .'

'The interview is over You are dismissed '

'None the less, I intend to say . . .'

'Do you wish me to have you forcefully removed? I have no further time for you. You have exhausted my patience. Is that clear? Now leave.'

Wirthof's mother was dying; at first he had refused to believe it, the stroke had occurred in her sleep and only affected her left side. Her speech was unimpaired, and, if anything, her mind seemed clearer than it had been for some years. Then she had a second stroke, and was unconscious for much of the time.

He stood by her narrow bed in the old nursery, looking down on the exquisite features, from which the stiff coarse hair spread out like an unbecoming headdress – why hadn't she looked after her hair? It had been pretty once, so soft, and now it was this coarse grey-white stuff, like wire wool: unbecoming. 'You must not die,' he told the inert form. The room smelled of formaldehyde and medicines. His school drawings were around the walls, neat and symmetrical, encircling the dying woman.

You must not die, Mother. It is unthinkable that you should die now, I have not had sufficient time with you, there has not been sufficient time, you are young still, you are not yet fifty. I had always intended to devote more time to you. Once I had settled all these other matters. There have been so many claims on my time, you see, with one thing and another. Mamma, surely you can't doubt my love. Are you dying to spite me? That is cruel of you. It is all very well for you to lie there calm and smug, you do look a little smug, Mamma, yes, you do: it is I who will have to do without you. Just when I need you. My own precious dear little Mamma, my little madonna. It is not kind of you to die and leave me so alone. How boring life is. It must end badly, that is the nigger in the woodpile. Yes. Was it worth the pain of bringing me into the world? You, who couldn't bear pain. Why did you have to? Not for my sake, I would gladly have forgone the privilege. For the momentary pleasure. Was it for that? For that pleasure? Really, Mother, *you*! So exquisite and refined, racked by that pleasure? You irritated me with your nervousness – you always had 'bad nerves', as you called it. Do you know that you are dying? And how do your nerves apprehend that fact? My dear precious little mamma, I can't spare you that – can I? It is not possible you are dying, you are just asleep. You will wake up and you will say, 'Konrad, Konrad, come and give your mamma a lovely kiss, my beautiful boy. I want to see you smile at me with your violet eyes. Give me a beautiful smile with your violet eyes, Konrad.' When we used to go to Gerstner's, in the afternoons, for chocolate cakes, how you loved chocolate cakes with cream. Elegant, in your furred pelisse. Your long veils. Your cool cheeks. You had to use rouge – you were always pale, like me. The first time you had an attack – in the park, photographing me, I had a chocolate cigarette in my mouth and I wore long trousers, I was six, and you felt 'peculiar' suddenly. I was so frightened when you fainted and they had to carry you to an ambulance and bring you home on a stretcher. And when I was ill, you couldn't bear it, I knew you couldn't bear it, I saw it in your eyes, the same expression as in the park: I made up my mind never to be ill, and I never was – was I? I knew you couldn't bear for me to be ill, with your delicate health, your 'nerves'. I remember – in the park – being frightened – what was it that frightened me? – and then the fear was in your eyes, you felt 'peculiar'. Your 'little peculiarities'! Never sleeping with your head towards the door. Holding your breath for a minute when you went out into the cold night air. Taking the flowers out of the bedroom because they poison the air. Washing your hands endlessly. 'Do it for your mother's sake,' you always said to me, 'do it for your mother, Konrad, for your mamma who loves you so, to whom you are more precious than gold. Ah – if you are not good, a little dwarf called Rumpelstiltskin will come and take you away, and what will your poor mother do then without you?' I was never a frightened child, not after the park. I made up my mind. You couldn't bear for me to be ill, and I never was. Not so much as a tummy ache. Wasn't that remarkable? I'd made up my mind. You fretted about my being so pale, and I said, 'All geniuses are pale, Mother, don't you know that, don't you know anything?' You laughed. Such an extraordinary child you'd brought into the world, a little genius of a child, a *Wunderkind*, never ill, good as gold. My many accomplishments – the time I was given my first pair of shoes and immediately ran, my legendary exploits. Never had a high voice that broke, mine was low from the start. You irritated me, Mother, with your little peculiarities. 'I do wish you would show more intelligence, Mother, you do sometimes make some very foolish remarks. I cannot bear for *my* mother to make foolish remarks.' 'That is no way to talk to your mother, Konrad.' 'Mother, I cannot bear stupidity. You must pay attention to what I tell you, and not always make the same foolish mistakes. Those stupid doctors of yours. What do they know? What good have they done you? Had you listened to me. I tell you, I don't trust those doctors.'

Four days after the second stroke she regained consciousness, but she could not speak. Her eyes looked up into Konrad's and said – It does not matter, my death is not a calamity, it is not a great loss for you, we have not been close, a little dwarf came and stole my baby boy who was good as gold. I have suffered with bad nerves all my life, Konrad, I lost you, Konrad, because I could not bear your pains and your fears. He had borne them instead, the dying woman thought, in some way the child had borne them, by some kind of *Wunderkind*'s magic he had taken his fears and those in his mother's eyes and hidden them all around his room, in secret places, in boxes, in receptacles, as he used to take the little hard stools from his diapers and hide them, under the mattress, in cupboards, under the floorboards, behind the curtains, her clever baby.

When she had died, her body and face were released from their torsion, from those muscular tensions that had afflicted her, and she looked young as when they used to go to Gerstner's together, except for her hair.

The ceremony of expulsion from the SS took place the day after his mother's funeral. It was conducted by Lüdenscheid at Bad Zoeltz before the three hundred assembled cadets, on a bright cold day, the mountains were of a crystalline sharpness. There was thick snow on the ground.

All the officers and men wore greatcoats, but Wirthof had to be in tunic and trousers for the ceremony. He couldn't control his shivering, his lips were blue, and as he marched forward under escort, while the long drum roll went on and on, his pale face disappeared into the sun glare. He was brought to a halt in front of Lüdenscheid and the other officers. A short announcement was read out. Greatcoats flapped, loose snow speckled the black uniforms. Another drum roll, building to a crescendo. Wirthof was commanded to step forward. His cap was seized by a junior officer who proceeded to rip from it the Post and Telegraph emblem of the unit on the uppers. Then Lüdenscheid himself stepped forward. With abrupt, violent, ritualistic movements, he tore the *Ritterkreuz* from Wirthof's neck, he took the loosened silver braid at the collar and ripped it off, first on one side, then on the other; he seized hold of the silver epaulettes and wrenched them from the shoulders. He pulled at the dark armband with the silver embroidery. He tore off the braid work of the sleeves. All this time the drums were rolling and Wirthof was shivering uncontrollably. When all decorations and insignia lay in the snow, and Wirthof looked like a tailor's dummy covered in cotton thread, Lüdenscheid said, 'You are removed and banished from this company. All awards and decorations are revoked.'

After this he was marched away, still shivering, between the lines of the assembled cadets.

Part Four

I must make a space in the mind, a clear space in which my thoughts can toss and turn. I must make order in my mind. What was yesterday? Yesterday I was in despair; ah yes; but in which kind of despair was I yesterday? (Since I have a choice of despairs.) The despair of being another? The despair of knowing I am in despair? The despair of not knowing? The despair of remembrance?

Memory is not the same as recall: recall has access only to what lies vivid and formed below the surface, but memory must reconstruct from fag-ends, memory deals in the flotsam of the mind, from scraps it builds hypothetical towers. Doubtful architectures! Somewhere between the future and the past is the man, but where? If I could re-enter my despair. But that takes courage. That is the desert and that is the limestone cliffs.

What is this story you are telling yourself, Kazakh? Will it make a movie? The story of Stefan Kazakh (as told to Stefan Kazakh). I must confess to becoming of late somewhat bored with the Jewish question. We have heard quite enough about Auschwitz. Couldn't you tell us how you made your money? That is always an interesting theme. It has more appeal.

I wonder what has happened to Leonie. The way you dwell on Leonie – admittedly she was a baroness and somewhat nympho from what you say – is surely unnecessary. Weren't you once married to Y., the actress? What was she like? I could tell you exactly, gentlemen, but it would be a trifle pornographic. While we would not wish to appear prurient. On the other hand. These days. A trifle is very nice. The lives of actresses are an endless source of fascination, wouldn't you agree? Try being married to one, gentlemen. Well, what about your other two wives, or is it three? Frankly, I forget. Wishful. Suffice it to say, Stefan Kazakh was three times married. Then he went to Vienna and had a breakdown. Regressive symptoms. Observed walking through the streets of Vienna talking to himself, occasionally slapping his face to the tune of 'Deutschland Über Alles'. In some respects, quite normal. Cessation is a tax matter. Any man is entitled to avail himself. Any man is entitled to cease. Freedom of the individual. Struggle against the encroachment of bureaucracy. I am entitled to cease. Unless we hear from you within seven days. Speak to my lawyers. Nobody can say it did not take a certain courage to do what I did. Is that so?

How are you ever going to think this through, Kazakh, if you keep letting your mind wander? What you need are guide tracks. Stick to the point. What is the point? Life is the quest for integration, which is another way of saying – Your life has been a quest for life, and what did you ever find that was not another form of dying? Take Wirthof, for instance; why are you so obsessed with the career of this footling Nazi? Wasn't even much good at that. Kicked out of the SS in disgrace. Bungled everything. I thought this was supposed to be your story, Kazakh, and it has become his. Who is he to occupy your mind so totally? And Leonie? And Lüdenscheid?

Wirthof suffered from what Goethe has called 'sensuous exaltation'; very prone to that, the Germans. The Austrians, too; to a lesser extent. The Austrians had the saving grace, especially the Viennese, of being more incompetent. Short bursts of sensuous exaltation, followed by boredom and collapse. A great nation for masturbation phantasies, spelled with a ph. Lovers of fairy tales. Aladdin and his magic lamp. Rub the lamp. And you have riches beyond the dreams of avarice. Not beyond the dreams of Germans circa 1933. The genie in the flatus. All you had to do was fart. And out it came – the genie slave. Magical and reprehensible. I suppose the essence of all fairy tales is the equivocal nature of the magician, the genie, the fairy, the wizard – the Jew.

The castle above Lake Bojh, the prototype of all fairy-tale castles; it stood on a vitreous cliff, and seemed to float on the mist that rose from the lake, a floating castle, occasionally screams were heard, nothing very unusual in that, it had been a lunatic asylum before. The way the mist rose, quite suddenly, as when you pour water into absinthe. When the mist rose far enough, the castle was gone. But in the village on the lake they still heard the screams and the firing squads. The old women – I say old because they looked old – didn't know if it was their sons who were screaming or somebody else's sons. They commended their souls to heaven whoever's sons they were, and even if they were communists. A hundred and fifty searchlights had formed a cupola in the sky above Nuremberg, and Wirthof had thought: it will be magnificent. Who could have told him he would end up in a castle above a lake in Upper Slovenia, not far from the iron works of Jesenice? In a place that had been a lunatic asylum, still was in fact, though all the lunatics had been moved into the east wing, which overlooked the yard where the executions took place. The lunatics all came to their windows to watch whenever there were executions, which was almost every other day, and they chortled and grunted and bellowed and shitted themselves. Wirthof was responsible for the lunatics because the major who commanded the castle had enough on his plate, what with executions every other day, and Jews dumped on him, without having to deal with lunatics as well. Wirthof didn't mind the lunatics, perhaps he remembered how his mother had been at the end, and he opposed one of the ideas of dealing with them, which was to shoot them; Wirthof had a special regard for lunatics, always had had, he regarded them as voyagers in the unknown, so he was reluctant to shoot them, and curiously enough the major who didn't mind shooting partisans and hostages felt superstitious about shooting lunatics. So the lunatics lived.

After his disgrace, Wirthof was packed off to Yugoslavia. I saw him off at the station. I and Leonie. Oh it was a real leave-taking; train wheels moved in our stomachs; steam hissed; soldiers waved from open windows, pregnant sweethearts clutched mementos to their expanding bosoms; and Wirthof, in Wehrmacht grey, a lieutenant again, minus *Ritterkreuz*, minus telegraph pole emblem, minus black and silver, was going to Yugoslavia. He still had the fur lining however, which he had transferred from his black greatcoat to his grey greatcoat. Consequently he wasn't shivering. As a matter of fact, he had managed to secure a sleeper, and though it didn't have rosewood veneered walls or Alpine brochures, and did rather smell of coal, it was back of the locomotive – it *was* a sleeper all to himself, and the fact that the radiator – this must have been because he was so close to the locomotive – heated up to furnace temperature wasn't the worst thing that could happen to somebody pale and with thin blood.

He lay on the upper berth, watching the white and whitening landscape, admiring the intricate workmanship of frost: sharp gusts of cold entered the dense heat of the compartment, bringing shivers to his gently sweating body. Thin as pencil lines the trees were; close to the track they floated in a snow mist, everything floated – the telegraph poles, the stacks of lumber, the little yellow two-roomed houses, the church steeples, the train itself. Late sunshine struck the distant slopes, now this side, now that, making golden green and russet patches on the ground; the sun disappeared, colouring the rim of the hills, giving them a brilliant edge, here the countryside was shadowed, but ahead it was still lit from an unseen source. The unusual play of light reminded him of those paintings of Leonie's, the ones he liked, the glowing ones of splendid girls in green and yellow fields; the others he hated – deformed faces, unreal, no relation to anything human. The trouble with Lüdenscheid was that he had no aesthetic sense. That was the truth of the matter. Ostrich-feather salesman. There were not enough outstanding men; great concepts foundering in a miasma of mediocrity and pettifogging bureaucracy. For lack of great men with noble vision. Lüdenscheid: the mind of a clerk. Dying in their thousands in Russia, single gloves, single shoes on their frozen limbs. Incompetence. All one could do was conduct oneself with honour. It was said to be very cold in Yugoslavia, he dreaded that, nothing else. I'm bored. I wouldn't mind dying, if it weren't for Leonie. A man must be able to abdicate – I wash my hands of it all, damn them! Upstarts and salesmen. The trouble with such men was that they lacked honour. Can't be taught, honour. Inbred. I never had to be taught anything. What did I ever learn at Gymnasium? Taught myself everything. Lüdenscheid conducts his outfit like a school, I'm well out of it, sneaks and bullies, no honour, no aesthetic sense. What can you expect of an ostrich-feather salesman with constipation? What a mess they were making of things, he thought. Anyway, I can abdicate. Any time I choose. I abdicate my life. Dignified. Only dignified thing to do in certain circumstances. A man has that right. A superior smile appeared on his face. It was a comforting thought that he could abdicate any time he liked, with dignity. His father had done it. You don't feel a thing. It just took a certain amount of resolution. Bang. All over. It was a way of showing your contempt. If they wanted to make a mess of things, let them: I abdicate, bang. That was all there was to it. A man could be free if he did not value his life unduly. A river curled below him, shimmering, darkening. Flashes from the train coloured the snow green.

Oh well, let the Jews have it all, I bestow it on them, the tradesmen: I will not soil my hands, it's my terms or nothing, I will not demean myself. I would like Leonie to think well of me. Yes. Yes. She must know that I die contemptuously: life is God-given, yes, perhaps, but a man is entitled to return a gift. I, Konrad Wirthof, cannot be bribed with the gift of life. However, he thought, it has not yet come to that: he could wait until the very last moment before returning the unwanted gift. Meanwhile, there was no reason why its less objectionable aspects could not be enjoyed. I shall do some skiing (he had brought his skis, they stood next to where his tunic hung from a hanger), and peasant girls might be refreshing, there was said to be a quite good house in Zagreb, though it might not be necessary to resort to professionals, a tin of coffee was a universal currency in wartime, and he had several such tins secreted in his leather luggage. It was not disloyal to Leonie. It was quite different from what he had with her. A man had need of pleasure. The biological imperative. A man's organs were external, a woman's internal, it made a difference. A man could sire a thousand children. To think of those hundreds of thousands of seeds slaughtered. They died in a woman's body. Woman's secretions killed them off. All those seeds in a woman's channel, and just one of them becomes me. A brutish business. The others must die. Nature dictates it. That is why one cannot be sentimental about life and death. It's a chancy business, at best. I would have liked to have a son. That is one thing Lüdenscheid is right about, a man should procreate a child before going to die. Still, I may not die. 'One way or the other,' he said out loud, 'it is a matter of supreme indifference to me,' and chuckled.

In the silvery field, the children rolled over and over in the grass, playing at the feet of the black men, over and over they rolled, intent upon their games, they felt no fear, there were hundreds of them, rolling, jumping, vaulting, leap-frogging, copulating, at the feet of the black men, sometimes they almost touched the toes of the black men, but there was no fear in Elysium, and then he noticed that the black men carried Schmeisser submachine guns, and as they began to fire into the happy cavorting children, who laughed at such games, he was afraid for his life, and ran, happy smiling bodies falling dead all around him, laughing and leap-frogging and dying, and he ran with all the effort of his legs, and he saw that the area they were in was surrounded by a high dark stone wall, and when he began to climb it he saw that it was covered in human excrement, which got on to his fingers and hands and body, but he climbed unaided to the top of the wall where he stood against a blue sky, a perfect target for the Schmeisser sub-machine guns, and he was not sure whether to leap or not. Below him was a path with people out strolling, women wheeling prams, fathers taking their sons for a walk, they took no notice of this grimy, faeces-covered figure standing on the high wall. He saw that all these people were going to the park, which was on the other side of the path; it had tall trees and swings, and children were playing there watched over by their parents, some of these children were crying in contrast to the happy dying children playing and bleeding at the feet of the black men, and he did not know whether to leap, and he felt himself hit by bullets but not yet dead, and still he did not know whether to leap or not, because really it looked very boring on the other side of the wall.

Was that Wirthof's dream, or mine?

Lüdenscheid never spoke of Wirthof in the course of normal conversation, if any of his conversation can be said to have been normal, but in a state of trance his former aide was frequently mentioned, bitterly, with anger, someone who had betrayed him. He took Wirthof's misdemeanour very personally. How could he have so misjudged a man? He had placed high trust in him, and had been given only duplicity in return. Another aide, with the face of a pig's bladder, now stood on guard while Kazakh administered treatments, the need for which was increasing. Betrayers lurked everywhere; no one could be trusted. Only the deal. In that he had faith. For Kazakh was bound to him by ties stronger than those of loyalty or obedience: by the ties of the deal, or reciprocity, of this for that.

And the dancing children, they too kept cropping up; the little boys' faces ardent with gallantry – obnoxious little gallants, with their flat-brushed hair, their white waistcoats, their thick stiff bow ties, their patent leather shoes – the effluvia of an effete bourgeoisie; the girls wore sixteen-button gloves; their dresses were of gauze and silk, and some had trains, they'd been taught how to gather up their trains gracefully and how to hold them while dancing. Ernst's hands were damp. He always wiped them on his trousers before shaking anyone by the hand. He refused to dance. They'd never get him to dance, if they killed him.

At the age of six he told his mother not to worry if Father died; he, Ernst, would look after her, he vowed it. He was sure Father was not a well man, with his narrow rounding shoulders, and his dancing walk. Unnatural for a man to walk like that. He'd died fifteen years ago, cancer. Towards the end, it was pathetic to see this sick old man demonstrating the quick-step, the mazurka, the polka, the waltz, the fox-trot to energetic children; his classes had diminished in size, and his old gramophone with the big trumpet wheezed and spluttered, as out of breath as the dancing master himself. Still he smoked sixty cigarettes a day, coughing convulsively through waltzes and polkas. Useless man. Young Ernst was sure it was a relief to his mother when he went. A waste of a man. His mother, however, was a strong woman. Eighty-one when she died six years ago. Once a year, regularly, he visited her grave. He'd had the inscription on the stone changed from 'Wife of the Dancing Master Lüdenscheid' – which was no great distinction, after all – to 'Mother of Obersturmbannführer Lüdenscheid', and each time he'd been promoted he'd had the inscription changed: Standartenführer, Oberführer, Brigadeführer, Gruppenführer. Tears trickled down his cheeks. She had not lived long enough to be aware of his triumphs. What consoled him was his belief in reincarnation, not that everyone was reincarnated, it depended on what the person had done with his life, no point in reincarnating the useless and the ineffectual, Nature did not make mistakes twice; but his mother, he felt sure, would be reincarnated, not his father though.

The defeats were having a terrible effect on him; Germany was being betrayed; enemies from within were destroying its fighting spirit; Paulus surrendering at Stalingrad was a betrayal, he should have held out to the last man, if necessary all three hundred thousand should have died. It was a failure of leadership. A commander must be prepared to die with his men. The most brutal measures must be used in countering the insidious seed of defeatism, planted by the Jews. There were still Jews in high places, he murmured darkly; until every last one had been rooted out Germany was threatened. Enemies of the state must be liquidated ruthlessly, and no longer would the state pay for the elimination of this scum. He had directed that in every instance of offences against the posts and telegraphs, bills for executions were to be sent to the heirs: board, per day (up to and including day of execution), 1.50 marks; transportation, 12.90 marks;

execution sentence 158.18 marks; fee for death penalty, 300.00 marks; postage, 1.84 marks; postage for statement of costs, 42 pfennigs. He would make the pigs pay. Loyal Germans should not have to bear the cost of the elimination of this filth. And so on, and so on.

After the treatments, he was always much improved. Had Kazakh heard of the youth elizir, Orchikrin? He had been taking it, and it had a remarkable effect. He was sure that German scientists were on the verge of discovering 'a natural substance' of unimaginable potency that would counteract the noxious toxins of city life, and revitalize the nation. Such a transfusion of natural energy would be a greater boon to the war effort than any secret weapon.

Of course he was quite mad.

Why did I carry on, alleviating that madness in dribs and drabs? Why did I not let him sink into the horror of his mind?

I had a plan. Stefan Kazakh had a plan worthy of such a dealer as he. When the time came, I would know. He must become so dependent on me that he can refuse me nothing, then I will make my demand. And what will that be? It will have no limit. For a man who is tied by the ties of such a deal as that between us is totally tied and can refuse me nothing. That was the plan of Stefan Kazakh.

Sometimes he insulted Lüdenscheid. A cheeky fellow was Stefan Kazakh, and it was important to know how much he could get away with. You are a mouldering man, Lüdenscheid. You are a crumbling edifice, Lüdenscheid. You are full of rubble, Lüdenscheid. You are debris and wreckage. You have the smell of refuse on your breath. Your veins and lungs are full of dust. You are a dust man, Lüdenscheid. (Or words to that effect.)

He smiled to hear himself so abused; his three freaks chortled; it was all part of the treatment, which was part of the deal.

'I do not expect you to love me Herr Kazakh. Only to keep to your deal.'

You are full of hubris, Lüdenscheid. You are full of shit. You nourish on the product of your bowels.

'Herr Kazakh,' said Lüdenscheid, smiling to hear himself so abused, 'your insults do not perturb me, why should they? they are only opinions. I am not vulnerable to the opinions of others. Your actions are what count, and your actions are determined by our deal. That you have a poor opinion of me is neither here nor there. Indeed, I find your scurrility reassuring; that surprises you? Why? It is a mistake, Herr Kazakh, to depend on love. A variable emotion at the best of times; not to be relied on. Our deal is much more satisfactory. A man can be betrayed in love. But a deal has clauses and sub-clauses that protect his interests. A deal cannot be unilaterally abrogated, as can a vow of love. I do not ask you to have feelings of regard for me, Herr Kazakh. Only to keep to our deal. I prefer to rely on your self-interest.'

'And supposing, Lüdenscheid, my self-interest becomes incompatible with your self-interest?'

'It is for me to see that it doesn't.'

'And supposing, Lüdenscheid, I lose interest in self-interest?'

'That is just bluff. I do not believe that a man ever loses interest in self-interest. If that happened, everything would break down, and it would be impossible to deal with anyone.'

'Do you not fear sometimes that it might happen?'

'No. I think you think you can outwit me. That does not bother me. For I am sure that you cannot. But I do not fear your lack of self-interest. All men have needs. The essence of all deals is a balance of needs.'

'Oh you are a mouldering man, Lüdenscheid. You are made of dust.'

'So are we all, Herr Kazakh.'

'In what way do I have need of you, Lüdenscheid? You do nothing for me.'

'Is that likely, since our deal stands? I am an empiricist. Why you have need of me does not concern me, it is a fact that you do. Perhaps you have need of my protection.'

'The protection of a hangman. Lüdenscheid? A curious protector.'

'Who better?' He had a point there, I suppose.

Wirthof arrived in Zagreb on Christmas Day. For the last lap of the journey it had been snowing and raining alternately, the snowflakes were of uncertain consistency, half way to being slush before they touched the ground. The station platform was crowded with troops, they looked shabby and weary. From their shoulder flashes he saw they were of an Austrian battalion; their boots were muddy and crusts of dried mud had formed on their greatcoats and trousers, they wore képis and had their steel helmets slung on their backs on top of their rucksacks, gas mask canisters dangled from belt rings. Bulky men, loaded like packhorses, slung about with weapons and grenades and flasks. He saw them passing cigarette stubs amongst themselves, drawing on them inside the half-sphere of their hands.

There being no such thing as a porter, he had to carry his own baggage; pushing his way through these apathetically huddled men, he drew glances on account of the smartness of his uniform, the set of his peak cap, the glittering jackboots, which he seemed concerned about muddying, judging from the way he sought to avoid puddles. His skis and leather suitcases were cause for amusement; too tired to sneer, the men just stared incredulously at this cavalier, oval Turkish cigarette dangling from lips, black soft leather gloves tightening over knuckles, fur-lined greatcoat draped over shoulders and billowing. They looked him up and down from the rigid postures of men who have learned the trick of not wasting energy on unnecessary movements, and they followed him with their eyes without altering their hunched-up positions, He thought: what a miserable bunch! And they had not even been up against a proper army. Were these the conquistadors?

Going through the waiting room the smell – he was, it must be remembered, excessively sensitive to smell – caused a wave of nausea in him; a urinous smell; a smell of bad teeth; a smell of sleep-soiled bodies, a smell of vomit; he had never seen so many people packed into such a space. It was impossible to make his way through. The whole floor space was occupied by inert forms, these sleeping lumps, these amorphous mounds, these rag-covered bundles, their body heat rising in swampy fumes. The way they lay, packed together in the contortionate positions of sleep, men, women, babies, children, it was impossible to tell what was a head or an arm or a leg, what was flesh and what was cardboard or cloth.

A steel-helmeted guard, seeing an officer with skis and leather suitcases trying to find a way through this lumpy bog, came forward, unslung his rifle, and with his butt cleared a path, digging and jabbing indiscriminately, with anger, muttering abuse. Wirthof formulated a reproof to the guard, but said nothing. It was very difficult without a porter. Why didn't they get out of the way? Becoming aware of what was happening, those ahead rolled clear of the soldier's jabbing rifle butt, leaving a way open for Wirthof. The guard was being unnecessarily brutal. Some of these Germans, peasant types, were unquestionably swinish. He would certainly reprove him.

When he had got out into the street, which offered a prospect of dour grey buildings and murky wet streets, he said to the guard, 'It was not necessary to be so rough with these people. Have you no humanity, soldier? A soldier should be hard, but ...'

'They're Jews, sir,' the guard said.

Jews? These were Jews? The manipulators of international finance, the conspirators of Zion?

'What are they doing here?'

'They're being transported to Jasenovac.'

'How long have they been here?'

'Five days. The boxcars haven't arrived.'

The fact that they were Jews cut off the dressing-down that Wirthof had been preparing for this guard. That they were Jews obviously constituted a provocation: this German had probably suffered at their hands, been exploited and humiliated by them in the past. It did not justify his brutality, of course, but it made it more understandable. Wirthof took another look at the Jews: how they clung together; even in the filth of this waiting room, body to body, compost heaps. They have no honour, submitting to such treatment: if I were one of them. He smiled to himself. What conjecture!

'Remember that you are a German,' Wirthof told the guard. 'Act like one.' The guard saluted, stiff-armed, and Wirthof gave him a bent-arm salute in return, his skis resting against his shoulder.

Of course there were no taxis. Damnable. What a place this was. A dead grey morning. A line of heavy lorries, their tarpaulin covers a broken skin of hoar frost, stood in deep slush. The streets were full of hollows and pot-holes; patches of oil and petrol formed a composite mire with snow, rain, horse dung, horse piss, bits of steel rusting: Wirthof couldn't find a clean space on which to put down his fine leather luggage. The rise in temperature had surfaced the ground in a brown-grey ooze, it made a series of converging streams and rivulets flowing down the camber towards the gutters. There were cold currents in the air, Wirthof sniffed them like a deer scenting taint. When he saw a staff car drawing up and officers getting out, he asked if he could have a lift into the centre.

'You intend to do some skiing, Lieutenant?' the driver asked with a hint of impertinence.

'That's right,' Wirthof said.

'I wish you luck sir,' he said, laughing, shaking his head.

The drive to the centre confirmed Wirthof's dislike of this town; never had he seen such a forlorn grey place, desolate streets, houses the same colour as the morning fog into which they disappeared, bare shop windows, very few people about – and those he did see were scurrying into doorways at the approach of a German staff car. Almost more depressing than anything else were the occasional signs of Christmas decorations, a few paper lanterns, some bunting, one or two fir tree branches. He had always hated Christmas.

Entering the main square, he saw the bodies hanging from the lamp-posts, necks lolling sideways, mouths open, tongues thick, lips black. They swayed very slightly in the cold air currents.

'Saboteurs,' said the driver, grinning. He dropped him off at the big hotel on the side of the square opposite the dangling corpses.

'Is this the only hotel?' Wirthof asked.

'The only one that's safe,' said the driver. There were pillboxes at the corners of the square, and a machine-gun enclosure of sandbags by the main entrance of the hotel. A porter, thin and bent, came out to take Wirthof's bags and skis.

Wirthof felt dismayed at the prospect of spending any time in this place; he went immediately to look for the transport officer; the big gloomy dining-room smelled of boiled vegetables and synthetic cream, two officers, a major and a lieutenant-colonel, were having breakfast with a third man who was not in uniform; the colonel said where the transport officer could be found, and asked Wirthof where was he headed?

'Bojh,' said Wirthof.

The three men exchanged looks.

'And where are you from, Lieutenant?' the colonel asked.

'Vienna, sir.'

'Ah Vienna,' the colonel said, and smiled, and the two other men smiled.

The transportation office was full; two staff sergeants were checking through the orders presented by waiting officers, and in a room beyond, its door open, a captain, with a reedy agitated voice, was yelling into a telephone that kept going dead, and he kept throwing up his hands and saying something about sabotage. When Wirthof managed to get near enough one of the staff sergeants to show his orders and ask if there was a chance of transport to Bojh that afternoon, since he preferred not to spend the night in Zagreb, he evoked generalized laughter; the staff sergeant told him politely that he'd do his best, but it seemed unlikely anything could be found for the lieutenant before tomorrow or the day after. There was a great shortage of transport, and Wirthof's orders did not have a top priority embossment, or even a special priority designation, only an ordinary priority stamp, which meant nothing, since all orders had one of those. 'I've been in Zagreb a week already,' a captain told Wirthof.

'Sheer incompetence,' said Wirthof loudly, hoping to register his displeasure with the harassed captain who was again holding a dead telephone. To the captain who'd been in Zagreb a week, he said, 'What does one do here?'

'Ping pong,' said the captain. 'It is the only form of recreation available. It is not advisable to go out in the streets alone. A few days ago a lance corporal was found round the back here, minus his private parts and with his head under his arm. The local partisans have picked up these habits from Pavelic's Ustasi. You know them, the Ustasi, from their charming practice of putting their hands in their pockets and showing you a selection of eyeballs and testicles. One is supposed to not be offended by this somewhat crude way of displaying their friendliness, indeed one is expected to respond favourably, since the eyeballs and testicles are those of our mutual enemy. But if you have no taste for such souvenirs, it's best to avoid the cafés. And if you don't like to see corpses dangling from lamp-posts first thing in the morning you'd best try and get one of the back rooms. Do you play chess?'

'Yes, I'm quite good.'

'Excellent. Excellent. We must have a game Where are you from, Lieutenant?'

'Vienna.'

'Ah – Vienna, yes, yes.'

It proved impossible to get a back room. For the first two days that Wirthof was in Zagreb he kept the curtains of his room drawn all the time, and played chess with the captain. He did not go out. On the third day, unthinkingly, he drew open the curtains. The temperature had dropped and the square was white. The bodies had frozen hard. They were quite rigid when they swayed. He studied these former receptacles of life: bodies; cold; indifferent to cold; still it was difficult – impossible – to put oneself in the position of being entirely indifferent to what was done to, or with, one's body, even after one had relinquished jurisdiction over it. After death one's remains did not belong to oneself; no longer *my* body, therefore why should I care? Difficult to think of it like that. The humiliation – the dishonour – of being hung like meat. Swinish. But it is not *me* any longer. But if such a thing as a soul exists. Great kings built mausoleums for themselves: even now it was done by some men: and of course one could make provisions in one's will, in that way one could continue to exercise an element of control. Reassuring thought that even after death one need not be entirely powerless. He who weeps most profusely for me shall have my fortune. But how to be sure one was not tricked? A bad arrangement. I don't mind dying, he reminded himself; but I shall resent it if it happens badly, really it should be possible to arrange such an important event so as to ensure one died appropriately, in accordance with one's own wishes and stipulations: I would also like to be able to choose my own mourners, and be able to correct any false impressions that might gain currency. People were so stupid: it was so easy to be misunderstood. Who knew what slanders one might be subjected to, after one's death? It was infuriating to think one would be in no position to rebut them, that one would have to rely on others for that. I have no sons. Oh what does it matter? The saboteurs hanging in the square, do they care? They will have monuments built to them. Yes. They will be remembered. Collectively, not individually. I wouldn't care for that. But who will remember *me*? Leonie? How can I be sure? How do I know she is not already unfaithful to me? Kazakh? Why should I care for the good opinion of a Jew? Insurance. Supposing his is the true God. One must entertain all hypotheses. Kazakh knows me, even if he doesn't like me. He will have to concede that I always acted out of honour. I have impressed that on him often enough. He scoffs at me secretly, perhaps he even despises me – no, no, that is not possible. Why should he despise me? Because I despisc him – ah, but he doesn't know that. Perhaps he does though. Do I despise him? What thoughts, what thoughts. I am indifferent to the good opinions of all men, as those frozen partisans are indifferent to the cold. Humiliating to be dependent on the good opinion of others. I can do without them. Yes. Wirthof felt considerably cheered by this thought, and he decided that what he did with his life was nobody's business but his, and therefore he need not concern himself with whether Stefan Kazakh, or anyone else, thought well or ill of him.

While Wirthof thought these thoughts – narcissistic even in his contemplation of death: how will I look? can I still love myself dangling frozen? – Stefan Kazakh (who attributes these thoughts to Wirthof, and therefore must take some responsibility for them) was concocting a plot to kill Lüdenscheid. He had become convinced of the necessity for this as the only means of terminating their deal. No other way offered itself to him. Of the usefulness of such an act he was not sure: one Lüdenscheid could be replaced by another. But this consideration notwithstanding, it was clear to him that it had to be done. Although he had regular access to Lüdenscheid, to kill him presented seemingly insuperable difficulties. During the treatments, the aide-de-camp was present with pistol drawn; at other times a bodyguard was always within call. An even greater deterrent was the knowledge of the retribution that would follow such an assassination.

But, somehow, it would have to be done.

At the same time, for one plan of action does not necessarily cancel out another, even if the other is its converse, Stefan Kazakh also had in mind to make a great demand of Lüdenscheid, one that he would not be able to refuse.

A deeply religious man was Dr Pavelic, head of the puppet state of Croatia. He lived in Zagreb, and heard Mass every day in his private chapel. It was said of him that he was an exemplary father and husband, and a devout Christian. The Pope received him. As, for that matter, did Hitler. His troops, the Ustasi, were armed with an extraordinary assortment of weapons: bludgeons, chains, knives, cleavers, axes, and also machine guns and mortars. The

Orthodox Bishop of Plaski was offered conversion to Catholicism as an alternative to garrotting, and chose the latter. The Ustasi did not confine themselves to the more conventional forms of slaughter, by means of guns and knives. Bishop Platon was prodded to death in a pond. Other schismatics were thrown alive over precipices, of which there were many in the area.

A man is never helpless. Stefan Kazakh's father said, situations of human making are capable of human solution.

In the hills of Elysium the belladonna children played, rolling over and over, leaping, vaulting, leap-frogging, copulating; they sang ring-a-ring-a-roses, dancing barefoot in the fluorescent snow.
   Let each man pretend; let each man pretend to be pretending; let each man pretend that the pretence that he is pretending is a pretence; let each man pretend that the pretence that he is pretending is a pretence, is a pretence; let each man pretend that the pretence that he is pretending is a pretence, is a pretence, is a pretence; in my dream I had a dream that I was dreaming, and in that dream I had a dream in which I dreamt that I was dreaming, and in that dream I dreamt that I was pretending to dream, and that this pretence was a pretence, and the pretence that it was a pretence was a pretence –
   How to determine the volume of the leg of a chair? How?

It is noticeable, Kazakh, even to me (and who am I to notice such things?) that your thoughts are becoming less orderly; moreover, your system of keeping the different areas of your life separated in accordance with some common-sensical arrangement (for after all, if everything floods together there can be no order) is not working. It is noticeable to me (and who, as I have said, am I to notice such things?) that you are becoming exceedingly disorganized in your thinking, no longer thinking purposefully but drifting hither and thither: hither and thither: is this businesslike? what profit is there in it? is it constructive, is it productive, is it remunerative, is it getting you anywhere? The rule is (how often you have propounded it): stick to the point, and do not allow yourself to be sidetracked, digressions are the very devil, nothing gets done, the mind flounders like chalk suspended in water.
   Whatever else might be said about me, nobody could say that I was not generous. True. True. You have contributed lavishly

to the coffers of the Society of Sceptics. You are leaving your eyes to the eye bank, your internal organs for research and/or spare parts' surgery. There's no waste in you. There's almost less waste in you than in a whale, whose eardrums are blown up and used as footballs and whose foreskin is used for golf ball bags. Your generosity, Kazakh, is phenomenal: whatever you slough off and have no further use for, you give away.

Lüdenscheid in the winter of '43–4 was an extremely sick man. He was truly mad, not mad in the way that I am mad in parts, my madness is a modest madness, it is nothing much really, it comes and goes – hither and thither – it is affected by damp and draught and by the closing prices (and is capable of being alleviated by self-slapping and other household remedies), it is a mouse of a madness, whereas Lüdenscheid's – Lüdenscheid's madness was the proselytizing sort that would seek to bring the entire world under its sway. Sometimes he called me his magician, or – with a collusive grin – his 'good Jew'. (A dangerous and daring allusion this, as he had had me declared a non-Jew.)

– I will kill you, Lüdenscheid/
– I will outwit you/
– I will rid myself of you/
– I will break our deal/
– I will make a great demand of you. (Strike out whichever is inapplicable.)

Leonie's flat was always full of refugees, who had nowhere else to go. It was actually more overcrowded than many apartments of comparable size that were let off as separate rooms. For Leonie could refuse no one. There were people sleeping in the kitchen, in the bathroom (a nice young couple, they conceived a child in the bath on a mattress of tiny ornamental cushions and under a covering of moth-eaten velour curtains), in the corridor, and in all the three principal rooms. There was much coming and going.

Leonie's guests were all told that they could be put up only on a temporary basis, and some had the good grace to seek alternative accommodation in due course; others, however, remained on a temporary basis for the duration of the war. It was not only accommodation that Leonie provided, but also consolation for those who had lost husbands, brothers, sons, wives, mothers (either by death or by Night and Fog). The Gestapo took no action against Leonie because they knew that she sometimes met General von Blitt, who would protect her if he was in the clear, and if he was not in the clear it was just as well to let him continue to see Leonie and perhaps incriminate himself.

Leonie was marvellous. She was always marvellous, in Stefan Kazakh's opinion, when Wirthof was not with her. She was cheerful and energetic, and busily organizing the Austrian Resistance – a wretched *nebish* of a Resistance, but Leonie gave little soirées on the floor of her bedroom at which she inquired of her guests if they would work for the overthrow of the Nazi regime, and most of them, out of politeness, said that they would, given the right circumstances and, of course, weapons. (Neither very likely to materialize.)

The Gestapo who kept a watch on the flat did not tremble at the sight of the conspirators coming and going, and did not bother to arrest any of them, hoping that one day Leonie might land a bigger fish, worth arresting. It is my opinion that Leonie was having an affair with General von Blitt, and that she considered it a cover for her conspiratorial dealings with him – for she maintained that she loved Wirthof; but I may be wrong about this, and perhaps she did not sleep with General von Blitt when she met him to discuss the assassination of Nazi leaders. It is also conceivable that General von Blitt pretended to be conspiring with Leonie in order to have a cover (for his wife, who was also an anti-Nazi) for his affair with Leonie, that is if he was having an affair with Leonie. In any case, it would seem that he told Leonie little or nothing about the actual conspiracy in which he *was* involved, for which he was later hanged by Hitler, on piano wires, from meat hooks, together with the other generals. Alternatively, Leonie was better at keeping secrets (from me) than I supposed.

Kazakh, Stefan: Austrian-born dealer; b. 1915; when he was four years old his mother, Jadwiga, ran off with a costume jewellery salesman and K. was brought up by his father, Staszek Kazakh, a construction engineer; K. entered medical faculty of University of Vienna where he came under influence of the psychiatrist and hypnotist Blumenfeld; in 1934 his father took part in the unsuccessful Socialist attempt to overthrow the Dollfuss government, and was killed during the shelling of the Floridsdorf settlement by government troops; K. abandoned his medical studies and went into business. He was associated with the late Baron Koeppler, and when the Baron was imprisoned by the Nazis, after the Anschluss, K. played a leading part in the negotiations for the banker's release. Before terms could be agreed, the Baron died. During the war a strange and equivocal relationship developed between K. and SS Gruppenführer Ernst Lüdenscheid, whom he treated by means of hypnotherapy for various ailments in exchange for the release of Jewish victims of Nazi oppression. It has been said that K. was involved in the plot to assassinate Lüdenscheid, but his exact role in this affair has never been established. After the war, he emigrated to England, where he became prominent in financial circles, specializing, initially, in the take-over of inefficiently run companies and re-establishing them on a sound financial basis. He was married three times, once to the actress Y., but all his marriages ended in divorce. In 1967, on a visit to Vienna, he suffered a mental breakdown and shortly afterwards experienced a religious revelation/took to drink/discovered the universal equation/ froze to death in an unheated hotel room/set up an institute of graphology to deduce the secrets of the soul from handwriting/became converted/died/died, having first published his life story, *My Story*, by Stefan Kazakh (as told to Stefan Kazakh)/ and thereafter, and thereafter – Though he did not achieve anything of importance in his lifetime, and all his endeavours were to prove futile, K. led a full and diverse life, and will be remembered for his quicksilver quickness, which stood him in good stead on many occasions and enabled him to survive the Holocaust, not to mention his three marriages, which, as a matter of fact, he didn't like to mention. Though he achieved nothing of importance, K. will be remembered for his death-bed utterance (held to be apocryphal by some authorities): 'The winners are the losers.' Alternatively, it is thought that he said – this is also considered apocryphal – 'The losers are the winners.' See Professor J. G. Bernard's 'Kazakhian Concept of Winners and Losers'. Another theory is that what he actually said was, 'The whiners are the losers', or possibly even 'the winers' (meaning wine-drinkers); not much credence has been given to the latter explanation as he was himself a gin drinker, though this has been held (by R. R. Fogelhoff among others) to indicate that he did at the end consider himself a winner, or winer, or even, possibly, whiner. It should be added that he died intestate, i.e. without his testicles, which he had previously had removed and vouchsafed to the Kazakh Institute of Artificial Insemination, another of his pet projects that unfortunately did not bear fruit. However, in other respects his influence was seminal, and those of us who had the privilege of knowing him will always remember his gay and cheerful bearing, notwithstanding his intestate condition, during those final days/months/years of black and total despair/hope. What kept him going during those last terrible/wonderful days/months/years was the thought that nobody, not even his closest friends, could accuse him of being stingy. Of this his intestate condition was ample evidence.

Why do you mock me, Kazakh?

Why do you shiver, Kazakh?

Why will you not let me have my story?

The castle stood on a vitreous cliff above a cold lake, and when the mist rose it rose with such rapidity that in a matter of moments there was no sign of a castle; this could have a disorientating effect on anyone unfamiliar with the area; but Wirthof attributed the tendency of the castle to be here one minute and gone the next not so much to any natural phenomenon as to the indubitable fact that Yugoslav plum brandy, of which he had drunk three-quarters of a bottle on the drive from Zagreb, was not Courvoisier, and consequently allowances had to be made, and this meant taking a fairly suave attitude to the sudden disappearance of castles, and to their equally abrupt reappearance. This sleepy suavity of his was actually the cumulative effect of five days of drinking between one and half and two bottles of Yugoslav plum brandy a day; in these five days he was at no stage actually drunk, only indifferent, and once he had attained this indifference its maintenance became his primary concern. He was careful not to drink so much in one go as to risk vomiting up the hard-to-come-by Yugoslav plum brandy, on the other hand he must not allow his blood alcohol level to fall below the level of indifference.

He spent most of those five days in Zagreb playing chess with the captain he had met in the transportation office. He was quite clear about everything that happened, but indifferent and even bored; he had a tendency to giggle when he thought of the lance corporal found with his head under his arm, and as for the Ustasi with their grisly pockets he was unable to suppress the bout of laughter that overtook him when he thought of the various possibilities suggested by their trophies: conkers, marbles, swapping: give you two schismatic priest's balls for a couple of Jew's eyes.

On New Year's Eve the square was suddenly full of balloons, red, pink, blue, green, yellow, orange, densely clustered, or drifting in pairs, or solitarily hugging the façades of buildings, an inundation of balloons, an avalanche of balloons – where had they all come from? People gathered at windows to watch them jostling down, forming a high multi-coloured dome over the square, each balloon bearing the slogan: *Smrt Fasismu – Sloboda Narodu*. When the Germans discovered that this was not a conventional New Year's message but meant Death to Fascism – Liberty to the People (by now the balloons were spreading through the city from rooftop to rooftop), half a dozen soldiers were ordered into the square to shoot down the subversive balloons; as they fired volley after volley into the thickly coloured air, the popping and squelching of burst rubber, and also the clinking of shattered glass (because their aim was not invariably exact), was supplemented by the peal of church bells, which took up this bang-pop-clang, bang-pop-clatter refrain and made of it a celebratory ding-dong-bang-pop-clatter anthem.

At the hotel, Wirthof threw open his window, drew his pistol and began firing into the dense spectrum – pierced, the shrunken balloons fell like dead birds of paradise, and soon at every window of the hotel German officers were joining in the sport, and the sky fluttered with ragged many-coloured skins, and the three-storey-long swastika pennons were riddled with bullet holes, and on a rooftop behind an unilluminated propelling pencil sky sign, twin church spires behind him, a Croatian partisan who had been blowing up balloons with a cycle pump put down his pump, picked up his rifle, drew a bead on the forehead of a German colonel, who was sitting on the window-sill of his room, one leg inside, one out, pistol in each hand, popping balloons with exclamations of delight, and the partisan fired and got the colonel in the left temple, making him perform a double somersault into the square. Whereupon, Wirthof, in an advanced state of indifference, drew the curtains again and resumed his game of chess with the captain he had met in the transportation office.

During the night tanks and armoured vehicles and lorries with field-gun trailers rumbled through the city, snow chains clanking, churning the snow into a chain-patterned dark-brown putty, and Wirthof watched the fragmented silhouettes of long, mounted guns on wall and ceiling and was plum brandy indifferent. A condition that he succeeded in maintaining all next day on the journey to Jesenice.

He had put on dark glasses to protect his eyes against the snow dazzle. For a while the road ran parallel with a shallow fast-flowing river; on the other side of it, hay was drying under the roofs of drying racks and women were working in the fields. Little orange houses squatted in the cold morning shadow of the mountain; the staff car passed through villages where the trunks of trees bore proclamations, and soggy notices of executions, drawing pins rusting; at one p.m. they saw groups of children in knitted caps and mufflers noisily leaving school, some of them jeered and threw stones or made sword lunges with their umbrellas at the fast-moving German staff car and then bolted for their lives.

The valley widened, it sparkled in many places, and Wirthof lolled drowsy and indifferent in the heated air which smelled faintly of petrol, leather, and gun-metal oil. At Jesenice the valley was narrow again and the road ran close to the side of the mountain, and they passed the iron foundry with its high black slag-heaps steaming, its dark belching chimneys. He placed the bottle of plum brandy to his mouth to reinforce the agreeable indifference: if we are ambushed, he thought, would I care? And he giggled to himself, and began to sing snatches of the *Konradlied*, adding words: 'and they found him, and they found him, headless in the snow, silly old so and so, in the snows of Jesenice, up to his ears, Professor Nietzsche, with his head under his arm, Konrad Wirthof, who didn't ought to have, come to Jesenice, Professor Nietzsche.'

First the castle was ahead of him, only turrets, flagpole and crenellations showing above the mist, and then after a couple of turns in the road, there was just blank grey sky. Their car took the road around the lake, it had not frozen over, and the houses along its shore were perfectly reflected in the water; the mist was fast rising; already it had cleared the tree tops, and presently, as the road began to climb steeply, Wirthof saw the castle reforming below him, piece by piece, and for some reason this also made him giggle.

On the cliff side the castle presented an aspect of red-roofed towers and turrets with narrow slit windows and loopholes, the towers were not all the same height, and were asymmetrically grouped; the approach road took a lateral loop, the gradient steepened, and the perspective changed as the car climbed at a divergent angle to the east wing, a sombre windowless façade of grey stone. Winding up and round, the road passed through a small wood, emerged in a village of lime-washed houses, and then continued for a couple of hundred yards as far as the eastern gate-house. Before opening the gates, the sentries examined Wirthof's papers with a degree of officiousness that annoyed him: Psychiat-rica something or other, the sign said by the side of the entrance. The car passed through, accelerating and then braking immedi-ately: the outer bailey was almost as crowded as the waiting-room in the railway station at Zagreb, only these people, two or three hundred of them, were in the open and did not lie still. They had woollen socks around their necks and over their fingers, some of them, and some of them were wrapped up in dark-brown blan-kets, or in crimson velour curtains, or in goatskins, or in heavy tablecloths, or in quilted bedspreads, or in sacking, or in Jewish prayer shawls, or in tarpaulin, or in greatcoats of the Royal Yugoslav Army, and strips of sheeting and old rags were bound around their shoes so that they all seemed to have bandaged feet. They were walking about, stamping their clumsily bound feet in the snow, massaging their arms, blowing on their hands. Some, too ill to walk, lay on the ground, in a huddle of feet-stamping relatives. A small boy of about eight was crouched by his mother, holding her up in a seated position, blowing on her body, panting and blowing, panting and blowing, with fearful rapidity.

Those who were not too ill to do so looked up as the car came through the gates and into their midst, making its slow progress towards the low arch, guarded by two sentries, beyond which, in the extensive stables, the armoured cars, the motor-cycles with side-cars, and the transport lorries, as well as the horses, were kept. A man in the greatcoat of the Royal Yugoslav Army carried over his shoulder a massive brass instrument, circular in design and convoluted, a bass tuba perhaps, a weighty instrument, which he did not put down in the snow.

Opposite where the vehicles were parked, a double flight of stairs led up to carved wooden doors: Wirthof went into the hall which had a vaulted ceiling with faded murals of trumpet-blowing angels.

'Lieutenant Wirthof,' he said.

The major in command of Castle Bojh, Ritzau, was a large man with large hands and a slab face, he had become fat above the waist and he wore a gun belt low on his belly, tight and snug under the bulge of belly flesh: he wore breeches and riding boots with spurs. He was playing cards with a captain and a lieutenant when Wirthof reported.

'I have a report on you, Lieutenant,' he said. 'You'll have to keep your nose clean while you're here.' He added, 'You've taken your time getting here.'

'There was no transportation.'

'Well, it doesn't say much for your initiative or keenness.'

'Is the major suggesting I should have walked?'

The slab face split and splintered into a laugh. He took in Wirthof's impeccable appearance, polished belt, glittering boots, violet eyes, his stance, at once insolent and effete, the aura of indifference, the smell of plum brandy about him. 'I am aware, Lieutenant, that until recently you held a higher rank. You will remember that this is not a rank you hold any more. Understood? Anything you want to know?'

'Yes, sir. What is the arrangement for officers, in the way of orderlies?'

'We are short of men, Lieutenant. You clean your own boots. There are two orderlies and they are amply occupied.'

'Perhaps I might have the loan of one of them, sir. My uniforms are all in need of pressing.'

'I suppose that's not something you could do yourself.'

'I have no experience of it.'

'You have any experience of fighting?'

'The major is well aware of my experience of fighting.'

'Oh yes – yes. You'll find it different fighting partisans. What is your opinion of partisan bullets, Lieutenant?'

'Like the local brandy, no doubt they do what they are meant to do, while perhaps lacking the bouquet one associates with the French brand. What, incidentally, is the situation there?'

'Yugoslav plum brandy,' said the major.

'I feared as much. What exactly am I expected to do here? My exact duties . . .'

'Kill partisans, those are your duties, Lieutenant.'

It got colder. In the morning the snow and slush and mud and horse dung and oil had frozen hard into a dirty-coloured rock-like substance in which chain marks and track marks and hoof marks and footmarks had become deeply engraved. Some of the Jews had died in the night. They were buried in a copse at the end of a long avenue of elm trees and their over-clothing was shared out among the diggers. The man in the greatcoat of the Royal Yugoslav Army played a brief requiem on the bass tuba. A man in a wide brimmed hat said *Kaddish* for the dead.

Wirthof had breakfast first, and then made his way down to the cells. He examined the heavy accounts ledger in which the prisoners' details were entered across five columns marked name, age, address, grounds, sentence. Under 'grounds' all the way down the page appeared the words 'espionage' or 'sabotage' in red ink, and under 'sentence' the word 'execution'. There were little ticks, with a date at their side, against the names of those on whom sentence had already been carried out.

There were ten cells off a corridor with small windows high up. The cell doors were of wood; each had a spy-hole at eye level and was secured by a simple hasp. Each cell also had a small door about one foot high through which food could be pushed in to the prisoners.

The first cell door was opened, by the removal of the iron toggle from the staple and the folding back of the hasp on its hinges. There were fifteen men in this cell. Each man was attached by chains to one of two rings in the walls. The sergeant accompanying Wirthof read out three names from his list, and those named got slowly to their feet and with a noise of chains embraced their comrades in turn. When they had concluded their leave-taking, they shuffled towards the door until their chains were taut; first their ankle clamps and then their wrist clamps were unlocked by the sergeant with a hollow key of the type used for winding clocks. Using a sharp stone one of the men scratched a few words on the cell wall, which was covered with many such scribbles. Much the same thing happened at the other cells. The twelve men due to be executed that morning were led into the yard. Where the lunatics were housed, faces had appeared at every window, and as the prisoners were placed against wooden stakes and their hands tied a great babble went up from the lunatics, screeching sounds, panting, crying, screaming, choking, blubbering sounds, dog sounds and reptilian sounds, the ululation of insects, a din of marrow bones and cleavers, a wail of Greeks.

The partisans were silent; each man gave the clenched fist salute before his hands were tied to the stake; as the members of the firing squad took their places and unslung their rifles one or two of the prisoners called out, '*Smrt Fasismu – Sloboda Narodu*', and began to sing the Red Flag; the prisoners in the cells joined in the song, their voices were heard contending with the screechings of the lunatics. Wirthof gave the commands, and the volley of shots abruptly ended all sound.

When it was all done, he stood for a while looking up at the silent faces of the lunatics, his nostrils twitching at the cold air currents coming down from the Karavanke and from the Julijske Alps and from pristine Triglav, highest of the peaks, and in the awesome pale morning light the Prehodavci Saddle resembled the back of a stricken white whale, and when he turned he saw blood running along the hard furrows in the ground, past him and around him, and he stepped carefully so as not to bloody his boots.

He went back into the castle, through the main hall, and up the broad stone steps without balusters, and then along the landing to the east wing where the lunatics were. They were standing about in oddly formalized attitudes, a chorus of the misbegotten, silent for the moment, all their vocal energies expended, sunk in their perpetual contrariety. They were all filthy, and stinking. There was excrement over the lower parts of the walls and on the floor, and the remains of food formed putrid piles. Wirthof walked through all this in his glittering boots and black soft leather gloves and the lunatics stared at him in astonishment, for no German soldier, let alone an officer, had ever come like this into their midst. And when he started to talk to them, not in the rasping sounds of command, but in a low, gentle, inquiring voice, like someone come humbly to the oracle, they cackled and farted with scorn and began to jabber their repetitious themes, and to make menacing gestures, their minds caught in a vortex, and he listened intently to their language, for Wirthof believed that the mad are travellers in the unknown and know secrets.

Every day he visited them. He arranged for workers to clean out their rooms and to empty their pails and to wash their clothing. He saw that they had sufficient food, even if it meant that the Jews out in the open had their meagre rations reduced. And he listened to their mysterious talk and began to detect patterns in it, to discover recurring themes, and with one lunatic, the one who sometimes thought he was Goering, he struck up a kind of conversation. Each day he greeted him, serious-faced, with the words, 'And how is the Field Marshal today?' And Goering replied with some such phrase as, 'The rest of time is rich on rooftops and in sparrows.' And Goering said he had been piloting his eyelids, he was happiest of all flying, and he had dropped many crunchers, and he screwed up his eyes tight, which Wirthof understood to denote bomb dropping – and said suddenly, with sly glee, 'The houses are all collapsed. I have pulled out their seacocks.' And he laughed maliciously. 'Blink, blink, blink,' he said.

'What is it like there?' Wirthof asked him.

He seemed almost to understand. 'Pieces,' he said. 'Pieces, geeses, gases, nieces, species, leases,' he said. 'White blubber. Sharp roses. Plop plop drowned, plop plop drowned –'

He puzzled over the meaning of their unintelligible actions and utterances, and made long lists of words and phrases that they used. The way they sat or stood, scratched themselves, picked their noses, sucked at a thumb or bit on a wrist, the way they picked at their scabs or pulled the thread out of clothing, wound string around objects, tore at the walls, ripped paper, sprinkled water, formed patterns and shapes out of garbage – all this was unintelligible but not meaningless. What were they telling him? They had secrets to tell, he was sure; had they not travelled farther than most and seen the pterodactyl? Flapping their arms and crawling on their bellies, what were they seeking to describe? Tell me, he demanded of the lunatics, tell me. And they gave him his answer, grinning, slobbering, farting – but you know; I don't know, what is it I am supposed to know? I do not know what it is you say I know; and they slobbered with laughter and farted with disbelief, and he thought damn them, damn them to hell and indifference, but again and again he returned to them, feeling sure there was something they knew.

He carried out his duties methodically, and always was very well turned out, spick and span, boots glittering, belt polished, uniforms pressed, unlike some of the other officers who sometimes did not shave for several days and replaced lost buttons with safety pins and made no effort to clean food stains and oil marks from their uniforms. Slothful, they were. The major in particular; the way he ate, dribbling from the mouth, wiping his greasy hands on the seat of his pants, and his mouth with his sleeve. Signing the execution orders, a kitchen smell of boiled turnips and ersatz lard came off him, and when he opened his mouth the faint peppermint smell of army-issue toothpaste was added. Some of the officers did not bother to clean up even for the executions and took them sloppily, without proper regard for the exact observance of ceremony, dispensed with drumrolls, and were angry with the prisoners, treated them roughly, denied them those extra final moments in which to compose themselves; in fact, just had them dragged out of their cells, stood up against the posts and shot.

Wirthof always observed the form for such occasions. He was meticulously turned out, accorded each man due to be executed a military salute, granted last requests such as the sending of letters or personal belonging to relatives, never dispensed with the drumroll, offered the blindfold, and made sure that all the men executed were in fact dead before they were buried, log-wise, in a pit. He considered any other way of carrying out an execution unworthy of an officer.

Morale was not good at Bojh. Except on the daily patrols, nobody ventured outside the castle confines. You never knew which village had fallen into partisan hands. The enemy was constantly on the move. It could choose where and when to strike, and then disappear back into the hills.

On patrols the men were nervy and on edge; a rifle shot could mean a solitary sniper somewhere up in the wooded slopes, impossible to pinpoint, impossible to flush out without risking the company in what might be a trap, or else it could mean the start of an attack, and if this was the case you never knew in what force the enemy was going to descend upon you. This type of warfare called for great coolness of judgment on the part of officers; few of them possessed it any longer, if they had ever had it, and their only answer to the guerrillas was the taking of hostages.

When he had been at Bojh two weeks Wirthof prepared a situation report for the major in which he recommended the cessation of patrols – their achievements were minimal – and the limitation of action to strikes against known enemy concentrations. But the major scarcely glanced at the report, and the patrols and reprisal actions and executions continued. If the partisans struck against German forces, the response was to strike against the villages. Every partisan was to be shot, that was the major's order: who was or who wasn't a partisan? In practice, it was up to the individual officer to decide, and his decision was liable to be arbitrary.

Wirthof hated this kind of warfare; he disliked the untidiness of it, it was messy, bitty, indecisive; he hated the fact that there was no definite line to hold, that you were all the time striking at a disappearing enemy, and he hated the country, the cold, the concealing whiteness, the very names of places: Črna; Vršič; Ojstrica; Vrba; Straža; Begúnjăčica; Mrzli; Zatrník – a wilderness of unpronounceable places. He had no sense of orientation in this country of labyrinthine valleys, now broad and sprawling, now narrow gorges; wide roads petered out at the edge of ravines; or took you in circles; villages of lime-washed houses all looked alike; a reasonable gradient for armoured cars suddenly became a precipice; a favourite tactic of the partisans was to lure a German patrol deep into these hostile regions of tangled forests and limestone rock walls and rotting tree trunks, where there was nothing to drink except melted snow, and every new vista was a duplication of the one before. In the previous winter several such patrols had just disappeared and their bodies were not found until the spring thaw. Worst of all, he hated and dreaded the cold – twenty below zero: it froze up rifle breeches, and what with the over-waxed Czech ammunition you could never be sure that your weapons would work.

Not surprising that the men were apathetic and sullen, fearful of expressing their dissatisfactions, distrustful of each other and of their officers – the planted Gestapo man was an expedient of which they all knew: so there wasn't even the relief of grumbling, or the sustenance of comradeship. Wirthof tried to establish some kind of contact with his men, but as a former SS officer he was treated warily.

In late February Lüdenscheid arrived on a tour of inspection of the occupied territories. Stefan Kazakh was with him. They travelled from Vienna in an armoured train, every second carriage of which contained troops of the Waffen SS; howitzers and anti-aircraft guns were mounted on open freight cars. From Zagreb to Bojh they travelled in an armoured vehicle, with an escort of tanks and motor-cycle outriders. Everyone at Castle Bojh had to smarten up for the occasion. The garrison, down to ninety-two men and seven officers, was lined up for inspection in the court-yard where the executions were normally held. Lüdenscheid did not show any reaction as he inspected these sullen men whose lacklustre eyes he sought to look into in the inspirational Führer manner – a look for each man – a technique frustrated somewhat by the fact that their eyes were lowered against the icy wind.

He kept them standing at attention for half an hour while he gave them the inspirational talk he had prepared and which no-thing could stop him giving, in the course of which it began to snow heavily. He told them they were fighting for the glory of Germany, that in their stoic acceptance of hardship and privation they were setting an example to history; in thousands of years to come men would marvel, etcetera. The men were occupied with the more immediate problem of keeping their feet from freezing. 'A German soldier who falls in the snowy wastes of Slovenia does not die,' he told them, 'he lives for ever in the hearts of his countrymen, he is an inspiration to the future . . .' The men stamped their feet as inconspicuously as possible, and though long before the end of the talk they were all stamping and shuffling, and one man had collapsed, Lüdenscheid carried on just the same, many of his words lost to the wind.

Lüdenscheid was not pleased with what he saw on his inspec-tion of Castle Bojh; he considered the officers and men slovenly and apathetic, which they were, and the place itself a pigsty, which it was. It offended his sense of tidyness to see the Jews dy-ing in the outer bailey, it was not orderly; and the presence of the lunatics in the east wing appalled him. The major with his food-stained tunic clearly disgusted him. The filth of this place made him blink even faster, as if the rapidity of his eyelids could anni-hilate the objectionable sights. He insisted on seeing everything. Every room had to be opened for him. His gloved hand ran along surfaces, disturbing the encrusted dirt of years. He looked up at the vaulted stone ceilings, tracing with his eyes the intricate con-fluence of trickles, and went stamping from room to room glaring around him, as if the next room, or the next, would reveal the source of these watery insinuations. He prodded at rotting purlins, and withdrew his hand with revulsion. In the kitchens he saw the rats rummaging in the potato peels and around the over-flowing refuse bins. He commanded, with a fierce head movement, the opening of lavatory doors, and stood, nostrils quivering, regarding the befouled pans, the piss-wet floors. His entourage moved with him, abashed and silent. He said nothing. At the end of his tour of inspection, he returned to the least objectionable room in the castle, the major's office and sleeping quarters, and ordered the removal of the major's bedding and other personal possessions.

'Major, you will find yourself other accommodation.'

'The Gruppenführer intends to stay here?'

'I intend to see this place restored to some semblance of military order.'

'Sir, there are ninety-two men, seven officers, an average of seventy prisoners, not to mention the four hundred Jews and the lunatics . . .'

'I have not asked for your observations, Major. This place is disgusting. It is dirty, Major. *Dirty*.'

'I have done my best, with the limited facilities . . .'

'Your best, Major, is a poor thing.'

He remained standing by the central iron stove, with its flue going up to the ceiling, hands extended over the rising heat, looking at the assembled officers of Castle Bojh through the quivering air; he remained in this position, silent, his eyes discouraging any flicker of movement or sound from the officers, until all the major's personal possessions had been removed from the room. Then with a single sweep of his arm he sent papers, files, ashtrays, ink bottles, pencils, corks, razor blades, rubber stamps, boot grips, riding crop, blotting paper, medicine bottles, dyspepsia tablets, boiled sweets and browning apple cores tumbling to the floor; and having cleared the desk in this way, he seated himself on its edge, and addressed the officers.

'I will say no more about the deplorable conditions in which I find this garrison. A number of steps will be immediately instituted to rectify this disgusting state of affairs. The lunatics and the Jews must be removed. Immediately. They have an unsavoury effect on the men's morale. The Jews and the lunatics will be taken to Jesenice. There they can wait until the boxcars arrive.'

'We do not have sufficient transport vehicles,' the major said.

'They can march,' Lüdenscheid said. 'Lieutenant Wirthof, you will take charge of the transport. You will need only three men on horseback with sub-machine guns to act as guards. The removal will commence at first light tomorrow. But first you will pick out a detail of the fifty fittest Jews, and having satisfied yourself that they are not suffering from any contagious diseases you will have them present themselves immediately to the quartermaster for cleaning duties. The remainder you will march to Jesenice. You will leave two men there to guard them, and return immediately.'

'How are they to be fed at Jesenice? There are two hundred lunatics and over four hundred Jews.'

'There will be less by the time you get to Jesenice. I will not have this garbage in a German garrison. They will have to make out as best they can until the boxcars, which, I may say, are disgracefully overdue – and I shall be looking into that too – arrive. You may leave now, Lieutenant Wirthof, and start making your arrangements.'

For the remainder of the day, SS Gruppenführer Lüdenscheid devoted himself to setting in motion a massive cleaning operation; he worked out, approximately, the total wall and floor area, and then he divided it into stone surfaces, wood surfaces, brick surfaces, and he calculated the rate at which one man could scrub wood, brick, stone, multiplied by fifty, and came to the conclusion that it would take fifty men thirteen and three-eighths hours to scrub the entire castle to his satisfaction. Gallons of disinfectant were sent for. A fire engine was commandeered so that its hoses could be used for hosing down the long corridors and winding steps after the scrubbing. A fumigation unit was sent for to treat the east wing when it had been vacated. Officers were sent chasing about the countryside to find an expert rodent exterminator.

As the work got under way, Lüdenscheid stalked around the castle, plum-brandy-soaked linen mask tied around his face, followed by his aides similarly masked and redolent, supervising every aspect of the cleaning. The troops were set to sprucing themselves up, and long lines of shivering soldiers clad only in their underwear were to be seen outside the laundry room, awaiting their turn to sponge and press their uniforms.

Nothing could be done about the wet and dripping ceilings with their twisting rivulets, and Lüdenscheid glowered darkly every time he was reminded, by the drip drip of water, or by the constantly moving wetness of walls, of the insolubility of this particular problem. Where dirt was too deeply implanted to respond to conventional cleaning techniques, Lüdenscheid resorted to more advanced methods: flame-throwers were brought in and resistant pockets of grime were burnt out, cauterized, with the fire men from the fire engine standing by to put out the flames.

The room he had taken over from the major had sulphur candles burned in it, and then with the windows wide open five men were put to cleaning and polishing every surface. Only when this had been concluded to his satisfaction, fresh linen placed on the bed and quantities of soiled underclothing (discovered lodged between bed and wall) burned, did he remove his face mask, take off his tunic and lie down on the bed.

When the orderly had removed the Gruppenführer's boots and been dismissed, Stefan Kazakh found himself alone with Lüdenscheid. 'Ah, Herr Kazakh,' he said, 'stay, I want . . .' His eyes closed with exhaustion, one of those overwhelming exhaustions which sometimes overtook him: he lay still, chest heaving, face unwrinkling; his gun belt was over the back of a chair by the stove, Kazakh was within a couple of feet of it – I could have reached out and taken the gun, I did reach out: he touched the leather holster, the securing button, unfastening it caused a click, which awoke Lüdenscheid. 'Ah, Kazakh, yes – I must have dropped off. You see what tasks are put on me. You see. One is surrounded by incompetence. Servile pigs they all are, the dregs. The flower of German manhood was wasted, criminally, wasted, in Russia.'

He got up. He began to pace, dressed in his peg-top trousers and shirt, and in stockinged feet. Exhaustion had had an effect of drunkenness on him, or perhaps it was the plum brandy fumes he'd been inhaling all afternoon. 'The blunder was in Africa,' he declared. 'That was the first blunder. I told them. The Führer was badly advised. Rommel should have been given the motorized formations and the supplies he needed. A calamitous mistake. The British could have been defeated, the Suez Canal captured, the entire Mediterranean coastline would have been in our hands – imagine, Herr Kazakh, the entire Mediterranean. Up through Persia and Iraq, nothing to stop us, we could have cut off the Russians from Basra, taken the oilfields. Cut off Murmansk from the body of the Soviet Union and taken it with a bold thrust from Finland. We'd have isolated Russia from America, the Japanese would have taken care of the American freighter fleet in the Pacific, and the principal ports, Basra and Murmansk, would have been in our hands. Only Archangel would have remained to the

Russians, and that is ice-bound much of the year. Imagine how we could have struck out from Mesopotamia! Captured the Caucasian oil fields – Baku! Lack of oil would have put the bulk of Russian armour out of action. Imagine, Herr Kazakh! And it was thrown away through short-sightedness, narrowness of vision, fear of decision, incompetence. We could have shattered the Russian colossus. Our nation cried out for the *Feldherr* – and there was none. The Officer Corps, entrenched in its outdated concepts, would not yield to men of vision. They could not see the simplest possibilities. No wonder the Führer became disgusted with them. Had I been given the opportunity, Herr Kazakh, I may say – I venture to think – things might have been very different. But as you see, as you see I was assigned to a minor theatre of war. I sat in Vienna censoring the posts – tapping the phones and issuing directives that nobody heeded. The Führer did not have sufficient faith in my military thinking. Repeatedly I advised the Führer. He disregarded my advice.' He gave a deep sigh. His eyes were damper than usual. It was grisly to see it: the man had had military aspirations; he had been frustrated in his ambitions; he had seen himself as the *Feldherr*, the military man of vision, and they had made of him a censor and a postman, and he was deeply sorry for himself. If only I'd killed him a moment ago, at least I'd have been spared this spectacle; and to find him addressing me in this way, with this intimacy, with all the expectancy of finding in me a sympathetic listener. He often made this mistake, brushing off my insults and gibes as mere tokens of opposition, assuming my essential responsiveness to his plight, his ailments, his burdens and problems.

At first light next morning, after the night's dead had been buried, the removal of the Jews and lunatics began. Lüdenscheid watched from his window, which was iced up at the corners, leaving only an iris of clear glass; his breathing kept obscuring the pane, and he had repeatedly to wipe it clear.

Wirthof, on horseback, was forming the Jews into some semblance of a marching column. The more fortunate wore several coats, one over the other, of varying lengths and different materials and colours, some wore caftans and wide-brimmed hats, and some had pieces of fur tied on their heads for warmth – old muffs some had for their hands and some had made fantastic turbans out of fox pelts, with head, paws, glass eyes at the top, and fox tail around the neck. The man in the greatcoat of the Royal Yugoslav Army still had his convoluted brass instrument slung on his shoulder. A little boy wore his dead mother's fur, trailing it in the snow. They marched in a shuffling gait, dragging their rag-bound feet. The lunatics were brought out last, moving on distorted limbs, arms whirling: windmills and grinders and contortionists and tumblers and climbers of rope-ladders and swimmers in the deep and broken bridges, and spinning tops. They were wild with joy at being released. They danced and shrieked. They performed their natural functions in full view of everyone, in an ecstasy of deliverance. The Jews shrank from them. The Jews beat their breasts and fell to the ground, to them it was the visitation of a curse. And among these nations shalt thou have no repose, and there shall be no rest for the sole of thy foot: but the Lord shall give thee there a trembling heart, and failing of eyes, and languishing of soul. They incanted the ancient curses of their Torah to themselves. And the German soldiers on horseback rode among them and forced them to move – out of the gates, out into the village. And the Lord shall bring thee back into Egypt in ships. Their lines stretched out: a shuffle-shuffle of cursed souls.

When they were gone from sight, Lüdenscheid remained by the window, allowing the glass to cloud over from his breath. 'Good,' he said in excellent humour, 'that has rid us of the children of Israel. Good. Good.'

The distance to Jesenice was about twenty-eight kilometres. Three hours out of Bojh some of the marchers began to drop on the wayside from exhaustion.

Wirthof could not understand these Jews, he felt a mounting anger with them: why didn't they run? There were only four Germans. If the Jews broke away and ran some of them were bound to escape. But they kept dragging themselves along, shuffle, shuffle, they kept on, a cursed people who cherish their chains, Wirthof fulminated to himself; damn them, damn them. He could not understand why they did not pull him and the three guards from their horses, and tear them to pieces. He despised them for not doing it. Evidently they preferred to die, with that on-your-head-be-it look in their eyes, and Wirthof thought Lüdenscheid must be right, they are cursed, they are the lowest of the low; they deserved to die. And about a third of them did before the marchers reached Jesenice.

The removal of the Jews and the lunatics was not the only task Lüdenscheid found for Wirthof. A German soldier who had been ill with fever and had difficulty in swallowing suddenly developed an extreme aversion to water – the sight of it caused violent contractions of the muscles of his throat. When it became known that some months ago he had been bitten by a dog, Lüdenscheid, who had been told of this, immediately cried, 'Hydrophobia.' The soldier died, and Lüdenscheid came to the conclusion that the partisans had intentionally infected dogs with rabies as a weapon of terror against the garrison. 'We shall nip their plan in the bud,' he announced. 'Lieutenant Wirthof, you will organize a round-up of all dogs in the area and these dogs will be slaughtered and their carcases burnt.'

'I strongly protest.'

'Perhaps the lieutenant is a dog lover.'

'Sir, I protest on the grounds that this is a totally unnecessary action, a waste of our limited manpower, and that it will expose our troops to needless dangers, since they will have to go about in small groups and go into isolated areas, where they will be highly vulnerable to attack. It would be much more practical, I suggest, for the men to be warned to take extra precautions with dogs and to shoot if attacked.'

'Your objection is dismissed, Lieutenant. This is an organized attempt to terrorize our troops, and it must be stamped out. You will carry out your orders.'

'Yes, sir.'

The dogs were duly hunted down over a period of several days, slaughtered, and burned on pyres. In the course of this, two Germans were killed by partisans, but Lüdenscheid considered it a very reasonable price for having averted a plague of rabies.

Lüdenscheid had had a dream, which troubled him because he never, never dreamt, and so he considered it a portent. He had with him, in addition to Kazakh, an astrologer and dream-interpreter (the three freaks had been sacked, one was in a concentration camp), a man with the face of a holed cheese. To him, in Kazakh's presence, he recounted the dream.

It was a dream of swans. A man had come to him with two swans, beautiful creatures, and asked him to keep them safe for a few days in a sideboard. As he loved swans, he agreed to this, but when the man had left, Lüdenscheid had misgivings. Now that he

348

looked at the swans again they seemed malevolent creatures, and not at all beautiful, and he felt sure they had been left with him in order to bring great harm upon him. He therefore decided to kill them, and did so by cutting their long necks with his dagger.

'What does it mean?' he demanded of the astrologer whose skin was holed as holed cheese, and who pondered for a moment before asking if the swans had seemed larger than swans normally are.

'No, smaller,' Lüdenscheid said.

'That is very interesting,' said the cheese-faced astrologer (who had formerly performed in cabarets but had been out of a job since the Goebbels edict). 'The swans are the Gruppenführer's enemies, and the man who brought them is clearly a Jew. He sought to plant his spies and agents in the Gruppenführer's house, represented by the sideboard. The Gruppenführer was quite right to kill them.'

Lüdenscheid choked slightly, and turned to Kazakh. 'What do you make of that, Herr Kazakh? You agree with my dream-interpreter? He's said to be first class.'

'I don't know the meaning of dreams,' said Kazakh.

'You can say if you agree with him or not.'

'I cannot really judge.'

'Herr Kazakh, I demand that you give me your opinion of the meaning of my dream.'

'You say the swans were very beautiful?'

'Yes, they appeared to be.'

'You must have been terrified when you had killed them?'

'Yes, that's true: it was a nightmare. Quite terrifying.'

'Then is it likely that they were spies? If they had been spies you would have felt relief – not terror – after you'd killed them.'

'What do you say to that?' Lüdenscheid demanded of the holed man, who only wanted to survive, only wanted not to be sent to a concentration camp, only wanted to make a living.

'It is my opinion that the Jew had cast a spell of terror on the Gruppenführer, but that the Gruppenführer was strong enough to overcome it.'

'I used to be fond of swans,' Lüdenscheid said, 'as a child I saw them on the lakes, lovely things, beautiful with their round delicate whiteness, yet fierce, quite fierce-looking in flight, their heavy wings pounding the water, magnificent creatures . . .'

'The Gruppenführer will agree that it is a familiar technique of the spy to masquerade in an appealing guise . . . After all, if they were swans and not spies why would the Gruppenführer have killed them?'

'Obviously they were spies,' said Lüdenscheid. 'They must have chosen that particular form to trick me, knowing of my great fondness for swans. Wouldn't you agree, Herr Kazakh?'

The cold closed its grip around Castle Bojh; massive spike icicles hung threateningly from eaves; in the now empty yards the snow was several feet deep, and the troops spent much of their time clearing channels for their vehicles to pass along, and every day work details from the population, guarded by soldiers, were employed keeping the main roads clear for military traffic, but old men and women and young children could not dig fast enough to deal effectively with the encroaching snow, and every night explosions in the hills produced new snow avalanches, which blocked roads that had been cleared the previous day.

Each morning Lüdenscheid called military conferences to announce new offensives against the partisans, and sent off exhortations, usually ignored, to the military commanders in other parts of Yugoslavia. It incensed him to be told of the impracticability of plans he had spent long hours working out during the night, poring over maps and charts. Again and again his postulated bold thrusts and daring crushing movements were frustrated at inception by factors such as the destruction of a railway line or the impassability of a particular road or the lack of adequate supplies. Communications were awful and hard to restore because actions intended to restore them got bogged down for lack of communications. Lüdenscheid's telegraphed directives arrived in garbled form, or not at all, his couriers were killed or captured, or when they reached their destination found it was no longer in German hands, or it was but the commander had not the slightest intention of taking any notice of Lüdenscheid's directives. Divisions that Lüdenscheid wished to deploy in a particular way had been captured or decimated by the time his 'orders' got to them, orders which in any case he was not authorized to give.

He had a tendency to conduct staff conferences as if they were meetings of the German General Staff, devoting much time to lengthy dissertations on the overall military situation. His officers had to remind him that his theories on the deployment of divisions and armies were not immediately enforceable, since in point of fact they had less than a hundred men at their disposal, some of whom must remain to defend the castle. Whenever he was told this, he fumed at the officer in question, accusing him of traitorous defeatism. 'If we cannot engage the enemy,' he declared, 'we shall starve him out, we shall contaminate his water supplies, burn his fields and villages.' It had to be pointed out to him that the enemy's water supplies were also the water supplies on which the Germans depended. Such considerations were of only marginal interest to him. 'If we cannot win,' he shouted, 'we do not deserve to win, and we shall go under, and a dark night of the soul will spread across Europe. That is why we cannot allow ourselves to be defeated. It would be the defeat of everything fine and noble and beautiful. The end of German *Kultur*. The long night of the infidels. That is why we cannot allow ourselves remorse in the execution of our duty. There are no noncombatants in this war, which is a war of survival for everything that we cherish. Therefore we must be ruthless and bold. If the enemy seeks to shelter behind women and children then we must slaughter women and children without compunction or remorse, knowing that we serve a higher purpose. If need be I shall make the snows of this miserable country run with blood.'

The officers had become accustomed to such perorations and listened to them in silence, after which they brought up more immediate problems such as a threatened outbreak of scurvy because of the lack of fresh vegetables.

'Lieutenant Wirthof,' Lüdenscheid said, 'I have always had a high regard for your soldierly qualities. You must know that. In the past you have shown exemplary courage and devotion to duty.'

'Yes, sir.'

'I have a task for you.'

'Yes, sir.'

'You will retake Zlogar.' He was damply radiant as he spoke.

'I would remind the Gruppenführer that Zlogar has been ransacked by the partisans. With the railway station at Zlat destroyed, and Jezerse put out of action, Zlogar is without strategic value. Its railway station is beyond repair and the railway tunnel has been blocked by dynamiting. The partisans have removed all food and equipment.'

351

'Strategic considerations are only some of the factors in assessing the value of an action. To retake Zlogar will serve as a boost to morale.'

'I would suggest to the Gruppenführer that to capture a village already ransacked by the enemy and impossible to defend with our present overstretched supply lines would be of little value as a morale booster or anything else.'

'Consider it in the nature of a punitive expedition. We must hit back at the enemy, and make him pay dearly for his successes. To retake Zlogar will be a great German victory.'

'The Gruppenführer cannot be serious in suggesting that the recapture of a wrecked railway station and a few peasants' houses can be of any significance. It means risking men and equipment . . .'

'Are you afraid of risk, Lieutenant?'

'We do not know in what force the partisans are defending Zlogar. They have two or three mountain divisions in the neighbourhood.'

'You can take forty men, Lieutenant.'

'Forty, sir?'

'And there is a battalion of Ustasi that you can use. The Ustasi also have an interest in retaking Zlogar.'

'I would rather not use the Ustasi, sir.'

'As you have pointed out, we do not have sufficient men. Lieutenant Wirthof, your orders from me are to retake Zlogar. I am not inviting your opinion. I will put it on a more personal basis. I make this demand of you, Wirthof. If you succeed, you will be totally reinstated, restored to your former position, your record wiped clean. I ask this of you, Lieutenant Wirthof,' he said in a cold ecstasy of command, eyelids quivering, damp face growing damper, pores outpouring; he glistened; like a fish he glistened, coldly.

'Zlogar,' said Wirthof, 'at least it's pronounceable, unlike most of the places in this God-forsaken country. It's just as well to die in a place that people can pronounce. Can you imagine how awkward it would be to have to say – Ah yes, he died at Trzic. You'll have to tell Leonie, you know. You think it'll shatter her, Kazakh?'

'I wouldn't worry about her.'

'She's very fragile in herself. My death will be a great blow to her. You must prepare her for the news. Not just blurt it out – eh? You must promise, Kazakh, that you will tell her gently. And then you must stay with her, because she will not necessarily react immediately. The grief can be delayed in such circumstances. She might collapse from the shock hours later.'

'Wirthof, there is no need to mourn yourself before you are dead.'

'It is hardly possible afterwards, Kazakh. I know you think this is a pose, but I truly don't care about myself. But Leonie receiving the news is something I find almost too unbearable to contemplate.'

'She might not be as grieved as you imagine.'

'That's an outrageous thing to say. I think that's a very contemptible statement, Kazakh.'

'All right, all right. Look: the chances are you won't be killed.'

'I have a presentiment. I always had a feeling I was going to die somewhere very cold. And Zlogar is cold, my God.'

'It doesn't follow, you know.'

'There is a sort of coincidence of circumstances about all this. You being here. Zlogar. Lüdenscheid. Lüdenscheid would like nothing better than for me to retake Zlogar for him, and die in action. That would redeem me in his eyes.'

'Well, don't do it for his sake.'

'I have been talking to the lunatics, Kazakh.'

'Yes?'

'You know what I always used to say – the mad are voyagers. Well, I was right. They see things we don't see. And when I look in their faces I can see they know something – they can see my death, Kazakh. It's like the blind can tell things that people with sight can't; they, the lunatics, have an awareness. They know.'

'Nobody can foretell the future.'

'That's your miserable rationalism. But the mad are not rational . . .'

'It doesn't follow that because they are not rational . . .'

'Oh we always used to have these arguments, ad infinitum.'

'Ad absurdum.'

'Yes, they were pretty absurd some of our discussions. Vienna is a great place for talkers. God, what talkers! What endless rumination – the onanism of the mind, the Viennese vice. I'm sick of all that, Kazakh. I'm sick of discussions, I have absolutely no theories any more. What a mess they've made, Lüdenscheid and his crowd. I used to think he was outstanding – the ostrich-feather salesman! Well, now, I tell you, I wash my hands of it all.'

'But you're going to Zlogar?'

'You make it sound like a skiing trip. With your capacity for logical thinking, Kazakh, can you suggest an alternative?'

'You could refuse.'

'Refuse an order?'

'Why not?'

'Apart from the fact that it wouldn't be honourable to refuse an order, it wouldn't serve any purpose, Lüdenscheid would undoubtedly have me shot.'

'Well, if you're so sure you're going to die anyway.'

'There's a difference. In any case, I see you don't refuse to treat him.'

'I have my reasons.'

'I always wondered what they were. They have never struck me as being very logical, for someone who prides himself on his logic.'

'For once, Wirthof, I am in agreement with something you say.'

'One is not free of a man like that until one is dead,' Wirthof said after a thoughtful moment of self-commiseration, an uncharacteristic expression of perturbation on his face, in his violet eyes.

'Or until *he* is dead,' said Stefan Kazakh.

'Regrettably, as far as I am concerned, the former is likely to precede the latter.'

'Somebody should kill him,' said Stefan Kazakh.

'Such men have magic lives. Not to mention bodyguards and steel-plated trains.'

'Somebody who was close to him could kill him.'

'Why don't you do it, Kazakh?'

'I don't have access to weapons.'

'That's not insuperable,' said Wirthof, taking the pistol from his holster and putting it down on the table between them.

'There'd be retaliation, if I did it,' said Stefan Kazakh.

'You see, your idea is not practicable.'

'You could do it, Wirthof. Have you never thought of it?'

'As a matter of fact, when I was doing my daily reports to him, he was always demanding that I should admit to a desire to kill

354

him. Not that I had any such desire, but he was so insistent – in the end I said, yes, I had. I hadn't thought of it really – beyond the impulse, which every serving soldier I suppose sometimes has, to kill a commander who is a swine.'

'You agree he is a swine?'

'Unquestionably a swine. But is one entitled to kill even an unquestionable swine? It's an interesting question, Kazakh.'

'You're in a position to do it, Wirthof.'

Wirthof laughed. I think for a moment he was seriously considering it, projecting himself forward into the situation of being the assassin of Lüdenscheid, weighing it against that quirky sense of honour of his, posturing, assassin-style, before the mirror of his mind. He had always wanted to do something remarkable, to be a general at thirty, to love Leonie, to decipher the language of lunatics, to understand more than can be understood with reason. But his imagination faltered at the idea of being the assassin of Lüdenscheid. He was not convinced that the asassination of the Gruppenführer of Posts and Telegraphs would be considered a great thing to have done, and so he smiled and said, 'You see, the Viennese vice: perpetual theorizing, Kazakh, I wash my hands of it all. Now, I'm going to write a letter to Leonie. Will you promise to see that she gets it, whatever happens? And then I must get ready. You wouldn't believe it, but there isn't even a map of Zlogar in existence, that's the sort of miserable place it is. Fortunately, I got hold of a 1929 Baedeker before I came here, and it is in that. Listen to this. "Zlogar. 1,112m. Townlet between the Karavanke and the Kamnik Alps, 18 km. N.W. of Kranj. Ski lift. Ski chairs. The climate is especially beneficial because of the solar radiation. Picturesque views of the Karavanke and of Mt Triglav. Situated in a natural declivity and surrounded by woodland." A most excellent place to die, Kazakh, wouldn't you agree?'

He always sought my agreement, a manner of speech. Agree with me, Kazakh. Agree with me that the core of the world could be made of jam, that lunatics can see beyond reason, that the future sends messages in the form of presentiments. Agree with me. Not a plea, a demand. He couldn't say please, of course. Couldn't say – if it pleases you. In the pre-dawn he was pale as the mountains: just a suggestion of glitter. As it happened, there was a full mad moon to complement his presentiment. Agree with me, Kazakh, that I am going to die. What relief would it have given him if I had agreed, joined him in his certain foreknowledge? He had his death all worked out: it will be like this: he didn't mind too much, as long as it happened his way. To die at Zlogar, wan and washing his hands of it all, suited him, and with me to take the message to Leonie. An excellent arrangement. Cold air currents smelling of the heights cut him about the face, and shivering into fur collar he turned and gave the signal to move off, sitting high in the cockpit of the armoured half-track, goggles up on his cap.

Snow churning under tracks and wheels and rising, the column began its ponderous crawl, through the courtyard, out of the gates, and down the steep decline to the lake, dull frozen and without images. On the lake shore the trembling trees disposed of their surplus snow on the passing vehicles. Red scrub bounded the lake, and under the ice, brown leaves were preserved like jellied fruits. The column was heading towards the lightest part of the sky, gathering speed, moving in a swell of noise, there were a few uncertain spots of colour on the Karavanke.

Hitting the main road, the valley broadened out; on both sides, yellow glowing houses beneath the forests: a sawmill; hay stooks; the wide undulation of a good sledge run; church steeples like high-piled ice-cream cornets; the landscape was impervious to the column's brute progress, spreading its hills to the soldiers. Past the ruins of a castle built by the counts of Ortenburg, and then under a railway bridge and through Zirovnica, and along by the hydro-electric power plant, parallel to the pipeline, beside the sluices, around the artificial lake: with daylight the Karavanke became speckled with changing colours, around Triglav rode a carousel of black clouds.

By now, Wirthof thought, Zlogar will have news of the approaching column. An hour out of Bojh the mountains closed in and the gradient began to increase in steepness and the road to wind upwards under an overhang of rock, he felt the narrowness of the gorge and smelled the heights, a natural tunnel overhead spouted icicles ten feet long, a petrified waterfall, he had a glimpse of eagles, and when the road did another loop a smoking black sun was in his eyes and he pulled down his goggles. The tail of the column was coiled below, and farther down, the Sava flowed strongly towards Lake Bohinj: another half hour. Indifference packed him in with its ice. One does not need to live, where is the necessity? He consigned his life to the indifferent peaks: I wash my hands of it. A gift that is an embarrassment can be returned.

Ten minutes later he had his first sight of Zlogar, a huddle of simple buildings in a scooped-out corrie of the mountain: behind it, perpendicular cliff, and at its sides smooth slopes backed by woods. The road they were on now began to loop down towards these woods – ample cover there: that was the place of rendezvous with the Ustasi. He had only forty men, but together with the Ustasi forces they could deploy in a semicircle and trap the partisans against the perpendicular cliff. It wasn't an easily defensible village, as the mixed garrison of Germans and Ustasi had discovered when the partisans had descended on them out of the hills. Still, they must have learned from their victory how not to defend this place, and they were hardly likely to put themselves in the same position as the garrison they had overrun and wiped out.

He surveyed the village and the surrounding terrain through field glasses: no sign of activity: was it possible they had not been warned? Or perhaps they had abandoned the village. Having ransacked it, wrecked the railway line and dynamited the railway tunnel, it was no value to them, or to anyone, except the two or three hundred people who lived there.

They descended fast, and Zlogar disappeared from sight behind the buttress of the hillside: he radioed to the tail of the column, which still had the village in view, to report any sign of activity, but the reply came back that there was nothing going on as far as they could make out. He saw, ahead and below, the beginnings of the woods where the steepness of the mountain flattened out into an extensive ledge – there must be several miles of these woods before the ground dipped again in ski-run slopes to the village. They drove fast, all gunners in a high state of readiness, until they had the shelter of trees around them; then Wirthof sent out men to scout the immediate vicinity, and had three armoured vehicles arranged in fortress formation, one ahead, one on each flank, so that their guns gave protection on all sides. At the rear, the rest of the column was winding in.

Wirthof looked at his watch. They were on time for the rendezvous; he was leaning out of the hatch, he pushed the goggles back up on his cap, took off the cap, and frowned into the bright dark deepness of the wood, its contrast of white and white bedevilled the eye, and it was several moments before he gave human form to the approaching snow shimmers, which turned out to be the Ustasi officers in white combat overalls. There were two of them. A little distance behind them came a third man, in white priest's cassock, and a sort of monk's cowl, a huge man, a rifle slung over his shoulder, and carrying a wayside crucifix that had evidently been chopped down with the axe that hung from his belt.

Wirthof spoke to the officers, 'Bring your men to the far edge of the wood, but don't let them come out of it yet. Take up your positions there, in as large a semicircle as you can form. I shall take my men down into the village. I shall see what sort of resistance we encounter. When I want you to attack, I shall fire a Very pistol. Don't move your men until you get the signal. Is that clear? How many of you are there?'

They nodded, smiling to themselves, humouring the questioner, not answering.

'How many of you are there?' he repeated roughly.

'Sufficient,' they said, smiling, ingratiating and non-compliant.

'You have understood what I said?' Again the circumlocutory smiles, which went all around the question without actually responding to it. 'All right,' Wirthof said, and signalled to the other vehicles to start up.

The track through the woods was just wide enough to allow the column to proceed in single file; the skein of branches of varying density above them, together with the passage of swift-shaped clouds, fragmented the sun and produced leaping lights and abrupt darkness. His eyes smarted from this rapid alternation of light and dark, and he was hardly able to tell if the quick white movements sometimes perceived were the eye's confusion or Ustasi. Back of hand extended horizontally before him to protect himself, he rode into the dazzle that marked the end of the woods, expecting gunfire as they came into the open, but there was no gunfire. The heavy vehicle was poised, cumbersomely, for a moment on the ridge, tracks churning, front wheels up in the air, and then it had set down and was over and on the dipping down track, buttressed on both sides by snow to the height of a man, its gun turrets traversing to cover the open slopes. He was head and shoulder out of the hatch, field glasses to eyes.

Zlogar was silent and without movement. Down – fast – in sudden sunshine. He picked out the sagging cables of a chair-lift, the torn-up railway tracks, the caved-in railway tunnel, the orange church, the *gostilna*, the Alpine hut for skiers. Still no gunfire and no movement.

Level with the first building, he raised his hand to slow down the column: no one to be seen, their guns covered every house. They proceeded along one street, and when the lead vehicle had come to the end of it they were in occupation of Zlogar.

Wirthof climbed down from the armoured car, and made a signal to the men in the rest of the column to dismount: they all jumped down off their vehicles, sub-machine guns at the ready, and went from house to house. Around Triglav the carousel of black clouds dipped and rose, dipped and rose: the cold air currents from the Karavanke threw up twisting snow streamers on the slopes, many-coloured, encircling the village with their aurora. Streaks of sun colour lay across the searchers, bulky men with gun-metal appendages on a nerve trigger – there were a few bursts of gunfire occasioned by glare and shadow, by a fugitive pig or chicken, by stiff fingers and tension. Rough and becoming rougher in their fruitless search the bulky cold men kicked open doors, swore, knocked over tables and chairs, smashed in windows, cleared shelves with rifle butts, stuck bayonets into mattresses and pillows, relieved their bladders in empty larders, ripped silk hangings in the little Orthodox church. In the *gostilna*, part inn, part town hall, they tore down the roughly drawn portraits of Stalin, Tito, Churchill and Roosevelt and the homemade flags of the Allies, they searched in vain for something to loot in this ransacked village.

At the wrecked railway station the twelve goods trucks, which had been the prize of this place, lay on their side, open bellied, spilling out vestigial flour, maize, beans, oil, carbide. Apricots and other fruit rotted on the ground amid torn steel and spent cartridges, and in the wreckage they came upon the bootless bodies of Germans and Ustasi decomposing under a skin of hoar frost. Scrawled over the sides of the trucks was the ubiquitous legend: *Smrt Fasismu – Sloboda Narodu.*

In different parts of the village, pinned to tree trunks and on front doors, they saw the partisan proclamation, 'In compliance with the Liberation Front's proclamation of May 28th, 1942, in re: action on the part of the anti-Liberation Front White Guard enemies of the Slovenian people, the individuals listed hereafter were sentenced to death and shot –'

In ten minutes Wirthof had made a complete circuit of the village, finding nothing. He stuck his pistol back in the holster, and scanned the hills through field-glasses. He made out the lines of Ustasi, a froth of movement on the edges of the wood, the hard glitter of weapons. Turning, he gave the order for the village to be burned, and men ran with petrol cans from house to house. He had possession of the village, and to burn it down, to lay waste to it, to render it uninhabitable was the task that he had been given. As the first house began to blaze, he stood watching the upward flight of cinders.

Continuing to sweep the surrounding countryside with his field glasses, he found himself peering into the sun – *as a child: our games: who can stare longest into the sun?* – and a lightburst obscured the perpendicular cliff, distorting vision as in a fractured mirror, and, blinded, he wrenched sideways. No relief: an after-vision of braided light patterns was superimposed on the landscape, which had become faint and distant, the village, the burning houses, the soldiers, the vehicles were all faint and distant. He blinked rapidly, rubbed his eyes, shook his head, closed his eyes for some moments and opened them again, but still the after-vision, vivid and burning, obscured all else, and the light patterns seemed to have a developing life that he could not control, mutations were occurring, little bursting pods of light oscillating from background to foreground in a way that made him giddy and feel nausea, he could not seem to recover his eyesight fully. In his mind, simultaneously with the lightburst an apprehension had occurred, and this forced him to place the field glasses to his eyes again and to attempt to examine the perpendicular glare. He saw nothing. He was blinded, all he could see were these bursting pods and behind them constantly reforming guilloches of light, and still further removed – no more than silhouettes – the mountains and the cables of a chair-lift disappearing into glare.

That was where the partisans were, undoubtedly, even though he could not see them, they must be *there*. He felt the heat of the burning village on his back.

They had reversed positions – a brilliant stroke – placing the Germans again in the declivity. His presentiment was strong. From up there they could shell the column with impunity. Though he still could not see he gave orders for the field guns to be turned and aimed into the bright convex sheen. What a fool to have allowed himself to be placed at such a disadvantage – it fitted entirely with his presentiment. Some satisfaction that his presentiment was so right. Now they were in the declivity where they could be shelled from above. The partisans knew the terrain, that was where they scored again and again. That his foreboding should have been so accurate! What he couldn't understand was why the partisans hadn't yet opened fire. What were they waiting for? He watched the crawl of clouds towards the sun: if it was obscured and this damnable after-vision went, he'd at least be able to see, instead of having to fight this action blind. He gave further orders, getting men and guns spread out and under as much cover as was available. Still he couldn't see.

He sent half a dozen men on foot back up the slope with orders for the Ustasi to spread out above the partisans, in positions from which they'd have a direct line of fire. He was reluctant to use the Ustasi, and repeated his order that they were not to open fire until he gave the signal. Speculative! Highly. He didn't know that there were any accessible positions above the partisans, affording a direct line of fire. Pure extrapolation. Intelligent extrapolation wins actions.

He didn't know the strength of the enemy. He didn't know where they were placed. It was a matter of extrapolation. To fight a presumed enemy in presumed positions. Because they must be there, where else could they be? And to muster against them this force of Ustasi – how many men? – whom he was ordering to take up positions that he didn't know existed, but presumed must exist, for the chair-lift must end on a plateau, and this plateau must be accessible from the woods to men on foot, if not to vehicles, and from this plateau it must be possible to direct fire on to any intermediary stop of the chair-lift, and if the partisans had got men and equipment up the perpendicular cliff face they *must* have used the chair-lift.

He was certain. It could not be otherwise. He must be right. And at the same time he was certain of nothing, not even of sight, the bursting pods were belladonnas, dancing and dying – sunstone, operculum, crocidolite; and the smoke of the burning village was the dishevelled hair of old women. He was waiting for the men he had sent back up the slope to get a good way up. The clouds were too slow, the perpendicular cliff was still obscured by the sun's glare (or was this blinding dazzle *behind* his eyes?), at any moment *they* would open fire, *they* would not wait for a shadow across the sun to reveal their positions. No use waiting any longer. Extrapolate and act. The enemy must be annihilated, seen or unseen. Principle of modern warfare. When the enemy is unseen, fire at presumed positions. Saturation shelling. Flatten them. They must be there. Where else could they be? Principle of modern warfare. Plaster the enemy with fire, even when exact positions unknown. Textbook stuff. First principle. Learned that at Wiener Neustadt. Opening fire ahead of the enemy usually decided the day. The commander who waits until a situation has become clarified comes off second best. A presumed enemy to be engaged as determinedly as an actual known one. Intelligent extrapolation decides the day.

He gave the order to open rapid fire from all guns – into the glare. It lasted five minutes, this concentrated barrage, this pounding of the mountain face, smoke spurted upwards in a dozen places, first thin and black and fire fast, then slowing into elegant loops and twirls as it stained the dazzling air, spreading out against sharp white hills, a lazy discoloration of the sky, a dark dyeing of the sun. In the middle of this barrage, he saw through his field glasses, through the after-vision of mutating light patterns, the Ustasi coming out of the woods and into the open, on foot and on horseback, many of them, many white blobs, an uncountable number of them, out of the woods and on to the cliff face, white flies – fast, along a downward tilting ledge, tilting down into the smoke. They had disobeyed his instructions. Furious, he gave the order to stop firing. As the noise of guns ceased, the air shivered with screams; smoke had blacked out the sun, and he could see. The dazzle had gone from behind his eyes and he saw the extrapolated enemy, children, women with babies, not all of them dead, through the gaps in the smoke he saw women demented, with bloody bundles in their arms, one, out of her mind, clutching something no longer whole, no longer living, something black and misshapen, which she carried – her hair white and widespread – to the edge of the plateau, and threw over, and herself after it, screaming. Sunlight punctured the smoke pall in places. Trees blazed, wood silver becoming orange, becoming fire, becoming ash. The cold air currents from the Karavanke curled the smoke and drove deep indentations into it and swept it from the plateau, and more was revealed: a natural cave: a burnt-out hut: piles of belongings – pack mules running loose, with pots and pans and bundles strapped to them. On the rocks above, a handful of men with red stars in their fur caps, one machine gun still operational trained on the line of Ustasi coming along the ledge towards the plateau. Through his field glasses Wirthof saw the hooded priest, the wayside crucifix held up before him high – The partisans were firing, moving about on the rocks. Wirthof counted four, five, seven men, the enemy.

On the plateau maybe forty or fifty women and children were still alive, attempting to climb up the sheer rock face, hanging on to ropes which others a little higher up had thrown to them. Wirthof rushed forward, waving his arms, shouting at the Ustasi: 'Back. Back. I gave no orders. I gave no orders.' His voice carried no distance at all. He returned to his armoured vehicle and ordered it back up the slope; it turned ponderously on the unlevel ground, lurched sideways, almost overturned, righted itself and started back through the blazing village and up, up the track; a quarter of the way up, the plateau was lost to sight behind a projection of the mountain: he heard gunfire, yells, the hard open syllables of Serbo-Croat, the fugitive Slovene vowels, now open, now closed, his ear heard the convergence of these sounds, the coming together of disparates, he heard women's screams and the cries of children and secret bell calls, and he heard many other sounds, no doubt, in his quirky inner ear, which had such confidence in its aural judgment.

By the time he got to the top, to the wood's edge, dozens of Ustasi were rushing along the ledge, which was broader than it had seemed from below, towards the plateau, he ordered his driver on, shouting at the white-overalled and snow-hooded figures to get back, to obey his orders; he was in command, he; none of them understood or wanted to: they grinned and burst into glottal speech and brandished their choppers and knives and rifles and kept on towards the ledge, even when he fired pistol shots over their heads they took it as a salutation and responded by yelling louder and firing their rifles in the air.

It took a long time to get to the point where the ledge began: no sign of the Ustasi officers, or of anyone in command, he couldn't seem to make anyone understand that he was in command, and that he was ordering them back, they'd be shot, he yelled at them, if they did not obey, but they just grinned and ignored him, and in desperation he pushed on, becoming wedged in this white horde pouring along the ledge, and was carried along in it, pushed on as if by a snow plough – there was almost no firing now from the partisan side, and nothing to be seen for men around him, and nothing to be heard but women's screams. The ledge became broader as it approached the plateau, widening into a promontory on one side and delving deep into the mountain on the other, and the white horde thinned around him sufficiently to show the slaughter.

Hardly any of the villagers were still left alive, only a few who had succeeded in climbing higher than the others up the rock face, and these were being pursued by Ustasi, and by German soldiers too, the men he had sent up with his orders were taking part in this: hands reaching up to grasp at feet and ankles, wrenching, pulling, bodies falling, and others setting upon these crumpled-up figures with knives and rifle butts and bludgeons. Wirthof was shouting for them to stop, to fall back; he was yelling something about disobedience to a superior officer and about the honour of the German soldier, and he pulled at one of his men who was pounding a child's skull with a rifle butt, and he was fumbling at his holster for his pistol, which he was prevented from drawing by the crush around him. 'Swinishness,' he shouted, turning like a whirligig. 'Swinishness. Swinishness.' A man with a red star in his fur cap came towards him on sagging legs, and Wirthof, having succeeded in drawing his pistol, took the man prisoner and told him to put his hands on his head, which he evidently didn't understand for he laughed and spat. Wirthof was furious. When a Ustasi tried to kill his prisoner, Wirthof shot the Ustasi between the eyes. The partisan found this incomprehensible, and spat. Wirthof shouted at him, 'You are my prisoner, you are under my protection. You understand? It is the duty of a soldier to protect his prisoner. You understand? I am a soldier. You are a soldier. We are brother soldiers. You understand?' The partisan did not understand. He spat again. Wirthof did not see that he was spitting gouts of blood. The man's incomprehension incensed him. 'This swinishness,' he said, waving his arms, 'is none of my doing. You understand? It is not my doing. I will show you. This is none of my doing. Je suis Viennois. Je suis soldat – officier – d'honneur.' In his fury at not being understood, he grabbed hold of the man and shook him violently and took his face in his hands, and he shouted at him about the sun having been in his eyes, and having been blinded by the glare, and that this – this swinishness – was none of his doing because he was an

364

honourable Viennese soldier, not a German, a *Viennois*, a *Viennese* of honour, and it was quite some time before he realized that the man he was holding and shouting at was dead.

Wirthof was missing for four days, presumed killed. In honour of him, the garrison of Castle Bojh was assembled and sang 'Ich hatt' ein' Kameraden'. Lüdenscheid made a personal recommendation to the Führer that Wirthof should be posthumously reinstated with the Knight's Cross, and have added the Oakleaves with Swords, the second highest order of gallantry in the land.

The truth is – I don't know what happened at Zlogar. Some of it must come from things that I read later, some of the details I must have heard at the time: for instance, the bit about Wirthof staggering around crying 'Swinishness', and trying to impress his Viennese honourableness on the dead partisan. Yes, that sounds like Wirthof. And, of course, it was very cold, and the sun was in his eyes when he gave the order for the artillery to open fire. How much else do I know? I know the locale, had no idea I knew it so well – I saw the area only once, after the massacre, but it seems I do know it, for it has described itself to me; yes, that is how it feels – *it* has described itself to me. Not that I have described it, that would presuppose some verifiable source, which I do not have, that is to say I have not been going around all these years with a photograph of the place in my mind, no, that has not been the case, if I have thought of Zlogar it has been with a paucity of detail – snow, whiteness, mountains, cold: no particularity at all, and this is why I say that it has described itself to me, and it has done so in a way that persuades *me* it was like this, which, of course, is entirely subjective, and it may be that if I went to Zlogar, or looked it up in a guidebook, the facts would contradict me. As for Wirthof's feelings, I have even less evidence for them. Can one ever get inside another person? And if so, is it of the other person that one has knowledge, or only of oneself inside that other person? That's one of those conundrums. Anyway, these are my thoughts, that is all I can say of them for sure, can I even be sure of that? Does the fact that I am thinking them make them 'my' thoughts? Futile speculation.

What kind of crisis of narcissism occurred in Wirthof at Zlogar? How could he, even with his capacity for not seeing what he didn't want to see, continue to esteem himself so inordinately, after Zlogar? There comes a point at which self-delusion is finally shattered by the force of reality, and then only madness can intervene to maintain the delusion. What choice was there for Wirthof after Zlogar? A lover whose love object – himself – has tarnished: a bathetic plight. Who can bear self-disgust? Not Wirthof with his violet eyes and dead-leaf hair. Can you, Kazakh, can you bear it? Everything is bearable, my father said. It is only pain. Only pain, yes. Therefore bearable. One can die because after all it is only death. One can live because it is only life. Everything is bearable and marvellous, Staszek Kazakh said.

Wirthof, at Zlogar, must have come, finally, to the untenable hypothesis, must have come at last to doubt in the all-possible, must have baulked, finally, at the proposition that the centre of the earth might be made of jam. What disillusionment. What grief. The end of magic, the beginning of terror. And Wirthof could not bear that. And supposing all this is true? And supposing he was everything you say? Still, he did kill Lüdenscheid, which is more than you did, Kazakh. Perhaps that was the ultimate hand-washing ritual on his part, the last fling at consummating his self-love, but do you allow yourself to arbitrate on love, its quality and its extent, with your record, Kazakh? Why are you so concerned with the career of this footling Nazi? Can you not give him credit for anything, for feeling horror at last? No, he was horrified too late. They all were, those belatedly decent ones, those super-efficient ones who somehow couldn't make the brandy bottles explode or place the briefcase accurately. Bunglers. Still, Wirthof did kill Lüdenscheid, which is more than you did, Kazakh. Can you trust your contempt? You make him contemptible, ludicrous – oh how the idea of his having a spark of honour sticks in your throat, how you muster all the forces of your derision at that possibility.

He turned up after being missing for four days. What happened in those four days? That is something at which your imagination peters out. How did he withstand the cold? How did he find his way back to Bojh? I don't know, those four days do not describe themselves to me, they are fallow in my mind, producing no images.

He was in an awful state when he arrived at the castle, almost unrecognizable, there were scabs of ice in his beard, his eyes were blue craters. What his intention was, I do not know. Lüdenscheid rose, there was a glowing expression on the Gruppenführer's face, he was in some state of exaltation – Wirthof had been restored to him, disobedience expiated; he looked as though he might embrace him, but contained himself.

'You've done well, Lieutenant Wirthof . . .' Perhaps if he had not said those words, he might have stayed alive. The phrase, uttered in that choked schoolmaster's voice, seemed to activate something in the exhausted man. Clumsily he reached inside his coat, an awkward fumbling movement. It would have been an easy matter to stop him. Even when he had drawn the pistol, there would have been time to stop him, he was so slow, his movements were so cumbersome, there was ample time for Lüdenscheid to get out the revolver that he kept in the drawer of his desk, but he did not do this, perhaps he preferred to rely on the chain of command, the strongly forged link. 'I order you . . .' he began, and then Wirthof fired the first shot, which went into the ceiling, and still there was time to stop him, to shoot him down, to fall on him, but Lüdenscheid did none of these things, he seemed held fast in the same slowness that had always impeded his articulation, he was suspended between words, choking a little, unable to complete the command with the necessary rapidity, his vocal cords clogged. Wirthof's second shot hit him in the thigh, and then the other shots followed rapidly, blood spouted from Lüdenscheid's neck, the next shot blew off the top of his head, still he wasn't dead, and Wirthof had to get up close to him, with a clumsy stiff step, catch hold of Lüdenscheid and steady the shaking pistol against the Gruppenführer's chest to place the final shot.

When he had done it, he seemed to regain some strength, sufficient to disentangle himself forcefully, for in the end Lüdenscheid had clung to Wirthof, clinging had taken the shot through his heart. Wirthof pushed him off, and fell back against the wall, and there formed on his face the smile of a small boy. 'You see, Kazakh, I have done it.' There was the noise of rushing boots outside as Wirthof turned the pistol on himself, pulled the trigger and scowled at finding the chamber empty. 'Damn.'

The guards seized hold of him and held him tightly, which was not necessary, he was not resisting, until the major came. The major's tunic was open, he had gravy on his chin, his stomach

swelled out against his braces as he drew breath; he was furious –
of course *he* would be blamed. His face was a blotchy red. He
shouted abuse at the guards – how had they allowed this to happen? He was hardly concerned with Wirthof. He looked
disgustedly at the dead form on the ground. You could see him
calculating the amount of trouble this would bring him. Best to
get it all over with quickly, before too many questions could be
asked; he jerked his head at the guards, who dragged Wirthof
out, lifting him off his feet. 'Kazakh! Kazakh!' 'I'm behind you.'
He was dragged down the corridor. 'Explain something to me,
Kazakh . . . Kazakh . . .' 'Yes, yes.' They were half carrying, half
dragging him down the stairs, apparently he'd fainted; the cold
air outside revived him as they dragged him through the court-
yard over the hard frozen ground, in a great hurry; they propped
him up against the post and he lolled like a drunk and had to be
secured with ropes to keep him upright. His head rolled back and
he opened his mouth wide as if to emit some tremendous sound,
but all that came out was a slight retching, and in the middle of
it he saw the two guards take aim, and at the last moment he
looked away, or was it that he looked up to where the lunatics
usually gathered at their windows? There was nobody there now,
no clamorous lamentation, only silence and me. Explain to me,
Kazakh. Explain to me. What had he wanted explaining?

What had he wanted explaining?

Stefan Kazakh walked through the castle gates, nobody to
stop him. It was quite easy. He just walked out. He took a few
steps slowly, experimentally, expecting at any moment to be
challenged, but nobody challenged him. He was out walking in the
village. Taking a walk. He walked. He had the terrors. That was
the first time, in all those years, that I was really afraid; Lüdenscheid was dead. Wirthof was dead. I was free of them both, and
I was afraid as I never was afraid before or ever have been since –

except yesterday, in Vienna, when I had that 'experience'. Dread of the possibility of life?

What was it he wanted explaining?

When Kazakh got to the downward sloping spruce wood along by the eastern walls of the castle, he began to run. An old grey day. No sky to speak of. Guipure of snow and branches overhead, snow underfoot, deep in places, sometimes sank into it up to his knees, couldn't make much speed. He cautioned himself: using up too much energy too fast. If I am going to cover any distance will have to preserve some energy. Must calm myself. I have been calm so long, must not lose it now. Imperative. What is this terror? Realizing he was out of breath, panting like a locomotive, after only a few hundred metres, he stopped. This won't do. Calm. Calm. Have always relied on my quickness; now must take this slowly, have only my own legs to carry me, must go at their speed, not mine. Cannot race ahead of my own legs. So Wirthof is dead. And Lüdenscheid is dead. Don't have time to think of that now. Must head for the mountains, find the partisans. Cold up there: sub-zero. Can I stand that? Wirthof was half dead after four days, and he had his fur-lined greatcoat, but no resistance to the cold. How he used to shiver always. Yet he stood it for four days, and came back to do what he did. Everything is bearable. It's only pain. Only death. Only life. Quite bearable, after all. What has to be borne must be bearable, by definition. That's what you say. Mist rising from the solid lake. Why did I run out? Had I stayed, I could have handled the major, a fool, I who could handle Lüdenscheid could surely have handled the major, I ran without thinking. Would have been more expedient to stay and bluff it out. Might have succeeded in getting myself a car; instead – having bolted – they will assume my complicity in the murder of Lüdenscheid, and will be out looking for me. If I'm caught, what do I say? Have left myself no room to manoeuvre. Not even a pinhead of room. A foolish thing for you to have done, Kazakh. The way it has turned out, I might just as well have killed Lüdenscheid myself. Why didn't you? I had a hand in it, I suppose; not enough of one – wish I had done it, I wish *I* had done it. That Wirthof should have done it in the end, that poseur and narcissist! He's dead, and you're alive, for the time being: oh you're very quick, Kazakh!

Mist over snow; objects robbed of their light are only aspects of themselves, incompletely realized: foetal in a landscape without depth: single-wall houses, without perspective: vapoury trees: mist however, can be useful to an escaping man; he, too, is robbed of some of his substance, which is helpful to an escaping man, and what is more, pursuers who have the advantage of motor vehicles and motor-cycles have the disadvantage of noise, they can be heard before they are seen, and Stefan Kazakh ran silent as fog, alert for every sound, keeping under the trees that skirted the lake, avoiding the roads.

He kept a steady pace, forcing himself to breathe as a runner, and his fear had a shape, an outline, boundaries, it was a country; he was running through this country of his fear, discovering its topography, or rather rediscovering it: for this was a country I have always known. So much, then, for my fearlessness.

The end of magic is the beginning of terror; I kept it tightly bound, as best I could. Who would have thought you could trust the hills. I had no choice, having forsaken my pinhead.

Stefan Kazakh had no clear conception of where he was heading, he was driven by the notion that he must go high, up into the mountains, where the Germans were loath to follow, and there, with luck, he might come upon a group of partisans, if he did not first freeze, or die of hunger or thirst. Once clear of the lake, he chose every steep gradient in preference to a lesser one, on the principle that while he was going up he was putting distance between himself and the Germans – if he kept to the valleys he would certainly run into the next German post, sooner or later.

As he climbed, winds from the Karavanke honing themselves on his face, he kept Lake Bojh below him for orientation; most of it was covered over by mist, but through the occasional gaps dull discs of the frozen surface showed like coins in a well.

After climbing for three hours, he was suddenly above the mist, he pulled himself up into a bright glittering sky of fearful dimension; distance like a disorder of perception opened up around him. This sudden multiplication of space almost made him lose heart and for several moments he just stood still and cried: how long since I had done that? Stood there – very close to despair, perhaps actually in despair – and wept. It seemed to me at that moment, surrounded by distance that was like a disorder of perception, that even the Nazis (whom I could handle: did I not have tricks, magical devices, gambits?) were preferable to this cold white prospect. I had a time of panic when I considered going back; I was not equipped for this journey through the country of my fear.

In a couple of hours it would be dark. Stefan Kazakh was at the bottom of a narrow gully, rising steeply to a col; the donkey track he had been following through the mist had led him to this point and then petered out. The rocky protrusions on both sides of the gully were veined with iced-up chimneys. Beyond the col there might be another track of sorts, or else a drop. He was not sure he could manage such a steep ascent, without ropes or stick. He took a few upward steps, and found himself slipping back, insufficient grip in his boots. He tried again, legs splayed this time to give his boots some purchase on the rocky sides of the gully, hands similarly spread so that he formed a letter X, and first in this posture then in variations of it he heaved himself up, hands, legs, back, elbows alternating in taking the bulk of his weight, making a coiled spring of his body, held by the pressure of its coiling, levering himself up by his feet and following with his body; towards the top the gully widened, and the resultant lessening of his hold, of his spring grip, called for greater exertion from him; pausing to gain strength it occurred to him that if he did not succeed in hauling himself up to the col by this method he would remain stuck like this, a horizontal wedge between the sides of the gully, until exhaustion forced him to ease the spring pressure of his body and he fell. The malevolence of the earth's pull, or the climber's ineptness – no matter which, one or the other would make him fall, maybe both. I would fall. Still, I had discovered some ways of not falling, making a spring of myself for instance; probably there were other means too. If the earth's malevolence was not supreme. (Or if I could outwit it.) His elbows cleared the top of the gulley, found firm ground, and he heaved himself up.

In the shallow depression on the summit he sat down hugging his knees, breathing hard. He was on one of the lower pinnacles of a chain of foothills at the base of a large mountain; below, a mucous vapour followed the downward curve of an old cart-track, which levelled out to a viewpoint, a small clearing with a log shelter. Rising, blown by the winds, he started towards this place. Closer, he saw that it was built like a bandstand, circular, and open between the peripheral arm rest and the projecting eaves; still, below the arm rest it was enclosed except here and there where wooden boards had rotted and come away. The shelter stood before an abrupt rock, and as he allowed the downward sloping track to speed him to a run he saw the Pokljuka Circles forming one after the other, and he saw the dusky Pokljuka luknja. There was the promised view from the shelter: Mount Stol, beribboned with a vapoury breath, Begunjscica and the steep rock walls of Smokuske stene.

Stefan Kazakh sat on the floor of the shelter where he was protected from the winds of the Karavanke which passed over his head, shaking the flimsy wooden structure. It was no less cold here, but at least he was not so exposed, and could take a short rest. It was going to be dark soon. The sun was sliding down behind the Karavanke, into Austria; pointers of refracted light moved over the high peaks from right to left, buoys of colour bobbed on the Alpine pastures of Rpecnikov rovt, and in the lessening daylight faint spots of man-made light became visible. He must make towards the nearest of these, he decided, and hope for the best: that they were not the lights of a German post.

He started off again, taking the continuation of the cart-track he had been on before, assuming that it would lead to one of these points of light. There could be no certainty of this in a country where cart-tracks sometimes ended, mysteriously, in steep drops: he'd have to take his chance. It was around this time, yes, round about the time I left the shelter and started on the downward cart-track, which might or might not lead to a friendly farmhouse, that the cheerfulness began in me; it did not displace the fear, but existed side by side with it, was its companion. It had the curious quality of being unrelated to anything that might be said to have caused it. I had no cause for cheerfulness, and my terror was unabated: you could say – I was in a state of terrified cheerfulness. It was unlike the condition I had been in these past years, which might be described, by contrast, as unterrified despondency. For the first time since leaving Bojh in the morning I experienced a sense of freedom, Lüdenscheid was dead, and Wirthof too was dead, and I was without devices. I would not say I was elated, far from it, on the contrary this freedom seemed like a fearful burden that had fallen upon me and might quite possibly kill me; this prospect, too, I regarded with something like cheerfulness, which is not to say that I was willing to die.

Kazakh, what happened to that cheerfulness? Where did you lose it again? Often, you have said to yourself, lying in a sweat of trivial apprehensions – of financial ruin, of loss of face, of some

372

impending humiliation, of sexual betrayal – but I was cheerful up in the Karavanke. If I could track the source of that cheerfulness, which ran parallel with my mounting fears and my failing strength; if I could find the secret of that mechanism. Such secrets Wirthof was interested in, the language of the mad. What was it he had wanted me to explain to him at the end? The universal equation, nothing less. Grandiose in all things, he would not have been satisfied with a lesser last wish. Kazakh, since I am about to die, explain to me the universal equation. Gladly, Wirthof. I've been meaning to do so all along. How forgetful of me. Just one moment and –

At nightfall, in a snowstorm, he came to a wooden farmstead; he approached it in a crazy zigzag of exhaustion; he kept falling, dragging himself to his feet, staggering on, falling again; each time he fell the pain of getting up increased in proportion to the fear of dying, and only a hair's weight separated them. Every time he fell, the length of time he remained on the ground – the snow piling up around him – increased. The snowfall was thick as walls; the farmhouse was intermittently seen. How do I explain myself? Who do I say I am? Not speaking their language, speaking only German, why should they help me? My complicated situation – how to explain that in a word? Why should they help me? He dragged himself to the door of the farmhouse and beat upon it with rapidly failing strength. It was not opened for a long time, and then a small bent old man with long moustaches was standing in front of him, and Kazakh could say nothing, he kept opening his mouth – but how could he explain himself? Who could he say he was? He wanted to say: help me. But he could not say it in this man's language – the truth is there was no language in which I could say those words. And so he said nothing, and then he said the only words that he knew: *Smrt Fasismu.*

Perhaps, after all, it was not necessary to explain anything. For these peasants did not ask for explanation. They took Kazakh inside before a fire and gave him stale crusts of black bread and some sour milk and a little goat cheese, and sat around watching him eat, making encouraging motions with their heads: an old man, an old woman, and two little girls. The little girls looked at him with great curiosity, especially when, having eaten, he began to weep. They giggled to see him weep. As soon as he had eaten, he fell asleep on the wooden floor in front of the stove, a melting snowman.

They woke him before dawn, all of them pulling and poking to rouse him, the little girls tickling the soles of his feet, the old man and the old woman shaking him, and they showed him with gestures that he must leave. They took him outside and pointed in the direction in which he must go to find the partisans, and the old man gave him goat cheese and sour milk to take with him, and one of the little girls came leading a mule, a scrawny animal, all its ribs showing, and the peasant smiled and nodded vigorously, and helped him up on to the animal's back. *Smrt Fasismu*, they all said, and gave the clenched fist salute.

It was a hardy animal, this mule, despite its thinness, it carried him upwards with a sure knowledge of the way, through mountain forests and harsh gorges and over swaying rope bridges, and he saw the deep fall of the Krma valley.

Soon after sunrise the German reconnaissance planes were out; he watched them swooping through the valleys, diving low over the beech trees, so low their bright wings almost touched the tips of the upper branches. In the late afternoon, he made out the line of a German patrol, but it was a long way below. That night, after eating the last of his cheese and sour milk, he bedded down in a mountain cave, keeping the mule close to him for warmth.

All day of the third day he saw no sign of human beings, and there was nothing to eat, and only melted snow to drink. His face was covered in cold sores. The mule was dying under him. Several times it stumbled and fell, and he prayed, 'Don't die yet, mule, stay alive a little longer, mule.' The mountains, this high up, for he was now at a considerable height, were polished by ice-action, glaciated to an arid shine. The mule picked its way along narrow tracks between the ice-sheets; in those moments when he was not out of his mind he would address the mule accusingly, and say to it, 'What a fool to trust myself to you, mule! Where are you taking me, mule?' And he said to himself, 'If this old mule dies, then I am done for.' It was a wretched animal that had been much eaten by lice, its coat was splotchy and diseased-looking and it was so thin that the tall man sitting on it appeared to impose a truly impossible burden on its back.

All day of the third day it managed not to die, and when Kazakh lay with it at night he praised it fulsomely, 'You are a great mule, a beautiful mule, how is it such a thin lice-eaten creature can carry my weight and not die? How is that, mule? How is it you can take such a weight as mine? You are a great beast of burden, mule. If only you will not die yet, if only you will refrain from dying a little longer, and take me wherever it is that you are taking me.'

He had entrusted himself entirely to the mule, to its knowledge of the mountains and to its strength; he was not really in possession of his mind any longer, and even if he had been I don't think he would have trusted it, and this went on another day and another day. On the morning of the sixth day, he lay sprawled out on the mule, a dead weight, his arms hanging down its sides almost to the ground, his head against its neck, and was only semi-conscious most of the time. It was shortly after the mule had eventually died, falling on its knees and then rolling sideways and depositing him in the snow, that two scouts of the 4th Proletarian Brigade found Stefan Kazakh and, though he was mumbling in German, decided not to shoot him, and took him back up to their commander, who had made his headquarters in a network of mountain caves only one kilometre from the spot at which the mule had died.

Stefan Kazakh was very well treated by the partisans, as soon as they found out who he was, whose son he was. 'The son of Staszek Kazakh?' There were questions, of course; but as soon as he had established indisputably that he was who he said he was, the political commissar conducting the interrogation embraced Stefan and kissed him with his walrus moustaches. The son of Staszek Kazakh! The slivovice was got out. 'Long live Stalin!' 'Long live Tito!' 'Long live the memory of Staszek Kazakh!' The partisan girls danced, clusters of hand grenades joggling at their belts. A celebration feast was prepared. The assassin of the tyrant Lüdenscheid must be feasted. No, no, they would not hear of denials. It was neither here nor there who had actually fired the shots; the Germans themselves had proclaimed Stefan Kazakh to be the assassin of Lüdenscheid – Wirthof was merely the helpless tool of the Jewish hypnotist.

As a matter of fact, the Germans held that I was the instrument of Jewish vengeance, the paid agent (paid with Koeppler money) of the Conspiracy of the Elders of Zion. That was their version. There were others. What was the point of denying them? I have never done so. Let the historians have their theories, their minutely researched reconstructions proving this or that. That, for instance, there was some kind of homosexual relationship between Wirthof and Lüdenscheid – and that his murder was not politically motivated at all.

It was a real feast the partisans prepared. Hen baked in clay. First the hen was killed – its neck slit joyfully, and its entrails removed: all of us watching bright-eyed, drinking, and the partisan girls danced, making the hand grenades in their belts jiggle in a way that caused us to roll about with laughter. Then the hen, feathers and all, was wrapped in clay and covered up in hot ashes. When the clay had been baked hard as earthenware, it was withdrawn from the ashes, struck with a rifle butt; it shattered to show the feathers stuck like a lining to the clay, and there was the chicken, brown and beautiful, producing in us a moment of reverential silence, which was broken by a salvo of salutations – 'Kazakh! Kazakh! Kazakh!'

They had their version of the slaying of Lüdenscheid, a bit fanciful, true, but it was no use trying to put them straight. Was I clear myself how it had happened? Are you clear now, Kazakh? All I know for certain is that I survived. That is indisputable. Is it? Is that so indisputable? I shiver – therefore I am. A dubious proposition. Need you become quite so metaphysical? The only reason for supposing that you survived is that you are, after all, here; if you go to the mirror you will see yourself. Which proves nothing, since you are a veritable hydra at growing new heads when it suits you to. Yes, this one is a good head, as heads go; intelligent, thoughtful – today you have your thoughtful head – a little grey, but it distinguishes you, to be perfectly frank this head suits you, it flatters you, it is a head for women to fall in love with (and divorce after two or three years); yes, this is undoubtedly one of your favourite heads, your going-out head, and it's the spitting image of me, except for a few small and unimportant details, like the fact that this is the head of a dealer, and for a long time now I have had an abhorrence of deals, for a long time now. I say *I* – but who am I to complain, since it was you who were so clever as to survive.

What I must do is think this thing through; that's what you've been saying – I know, I know. All right, all right. At the heart of it is the fact that you could never allow Wirthof even a spark of honour. That ridiculous poseur! Maybe that's what he was, and maybe the slaying of Lüdenscheid was a homosexual act, on some level or other, but why should it concern me? Why should it continue to concern me? Does he ask me for charity? Wirthof, who never could say please? The whole thing is academic. Besides, it would be a perversion of the whole concept of charity to think charitably of him, and, anyway, I can't do it. I can't and that's all there is to it.

The Viennese were lucky, not much damage to their city – not like Berlin. The bridges over the Donau were down, all except one, and the high-pitched roof of the Stephansdom blazed for three days, but the outer walls and the main spire withstood the flames; and the chariots of the Parliament building were intact though the roof was shattered, and at the University the main stairs sagged a little in the middle and the balusters were mostly gone and the coping was somewhat contorted and some of the statues were headless; at the Volkstheater still erect pillars supported a mass of rubble, once a balcony. There *was* damage, and the Viennese did starve for a time, and shiver – all the trees in the parks had been stripped of their lower branches for firewood, which you saw people wheeling through the streets in perambulators. There were new graves at street corners and in the Prater, where the Riesenrad was like some burnt effigy of their past. None of it was enough for me. They had not suffered nearly enough for me. Why, they had almost thirteen hundred calories a day: bean soup; pea soup; biscuits; once in a while they had a piece of sausage – not nearly enough of them died of hunger. My lovely bridges across the Donau canal were all wrecked, their tangled ends like severed arms with blood vessels and nerve ends protruding. It has all been restored. There is not enough sign of damage in this city.

I looked for Leonie in April 1945. I still had a letter for her from Wirthof. She was nowhere to be found, and after a while I gave up looking for her: I was no longer their messenger: she did not interest me very much any longer, I discovered to my astonishment, and I burnt Wirthof's letter without reading it. I was not even curious what he had said to her, what kind of pose he had struck for her benefit before going off to be killed, as he had thought, at Zlogar. I knew all his poses, didn't I?

Stefan Kazakh was very tired yesterday in Vienna, lately he had had many of these attacks of exhaustion, which felt as if he was being violently robbed of some essential part of his energy. Yes, I am often tired these days for no reason. It must be age, I am no longer as quick as I was. And so much of my energy I spend recklessly, with a gambler's passion for doubling up when he is losing. If I risk all, perhaps I can regain my losses; perhaps I can do it all in a flash. But then perhaps after all a flash is not long enough to restore a world so destroyed, perhaps it demands more effort, more pain, more cost. If only I had more energy, but I have wasted it prodigiously, as I have wasted my time, which is the time of my life, I have no other.

The way – sometimes – Wirthof still glitters in me, on my energy, in my time: that mica glitter of his: that is the source of my exhaustion; if only he would glitter less I would not have to despise him so much, and how much time and energy I spend on despising him, it should be possible to despise with less effort surely, if only he would glitter less, but there seems to have been a bargain struck between us, and I don't know how to get out of it, surely it cannot hold for ever.

Other Panthers For Your Enjoyment

Top Excitement

☐ **Patricia Highsmith**   **A TREMOR OF FORGERY**   30p

North Africa in high summer. A New York script writer commissioned to work on a film script. A film director to come – who doesn't. And an ex-wife not to come – who does. In between there's booze, sex and murder. In other words, it's that old Highsmith magic as ever working at the top of its sinister power.

☐ **Peter Dickinson**   **A PRIDE OF HEROES**   25p

An English stately home, a lion kept in a pit decorated with an obscene frieze, two old heroes fighting a moonlight duel with antique – but lethal – pistols. A crazy situation for very macabre murders. 'Dickinson is the most original crime novelist to appear for a long time' – Francis Iles, *The Guardian*

☐ **Len Deighton**   **THE IPCRESS FILE**   35p

The bestseller that started a new trend in spy fiction. 'Len Deighton really is something special' – *Sunday Times*

☐ **James M. Cain**   **THE POSTMAN ALWAYS RINGS TWICE**   25p

One of the handful of thriller classics, or, how to get away with homicide – and still pay the sinister price.

☐ **James Graham**   **A GAME FOR HEROES**   30p

The game begins one savage morning on a Channel Island when – 'The bodies started to come in with the tide just after dawn, bobbing in through the surf to the beach a hundred feet below my hiding place.' Take it from there and you have one of the most driving adventure novels you've ever read. 'Outstanding' – *Evening News*. 'Chair-gripping suspense' – *Scotsman*. 'Powerful – it crackles' – *Books and Bookmen*

☐ **Chester Himes**   **THE REAL COOL KILLERS**   25p

'Harlem *must* be like this' – *The Sun*. Even the realist and coolest of killers lose their cool when they get Detectives Grave Digger and Coffin Ed on their tails. 'Like a flick knife, it is tough, weird, wicked, vicious, and quite un-put-down-able – *The Scotsman*

War

☐ **James Clavell**   **KING RAT**   40p
Rat-like humans in a notorious Japanese POW camp. King Rat
is an every-man-for-himself US sergeant who lives high at the
expense of others – and finally pays the brutal price.

☐ **Hugh Wray McCann**   **UTMOST FISH**   30p
A *very* odd episode from world war one. Equatorial East Africa,
well-officered, highly professional German troops, and against them
a handful of green Britishers. Result – not what you might think.

☐ **David Forrest**   **THE LAST BLUE SEA**   25p
The second world war – the Australian Expeditionary Force
(amateur soldiers if ever there were) against the hair-trigger-trained
Japanese in tropical, unexplored Papua.

☐ **Gore Vidal**   **WILLIWAW**   25p
US naval war in the Arctic. The Japs are bad enough, but then
Nature takes a murderous hand in the game. The pace never lets
up. By the author – surprisingly! – of MYRA BRECKINRIDGE.

☐ **Ray Rigby**   **JACKSON'S WAR**   35p
A war like no other; skilfully waged by 'NAAFI troops' hundreds
of miles behind the 8th Army battle line. 'Permissiveness' may well
have hilariously begun here.

☐ **J. P. W. Mallalieu**   **VERY ORDINARY**
                                      SEAMAN   25p
By a writer who was there – life below decks on the high seas
during the last war. Many grim moments, but the ability of the
common seamen – most of them 'civilians in uniform' – to forge a
warmly human world in their stark, confined quarters makes this
one of the most triumphant books ever published.

Highly-Praised Modern Novels

☐ **John Fowles** **THE FRENCH LIEUTENANT'S WOMAN** 50p

Although Fowles is an English – and *how* – writer his novel has been on the American bestseller lists for months. To read it is an experience. 'When the book's one sexual encounter takes place it's so explosive it nearly blows the top of your head off' – *New York Saturday Review*

☐ **David Caute** **THE DECLINE OF THE WEST** 50p

A newly independent African state in bloody turmoil, and the world's adventurers – male and female – home in like vultures. Strong reading.

☐ **John Barth** **THE SOT-WEED FACTOR** 75p

The story of a mid-eighteenth century man of fortune, told in a modern spirit by one of America's great writers. 'Most magnificent, totally scandalous' – Patrick Campbell, *The Sunday Times*

☐ **Elizabeth Bowen** **EVA TROUT** 35p

'Elizabeth Bowen is a splendid artist, intelligent, generous and acutely aware, who has been telling her readers for years that love is a necessity, and that its loss or absence is the greatest tragedy man knows' – *Financial Times*

☐ **Norman Mailer** **THE NAKED AND THE DEAD** 60p

The greatest novel from world war two.

☐ **Mordecai Richler** **COCKSURE** 35p

Constantly reprinted by public demand. The brilliant satiric picture of a tycoon whose business and sexual appetites know no limits.

To-day's Fiction

☐ **Alexis Lykiard**　　　　　　**ZONES**　　　　　30p
A young man's mental and erotic awakening, and his free-wheeling
swing from London to Paris to Spain. 'Bursting at the seams with
vitality' – *Sunday Telegraph*

☐ **Donald Barthelme**　　　　　**SNOW WHITE**　　　30p
The novel with the big underground reputation. 'A wised-up story
of our time' – *Newsweek*. The lady is a tall dark beauty. She lives
with seven men who, to earn their daily bread, do various odd jobs,
and in between make love to the tall dark beauty in the shower –
more or less one at a time. 'No matter what you look for in a
book you can find it here' – *Boston Herald*

☐ **Colin Spencer**　　　　　　**ANARCHISTS IN
　　　　　　　　　　　　　　　LOVE**　　　　　　30p
They were young, and unattached – and *very much* uncommitted;
and passionate love-making on the night beaches of summertime
Brighton was their be-all.

☐ **Julian Gloag**　　　　　　　**MAUNDY**　　　　　40p
Maundy is a young man starting on a banking career . . . but his
fate is hallucination, rape and final destruction. 'Fantastically
clever; it illustrates a case of obsessive sanity falling to bits in
slow motion: coldly erotic' – Kay Dick, *Queen*

☐ **James Leigh**　　　　　　　**THE RASMUSSEN
　　　　　　　　　　　　　　　DISASTERS**　　　35p
Rasmussen is a second – maybe third – generation American in
southern California where he runs a liquor store. Rasmussen is
by no means an eccentric, but the mob that suddenly home in on
his rather staid life by god are. Order is finally restored by a local
fascist and his thugs and – hold it – a bowling team. Only
California could be like this.

☐ **Ivan Gold**　　　　　　　　**SICK FRIENDS**　　50p
Not since Henry Miller has any writer explored so frankly the
limits of love and sex. Its outspokenness may startle, but it is not a
'shocking' book – simply an honest one.

Some British

☐ Piers Paul Read   **THE JUNKERS**   30p
An exciting and important novel about love and danger in today's
divided Europe by one of Britain's finest young writers.
'Dazzling' – *Financial Times*. 'Compelling' – *The Observer*

☐ James Plunkett   **STRUMPET CITY**   50p
All big city life (Dublin is the city in the case of this wonderful
novel) is here – from saints (?) to sinners. The sinners need no
question mark – they're precisely what they're described as. A big
novel if ever there was one. Reviewers hailed it as the greatest novel
since DR. ZHIVAGO.

☐ Philip Callow   **THE BLISS BODY**   30p
Colin was young and wanted a woman – then he met Leila,
attractive, sexy, experienced. She was also married; which didn't
stop either of them. But there's always a price. *The Observer*
described the author as a 'confident successor to D. H. Lawrence'.

☐ Colin MacInnes   **WESTWARD TO
LAUGHTER**   30p
MacInnes sails westward in splendid style to murder, rape, piracy and
rebellion in the 17th century Caribbean. It's a novel that's got
something for everybody, and it 'takes the reader by storm' –
Spectator

☐ Simon Raven   **THE JUDAS BOY**   30p
Ambiguous sex, possible danger, final betrayal – Fielding Gray goes
to Greece on a TV fact-finding mission and is there seduced – quite
literally seduced – by a corrupt, golden boy who's the paid agent
of an American undercover man. 'Cynical and civilised' –
Evening Standard

Obtainable from all booksellers and newsagents. If you have
any difficulty please send purchase price plus 6p postage per
book to Panther Cash Sales, P.O. Box 11, Falmouth, Cornwall.

I enclose a cheque/postal order for titles ticked above plus 6p
a book to cover postage and packing.

Name...

Address ....

....